Magnolia Landing

Jessica Manning

Created by the producers of **Wagons West, White Indian, and Saga of the Southwest.**

Chairman of the Board: Lyle Kenyon Engel

BANTAM BOOKS

TORONTO • NEW YORK • LONDON • SYDNEY • AUCKLAND

MAGNOLIA LANDING

A Bantam Book / published by arrangement with Book Creations, Inc.

Bantam edition / February 1986

Produced by Book Creations, Inc.
Chairman of the Board: Lyle Kenyon Engel

ISBN 0-553-25419-7

Published simultaneously in the United States and Canada

PRINTED IN THE UNITED STATES OF AMERICA

H 0 9 8 7 6 5 4 3 2 1

To the people of New Orleans,
past, present, and future.

Masters, give unto your servants that which is just and equal; knowing that ye also have a Master in heaven.

—Colossians 4:1

Introduction

The 1830s marked the golden age of New Orleans. The city had gained full stature as a place of sin and gaiety unique on the North American continent. Creoles of French and Spanish blood, pirates, river gamblers, whores, politicians, voodooists, thieves, plantation owners, and people of the various color gradations, free or slave, made up that diverse community and contributed to its allure.

Epitomizing that age of intemperate society was a place called Magnolia Landing—an area composed of six sugar plantations situated some thirty miles upriver from the Crescent City. Against a backdrop of passion, power, and privilege the inhabitants of that wealthy community acted out the various roles to which they had been born and added to the legend of New Orleans as "the wickedest city in the world."

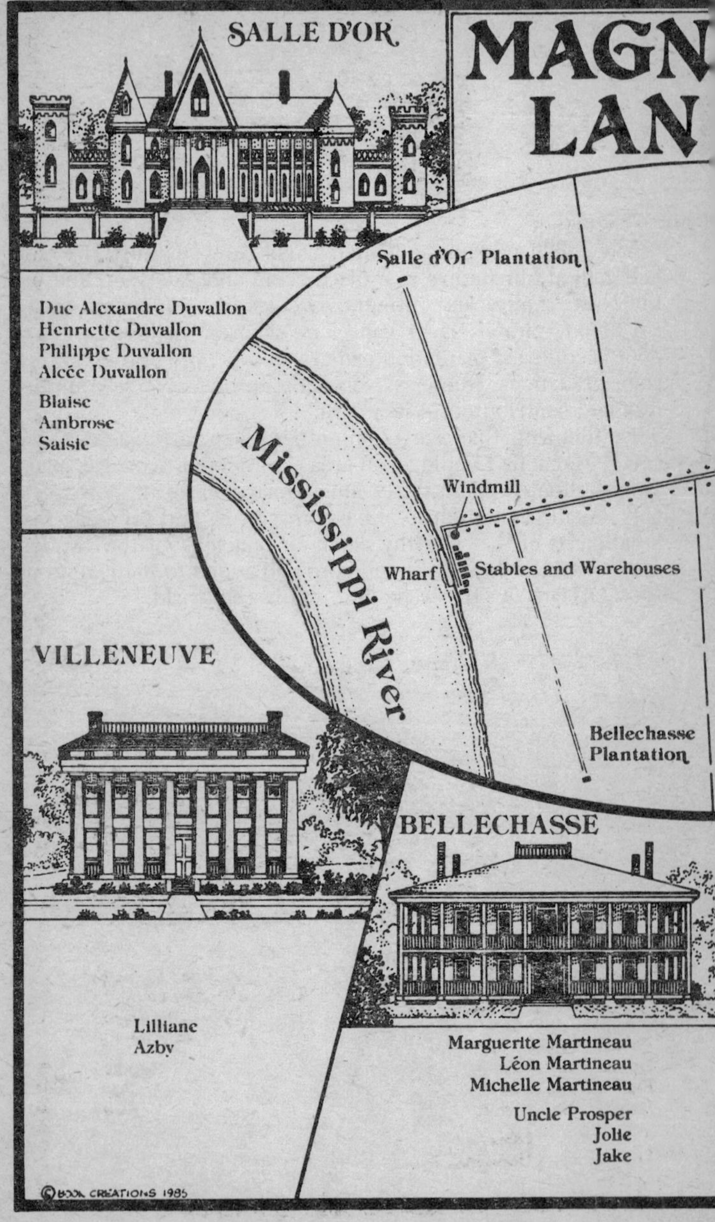
SALLE D'OR
MAGN
LAN
Salle d'Or Plantation
Duc Alexandre Duvallon
Henriette Duvallon
Philippe Duvallon
Alcée Duvallon
Blaise
Ambrose
Saisie
Mississippi River
Windmill
Wharf
Stables and Warehouses
VILLENEUVE
Bellechasse Plantation
BELLECHASSE
Lilliane
Azby
Marguerite Martineau
Léon Martineau
Michelle Martineau
Uncle Prosper
Jolie
Jake
©BOOK CREATIONS 1985

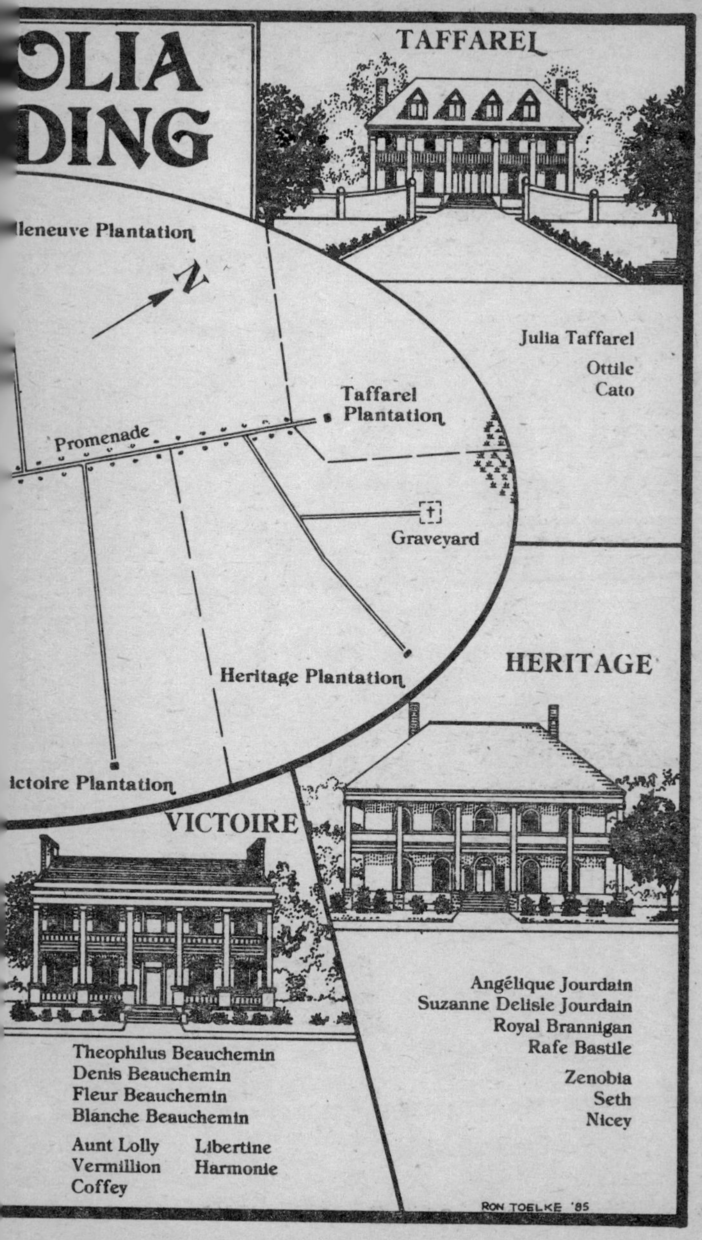
OLIA
DING
TAFFAREL
lleneuve Plantation
N
Taffarel
Plantation
Promenade
Graveyard
Heritage Plantation
ictoire Plantation
Julia Taffarel
Ottile
Cato
HERITAGE
VICTOIRE
Angélique Jourdain
Suzanne Delisle Jourdain
Royal Brannigan
Rafe Bastile
Zenobia
Seth
Nicey
Theophilus Beauchemin
Denis Beauchemin
Fleur Beauchemin
Blanche Beauchemin
Aunt Lolly
Vermillion
Coffey
Libertine
Harmonie
RON TOELKE '85

Prologue

May 31, 1830

A dense fog hung over the river like a shroud. Although the steamboat was behind schedule, it was forced to proceed at half-speed. The pilot, a seasoned riverman, carefully navigated his ship through the heavy mist in an effort to avoid floating trees, logs, and other debris.

The mist was parted by a sudden wind, and what appeared to be a Greek temple materialized on the east bank of the Mississippi River. It was not a Greek temple, but the columned residence of a sugar plantation—one of the many that lined the banks of the river. In these fantastic castles, self-crowned royalty lived in a grand manner. If they had had a coat of arms, it would have been designed to incorporate the sword-shaped leaves and tasseled tops of the sugar cane. That luxuriant crop allowed them an opulent lifestyle as latter-day lords of the most consummate system of feudalism in America.

Royal Brannigan stood on the upper deck of the *Belle Créole* and watched the paddle wheel churn the muddy waters of the Mississippi into a coffee-colored foam. He flipped open the heavy gold lid of his pocket watch with his thumbnail and smiled in remembrance as he gazed upon the most unusual clock face. Instead of numerals, twelve miniature cards—ace through queen—marked the time. It was just after four o'clock in the afternoon; with luck, the ship should reach Magnolia Landing by sundown.

Royal would have liked to visit the fabled community before this. But one did not visit Magnolia Landing. One either lived there or was an invited guest. That exclusive area was the subject of much discussion in New Orleans—the beautiful setting, the extraordinary wealth, the fabulous parties, and the colorful inhabitants. Well, today Royal was going to Magnolia Landing of his own accord, albeit under very unusual circumstances. He knew that he would not be welcome, but they would have no choice but to tolerate him.

Royal was well over six feet tall, with lusty good looks and an expressive, athletic body. His deep-set blue eyes were the quintessence of his Irish heritage. The corners were cross-hatched with tiny lines of concentration that belied his age of twenty-four. Royal's hair was thick, black, and as smooth as paint. His broad nose was saved from appearing pugilistic by a sharp, high bridge and refined cheekbones. His sensually sculpted mouth seemed never to rest; even when his other features were totally relaxed, his mouth seemed to carry on a life of its own, curling upward in easy humor or puckering in the anticipation of pleasure.

But perhaps Royal's most striking feature was his hands. They were large and powerful, yet gently formed, as if crafted by a master sculptor. The backs were broad and delicately patterned with light blue veins, and the palms were smooth and deeply etched by Royal's heart line, head line, and life line. Although his thumbs were thick, his fingers were narrow and tapered into blunt, squared tips that were lightly callused, with nails neatly cut and manicured. From time to time he would glance at his well-tended hands with a secret smile, as if they were a source of private amusement.

His basic garments were somber enough, but the total effect was dazzling. He wore a smartly tailored knee-length black broadcloth coat. His white shirt was cut low, with a loose collar and a frilled bosom partly concealed by a vest intricately decorated with hand-painted flowers. His shirt-front sparkled with a huge diamond stud called a headlight. His black trousers were so tight that they looked a part of his long, well-muscled legs. His highly polished black boots were made of Italian leather, and his underwear came from Paris.

The gentleman's dress made his profession apparent to almost everyone on board, excepting the two middle-aged women who were seated on folding chairs on the cabin-deck promenade. They eyed Royal with unconcealed interest while carrying on a speculative conversation in rapid French. The women, residents of Magnolia Landing, were bound together by age and Creole tradition more than anything else. In appearance and personality they were as dissimilar as traveling companions could be.

The elder—by less than a year—dominated the conversation to such a degree that the dialogue was close to being a monologue. Marguerite Martineau was a garrulous spinster of forty-eight who was obsessed with fashion, bloodlines, and gossip. She had once been beautiful and might still have been called attractive but for her determination to hang on to her youth. She favored clothing far too young for her, wore a surfeit of cosmetics, and darkened her graying hair with coffee. These affectations aged her far more ruthlessly than had her accumulated years.

Marguerite brandished a feather fan that had been dyed to match her traveling costume of pink silk. She employed the fan so effusively that as it fluttered about it took on the resemblance of a tortured bird held captive by her grasping hand.

Marguerite narrowed her eyes into slits and hissed, "Who do you suppose he is? The captain told me he was going to the Landing. I wonder whom he's visiting there? No one I know. Perhaps he's not a guest. But what kind of business could he be involved in? A man who looks like that!"

Henriette Villeneuve Duvallon was the very antithesis of her friend. She was a plain, unadorned woman who took few pains with her toilette. Once Henriette had been almost pretty, and the vestiges of her youth were still visible, albeit diminished by pinched lines of anxiety. She had a tight, pressed mouth, tidy little curls, and skin so scrubbed that it looked varnished. She held her body rigidly straight, as if she were wearing an iron brace.

In lieu of jewelry Henriette wore a crucifix. She wore it whether she was attired in a day dress or a ball gown. She didn't remove it even when she went to bed, for if she took it off she felt as if some physical part of her had been cut away. Clutching it tightly in her tiny hands, she offered a shy contribution. "I'm sure I've never seen him before, Marguerite. I would have remembered."

Marguerite licked her thin, liver-colored lips and continued. "Perhaps he's the son of a wealthy West Indian planter or a European exile from the Revolution. I've never seen such unusual clothing before."

"Perhaps he's an American," ventured Henriette.

"Nonsense," Marguerite snapped. "He couldn't be an American. He appears civilized! Look at him! The way he moves, his poise, his bearing. Hardly a pagan!"

Henriette timidly put forth an opinion. "Actually, Marguerite, I have met some Americans who were quite nice."

Ordinarily the comment would have invoked a barrage of shrill argument from Marguerite, but she was deep in thought. How could she discreetly open a conversation with the young man? There was no other way she could find out whom he was visiting at the Landing. And if he were an American, she supposed she could lower herself to speak the barbaric tongue. After two decades of dealing with the Americans, both Marguerite and Henriette had become somewhat bilingual.

As for Royal, even though he did not understand French, he knew that he was the subject of the women's conversation. He turned and flashed them a bright if automatic smile. Henriette became flustered. But Marguerite, seizing the opportunity, let her fan drop to the deck. Royal had no choice but to retrieve it and then introduce himself.

A look passed between the two women. He was an American after all. Marguerite didn't hesitate to employ English. She introduced herself and, almost as an afterthought, Henriette. Before Royal could get away, she launched into her interrogation. "Then you are an American, M'sieur Bran-ee-gan?"

"Yes," Royal replied without a trace of embarrassment. "Second-generation Irish. Born and raised in Pennsylvania." Royal had a soft lilt to his voice—an accent rather than a brogue. The words rolled easily off his tongue, giving the listener the impression of sincerity.

"Such a long way from home," Marguerite said encouragingly, but Royal merely nodded in response. She began working her fan again. "And you're traveling to Magnolia Landing?" Royal nodded once again. Marguerite sniffed with frustration, but Royal's lack of communication only made her all the more determined. She nudged Henriette sharply in the ribs for support.

"We're from the Landing," Henriette announced a bit loudly. "We know everybody there." Royal shifted his weight uncomfortably, and Marguerite was afraid he was about to make an exit.

But Royal said, "I've never been to Magnolia Landing before."

Marguerite pounced on the tidbit of information like a starving dog after a morsel of food. "Then you know nothing of the history of the place, M'sieur Bran-ee-gan?" He shook his head, and Marguerite knew that she had him. He couldn't politely take his leave now. And by honing in on each plantation, she would be able to find out exactly where he was going and for what purpose.

"Go on, tell, Marguerite," urged Henriette. "You're much better at it than I."

Marguerite was in her glory. She cleared her throat and eagerly began her encapsulated history of the place. "The Landing, as we call it, is a very exclusive community—"

"And we raise sugar cane," interrupted Henriette.

"That's right. We raise sugar cane. Our annual harvest accounts for one-eighteenth of all the sugar and its by-products sold on the New Orleans market."

"And the best quality," Henriette added enthusiastically.

Marguerite obviously relished her role as instructress. "Originally all the land at Magnolia Landing was owned by one man, Julius Taffarel, but he lived too high and mighty. After he died, his daughter, Julia Taffarel, had to sell off large sections of the land, until there were six plantations in all, including Taffarel."

"Which is in a disgraceful state of disrepair," interjected Henriette.

Marguerite pursed her lips in distaste. "Yes, it's—how do you say? An eyesore. But I suppose nothing is to be done until Miss Julia dies and the house and grounds are sold to a more responsible owner."

"Miss Julia's not quite right in the head," said Henriette. "It was her mama who planted all those magnolia trees. Why, she must have been even crazier than Miss Julia."

Marguerite continued, "Julia Taffarel is a recluse and, yes, a bit strange. She *never* has visitors. So I don't suppose you could be going there."

Royal responded by asking, "On which plantation do you ladies live?"

"I live at Bellechasse," said Marguerite, "with my nephew and his wife, Léon and Michelle Martineau. Léon's on board, too, although for the life of me I don't know where he's got to. His wife comes from a very old, very distinguished Spanish family, the de Venturas, although the younger generation these days—" She caught herself and, clearing her throat, returned to the original question. "Henriette and her husband—the Duc Alexandre Duvallon—live at Salle d'Or, and they also own Villeneuve."

"Which belonged to my parents," Henriette managed to put in.

Marguerite shot her a withering glance and continued. "That leaves three. Victoire, which is owned by Theophilus

Beauchemin." She paused, but there was no response from Royal. "Heritage, which belongs to the Jourdains." She paused once again. Still no reaction. "And, of course, Taffarel."

When Royal didn't respond, Marguerite leaned forward, working the fan so vigorously that it threatened to escape her grasp. "Tell us, M'sieur Bran-ee-gan, at which of the plantations are you to be a guest?"

"I am to be nobody's guest, madame," Royal replied stiffly. "I'm going to Magnolia Landing quite uninvited."

"Then you're a businessman!" Marguerite exclaimed.

"No, madame, I'm a gambler. And I'm going to Magnolia Landing to collect a debt. Now, if you'll both kindly excuse me . . ." Royal made a hasty retreat before Marguerite could initiate another line of questioning.

Marguerite, sputtering with outrage, switched back to French. "An American and a gambler!"

"Marguerite, please don't mention this to Alexandre," begged Henriette, clutching her crucifix. "I don't know what he would say if he knew that we conversed with such a man."

Marguerite eyed her friend with exasperation and growled. "We still didn't find out where he was going!"

The fog began to lift, and the steamboat was able to proceed at a faster speed. The *Belle Créole* slid over the current past wide lagoons, mist-shrouded swamps, and inlets that led to sunless marshes and hidden bayous. Herons and snowy egrets swooped down and came to rest amid trees draped with moss that resembled tattered gray garments. Alligators, the guardians of the riverbanks, lifted their heads and eyed the passing ship with lazy menace.

As Royal was walking along the promenade, he saw the captain of the steamship coming toward him. He braced himself. Captain Bartolomé Calabozo was a strutting cock of a man who exuded manufactured geniality. Short and chunky, he was crowded into a too-tight uniform of his own design—royal blue silk decorated with yards of ornate gold braid. More social director than captain, Calabozo nonetheless took his duties seriously and saw to it that his passengers—at least the genteel ones—had nothing to complain about. No doubt he had observed with apprehension Royal's brief exchange with Henriette and Marguerite.

Nodding Royal aside as if to impart a great secret, Calabozo remarked, "People from the Landing don't like Americans."

"I'm used to a certain amount of prejudice," Royal replied. "Of course that doesn't keep them from being inquisitive. And given your destination, I can't blame them."

Royal found himself smiling at the man's transparent curiosity. His motives were exactly the same as those of the ladies—he wanted to find out the details of Royal's trip to Magnolia Landing.

Royal ignored the ill-disguised request for information and, hoping to distract the captain, remarked, "Nice ship."

"Nice!" Calabozo sputtered and pulled himself to his full height of five feet. "*La Belle Créole* is a beautiful ship!" He fondled the wooden railing affectionately, as if touching a woman. "I named her myself. She's my home as well as my livelihood. She may be small, but she's pretty and very, very demanding. I'm true to her six days a week, but on Sunday, when we tie up in New Orleans . . ." He dropped his voice to a whisper, as if the ship could overhear him. "I am unfaithful to her."

"Who's the lucky other woman?" Royal asked solemnly.

"Personally, I favor Odalisque."

Royal winced at the captain's mention of the most expensive gambling, drinking, and whoring establishment in New Orleans. After all, it was his visit to Odalisque two nights ago that had initiated the fateful events that were now taking him to Magnolia Landing.

"The fog's lifting," Calabozo said. "We should reach the Landing by sunset." He glanced uneasily at Royal, trying to form the words for the request he was about to make. The young man anticipated him.

"Don't worry, Captain. I intend to stay on board until everybody has disembarked; then your men can unload my . . . ah . . . freight."

The captain visibly relaxed, and his hearty manner returned. He took Royal's hand and shook it vigorously. "I am much obliged, M'sieur Brannigan. You are a gentleman after all," he said, then hurried away.

"Am I?" Royal said to himself. "The test of that is yet to come." The faintest trace of a smile clung to his lips.

He descended the stairs to the main deck, then turned and headed aft. Two young men were standing in the shadows of the staircase. At first glance they looked related, but as he neared he realized that they had simply been cut from the same bolt of expensive cloth. They were both in their early twenties, handsome, and impeccably turned out. Their suits were of the latest fashion, differing only in color. The one wearing cerulean blue was smoking a small cigar, while the other—attired in bottle green—was sipping from a silver flask.

They were not friends, Royal thought. Rather they sought out each other's company because of their similar backgrounds. In all probability they were the sons of plantation owners at Magnolia Landing and had come below together to drink and smoke out of view of friends, relatives, or neighbors who might be on board. He guessed that one of them was the nephew of the garrulous matron he had talked to earlier.

The young men, too polite to stare, offered Royal no more than a cursory glance as he passed, yet obviously their curiosity had been aroused by the appearance of this handsome, oddly dressed stranger.

The main deck of the stern-wheeler housed fireboxes, firewood, engines, cargo, and low-paying deck passengers. Here the noise of the engines and the heat of the boilers were almost unbearable. The passengers, mostly plantation workers and slaves, their faces dulled by servitude, clung to the railing in an effort to escape the cacophony and the temperature.

Royal proceeded to the area where the freight was stored. Sheets of canvas had been unfurled from the beams above to protect the cargo from the rain. A drop of sweat slid down Royal's forehead and into his eyes. He brushed it away with an impatient gesture, then pulled a section of canvas aside and entered.

Hanging lanterns cast a dim red glow over the tightly packed barrels, crates, and trunks being delivered to the wealthy inhabitants of Magnolia Landing. Royal scanned the goods as he threaded his way through the narrow aisles, looking for his own freight. He inhaled deeply as he passed a dozen kegs of brandy from Spain. The rough wood could not contain the heady aroma of the spirits. He bent low to avoid a collection of Indian temple bells suspended from the deck beams. A large painting imported from France leaned against a stanchion. The heavy wrapping paper was torn in one corner, and Royal could just make out a voluptuous shepherdess tending her flocks in an idyllic meadow.

He turned into another aisle, where earthenware jars containing fancy foodstuffs were lashed together with lengths of twine. Brown sacks of coffee and cocoa beans were piled on top of each other like overstuffed pillows. Great bunches of bananas from the Caribbean were suspended from bamboo poles, their yellow fingers forming great cupped hands.

He stepped through a pair of ornately carved doors snatched from some Chinese palace, and ducked to miss the rattan cages holding a variety of tropical birds. The brilliant, iridescent color of their plumage was startlingly evident even in the gloom. They watched the intruder with wary, unblinking eyes.

Royal bumped into a large crate containing a crystal chandelier, and its prisms rattled menacingly. The seal that had been burned into the wood read: BRANNIGAN GLASSWORKS. The young man smiled without humor. The chandelier had been made at his father's glass factory in Pennsylvania. It was as if the product had been willed there by Terrence Brannigan to remind Royal of his continuing disapproval. Royal turned abruptly away from the crate and saw his luggage. It was stacked alongside his other piece of cargo—the reason for his trip to Magnolia Landing. Small parcels had been placed on and around the long, black container, no doubt to hide the offending box from the passengers.

The coffin, constructed of ebony and decorated with silver fittings, might have been purchased for a lifelong friend or a dearly beloved family member. But this coffin did not contain someone near and dear to Royal, or even a distant relation. It held the body of a young man he had known for only a matter of hours, but his death had completely altered the course of Royal's life.

Transfixed, Royal stared at the black box as if he didn't quite believe it existed. Then, without warning, the horror of the recent past seized him. The beating of his heart turned into a deafening pounding. Blood rose to stain his face, and his flesh burned with a sudden fever. The coffin shifted out of focus as driblets of sweat poured into his eyes. He shut his eyes, hoping the vision would go away, but when he opened them again the coffin was still there. It was not a figment of his imagination.

With the slow, dreamlike movements of a somnambulist, Royal moved closer to the coffin. He withdrew a linen handkerchief from his breast pocket and wiped a bit of grease from the silver handle. As he did, the ship lurched sideways. Royal grasped the handle to keep from falling. The canvas bulged and snapped, and the lanterns began to swing back and forth, casting eerie shadows. The tropical birds squawked and fluttered about their cages, and the Indian temple bells tolled a dull, metallic knell.

Royal's face became blistered with drops of perspiration. The ship righted itself, but he still held on to the silver handle, gasping for breath. His fingertips went cold, as a strange, insidious odor filled his nostrils. The overpowering aroma of dead flowers rushed at him like a sudden blast of wind. Flower petals—thousands of them—had been stuffed around the body like fanciful packing material. The undertaker had explained that the petals would disguise the scent of death during the thirty-mile trip to Magnolia Landing. Royal had agreed to the fantastic scheme, and the undertaker had exacted a fine price for his efforts.

But the trip was taking longer than expected, and now something lurked behind the cloyingly sweet scent. The ghastly odor of putrefaction, whether real or imagined, assaulted Royal's senses, searing the lining of his nostrils.

He let go of the handle as if it had become suddenly hot. He pressed the handkerchief over his face, and his whole body began to jerk in a convulsive shudder. He dropped the handkerchief and groaned. Memories, recent and raw, crowded into him so fast that he could hardly breathe. He pressed his hands over his ears, hoping to ward off the sounds that he knew were coming—sounds that he feared would haunt his dreams for the rest of his nights. His head became filled with the murmur of voices, hushed at first, but growing in volume until they became a clamor. He heard the shattering glass, the sharp click as the safety catch was released, then the explosion as the pistol destroyed the handsome face, reducing it to a pulp of blood, bone, and brains.

Someone touched Royal's shoulder. He whirled around, his eyes wild, perspiration streaming from his face.

"Excuse me if I startled you," the captain said, then glanced at the coffin, the object of Royal's consternation. "How did your friend die?"

Royal replied softly, "I suppose you could say I killed him."

PART ONE

Chapter One

The afternoon sun made its appearance at last, and its rays were surprisingly intense. A quartet of crows silhouetted against the lemon-colored sky appeared as black-gloved hands applauding the efforts of the day. Shafts of sunlight filtered through the leaves and burned away the raindrops. Thin wisps of steam rose from the trees, then quickly evaporated.

Seth, a Negro boy of eight who belonged to Heritage Plantation, sat in the crotch of a magnolia tree and waited patiently. His dark eyes peered through the foliage and remained focused on the bend in the river where the steamboat would first appear. The tree, nearly one hundred feet tall, was one of a matching pair that grew next to the dock and marked the entrance to the tree-lined corridor known as the Promenade. Stationed at various points down the long alley of flowering trees were a score of black boys who awaited Seth's call—"Steamboat a-comin'!"

When the signal came they would relay it to the slaves from the six plantations at Magnolia Landing. Thus alerted, plantation carriages would begin rolling toward the dock to meet the guests and returning residents and pick up goods brought from New Orleans.

To while away the time, Seth had brought along his homemade banjo. He leaned against the tree trunk, his face a mask of concentration as he tuned up. Although he was odd in appearance, his expertise at playing the banjo gave him a certain position in the younger slaves' community. Seth was small for his age, thin as a cinnamon stick and just about the same color. His features were scrunched up in the center of his face, giving him the appearance of a little old man. His eyes, however, were bright and intelligent, and his little pinched mouth was usually bursting with impertinent opinions.

Seth began a traditional mournful slave song, but beneath his fingertips the strings sang and throbbed until the plaintive tune became one of rebellion, expressing the discontent the slaves felt with their loss of freedom. His voice was raspy but held a power that commanded attention.

"Nobody knows who I am.
Nobody knows who I am.
Nobody knows who I am
Till de Judgment Mornin'!"

The beat became more powerful, transforming the message from a simple complaint into a forceful statement. Seth's song was picked up by the other slaves nestled in the branches. The boy chorus began shouting and clapping their hands in counterpoint, until the entire line of trees shook with defiance.

"Nobody knows who I am
Till de Judgment Mornin'!"

Julia Taffarel cocked her head to one side and listened. The combined voices of the slave chorus drifted across the grounds of Taffarel Plantation and floated inside. "My, my," she remarked aloud. "The boys are in fine voice today." She listened for a moment longer, then continued slowly through the first floor of the big house.

Although her fifty-nine years had exacted their toll, Julia was still a beautiful woman. Her hair, totally white, surrounded her face like a bursting halo. Her skin was delicately lined like old porcelain, and her eyes, which were as blue as robins' eggs, now lay in delicate nests of wrinkles. Her carriage remained erect, and her graceful movements belied her age. She wore a faded gown of damson silk held together by clever stitchery. Encircling her neck was a ruffle of lace, but not even the starch or meticulous ironing could disguise the fact that it was yellow with age. From time to time she would stop and examine a remaining piece of furniture or a painting, then recite some little anecdote connected with it.

As usual, Julia's audience for this late afternoon ritual were her only friends—Ottile and Cato. The couple had been at Taffarel almost as long as Julia herself. Julia had been nine and her brother Claude six when their father, a widower, decided that the children each needed a personal slave. He had bought the young Negro couple at a slave auction and delivered them to Taffarel. But instead of becoming subservient, Ottile and Cato had become a second mother and father to the youngsters. Julia had freed all her slaves six years ago, but the couple had stayed on, along with most of the field hands.

Now the couple dutifully trailed behind Julia, listening to her somewhat rambling recitations. Although they were a decade older than their mistress, they were both healthy and sharp of mind, and they pampered Julia as if she were still an indulged child. They had lived as husband and wife for more years than they could count, and like their mistress, they were both unstooped.

As Julia moved down the shadowed hallway, her feather-light footsteps made a tap-tap sound on the cypress floor, now bare of carpets. She paused at the end of the hallway, traced her fingers over the carved surface of a huge mahogany armoire. The wood was warped and split in several places, and the fine linen that the cupboard had once held had long since been discarded. The shelves had been removed, and the armoire was now used to store seeds and gardening tools.

Julia wet her lips, and when she spoke, her voice was light and musical—the voice of a young woman. "Papa had this imported from the West Indies for my eighth birthday. Originally it was put in the nursery to house my dolls. I thought it dark and ugly and wanted it whitewashed, but Papa wouldn't hear of it. And so it was brought downstairs and Papa ordered another made of bleached pecan." She frowned. "I still don't like dark wood."

They entered the grand foyer. The sun streamed through the fanlight over the door with such unexpected brightness that all three blinked. The foyer was completely barren of furniture or ornaments, except for a single mirror—the only remaining mirror at Taffarel. The Creoles were very fond of mirrors because they were regarded as symbols of luxury and refinement. At one time the big house had boasted at least three in every room. This last mirror rested in a gilded oval frame, but the silver backing had flaked, and any reflection appeared as if viewed through a snowstorm.

Julia started at seeing herself reflected in the bright glare. She shaded her eyes with a hand that was no longer delicate, but coarse and callused from years of toil. "Mirrors are such truth tellers," she exclaimed, and looked away.

She reached the closed doors leading to the parlor and said, "Oh, I knew I was coming here. On days when I feel . . . disassembled, having supper with Claude always helps to put me back together."

She opened the doors and entered the dark room. Cato hurried in to light a lamp. The exquisite chandeliers that had hung in the parlor were among the first things to be sold years earlier. The lamp illuminated the portrait of Julia's brother, Claude, above the marble fireplace. Julia smiled at the portrait.

Ottile went to get the tray she had prepared in advance for Julia's supper. Every day Julia dined in a different room, and she always dressed for dinner. It mattered little to her that she wore ruined finery, or that her dresses had been patched again and again. It was an ingrained habit as constant as Ottile's savory Creole dishes and Julia's unfailing appetite. The only thing that had changed over the years was that Julia ate her meal at an earlier hour. She now retired when twilight fell. She liked to sleep through the darkness so that she could see more of the day.

The windows of the parlor had been boarded up. Stacked next to the walls were sacks of shelled corn that would be used to feed the remaining livestock. As Cato moved about the room, a group of mice scurried to safety, scattering balls of dust in their wake.

Cato removed the sheet from an oversized armchair of threadbare brocade, and Julia sat down. He moved a *bombé* side table next to her, then set the lamp on the ledge of the marble fireplace, adjusting the flame so that Julia could see the portrait clearly. In the flickering lamplight the face seemed to come alive. The dark eyes sparkled with mischief, the black curls stirred in the wind, and the high cheekbones shifted as the lips expanded and contracted. He looked idealistic—a young man meant for heroic deeds.

"I remember," Julia said, "when you posed for the painting, Claude. The artist was talented, but not talented enough to capture your beauty. You hated posing for so many long hours. But I insisted. I'm so glad now that I did."

Without averting her gaze from the portrait, Julia said to Cato, "Everyone who visited Taffarel always remarked that he was the most handsome man they'd ever seen."

Cato did not reply to his mistress's words, but punctuated them with *Ahas*. Ottile arrived with Julia's tray, and the room was suddenly filled with a spicy aroma. On the tray were a bowl of crab gumbo, several ripe figs, and a bottle of wine. The plate and bowl were edged in gold, the last pieces of what once had been a service for fifty. Also on the tray were a vase containing a freshly cut flower and a soft linen napkin. Julia insisted on maintaining a semblance of gentility.

Ottile and Cato left Julia to her supper but remained outside in case she should need them. They sat side by side on the bottom step of the winding staircase, holding hands and seemingly content with their time and place in life. They listened in silence as Julia chatted with the portrait, discussing the past with her absent brother.

Julia knew that her faithful servants listened to her, and every so often she would speak in the direction of the doorway, asking them for confirmation of her thoughts. Ottile and Cato would always reply in unison, "Dat's right, Miz Julia," smile, and look at each other knowingly. Then, a few moments later, Cato would surreptitiously glance over his shoulder, as if checking for ghosts.

Julia, left with little else but her memories, sometimes found herself looking forward to her own death. But she still had duties to perform and certain essential responsibilities to see to. She finished her supper and poured herself a glass of wine. Her eyes brimming with tears, she toasted her brother's portrait and murmured, "Claude, you were the most beautiful man in the world."

At Bellechasse Plantation, Michelle Martineau lay naked in the center of the huge mahogany bed, flexing and unflexing her long, supple legs in pleasure. A stray breeze slipped through the jalousies, stirred the mosquito netting, and stroked the glistening flesh on the beautiful young woman who rested on the blue counterpane. Michelle imagined she was adrift on waves of powder-blue silk, while above her billowed sails suspended from the sturdy masts of the four-poster. The illusion was enhanced by the *ciel de lit* that hung over the bed. These canopies were made especially for Creole brides and were always of pale blue silk, gathered in the middle by a gilt ornament and trimmed with lace. Across this counterfeit heaven, fat cupids armed with bows and arrows chased one another.

Although Michelle and Léon Martineau had been married a full year, the *ciel de lit* remained hanging over their bed. At a time when most couples began to tire of the physical pleasures of marriage, Michelle and Léon remained wildly, passionately in love, more sexually attracted to each other than ever.

Michelle closed her eyes tightly and pursed her lips to kiss a man who wasn't there. For a moment she saw nothing but blinking stars, and then *he* appeared. She could see him as clearly as if he were lying beside her, his chestnut hair falling over his dark blue eyes, his lips—wet, parted—waiting for hers. She tightened her thighs and pressed her abdomen against the soft bed cover. She breathed one word, drawing it out to three distinct syllables, "Lé-oooo-on."

Léon was due to return from a trip to New Orleans on the steamship *Belle Créole* and had been gone for two whole days. Michelle was anxious not only to make love to her husband but for the presents that she knew he would be bringing her.

Well, she would have a present for him too!

Michelle scrunched up her pretty gamine face in concentration. How could she best surprise Léon when he arrived back home? In one quick movement she rolled over, arched her back, and sighed. She touched the tip of her finger to her throat. Her flesh was damp with a light sheen of perspiration. She ran her finger down between her breasts and over her ribs. Then touched the finger to her lips. It tasted sweet, like sugared water. Perhaps she would make herself up like a whore and wait for him naked on the veranda, in a seductive pose. No. That was out of the question. The slaves might see her, and they would surely tell Aunt Marguerite. And then there would be the devil to pay.

Michelle pushed apart the netting and swung out of bed. She stood on her tiptoes and stretched while emitting a soft gasp of exhilaration. Then she hugged herself tightly, spun around, and cried out in the sheer delight of knowing that she was no longer a little girl. Thanks to Léon she had discovered that she was made of flesh and blood, and she luxuriated in her newfound womanhood.

She skipped across the soft Persian carpet that covered the floor of the master bedroom and stopped abruptly in front of her rococo dressing table. The pink marble top was littered with bottles and jars of cut crystal containing Michelle's collection of perfumes and cosmetics. The mirror above was framed by a swirling confection of gilt bronze. Michelle sat down and smiled at her reflection. She reveled in what she saw. Her hair was as dark and shiny as a raven's wing. Her eyes were like pieces of black onyx. A pert nose, slightly pinched by disdain, and a soft, puckered mouth completed a perfectly symmetrical arrangement in a delicate, heart-shaped face.

Michelle opened one of the jars and, while flirting with her reflection, decided to darken her nipples with rouge. She daubed a bit of carmine on each nipple, then began blending in the color with slow, circular motions. Her breasts tingled beneath her touch, and she wished that the hands that touched them were not hers but Léon's.

"Hurry, Léon!" she breathed. "Oh, please hurry home."

Michelle got up and nervously paced the floor. Perhaps she would hide in the attic and make Léon come looking for her. But she quickly dismissed that idea. It would take hours before he found her, and she was anxious to make love. Besides, she had done that before. Michelle and Léon considered themselves adventurous and had promised each other they would never repeat the same sexual experience twice.

Once, during a dinner party at a neighboring plantation, they had slipped away and made love in the host's carriage, afraid that at any moment they might be caught. The sensation had added to their enjoyment. In the months since, there was hardly any place on the plantation where they had not indulged themselves. They had used the slaves' quarters, and once when Aunt Marguerite was having tea with Henriette, they had even made love in her bed.

"I have it!" Michelle exclaimed. There was one place neither of them had thought of—until now. She quickly powdered her body with a fine milled talcum, then put on slippers and a satin robe. She blew her reflection a self-congratulatory kiss and went down the back stairs to instruct the house servants that they were not to clean up anything they found amiss, or go near the back of the house. Leaving the puzzled slaves behind, she dashed through the hall to the foyer. She gathered a bunch of day-old roses and began strewing a trail of petals from the front door in a zigzag maze through the rooms to the back of the mansion and the hothouse. She pushed open the door, and the rich, warm scent of growing things made her senses spin. She continued dropping the flower petals until she reached a place at the back where empty burlap sacks were piled high. She took off her robe and, giggling with anticipation, spread it on top of the makeshift mattress. She plucked gardenias and rubbed them over her flesh. Then she stuck a hibiscus behind each ear and sat down. While waiting for Léon to arrive she plaited violets into the soft hair between her legs.

* * *

There were no fancy outbuildings at Victoire. The only separate structure was the kitchen. For safety, as well as to keep the heat out of the house, most Creole kitchens were separate from the main residence. The kitchen at Victoire was constructed of brick and attached to the rear porch by a loggia. It was not just a place where meals were planned and cooked, but was acknowledged by slave and master alike to be the heart of the plantation.

Its popularity was mainly due to the plantation mammy—Aunt Lolly. The formidable slave ruled over Victoire with a firm but loving hand, and the kitchen was her royal chamber. At that time of day her voice, as rich as apple butter, could be heard above the kitchen clatter.

"Vermillion! Don't let dat oyster stew come to a boil too quick or yo' scalds de milk. Libertine! Put dat chicory through de grinder again. I wants it fine. Harmonie! Yo' burn dat rice and beans and I sends yo' back to de cane fields. Fan my brow! If I didn't oversee de cookin', I don't suppose anything comin' out of dis here kitchen would be fit to eat."

Aunt Lolly was a rotund woman of generous proportions just short of five feet tall. She was the color of a burned tree stump, and her round face was usually broken by a huge smile. A bright madras tignon was neatly tied around her head and pushed high by a comb worn underneath. She was dressed, as always, in a voluminous ruffled shift of red cotton and a spotless white apron stiff with starch. Around her neck hung a rosary and a chamois bag containing voodoo charms. The smell that emanated from it was unpleasant, but the family had got used to the odor, and it had become almost aromatic to them. Aunt Lolly divided her religious attentions between the Christian gods and those worshiped by the voodooists; she believed in giving equal time to both . . . just in case.

Working a palmetto fan about her face, Aunt Lolly sashayed around the kitchen, keeping a sharp eye on everything and from time to time glancing at the grandfather's clock next to the doorway. As her ruffled skirts rippled and her heavy shoes flap-flapped on the smooth stone floor, she kept up a running diatribe, criticizing, cajoling, and admonishing her helpers to pay attention to what they were doing.

The three grandchildren of the plantation owner, Theophilus Beauchemin, were also in the kitchen, performing their assigned task of clarifying the drinking water. Denis, Fleur, and Blanche stood on stools next to huge jars called *ollas*, which had been filled with water from the river. A lump of alum had been dropped into each, and the children had to stir until the water was purified.

"Denis! Fleur! Don't yo' let up on dat stirrin', now. Blanche! Yo' gets back up on dat stool. I told yo' no sweets befo' dinner. If yo' don't stir de water, den de water don't get clarified. Now, does I make myself clarified? I do believe dat little gal could live on sweets . . . if I lets her."

The grandfather's clock began striking the hour of six, its heavy gong sounding over the rattle of pots. For a moment the chatter of the kitchen help ceased and everything came to a stop. Spoons were stalled in mid-stir and gossip in mid-sentence. It was time to prepare the master's before-dinner drink.

"Upon my misery! It six o'clock! Denis, get down dat tray and de whiskey. Careful, don't drop dat decanter or I skins de hide offen yo'."

Aunt Lolly ran her fingers through Denis's hair, squeezed Fleur, and then picked up Blanche, cradling her in huge arms that resembled great loaves of bread. "Whose turn is it to tote yo' grandpa's whiskey today?"

"It's mine!" Blanche shouted. "It's mine! It's mine!"

"I thought yo' did it yesterday, sweetbread?"

Blanche shook her head violently. Aunt Lolly looked at Denis, who, being the oldest and the only male, always acted as spokesman for the trio.

"It's my turn, Aunt Lolly, but Blanche can take it."

A dazzlingly bright smile split the mammy's face. She appreciated the way Denis usually deferred to his sisters' wishes. After releasing Blanche, she went to prepare her master's drink. She filled a tall glass two-thirds full of whiskey and added clarified water, then garnished it with a sprig of fresh mint. She placed it on a lacquered tray and turned around. Blanche was waiting to receive it.

"Now, if yo' don't spill none, honeysuckle, dere'll be an extra measure of pudding fo' yo' after dinner."

"I won't," promised Blanche.

The children proceeded to line up. Denis and Fleur positioned themselves on either side of Blanche, ready to catch the glass and tray in case she tripped.

Their grandfather, Theophilus Beauchemin, now seated in his rattan fan-backed chair on the veranda, was accustomed to their attentions. This was his favorite time of day, a time set aside and belonging exclusively to *la famille*. Any moment now, he knew, his three grandchildren would appear bearing his before-dinner drink. Rather like acolytes paying homage to their priest, they would gather around his feet, and the ceremony of questions and answers would begin.

The questions, gathered through the day like so many wildflowers, were formally presented each afternoon for the expected answers. After all, they believed he was the wisest man in the world.

Denis: "If I untie my navel, could I manage to pull myself inside out?"

Fleur: "Do the trees hold up the sky?"

Blanche: "Is the grass the earth's hair?"

Theo tried to take each question seriously and answered them as well as he could. The ritual almost always ended with speculation concerning the local legend—the ghost of Magnolia Landing. Throughout the years, various slaves, residents, and visitors claimed to have seen the ghost. Descriptions varied, but all were in agreement that it had long hair and skin as white as a shroud. Many Creoles as well as Negro slaves used the ghost as a threat to keep their offspring in line, but Theo used no such measures with his grandchildren.

At sixty-one, Theo looked the part of a high priest. He was a vital, attractive man with a full head of hair and a luxuriant beard, now as gray as a winter dawn. His eyes were dark and alert beneath bushy brows, and his face, weathered by the seasons and burnished by the sun, appeared to have been carved from oak. Theo considered himself a fulfilled, even a fortunate, man. From time to time he suffered private moments of anguish when his eyes clouded over with a mist of tears. But he fought to keep himself from becoming immersed in past tragedies, and he never gave in to his grief. He had to set an example for his grandchildren. For them he had to be strong, so that he could infuse their young lives with a zest for knowledge—the greatest gift he could bestow upon them.

Theo's eyes sparkled with anticipation. He wondered what queries the "Terrible Trio" would bring to him that afternoon. He looked forward to each new day as he did to each new question. They were all different, imaginative, and surprising. And he knew *that* kept him young.

Theo sighed with pleasure when he saw them coming

toward him, the sun at their backs. Denis was tall for his twelve years and as narrow as a stick. He hadn't yet filled out and appeared to be all arms and legs. Of the three children, he most resembled his father. His hair was the color of licorice and fell in an unruly swatch across his forehead, shading a pair of eyes that were as green as the skin of a lime. A spattering of freckles covered his slightly off-center nose—the result of a bad spill when he was a toddler. Denis was a natural-born leader, and in spite of his position in the family unit, he had developed his own brand of democracy in dealing with his younger sisters. He never engaged in the usual older brother antics of teasing or mistreating them, but instead had assumed a responsibility for their well-being in a truly adult manner.

Fleur at nine seemed to have none of the childhood drawbacks of that age—she was neither awkward nor boisterous. Instead she was a poised little lady, a miniature Southern belle. She was already a beauty, and although it seemed inconceivable to those around her, each passing day made her even more so. Her hair was the color of corn silk, but full-bodied and bouncy. Her eyes were large, wide-spaced, and hyacinth blue. Her mouth was a neat cupid's bow, and her lips were uncommonly red. Fleur seemed all rustle and flounce, but inwardly she was a serious, circumspect youngster who enjoyed acting out the adult role she had created for herself.

Blanche was seven and the pepper in the family stew. Plump and giddy, she was a source of amusement to everyone around her. Her tawny flesh was like soft taffy, and the mass of untidy curls that was her hair resembled freshly buttered popcorn. Her dark brown eyes glistened in her buttery roll of a face. Perhaps in compensation for not having parents, Blanche had developed a sweet tooth. Although she loved her older brother and sister, she had a tendency to view them as a threat to her "just desserts."

Mindful of Aunt Lolly's promise of an extra portion of pudding, Blanche managed to deliver the drink to her grandfather without spilling a drop, and he congratulated her on her efficiency. Blanche seated herself closest to her grandfather so that she could press her chubby cheek against Theo's leg. Denis hunkered down in a squatting position, wrapping his arms around his knees. Fleur stationed herself farthest away, arranging the folds of her dress so carefully that it resembled an open parasol.

"I have something to tell, Grandpapa," Denis said, barely able to contain himself. His adolescent voice was both rough and squeaky in the course of the same sentence.

"Tell, tell, tell!" burbled Blanche.

"Hush, Blanche," cautioned Fleur. "Screaming is most unbecoming."

Theo stifled a grin. "What is it, Denis?"

"Coffey saw the ghost." His voice was tinged with excitement and envy.

"Our Coffey?" asked Theo, referring to the adolescent son of Vermillion, one of the plantation cooks.

"Yes," Denis went on breathlessly. "He went possum hunting last night, and around midnight he saw the ghost in the woods behind Heritage."

"And what was the ghost doing in the woods? I assume he wasn't possum hunting, too."

"Just walking along. Coffey saw it and hid behind a tree. He said it had skin as white as a piece of paper, and long, white hair, as long as a woman's. But it didn't have any . . . any . . ." Denis looked embarrassed. "You know."

"He means breasts," supplied Fleur.

"So Coffey has ascertained once and for all that the ghost is male," Theo put in with some skepticism. The young slave was given to making up extravagant stories.

Denis nodded. "I wish it had been me, Grandpapa. I wish I'd seen the ghost. But you won't let me go out at night."

"You're just a child," admonished Fleur.

"That's because there are things besides ghosts prowling the countryside, Denis," said Theo.

"He means criminals," explained Fleur. "Thieves and killers."

"Killers, killers," Blanche chanted until her grandfather touched her cheek as a signal for her to be quiet.

"Well, perhaps one night soon you and I will take a little walk around the Landing," offered Theo. "Perhaps we'll even see the ghost, Denis."

"I thought you didn't believe in ghosts, Grandpapa?" asked Fleur.

"I've never seen it, Fleur. But that doesn't mean it doesn't exist. I've lived long enough now to know there are certain things in this world that can't be explained."

Denis closed his eyes and clenched his fists. His words

were almost a prayer. "Oh, I do hope I see it before summer's end, Grandpapa."

"Me too! Me too!" shrieked Blanche. Even Fleur looked wistful. She also wanted to see the ghost, but she was too much "grown-up" to admit it.

Theo surveyed his grandchildren with amused affection. "Well, then," he said, directing his remark at Fleur, "I hope you *all* get your wish."

Aunt Lolly appeared at the door to tell them dinner was ready. Theo always ate with the children. It was earlier than he preferred, but he did it to accommodate their bedtime. He had vowed long ago to give them as much time as possible, in order to teach them to think independently and to be kindhearted and respect education, so that when his time came to pass on from the world, they would be well equipped to deal with whatever life had in store . . . even ghosts.

Holding on to the railing, Royal made his way forward, anxious to get as far as possible from the cargo area and Captain Calabozo. As he threaded through the steerage crowd, there was a commotion on the river and everyone leaned over the railing to see what was the matter. Three canoes filled with Indians, their faces painted in a grotesque manner, were floating downriver toward the steamer. The Indians stopped paddling some distance away and began chanting in frightened voices, *"Penelore! Penelore!"* Several passengers laughed derisively. Royal, whose experience with Indians was limited, naïvely asked a ruddy-faced man who reeked of whiskey, "Are we under attack?"

The man threw back his head and howled, filling the air with an alcoholic miasma. "No, good sir. The Choctaws aren't attacking—they're protesting." Speaking directly into Royal's face, the man explained, "*Penelore* means fire canoe. The superstitious savages believe that the steamboats are the work of evil spirits."

The *Belle Créole*'s pilot responded to the situation by blasting the steam whistle several times in rapid succession. The passengers cheered as the Indians began paddling toward shore in a panic. The red-faced man laughed again and offered Royal a drink from a cloudy bottle.

Royal declined with thanks, then moved along. A high wind had come up. Its gusts whipped down smoke from the steamboat's stacks and flattened the tall grasses on shore. The ship lurched from side to side as the river's current twisted and turned like a water snake.

Royal found himself near the bow. Two male passengers in tattered and sweat-stained clothing were sitting on a low stack of firewood, immersed in a game of chance. They were squinting in concentration at the greasy, dog-eared cards they held in their hands.

Royal, a puzzled look on his face, stared at the older man and murmured, "Charlie?"

They noticed Royal. The older man grinned. "You want to join us, son?" When Royal didn't answer, he offered, "If you don't know the game, we'll be glad to teach you."

Royal shook his head. "No, thank you. I . . . I'm sorry—for a second I thought you were someone else."

The younger man nudged his companion and whispered in a hoarse voice that carried to Royal's ears, "Don't be a fool, man. Don't you recognize him? That's Royal Brannigan."

Royal turned away. As if of their own will, his fingers moved to his vest pocket and withdrew the gold watch. He thought of Charlie Hazard, and of his youth. . . .

Royal had grown up in a small town on the Monongahela River, twenty miles south of Pittsburgh. He was the youngest of four sons produced by Terrence and Finola Brannigan, emigrants from Waterford, Ireland, home of the world-famous crystal. Dissatisfied with their lot under the yoke of the English, the couple had come to America and settled in the town that later was to bear the name Glassboro, in honor of the glass manufactory they established there.

They had started small—bottles, paperweights, furniture knobs, and an occasional piece of hand-cut crystal. The area was accessible to water transportation, and there were ample supplies of sand for the glass, as well as wood for fuel. These natural advantages, combined with Terrence Brannigan's perseverance, caused the business to grow rapidly. Eventually he was able to import more skilled workers from Ireland and greatly expand production, turning out pressed-glass bottles and tableware, in addition to hand-blown specialty items.

The company became the first in America to manufacture cut glass commercially, and in 1810 it turned out the first cut-glass chandelier produced in the nation. The work was of such high quality that, in 1817, Brannigan Glassworks filled an order for President Monroe and became the first American glass factory to make a crystal service for the White House. In 1829 it was similarly honored by President Jackson.

Success in the New World did not, however, ensure happiness within the Brannigan clan. As a husband and father, Terrence Brannigan was a petty tyrant. He treated his wife like a drudge and allowed her few basic comforts, let alone the luxuries he could well afford. As for his sons, he never let them forget that they had been brought into the world for one purpose only—to perpetuate the Brannigan Glassworks Company. His favorite and oft-used words were "duty," "quality," and "frugality."

From the very beginning, Royal rebelled. He was a normal high-spirited boy, and Terrence, try as he might, could not stifle his youngest son's personality. Early on, Royal developed an interest in gambling. He would bet on anything—a sudden change in the weather, how many marbles were in someone's pocket, whether he could get a girl to kiss him. He almost always won.

Royal enjoyed a close, loving relationship with his mother. Perhaps Finola's indulgence of her favorite child was her own form of rebellion against her domineering husband; but whatever her motives, she always strove to hide Royal's various escapades from Terrence—not entirely with success, for often the boy was found out and punished for his "transgressions."

Once his father had caught him playing dice with his schoolmates. As usual, Royal was winning and had a pocketful of pennies. His father was outraged. He made the boy pull down his trousers and, to Royal's acute embarrassment, whipped him in front of the small audience, which included his brothers. Tears streamed from his eyes, but he would not cry aloud. When his father had finished, Royal demanded to know what was wrong with gambling. After all, he had been winning, hadn't he?

His father, paraphrasing the Bible, replied that it did not matter if he won, if in the process he lost his immortal soul. Then he went on to pronounce gamblers, whores, drunkards, and thieves the bane of humanity.

The incident did nothing to break the boy's spirit. In fact, it reinforced his recalcitrant nature. As Royal entered adolescence, the battles against his father's domination did not abate, and he continued to steal his pleasures wherever he could.

Terrence Brannigan had his conspirators. The Irish community was small, with only one Catholic church and school—which was supported in the main by Brannigan and attended by his workers and their children—and the nuns and priests, as well as many of the glassworks employees, deemed it their duty to report every infraction. The old man, in turn, continued meting out punishment.

When Royal was eighteen, his mother became seriously ill. Finola had never been a strong woman, and the rigors of bearing one child after the other and raising them in the harsh atmosphere of the Brannigan household had weakened her. In addition, Terrence had compelled her to continue working in the showroom of the glass factory. It was inevitable that she would have a physical collapse. Yet when she did, Terrence did not send to Pittsburgh for a decent physician, but allowed a local charlatan to treat her. The "doctor" adhered to the use of purgatives, and Finola continued to weaken. Royal begged his father to bring in another doctor, but Terrence was adamant. A few days later, Finola died.

On the evening following his mother's funeral, Royal got drunk at one of the local taverns, and on his way home he broke into the showroom of the glass factory, grabbed a length of wood, and began breaking everything in the place.

The glass workers who lived nearby heard the commotion and called the police. Royal was apprehended, but instead of being taken to jail, he was held at the showroom until his father and brothers arrived. The police were sure that Mr. Brannigan would not want to press charges.

But Terrence surprised them all. He decided that his son should pay for his crime. A term in prison, he said, would "make a man out of the boy." Even Royal's usually staid brothers were appalled at this decision and pleaded with their father to change his mind. Terrence, however, would not be moved, and Royal was sentenced to one year in the Pennsylvania State Prison.

That was how he had met Charlie Hazard. Despite the terrible conditions in prison, Royal had found a friend who would change his life forever.

Charlie was a gambling man. He had worked the steamboats, and his playing grounds included the Mississippi, Missouri, and Ohio rivers and their tributaries. Charlie had made and lost a dozen fortunes. At one time, he claimed, he had been worth over a million dollars, but Lady Luck had suddenly dropped him, and now he was imprisoned for a slew of gambling debts he couldn't pay. At sixty-four he was still handsome, and even in prison clothes he retained his dapper air. He had a mane of snow-white hair, a rough-hewn face, and a twinkle in his watery blue eyes. He did, however, suffer from a bad cough, which the dampness of the prison cell and an ever-present cigar didn't help.

Charlie was a favorite among the guards and was allowed privileges because he taught them various crooked gambling techniques, such as how to deal from the bottom of the deck, how to mark cards, and how to play three-card monte. Charlie made it clear to Royal that he didn't approve of these tricks and never used them himself. A professional gambler, he proclaimed, was a "square" player who relied only on his skill and Lady Luck. Charlie believed that a real gambler was an artist, a mathematician, and a philosopher all rolled into one. Royal had not been in jail more than a week before Charlie took him under his wing, declaring he would teach the eager young man everything there was to know about gambling.

They proceeded methodically. First the old gambler taught Royal every legitimate game he knew, then he worked on developing the boy's skill and finesse. Royal learned how to spot the cappers, shills, and tricksters, the "sure-thing" players who ran "brace" games, as well as those adept at palming cards and "laying the bottom stock"—dealing from the bottom of the deck. Royal learned to keep an eye out for such mechanical cheating devices as vest, table, sleeve, and belt holdouts, "shiners" for reading hands held by opponents, and rings fitted with needlelike points for making tiny indentations in the back of cards. These and other appliances of a like character were known to the trade as "advantage tools."

Over and over again, Charlie admonished Royal to be an honest gambler, because, he said, honest gamblers lasted longer. Finally he taught his pupil a measure of "social polish." A man should be flashy, Charlie said, but not vulgar, and should enjoy the best that money could buy—fancy clothes, good wines, and pretty women.

During their time together, the two men became close friends and confidants. Royal told Charlie of his family problems, his determination not to return to Glassboro, and his plan to become a riverboat gambler. Charlie admitted that the young man had the natural talent to be a success, but warned him that gambling was a lonely life. Lady Luck was an all-consuming mistress, he said, who would leave him no time for the simpler pleasures of life, such as marriage and family.

When the time came for Royal's release, the old man called for his valuables, and when he unlocked the metal box there was only one thing inside—a fancy gold watch with a face depicting playing cards instead of numbers. He presented this to Royal and told him that it would bring him good luck only if he never put it in the pot. Inside the watch was a gold coin worth ten dollars. "Always keep a little something aside for the toll," said Charlie. "You never know when you're going to have to pay the ferryman." Royal was touched by the gift and promised that as soon as he made enough money he would pay off the old man's debts and get him released from prison. Then the two of them would work the rivers together.

As Charlie's friend, Royal had been able to enjoy a few privileges, which included better food and the frequent use of bathing facilities. Although he was thinner now and looked older, he was, if anything, even more handsome. His face had lost the ambiguous lines of youth and had taken on definition. The mourning clothes that he had been wearing when he was arrested now awaited him. The wife of one of the guards had pressed his suit, washed his shirt, and polished his boots. Charlie, who was allowed to see Royal for a brief farewell, remarked that Royal should always dress in black—perhaps with a bright vest or a piece of jewelry to provide contrast.

The men said goodbye, and Royal was released.

Outside the prison, Terrence Brannigan was waiting for his son. Sitting in the driver's seat of a modest carriage, he watched Royal exit through the gates and start to cross the road toward him. As soon as Royal saw his father, however, he stopped. He stared at him hard for a few moments, and then walked on. The old man followed him for several blocks in the carriage, but Royal did not turn around or acknowledge him in any way.

That afternoon, Royal purchased a steamship ticket for Louisville, Kentucky. The moment he stepped aboard that fancy Ohio River stern-wheeler, complete with its gingerbread decor and social hall filled with felt-topped tables and gambling men, Royal knew he was finally home.

It didn't take him long to get into a game and figure out who was straight and who was crooked. He played modestly at first; then, as he began raking in the pots, he placed higher bids, always quitting when he was ahead.

The pattern of his existence was thus established. In the following weeks and months, he bought himself several expensive sets of clothing, always in black but with a bright vest. He booked himself into the best cabins and gambled his way up and down the Ohio. He not only had phenomenal success at winning, but his dress, his manner, and the fact that he had appeared from nowhere combined to create an air of mystery that Royal found to his liking.

It took several months, but Royal was able to acquire the huge amount of money Charlie Hazard owed his debtors. Bearing a bottle of brandy and a smart new suit of clothes for his friend, Royal went to the prison to pick up the old man. But just before his scheduled release, Charlie Hazard had died of lung failure; Royal arrived only in time to save him from a pauper's grave.

One of Charlie's gambling cronies had somehow gotten wind of his demise and was also on the scene. St. Louis Sam was a scarecrow of a man. Although he was somewhere in his fifties, his hair was still bright red, the texture of straw, and seemed to be made up entirely of cowlicks. His face was long and sad, and he had jug ears and eyes so pale blue they resembled skimmed milk. St. Louis Sam had fallen on hard times and was pleased when Royal was able to spring for a decent burial for Charlie. The two men stood sharing the bottle of brandy as they watched Charlie's coffin being lowered into the grave. Then Sam offered Royal a hundred-dollar bet that Charlie was not in the box. Royal looked at him quizzically, and Sam grinned. "I wouldn't take the bet if I were you. I've known Charlie to squeeze out of tighter spots than that."

After Royal saw that St. Louis Sam had a good meal, a bottle of whiskey, a decent hotel room, and some money in his pockets, the men parted.

"May God watch over you, Sam."

"And may the same God watch over you, Royal."

St. Louis Sam's whispered words echoed in Royal's memory. Without a backward glance at the two card players, he returned to the cabin deck and forced his thoughts to the present. There was no room in his life for nostalgia.

Chapter Two

The Duc Alexandre Diron Duvallon stood at the top of the grand staircase at Salle d'Or, snorting with impatience. As he descended he made a whimpering sound with each step. At the bottom he grasped the heavily carved newel post, looked up, and glared at an empty space in the ceiling. It was reserved for a chandelier he had ordered months earlier from the Brannigan Glassworks in Pennsylvania and which had yet to arrive. Rather like a recalcitrant child the Duc stamped his foot. He was convinced that the chandelier would not come in time to be installed for the midsummer ball, an annual social event at Salle d'Or. He was further annoyed because the steamboat was late. His wife, Henriette, and his son, Philippe, were both on board, and that meant supper would have to be delayed until their return. Duvallon demanded that his household be run on a precise schedule. There was no room in his well-ordered life for late deliveries or postponed meals.

The Duc was a small, compactly built man with angular features. His black hair was just beginning to gray, and the sharp widow's peak added an incongruous touch of femininity to his appearance. Although he was forty-six, his face was unlined and retained its high color. He sported a carefully trimmed mustache beneath a prominent but well-formed nose. He was always impeccably dressed, right down to the gloves he invariably wore. He might have been called handsome if it were not for his dark eyes, which were restless and full of secrets.

The Duc's ruthless financial expertise had made him the richest of the Magnolia Landing residents, and Salle d'Or was the largest and most ostentatious of the plantations. For several months the big house had been in the throes of redecoration. The Duc, not one to stint, was adding extra rooms and ornamentation.

He spun on his two-inch heels and swaggered toward the front door, which was partly open. He called harshly to a slave who was standing on the veranda. "Has the steamboat been sighted yet?"

The slave replied, "No, m'sieur." He was a sixteen-year-old griffe, as the Creoles called those with one-sixteenth Negro blood, and his name was Blaise Christophe. The surname came from his previous master, who had been his father. He was an extremely good-looking youth with light brown hair, pale blue eyes, and skin the color of honey. Blaise moved to the other side of the column, probably hoping to keep out of his master's line of vision and therefore avoid his anger. He was saved from an impending explosion by the appearance of Alcée, the Duc's daughter.

"Are they coming, Papa?"

The Duc's agitated expression altered. "Not yet, *ma chérie.*" He grinned, obviously delighted to see her. The Duc doted upon his daughter, and though he would never admit it, she was the most precious thing in his loveless life.

Alcée Duvallon was fifteen and quite lovely. She possessed her father's dramatic dark features, but they were softened by her mother's large green eyes, chestnut hair, plump cheeks, and generous mouth. Her skin had the texture of a rose petal, and her softly curved lips seemed always on the edge of a smile, as if she knew some delightful secret.

She embraced her father, and as she did she waved behind his back to Blaise. It was a warm and intimate gesture.

Alcée took her father's hand and, pretending to scrutinize it, said in a low, sweet voice, "Now, Papa, stop fretting. The steamboat's late, and supper will keep. Goodness, even you can't control the elements."

"More's the pity," the Duc replied in all seriousness.

They walked back into the big house. The Duc trained his eyes upon the foyer ceiling.

"Papa, I'm sure the chandelier will arrive in time for the ball. That's weeks away."

"The company is usually so prompt," he complained.

"But you ordered such an unusual piece. That has to take extra time. Who knows, it just might be coming with Mama and Philippe."

"I am not so optimistic!"

Alcée sighed, took her father's arm, and guided him toward the library. Alcée loved her father, but she didn't approve of him. She disliked his business methods, his treatment of the slaves, his cruelty to her mother, and the way he had shaped

Philippe's personality after his own. She knew that her ability to manipulate him kept the household running smoother and often saved her mother from bearing the brunt of his ill humor.

The library, like the rest of the house, was decorated with an overabundance of furniture and bric-a-brac. Alcée poured her father a glass of brandy and diverted him onto another line of thought with a casual mention of the upcoming midsummer ball.

"I'm really looking forward to the ball," she said with manufactured enthusiasm.

"And so you should. Why, every eligible young bachelor from New Orleans will be attending."

Alcée pursed her lips and turned away to keep her father from seeing her exasperation. The Duc began ticking off the names of those he approved. "Louis Perrault, a handsome young man! Pierre Listeau, what a good swordsman! Ferdinand de Morales, most enterprising! Jean-Baptiste Trémoulet, very athletic! Charles Danezac, a real scholar! Jean-François Frèret, impeccable manners!" The Duc cocked an eyebrow. His daughter's lack of interest in such a prestigious list dismayed him, but he blundered on. "There's Robin Arnaud, an accomplished dancer. And the Ballard twins, André and Arsène. How could you choose between them?"

"Papa," Alcée pleaded wearily, "I *know* who's coming."

The Duc poured himself another brandy. His daughter's indifference mattered little. He intended to select her husband just as he had selected his own wife—with an exacting eye to bloodline, bank account and, as in Henriette's case, property. Alcée, he was confident, would come to love whomever he chose.

"I almost forgot Gilbert Gadobert," he said. "He has the virtues of all the other young men combined."

"Gilbert Gadobert!" Alcée exclaimed. "Papa, he hasn't any chin. You can't honestly want a brood of chinless grandchildren, can you?" Before he could reply, Alcée kissed him on the cheek, saying, "You enjoy your brandy, Papa. I'm going to the veranda to see if the steamboat has been sighted yet. Now, stop fussing. I'll be perfectly charming to all the young men, even the chinless ones. And I'm sure Mama and Philippe will arrive at any moment, probably bearing the chandelier." She gathered up her skirts and hurried out of the library.

The Duc sighed. Alcée simply didn't realize the importance of her position in society. He started to pour himself a third brandy, and as he did, the cut-glass goblet caught the light and cast a prismatic pattern against the wall. Once again he was reminded of the overdue chandelier. He muttered a curse and hurled the glass into the fireplace.

At Villeneuve Plantation, the kitchen door slammed open with a loud bang, and a young slave, Azby, announced in a breathless voice, "Mama, the fog's gone! Steamboat's a-comin' soon!"

His mother, Lilliane, in the act of removing a loaf of bread from the oven, was so startled that she dropped it on the floor. The bread landed upside down, causing her more consternation.

"Azby! Look what you made me do! A loaf upside down means the devil's coming round."

She picked up the fallen loaf, brushed it off, and set it on the table right side up. "You know better than to be making so much noise around the house. M'sieur Philippe would whip you if he were here." Hoping to avert possible disaster, she took a handful of salt and sprinkled it in a circle around the bread.

Then Lilliane looked at her son, and her face softened. Azby was seven years old and the only bright spot in her life. He was a gleaming gold color, with curly chestnut hair, huge gray eyes, and a mouth made for grinning. At that moment his eyes were brimming with tears and glistened like pieces of highly polished silver.

"M'sieur Philippe's not here now," he protested weakly.

Lilliane, almost bursting with tears herself, knelt down and gathered her son in her arms. "He will be soon," she replied softly. Then she rolled her eyes and put on an exaggerated expression of mock servitude. "And yo' know when M'sieur Philippe is at de Landing, he most always stays here to keep an eye on us niggers!"

Azby knew that his mother was putting on a show solely for his benefit, and he managed to grin in response. He also knew that his message was unwelcome. His mother dreaded Philippe's visits to Villeneuve. Although the little boy did not understand the physical aspects of their relationship, he knew that Philippe used his mother as a concubine. And he knew that his mother didn't like it.

"Come on, now," Lilliane said. "Come sit down, and I'll fix

you a slice of fresh-baked bread with butter and swamp honey."

Azby gazed at his mother in adoration. She was the only person in the world who loved him and shielded him from childhood hurts. "Mama, you're the prettiest mama I know."

Lilliane was touched by her son's words. There were times, though, when she cursed her own beauty. Lilliane was a twenty-one-year-old quadroon, and her mixed blood was evidenced in her features. Her skin was tawny, and her abundant hair, which she kept hidden beneath her tignon, was a vibrant auburn. Her eyes were large, light gray, and slightly slanted, giving her face an exotic appeal. A long, graceful neck and a full, voluptuous figure caused men of all colors to turn their heads and women, both free and slave, to cluck their tongues in disapproval.

Had Lilliane been a free woman of color she could have been a Siren of the Ramparts—one of the young mulatto women who were kept by wealthy Creole gentlemen. But she was not free, and she was no longer a virgin.

Lilliane had been born to a mulatto slave woman owned by a wealthy Creole family. Her father, whom she had never known, had been white. Raised to be the companion of twin daughters, Lilliane had been taught correct speech, manners, and deportment—qualities that would later cause her much heartache. When she had been barely fourteen, her owner and most of his family had perished during one of the recurrent yellow fever epidemics, and the executors of the estate had seen fit to dispose of the slaves for ready cash. Lilliane had been separated from her mother and sold at auction to Philippe Duvallon, who had brought her to Villeneuve rather than Salle d'Or, so that he could conduct his exploitation of her well away from the disapproval of his mother. Philippe was the only man Lilliane had ever known intimately. She had never experienced tenderness or felt passion. She believed that Philippe knew she was repelled by him, and that that was part of his attraction to her.

She glanced at the ceiling. Hanging from the beams were strips of flypaper—cut lengths of newspaper that had been dipped in molasses. They were polka-dotted with dead insects, and those that had been recently caught were struggling to free themselves, ultimately at the cost of a leg or a wing. An ironic smile crossed Lilliane's lips. She, too, was trapped. Unless Philippe married and brought his wife to

Villeneuve, her situation would never change, never improve. It could only become worse. Still, she had her son. When her feelings of bitterness surfaced, they were immediately dispelled by Azby. Lilliane loved him with every fiber of her being, and his very existence made her own tolerable.

She got up from the table and said, "You go play until dark. I'll fix you something good for dinner."

"Can't I stay with you, Mama?" the boy pleaded.

"You can't be with your mama all the time, Azby."

Lilliane knew that Azby didn't like playing with the other slave children. They resented him for being lighter than they and for speaking more like a white boy than a slave. Though Azby was often the brunt of cruel jokes, Lilliane felt that he must learn to deal with the world. It wasn't a happy place for a person of color, nor, she suspected, would it ever be.

"Go on," she said, and handed him an empty canning jar. "Catch me some fireflies. They'll be out soon."

Azby's face brightened. "I'll catch you a whole jar full, Mama."

She watched him hurry away toward the peach orchard, and her heart went with him.

Even though Lilliane was in a distasteful position, there were advantages to her life at Villeneuve. Her duties were few. The grounds and the buildings were scrupulously maintained by slaves from Salle d'Or. Mainly she just had to care for herself and her son and please Philippe in bed when he visited the big house. Lilliane had a good deal of free time to pursue her own activities. She had a fine hand with a needle and made patchwork quilts, fabric dolls, and ruffled aprons, all of which were taken by Juba, a male house slave, and sold on the market in New Orleans. The money she earned was hidden away for a very special purpose.

Lilliane went to her and Azby's small room down the hall from the kitchen. Most of the rooms at Villeneuve were closed off, except for Philippe's quarters, and she saw those only when he summoned her. Lilliane was glad that at least Philippe never came to her room. It was her sanctuary—a place where she hoarded her secret dreams for Azby's future.

Lilliane sat down on the rocker near the window. She took up her sewing, and as her fingers nimbly worked, her eyes began to burn and tear. She was afraid that she was developing eye problems, and she prayed that God would grant her the time to earn enough money so that she could buy her son's freedom from his father—Philippe Duvallon.

Driven by the scent of roasting meat, a stray male dog with a battle-scarred yellow coat hurried through the field of sugar cane toward the plantation called Heritage. He was salivating heavily as he approached the driveway leading to the big house. He broke into a trot until he reached the elaborate wrought-iron gates, where he stopped. The gates were open, as if the owners were expecting him.

The mongrel lifted his muzzle, sniffed suspiciously, then slipped inside. Keeping low to the ground, he moved cautiously through the gardens, then gingerly crossed the lawn bordering the big house. He stopped, lifted his leg, and relieved himself against a rose hedge.

At the same time, a figure noiselessly crept along the other side of the hedge, deep in the shade of the veranda. Large hands carefully parted the bright crimson flowers that concealed curved thorns lurking beneath the leaves. Dark, hooded eyes blazing with anger peered at the dog. A stone, scooped from one of the flower boxes, was flung through the air. It struck the dog directly between the eyes. The stunned animal yelped in pain and staggered in a circle. Recovering, he snarled at his assailant before breaking into a run away from the big house and the roasting meat.

Zenobia grunted with satisfaction as she watched the dog's departure. She was a Negro slave in her middle forties who had served in her younger years as mammy for the plantation children, and now she functioned as housekeeper. A tall, muscular woman with an erect carriage and detached manner, she had prominent cheekbones, a long neck, and large, sculpted lips that testified to her Senegalese ancestry. She was as black as if she had been carved from ebony. On her head she wore a tightly wrapped tignon and a pair of gold hoop earrings. A simple shift of brown cotton and the inevitable white apron were her only garments. She had never worn shoes. Her feet were large but gracefully formed and cushioned by soles that were as tough as tanned leather.

As she continued along the veranda a voice called from the sewing room, "Zenobia, what was that terrible noise?"

Zenobia stepped through the French doors. The two women looked up expectantly. Now that the weather was clear, the steamboat would be docking soon, bringing to one a husband and to the other a brother.

"Jes' a stray dog," Zenobia said.

Angélique Jourdain was the first to react. "You and your stray dogs, Zenobia. I suppose you routed this one with a rock?" The slave's black-as-flint eyes remained impassive as she nodded imperceptibly.

"The poor thing probably just wanted something to eat," said Suzanne Jourdain.

"Stray dogs bring bad news," Zenobia grunted, then moved through the sewing room collecting two empty cups and the remains of several small iced cakes that had been picked over but not eaten. Without another word, she left the sewing room.

When the door was closed the two women looked at each other and broke into girlish giggles.

"Zenobia and her stray dogs," Angélique laughed.

"Zenobia and her stray omens, you mean," amended Suzanne.

They burst into another fit of giggles, then, struggling to control themselves, returned to their needlepoint. The women, seated in a pair of matching Queen Anne chairs, made a startling impression. A stranger entering the room would have been struck not only by the magnitude of their beauty but by the sharp contrast between them.

Angélique Jourdain was twenty, two years younger than her brother, Jean-Louis, the owner of Heritage Plantation. Silver-gold hair crowned her head. Her eyes were extraordinarily large, slightly protuberant, and pale green—the eyes of a visionary. Her gardenia-white complexion was flawless, so clear and shiny that it might have been polished. She had a narrow, authoritative nose and a wide, sensual mouth. Her smile was self-contained, catlike, and the way she held her head bespoke a certain arrogance and recklessness.

Jean-Louis's twenty-one-year-old wife, Suzanne, was also a stunning woman, though in a more modest way. Her face was longish but relieved by huge, wide-set blue-gray eyes flecked with green and amber that shone like pieces of mother-of-pearl. Her features were sharply chiseled, and her hair was black and glossy against her pale skin. She had the expression and deportment of a woman who had accepted herself and her position in life, though her gaze hinted at an incipient danger lurking beneath an outer calm.

As they sat near the window working on their needlepoint, the sunlight began to fade. Suzanne left her chair and moved about the room, turning up the lamps. It was a large, pleasant room, smelling of roses and beeswax. The walls were paneled with fruitwood, and an Oriental carpet graced the highly polished wood floor.

"I hope the gowns we ordered for the Duc's ball are on board," said Suzanne. "Perhaps Jean-Louis will be bringing them home."

Angélique, who dealt more realistically with her brother's unreliable nature, replied, "*If* he comes home tonight."

"But he promised he would," Suzanne said, her tone not altogether convincing.

"Then I'm sure he will," her sister-in-law automatically responded. "After all, he did promise."

They avoided looking at each other, and something unspoken separated them like a curtain.

Zenobia entered, telling them dinner would soon be ready.

After the two of them went upstairs to change, the slave, more practical than her mistresses, began turning down the lamps. Curious, she examined their needlepoint. Suzanne was executing a precise design with small stitches, using subtle colors that blended into a delicate floral design. Angélique employed bold contrasting colors and larger stitches, in a stark design that portrayed an avenging angel with a flaming sword, slicing through the heavens to wreak havoc on earthbound sinners.

"Steamboat a-comin'!"

The jubilant call rang out and was echoed and reechoed down the long corridor of trees. The Negro boys, their duty done, scrambled out of the magnolias, dropping to the ground like so many pieces of sun-ripened fruit. Racing one another to the wharf, they sprinted en masse down the Promenade.

The river changed from muddy brown to green as the *Belle Créole* drew closer to shore, its bells clanging and whistles blowing to announce its successful, if late, arrival. As if in greeting, the low clouds released the setting sun, tinting everything on shore a crimson gold.

Royal stood atop the hurricane deck, well away from the other passengers. He had the odd impression that the wharf was moving through the shimmering red light toward the ship, instead of the opposite. He gazed at the buildings clustered near the landing; they had been built high on an embankment in order to accommodate the rise of the capricious Mississippi. There were several warehouses, a windmill, a post office, and a livery, all so close together that they looked like one structure. The buildings were framed by huge trees bowed down by Spanish moss, and around the base of each was a variety of flowers. Poincianas burst into flame; lacy ferns, shimmering in the light, became filigrees of gold; birds of paradise looked as if they were ready to take flight. The entire place appeared as unreal as a stage setting.

The paddle wheel backed water as the *Belle Créole* glided alongside the wharf, a half-dozen deckhands leaping nimbly ashore and securing mooring lines. From his vantage point Royal saw that Captain Calabozo had stationed himself on the shore side of the already lowered gangplank, striking a pose that resembled a ship's figurehead. With a great fuss, he helped the Creole women—Henriette and Marguerite—descend the last few feet of the gangplank. They spent a moment talking, and the captain's face went red and apologetic. Royal assumed that they were complaining about his presence aboard ship. Then the women disappeared around the corner of the windmill, apparently to where carriages awaited them.

The Negro boys stood aside until the last of the passengers had disembarked, then hurried to the loading area to see if there were any small packages they could carry home. A deckhand good-naturedly distributed those items that were unbreakable and of a moderate size and weight. Grinning with self-importance, the boys clutched the packages to their chests and broke into a run, knowing that at the end of their journey a coin awaited them from their master or mistress.

The wharf had suddenly come alive with activity, and the stage setting took on a semblance of reality. Burly blacks and mulattoes unloaded the bulkier cargo, then carted the various goods through the swarming throng. Some of the disembarked passengers milled about on the wharf, sweating under their heavy garments and trying to avoid being jostled by workers while they gathered their belongings and found their rides to the various plantations of Magnolia Landing.

* * *

Léon Martineau, anxious to see his wife, Michelle, jumped from the carriage before it had fully come to a stop in front of Bellechasse.

"Léon, contain yourself," admonished his aunt Marguerite. "Remember that you're a gentleman."

Léon did not apologize. Instead he ordered the driver to bring the luggage and the gaily wrapped presents into the house. He extended his hand to his aunt. He intended this gesture to be his final act of Southern gentlemanliness for the evening. Léon was most anxious to be rid of Marguerite. All the way home from the Landing he had endured her nonstop tirade, which included the inconsequence of Henriette Duvallon, their encounter with the American gambler, her worries about the decreasing quality of the passengers on the *Belle Créole*, and her agitation over the extravagant gifts he had bought for Michelle in New Orleans.

As Léon waited for her to smooth the folds of her dress, he brushed dust from his cerulean blue suit in a gesture of impatience. They walked up the stairs to the veranda, and the main doors to the big house sprang open as if by magic. The corps of house slaves, in perfect alignment, stood in the foyer awaiting orders. Léon ignored them, but Marguerite marched down the line like an inspecting general, stopping from time to time to point out an infraction of dress or demeanor.

Léon's eyes fell upon the gilded wood console. The roses in the Bohemian glass vase were bereft of blooms, the long stems evidently having been decapitated. Then he noticed a cluster of rose petals on the floor, which signaled the start of what appeared to be a trail leading somewhere into the house. Marguerite noticed the object of Léon's attention. She glared at the house slaves. "*Alors!* What is this mess? Why hasn't it been cleared away?"

The slaves immediately broke rank. Léon held up his hand and, smirking, said, "No, don't bother. I'll do it." He impulsively kissed his aunt on the cheek and recited from Robert Herrick, the seventeenth-century English poet:

"Gather ye rosebuds while ye may,
Old Time is a-flying;
And this same flower that smiles today,
Tomorrow will be dying."

Marguerite snorted, "English poets, indeed! It's all that European decadence." Perplexed by her nephew's eccentric behavior, she turned her irritation toward the slaves. "I am exhausted," she announced to the assemblage. "I am going straight to my room, and I am not to be disturbed."

Léon bid her good evening and, his heart beating with anticipation, moved slowly through the main floor of the house. He took his time, gathering each petal and stuffing it into his pockets. He was infused with the excitement that comes from putting something pleasurable off just a little bit longer.

By the time he reached the door to the greenhouse, his pockets were bulging with rose petals. His trembling fingers touched the brass doorknob, and he was grinning with delight. What a woman! What imagination! He licked his lips nervously and eased the door open. The heavy languor of the flower-drenched air rushed at him like a warm, sensuous embrace. He shuddered with expectation and, bending low, followed the trail of petals down the aisle between the tables of thriving floral plants. He was too eager now to gather the strewn petals and could barely contain his rapid breathing.

The far end of the greenhouse was lit by flickering candles, creating a churchlike atmosphere. In the center of this carnal shrine Michelle was frozen in a position of supplication. A nude madonna!

Léon swallowed hard and expelled his breath in a deep sigh. He began walking toward her. His movements were slow, labored, dreamlike. His eyes were glazed and shining. His chest was heaving. He unloosened his cravat and fumbled with the buttons of his shirt. By the time he reached her, he, too, was naked.

Reverently, Léon knelt in front of her, then pressed his hard, compact body against her soft, yielding flesh and slowly pulled her to the ground.

"You found me," Michelle whispered.

When the carriage arrived at Salle d'Or, Philippe, a little bit drunk, began railing at the slaves who were unloading the crate containing the eagerly awaited chandelier.

"Steady, you black bastards—keep it steady! You niggers break one crystal on Papa's chandelier and I will personally whip the hide right off your backs." Despite the harshness of his words, Philippe was smiling. He loved to give orders to the slaves.

Henriette, anxious to get away from her bullying son, hurried up the steps. She paused on the veranda and said, "I'll run and tell Alexandre we're home so that supper can be served." She glanced nervously at Philippe. "Don't be long. You know how cross your papa is when he's kept waiting."

"Papa's humor will be considerably improved when he hears that the chandelier has finally arrived." Philippe laughed, then went to lean against one of the columns, sipping from his silver flask as he watched the slaves struggle up the stairs with the chandelier. He smiled smugly, and a bit of brandy dribbled down his chin, staining his elegant bottle-green suit. He cursed and threw the flask into the azalea bushes. After seeing that the chandelier was carefully placed in the foyer for installation the next morning, Philippe went directly to the dining room.

The dining room was a cavernous space, designed and decorated with little regard to the joys of eating. The dark fabric that covered the walls and ceiling was printed in dull, muddy colors. The woodwork was mahogany, with a profusion of baroque friezes, cornices, and pilasters. The furniture was ponderous and ugly, and the room was poorly lit by a monstrous chandelier of brass that resembled a great golden spider. The place looked less like a plantation dining room than a bleak chamber in a Gothic castle.

The Duc and Alcée were already seated at the table. "Where's your mother?" the Duc asked sharply. He turned to one of the slaves standing at rigid attention next to the sideboard. "Fetch Madame Duvallon!" Then he abruptly stood up, jiggling the wineglasses on the table. "Never mind. I'll fetch her myself!"

He started for the door, but at that moment Henriette entered. She had spent a few minutes praying at the *prie-dieu* in her bedroom. She looked serene, untroubled—almost as if she had taken a drug.

"We've been waiting for you, madame." The Duc went to her, a poisonously sweet smile on his lips. He kissed her dry cheek, then slipped his hand behind her neck. Though it appeared to the others that he was affectionately guiding her to her seat, in reality the Duc's strong fingers were ruthlessly kneading Henriette's flesh, sending flashes of pain through her skull.

"You've managed to delay supper once again, madame. The pompano will be overdone. The turtle soup will have gotten too thick, and the duck will be dry and the crawfish tough. But no matter. You're here now, and our little family is complete." He pushed her against the back of her chair. "Do be careful, madame," he said with concern. Then he released his grip and pulled out the chair so that Henriette could be seated.

The Duc took his place at the head of the table and snapped his fingers at the male slave who served as the wine steward. The griffe, Blaise, stepped forward to fill the Duc's glass with the blood-red Spanish wine he so favored. For this duty the slave's brawny body was encased in a snug uniform of dark green lawn trimmed in lace. Blaise moved around the table to the Duc's right, where Philippe sat, then on to Henriette. She covered her glass with the palm of her hand and shook her head. The final glass to be filled was Alcée's. "Just half, please," Alcée said, and when he had done her bidding, she added, "Thank you, Blaise."

The Duc frowned at Alcée. "It isn't necessary to thank them or call them by name, *ma chérie*." Alcée didn't respond to his criticism.

Throughout the hurried supper the Duc belittled his wife, making sport of her until she was almost reduced to tears. Even before coffee and brandy were served, he prodded Philippe to tell about his exploits in New Orleans. Philippe was sufficiently drunk that it amused him to embarrass his mother and sister by describing his sexual conquests in the coarsest terms. The Duc was also amused, but Henriette and Alcée stared uncomfortably at the table.

Alcée usually protested her father's and brother's rude behavior, but tonight she said nothing. She had grown tired of defending Henriette and, as always, was just a little bit afraid of her father and brother when they were drinking. Interrupting one of Philippe's indelicate stories, she stood up and said, "You will excuse us." She nodded to her mother, and Henriette also stood up.

"You are excused, *mes chéries*," the Duc said, laughing at his son's adventures.

Henriette quickly mounted the stairs, went to her room, and knelt at her *prie-dieu*, where, in the flickering candlelight, she prayed fervently to her favorite saint—Saint Roch, the patron of plague victims and impossible favors. The popular belief was that the good saint might grant what one wanted but always took something away. Henriette closed her eyes tightly and intoned, "Oh, dear Saint Roch, my beloved saint of impossible tasks, please protect Alcée from those who would corrupt her." Tears streaming down her face, she beseeched, "Do not turn your back on me. Give me this and take something from me. Just protect my sweet Alcée, and you can have my life if you so wish it. I ask this in the name of the Father, the Son, and the Holy Ghost. Amen."

As for Alcée, she stomped and sputtered around her own room in a perfect imitation of her father. "I will not be forced to marry anyone," she vowed. "Not Robin Arnaud, not Louis Perrault, not anyone! Not even the Ballard twins!" She laughed in spite of herself. She knew that no matter what her father decreed, it was too late. She had already given her heart away.

Royal checked his pocket watch. His face was flushed, and he was controlling his anxiety with difficulty. He had been waiting aboard the *Belle Créole* for an hour and forty-five minutes while all the carriages had been loaded and the people whisked away. The wharf was empty now, save for a few slaves. Royal decided it was time to leave the ship.

Just then he saw Captain Calabozo striding toward him. The little man was sweating profusely. "I've secured a carriage to take you to the plantation, M'sieur Brannigan," he said. "But I'm afraid it will cost a bit more to load your . . . cargo."

"And why is that, Captain?" Royal asked evenly.

"The Negroes won't touch the casket. They're very superstitious. My men, however, will bring it ashore and put it onto the wagon . . . for an additional fee."

"How much?"

Calabozo shrugged his shoulders.

"I don't have the time to haggle, man," Royal said sharply. He withdrew a packet of money from his inside pocket, peeled off several bills, and waved them in front of the captain's face. "This should more than cover the additional fee."

Captain Calabozo palmed the money, signaled to a group of his men who were waiting near the cargo area, then shouted for another to bring around the horse and wagon.

Once Royal was satisfied that the coffin and his luggage

were secure, he climbed up to the wagon seat and asked, "How do I get there, Captain?"

Captain Calabozo replied, "Just beyond that windmill is the Promenade, the entrance to Magnolia Landing. You can reach all the plantations from there. They're identified at each turnoff."

Royal drove off without another word. As he rounded the windmill, he reined the horse to a full stop. He was struck, as were all visitors to Magnolia Landing, by the sheer majesty of the Promenade. The twin line of giant magnolia trees stretched as far as the eye could see. They were in full flower, and the white blossoms resembled delicate cups of fresh cream tinged pink in the twilight. The crowns of the trees were so crowded with blooms that they almost seemed like rows of tethered clouds.

Royal sat there, drinking it all in. The alley between the trees had been paved with tons of crushed seashells that glittered like semiprecious gems, and the night air was so fermented with the spicy aroma of the magnolias that it made him lightheaded. He knew that he would remember his first view of Magnolia Landing for the rest of his life. Gently he snapped the reins, and the wheels began to roll, carrying him down the sylvan corridor.

An amorphous lemon-colored moon became superimposed on the dark magenta sky. The eerie glow of the evening accounted for the distortions Royal seemed to see. The magnolia trees appeared more closely crowded than they actually were, and the roadway became darker and narrower.

Royal had always been an outsider, a man on the run from society, but until this moment he had not recognized his loneliness. Since leaving prison, he had lived in a world devoid of friendships. As time passed, he had become used to his singular existence and had become almost fond of his loneliness, as one might of a somewhat shady friend.

A mongrel yellow dog darted across his path. The startled horse raised itself on its hind legs and pawed at the air with its hooves. "Easy, boy, easy," Royal crooned. He managed to calm the animal, and it picked up an even, rhythmic pace once again.

He drove through a bank of drifting fireflies as in the distance a whippoorwill sang its deliberate call. Its night song was repetitive, almost hypnotic. The muted clip-clop of the horse's hooves against the crushed seashells, combined with the overpowering scent of the magnolias, served to stir Royal's memory. Scenes from the recent past rushed down the darkened corridor toward him like images conjured by a fevered dream. . . .

Chapter Three

The first link in the chain of events that had brought Royal to Magnolia Landing was the purchase of the boutonniere. When in New Orleans, Royal always stayed at the Plantation Hotel, where he kept a suite of rooms. That Saturday night, two days earlier, he had stopped, as usual, to buy a flower for his lapel from the little girl in the lobby.

Even for New Orleans Minette was an odd-looking creature. She was a wisp of a girl, no more than twelve—a quadroon, or perhaps an octoroon. Her pale skin was extravagantly freckled, and her blue-gray eyes were so large that her other features seemed inconsequential. The dress she wore appeared to be made of patches upon patches of fabric and was decorated with scraps of ribbons and lace. Her total appearance reminded Royal of a mosaic, an entity put together with bits and pieces of color and texture.

Minette exhibited her flowers in a miniature ship on wheels, complete with canvas sails, that evidently had once been the elaborate toy of a wealthy child. Now discarded, it showed the wear and tear of that spoiled youngster. The sails were tattered, the paint scarred, and only three of the original wooden wheels remained. The fourth, somewhat larger than the others, had been a metal lid. The hull of the ship held the various jars, which were filled with muddy Mississippi river water and kept the blooms surprisingly fresh. The ship also served as a repository and napping place for a ragged calico cat.

Minette suggested that Royal buy a pink magnolia because it matched the color of his embroidered vest, and the message imparted by that particular color and bloom was: "I am alone but I don't want to be." Royal laughed, accepted her selection, and gave her a generous tip. As he continued on his way, she called after him, *"Bonne chance, M'sieur Brannigan. Bonne chance!"*

The sky rumbled like the empty belly of a beggar, and each breath of wind that touched Royal's face whispered rain. As he walked down Chartres Street, he took a deep breath and inhaled the perfume of the city. The pungent aroma of New Orleans combined the smell of crayfish and brine, Creole cooking, exotic spices, and the perpetually brewing chicory-laced coffee. He sucked the air down his throat, and it charged him with a sudden energy. His veins and arteries pulsed, and he felt as if his heart were going to explode from his chest like Christmas fireworks. Every night in New Orleans held its own peculiar feeling, but he sensed that tonight was somehow special.

Since it was Saturday night and there was a full moon, the streets and banquettes were more crowded than usual. Everyone seemed to be smiling, which didn't surprise Royal, for he was of the opinion that just being in New Orleans was reason enough to celebrate.

He encountered a group of Portuguese sailors laughing and spitting sprays of alcohol at one another. They were swarthy, curly-haired men, and each sported a golden earring. One of them carried on his shoulder a spider monkey in a miniature sailor suit. As Royal passed, the animal tipped its hat. The men were probably on their way to one of the many whorehouses on the waterfront.

A jagged fork of lightning bounded across the horizon and left a sulfurous tang in the air. The sound of thunder was still distant but was increasing in volume by the minute. Stray cats darted for cover as the moon suddenly vanished in a mass of swirling clouds.

Royal turned at the corner of Canal Street and quickened his pace. The night was charged with excitement, and he could feel its magic infuse his being. It was a feeling he had experienced many times before. It was the special knowledge that capricious Lady Luck was walking beside him.

The dominant vice in New Orleans was gambling. Everyone indulged in it. In the evening, when the business day was over, fortunes were lost and won and lost again at the gaming tables. New Orleans boasted more gambling houses than Philadelphia, Baltimore, Boston, and New York combined.

Royal moved quickly past the lower-class gambling establishments, cafés, ballrooms, and coffeehouses, all of which catered to the rougher elements of the city's population. They were not for him. He was headed where the games were played for the highest of stakes.

The sky opened and the rain began to fall. First a light spattering of drops, then bigger splashes, then it began coming down in silver-gray sheets. Royal ducked under the bright red awning that marked the entrance to Odalisque. A Negro doorman in a crimson uniform opened the etched-glass door, and Royal stepped into a world of abundant decadence.

Odalisque was designed for the rich and the debauched. It was a place where professional gamblers, plantation owners, monied tourists, visiting dignitaries, high-priced courtesans, and thrill-seeking politicians could eat, drink, gamble, and fornicate in hedonistic splendor, all under one pink-tiled roof. At Odalisque gratification was the order of the day, and the only commandment recognized there had been amended to two words: "Thou shalt."

Those who came to Odalisque expected and received the best—the finest wines and liquors, exquisite Creole cuisine, and beautiful whores who catered to any outlandish taste. The sumptuous rooms were sprayed hourly with expensive perfumes, and the pop of champagne corks sounded twenty-four hours a day.

Odalisque herself, the owner of the casino, was a "straight shooter." She ran an honest gambling house, and woe to anyone she caught cheating. There was also a certain amount of discretion at Odalisque—something practically nonexistent elsewhere in New Orleans. It was understood that what went on within those elegant walls was not to be included in the next day's gossip.

After passing through a narrow hallway with cloakrooms on both sides, Royal entered the front bar. He recognized many people and acknowledged a few of them. There were women with whom he had slept and men with whom he had gambled, but he stopped to chat with no one, making his way toward a space at the end of the bar. Generally gamblers preferred to travel in pairs or in teams of three or more, but Royal was a private man and a rare gambler—the consummate loner.

The bar was a polished work of art. Sculpted from rosewood and complete with gleaming brass fixtures, it was well over twenty feet long. Behind it were shelves of fancy glassware and paintings of buxom enchantresses coyly posed in the nude. The bartender, a handsome young quadroon, greeted Royal and served him an Irish whiskey.

Drink in hand, Royal wandered through the gaming rooms. Each room was decorated differently, but the color scheme was always in a shade of red. Everywhere were gilded mirrors, marble side tables, alabaster vases, and divans heaped with silk cushions. The brocade-covered walls were hung with erotic paintings. Each room was dedicated to a particular gambling *spécialité*, whether it be roulette, *rouge et noir*, faro, casino, whist, keno, even the newly popular poker. The chatter of conversation and the clink of glassware were augmented by the shuffle of cards, the spin of wheels, the rattle of dice, and the jingle of coin.

The red felt tabletops were covered with enormous piles of gold and silver, stacks of paper money, private issue, multicolored chips, and even precious gems. People stood shoulder to shoulder, gambling their newly won fortunes or their last dollar on the spin of the wheel or the turn of a card. It was a heady atmosphere, charged with speculation and greed.

Royal was in his element. There was only one thing that detracted from his pleasure—most of the bar ware, and all the chandeliers and light fixtures, were from his father's glass factory. He moved in and out of the rooms, quietly observing the action. His favorite game was poker. He felt it was an exercise in skill rather than chance, provided the players were honest and the cards unmarked. But he was in no hurry to play. After so many weeks of working the river, he was enjoying the ambience of the lush gaming house. He decided to head for the main salon, where Odalisque usually held court. He wanted to pay his respects to the proprietress. Guided by the music of a string ensemble—harp, violins, and cello—he found the entrance and looked inside.

The black and white checkered floor made a splendid backdrop for the colorful costumes of the patrons. Garnet silk, turquoise velvet, emerald satin, and topazine linen splashed color against the stark pattern. The effect was completely dazzling. For a moment Royal had the impression that the people were frozen into position like pieces on a gigantic chessboard. Then, as he stepped through the doorway, the figures suddenly became animated.

The main salon had two stories. Staircases led to a balcony, which ran the length and breadth of the room and opened onto private chambers used for gambling or activities of a more intimate nature. Three huge crystal chandeliers with illuminated red globes resembling overripe plums hung from the ceiling.

Royal made his way through the swirl of color and conversation toward Odalisque. Once, countless years earlier, Odalisque had been pretty, but now her features were obscured by layer upon layer of fat. Although her body was huge, it was not without a certain attraction. The fat was distributed in the right places. Her immense bosom overflowed the décolletage of her scarlet gown and was more than matched in girth by her hips.

She attempted to hide herself under heavy makeup, an outlandish wig of flaming red, and a coral gown so intricately sequined, embroidered, beaded, fringed, ruffled, and tasseled that it did indeed have a tendency to defy the eye to concentrate on the true contours of the wearer. Her nose, short and spongy with broad nostrils, bobbed above a self-indulgent mouth that had been tinted burgundy. Fuchsia eye shadow set off her small black eyes, and a daub of vermilion wounded each bunchy cheek. As a final garish touch, a beauty patch in the shape of a heart had been pasted on her chin. Royal thought the total effect was that of a burning bush, but definitely not the biblical kind.

As always, Odalisque was seated on a huge chair affixed to a wheeled platform that was pushed around the rooms by a muscular black slave named Mataché, who was rumored to be her lover. Royal had never seen Odalisque walk, yet he had heard that she was not a cripple, just fat. On her excursions around the club, Odalisque was proceeded by a Negro slave boy called Boudin, who was costumed as a Turkish harem attendant. Deftly balanced atop his turban was a silver serving tray containing an assortment of the soft chocolates that Odalisque favored. From time to time she would spear one with an extraordinarily long fingernail, pop it into her mouth, and seemingly swallow it whole. Odalisque claimed she never slept, and Royal believed her, for all the times he had gambled at her casino he had never known her not to be in attendance.

Odalisque saw Royal, signaled Mataché, and the overburdened chair came to a halt in front of him.

"Haugh!" she bellowed. "You're cetainly a handsome devil, Royal Brannigan. How are things with you? Haugh? Haugh?"

Royal bussed both her swollen cheeks. "I'm fine, Odalisque. You look as spectacular as ever."

"Haugh!" Odalisque snorted, and speared a chocolate. "I love to be complimented," she replied with calculated coyness, "by tall . . . handsome . . . young . . . men."

"Even more than you love chocolate?" Royal teased.

She turned to her lover. "Mataché, see that Royal has everything he wishes. Food, liquor, women . . . whatever. And it's on the house. Tonight, Royal, you are the guest of Odalisque."

Royal bowed and kissed her stubby, bejeweled hand. "Thank you for your hospitality. The food and drink I will accept." He raised his head and looked directly into her eyes. "But there's only one woman here who totally fascinates me." He glanced at Mataché. "Unfortunately, she's not free."

Odalisque's face beamed with pleasure. Not trusting herself to be discreet, she speared three chocolates in a row and crammed them into her mouth before replying. "Mataché, wheel me away from here before I forget I'm a lady. Go on, Royal, break a few hearts—just be careful not to break my bank."

As Royal moved across the marble floor, the music changed. The sedate string ensemble was replaced by a German brass band, and the subsequent martial sounds put Royal on edge and instilled an air of tension to the already high-strung crowd.

Royal noticed that his glass was empty. He went to the bar and, taking advantage of Odalisque's hospitality, ordered another. As he took the first sip he became acutely aware that somebody was staring at him. He turned to his left, and his gaze came to rest upon a young Creole gentleman.

The man quickly turned away. He was tall, impeccably dressed in a suit of apricot silk, and strikingly handsome. Royal had seen him here before and had heard his friends address him as Jean-Louis, but the two of them had never spoken. Standing on either side of the young Creole were two women Royal recognized as employees of Odalisque. One was a pretty mulatto named Persipanie, and the other a pale redhead who called herself Pearl Precious. They worked as a team, and in times past both had tried to persuade Royal to bed them, but Royal had graciously declined.

Turning his attention back to his drink, Royal reflected that there was something about the young Creole that offended him, but he couldn't quite put a name to it.

"I had always thought," Jean-Louis said in a loud, brittle voice, meant to be overheard by Royal, "that Odalisque ran a casino for the select. But I discover I've been deluded, for here we find ourselves rubbing elbows with an American!"

Royal stiffened, and a hush fell over the bar. The people at the nearest tables grew suddenly quiet. All eyes were directed toward Royal, but he continued sipping his drink as if he had not heard the Creole's insult.

Jean-Louis persisted. "The barbarian must be hard of hearing."

The Creole's second remark gained him even more of an audience, including Odalisque. The hefty proprietress, determined to avoid trouble, ordered Mataché to wheel her to the bar.

Royal finished his drink in one gulp, set the glass down, and walked toward the insolent Creole and his companions. As he neared them he saw that the rose-colored light had been most flattering to Jean-Louis. There were coarse threads of gray in his blond hair, and his face was bleached from dissipation. His brown eyes were no longer young, and they seemed unnaturally bright. And his fine nose was scarred by small, broken veins. Royal suspected that alcohol wasn't the only thing that kept this man going; doubtless he also indulged in Get-Lively Powder, or some other brand of opium-laced snuff.

As Royal stared insolently, Jean-Louis's self-satisfied expression began to turn sour, but he would not deign to notice the other man. Royal observed that the Creole's elegant apparel did not disguise the fact that his body had grown soft. His shoulders slumped, and a flab of belly hung over the waistband of the too-tight pants. And, Royal noted with distaste, he reeked with the overpowering scent of sandalwood.

In a steady, clear voice, Royal said, "I choose to ignore the unpleasant aspects of life. For instance, if I am standing on a street corner and a passing donkey breaks wind, I choose not to acknowledge that beast's ill manners, for I know he cannot help it."

By now even the band had stopped playing. Everyone's attention was riveted to the bar and the exchange that was taking place. Odalisque obviously was reluctant to intervene; both men were frequent customers and big spenders. She couldn't afford to offend either of them.

Jean-Louis's response was predictable and typically Creole.

He picked up one of his gloves from the bar and, with a sneer of defiance, struck Royal across the face. "Foreigner! I demand that you give me satisfaction beneath the branches of the Dueling Oaks!"

"I accept the challenge," Royal replied. "But first I must give you a history lesson. It is you who are the foreigner. Perhaps you've forgotten that the United States bought your country lock, stock, and barrel."

Before Jean-Louis could reply, Odalisque rolled to their side. "Gentlemen, gentlemen," she cooed, "don't be foolhardy." She gestured toward the shuttered windows. "You would both be drowned in this terrible deluge. Besides, much as I would regret it, neither of you would henceforth be welcomed in this establishment. I have my own good name to look after."

The men glanced at each other, then turned back to Odalisque. They had not expected this.

"Why not a game of chance instead?" she added slyly.

Royal said, "Since he started this unpleasantness, the game must be by my choice . . . unless he prefers pistols, of course."

"I defer to madame," conceded Jean-Louis.

Royal smiled. "Then I say poker."

"Poker is not a gentleman's game!"

"I am not a gentleman."

Odalisque said hurriedly, "Poker it is. I shall have one of the private rooms made ready for you."

A short time later, the two young men found themselves in a small room on the second floor, seated at a round oak table with a scarlet felt top. An oil lamp hung low between them, its brass shade casting a pool of light the exact circumference of the tabletop. Standing sentinel next to a well-stocked bar was a Negro waiter wearing a blood-red uniform that matched the room. The only others in attendance were Jean-Louis's two female companions, Odalisque and her two male attendants, and the house dealer, an uncommonly slender white man with thin black hair and a cadaverous face.

"Gentlemen, we are at your disposal." Odalisque pointed to the man standing next to the bar. "Jocko will see to your food and drink needs." She indicated the thin man. "This is M'sieur Valentine. He is the best dealer in the house."

Jean-Louis said, "I would like a bottle of champagne for me and my companions."

Royal said, "I'll have an Irish whiskey, please."

While waiting for the drinks, Jean-Louis took off his watch and rings and placed them on top of his gloves. Royal loosened his cravat and flexed his fingers. He felt lucky.

The drinks arrived, and the dealer asked, "How many chips would you like, gentlemen?"

Jean-Louis responded, "Ten thousand dollars' worth." He took out a large roll of five-hundred-dollar bills, peeled off twenty, and tossed them to the dealer.

Royal raised his eyebrows but said nothing. He withdrew a blank check from the Louisiana State Bank, wrote in the amount of five thousand dollars, and slid it across to the dealer.

The dealer gave each his chips, and it was agreed that the game would be seven-card draw with a hundred-dollar ante. The dealer tore open a fresh pack of cards, shuffled them deftly with his long, bony fingers, then dealt seven, face down, to each man.

Persipanie stroked Jean-Louis's cheek, and Pearl Precious nibbled at his ear, but that didn't seem to distract him. His attention was completely focused upon his hand.

Royal arranged his cards. He had only a pair of jacks.

Jean-Louis started the bidding by tossing a red chip—worth five hundred dollars—into the pot.

Royal said, "I'll see you and raise you five."

Jean-Louis replied, "I'll see your five and stick."

"How many cards would you like, M'sieur Jourdain?" asked the dealer; Royal realized it was the first time he had heard the man's last name.

"Four."

"And you, M'sieur Brannigan?"

"Five, please."

Jean-Louis suppressed a grin. Obviously his opponent held no better than a pair. He flipped a red chip toward the pile. "I'm in with five."

Royal's new cards had brought him nothing. He knew that his pair of jacks was hardly a winning hand, but he decided to bluff the Creole. He pushed two red chips toward the pile. "See you and raise you five."

A flicker of a smile played upon Jean-Louis's lips. "Very well, m'sieur. I'll see you, and raise ten."

Royal knew instantly he'd been had. He had underestimated his opponent.

"It's yours," said Royal.

"Your reputation has exceeded you, m'sieur."

If Royal was angered by the remark, he didn't show it. "Another hand?"

Jean-Louis raked in his chips, smiled, and nodded to the dealer.

Odalisque pursed her lips in surprise. She sent Boudin scrambling for another tray of chocolates and settled back for what she hoped would become an exciting *and* expensive game. After all, the house would collect ten percent of the winner's spoils.

The first hand had been dealt at exactly nine thirty-five. At ten minutes past twelve the two men were still at it, Royal still losing but far from broke. The room had become stuffy. Odalisque ordered Mataché to draw the draperies and open the windows a few inches. The storm had abated, but the rain continued.

Royal won the next several hands, whereupon Jean-Louis called for a break and Royal acquiesced. Royal asked for a pot of coffee and some sandwiches, and Jean-Louis ordered another bottle of champagne, then disappeared into one of the bedrooms with the two whores. Royal wondered how the Creole could consume so much alcohol and still remain alert and sober to all appearances. He had to admit that his opponent was an expert player, perhaps one of the best he had ever faced. Still, he had seen and beaten better.

Royal went to the balcony and smoked a cigar while watching the revelers below. He wished that he could join them. Of course he could leave the game . . . though that would be admitting defeat. Still, he had walked away from games before; why couldn't he walk away from this one? What made him so committed to bringing the arrogant Creole to his knees? He simply couldn't fathom his reasons.

After a while he walked back to the table, and the waiter served him. Royal ate and drank his coffee slowly, and when he was finished he checked the time. Jean-Louis had been gone thirty minutes.

Odalisque was also growing impatient. "Where is M'sieur Jourdain?"

"He's busy with the two young ladies, it seems," Royal replied.

Just then Jean-Louis reentered the room. His eyes were incredibly bright, almost glowing. The women, however, looked the worse for wear. The trio was followed by a new couple. The girl was another of Odalisque's whores, an attractive blonde named Félice, whose company Royal had enjoyed several times. The man was someone Royal recognized from his rounds of the New Orleans clubs. His name was Corso Lajeunesse; he was a swarthy, good-looking Creole in his early thirties who functioned as factor—a commissioned business agent—to several of the leading sugar plantations. Royal had heard he was a former rough-and-tumble riverman who had wangled his way to his newly respectable position.

"I've asked some friends to watch," Jean-Louis announced. He neither requested Royal's permission nor apologized for the intrusion.

Félice smiled uncomfortably at Royal. She appeared embarrassed to be in Lajeunesse's company. For his part, the factor barely nodded in Royal's direction, then turned his attention to the bar.

Royal said, "Shall we begin?" He was irritated with himself that he had been unable to keep the impatience out of his voice.

Jean-Louis flashed him an insincere smile. "So anxious to lose? *Eh bien,* I shall be more than happy to accommodate you, m'sieur."

Because of the presence of his friends, the liquor, and the brief sexual experience—and, Royal suspected, more Get-Lively Powder—Jean-Louis was oozing with self-confidence. He attempted to bluff Royal by raising the pot again and again when he had a poor hand. In the few hours they had been together, however, Royal had gotten to know something of the man—his eccentricities, his motives, his conceits; the Creole, he realized, was bluffing in order to show off for the spectators, and as a result Royal now won hand after hand.

Jean-Louis began to sweat more heavily. It was the kind of perspiration peculiar to drinkers and drug-takers. Globules of oily condensation formed on his forehead, temples, and the rim of his upper lip. He called to the waiter for a hand towel and, after drying his face, carelessly tossed the towel to the floor. Then he resumed the game with his usual jauntiness, even though sweat still crawled down his temples like spiders.

Royal continued to win. Lajeunesse as well as the whores urged Jean-Louis to concede, but he stubbornly refused. Toward morning Jean-Louis ran out of money. He offered up his gold pocket watch and several rings, saying, "I realize that these items may not suit your personal taste, m'sieur, but I assure you that they would easily bring seven thousand dollars on the open market."

Royal replied sharply, "You are correct, m'sieur. They are not to my liking. I am afraid the game is over."

"M'sieur, you cannot deny me the chance to win back my losses!" Jean-Louis sputtered. "Only a barbarian would deny a gentleman his rights!"

Royal, angered by Jean-Louis's remark, replied in a tight, controlled voice, "Very well, I will accept your baubles in lieu of cash."

Jean-Louis did not reply, but a shudder racked his body, and his eyes became suddenly haggard. He looked toward the windows. The storm had been swept out to the Gulf, and the rain was reduced to a mere drizzle.

In that brief instant Royal felt sorry for the man. But then Jean-Louis turned to him and said, with a sneer, "There's a proverb among our niggers: Never call an alligator 'long-mouth' till you pass him by."

Royal asked for another pot of coffee. Jean-Louis smirked. No such sobering drink for him. He ordered not one, but two more bottles of champagne. While waiting to be served, Jean-Louis pushed back his chair, got up from the table, and began waltzing around the room with first one whore and then the other. Considering the Creole's financial position, Royal wondered if his erratic behavior might be due not only to alcohol and drugs but to some mental aberration.

Another hand was dealt. By now the Negro boy, Boudin, was asleep at Odalisque's feet. The proprietress rested her head against the hard abdomen of Mataché. The dealer, apparently used to long, tedious hours, showed no signs of fatigue as his skeletal fingers dealt each card with the subtle rhythm of a sacramental rite.

Royal was dealt a full house and won the watch and rings.

Lajeunesse bent low and whispered in Jean-Louis's ear, again advising him to quit the game. But the Creole shook his head.

"M'sieur," said Royal, "you're out of funds. The game is over."

Jean-Louis retorted, "The game is over when I say it is over!" He said to Odalisque, "Madame, I wish to make use of your writing room."

"It's at your disposal, M'sieur Jourdain."

"M'sieur, I shall return in a moment."

Jean-Louis grabbed the factor's arm and pulled him toward the door. As he exited, he called out, "I want another bottle of champagne, buttered toast, and a pot of your best caviar waiting for me."

The men were gone a quarter of an hour. When they returned, Lajeunesse's dour expression contrasted sharply with the triumphant look on the other Creole's face. Jean-Louis strolled over to Royal and dropped a folded paper on the table in front of him. Puzzled, Royal opened the paper and read it. It was an informal but nonetheless binding deed to Jean-Louis's plantation, Heritage—the house and holdings, including the land, the slaves, and livestock. It was signed in Jean-Louis's flamboyant script and witnessed by his factor, Corso Lajeunesse.

"That is my final wager, m'sieur. Everything I own against everything you've accumulated thus far."

Royal was shocked. He couldn't believe that the Creole was serious. The expression on Jean-Louis's face told him different. "But this is madness! I urge you not to make such a foolish bet."

Jean-Louis's eyes blazed. "M'sieur, would you dare to turn down my wager? You are completely without pedigree."

"But what if I should win?" argued Royal. "Be realistic, man!"

Jean-Louis lifted his glass high and with a mocking laugh said, "Realistic! I'm never realistic. We all create a world for ourselves which makes it possible for us to live. And I have created mine with more imagination than most." He paused and added, "But then you Americans don't understand imagination."

Royal stared at the Creole for several moments and finally said, "Take your seat, m'sieur, and let us finish the game."

Everybody moved closer. Even Boudin woke up and rested his chin on the table edge.

Jean-Louis sat down, spread a thick glob of caviar onto a triangle of toast, and bit into it. He chewed slowly, his eyes never leaving Royal. Royal pushed the deed to the center of the table and stared at it as if it were something alive. Then with both hands he pushed the accumulation of his night's winnings—chips, jewelry, and watch—worth nearly twenty thousand dollars, across the red felt until they surrounded the piece of folded paper. Without looking at the dealer he gave the order, "Deal!"

The dealer stood up for this last and most vital hand. The pale amber glow from the low-hanging lamp made his face look like a death mask. The first card cut through the air and landed in front of Royal. Royal gritted his teeth and, not waiting for all seven cards to be dealt, picked it up. It was the ace of spades.

Jean-Louis's first card landed between his outstretched and trembling hands. He snatched it from the tabletop.

One by one, the rest of the cards were dealt, each picked up as soon as it fell. Obviously Jean-Louis had a good hand; he could scarcely contain his excitement. Royal's expression was unreadable.

"Oh, I can't bear the suspense," cried Pearl Precious. The other whores shushed her.

"How many cards, M'sieur Brannigan?" the dealer asked.

"Two, please," Royal replied.

"And you, M'sieur Jourdain?"

Jean-Louis said loudly, "None . . . thank you."

Royal silently prayed that Lady Luck was still his companion. He cupped his final two cards in his hand and, hardly daring to breathe, turned them toward him.

"I call," Jean-Louis said sweetly, and with a broad smile of satisfaction laid his cards on the table. Four kings—an almost unbeatable hand. The whores began applauding, and even the dour Lajeunesse smiled. Jean-Louis encircled the pot with his arms, like a child embracing a favorite toy.

Then he looked up and met Royal's gaze, which caused his eyes to dilate with terror. Royal spread his cards on the table. Four aces.

The applauding stopped. Jean-Louis's mouth fell open. Slowly he uncurled his arms from around his treasure. The incandescence faded from his eyes, leaving them opaque. With a painful effort he rose from the table. Visibly summoning his last ounce of *joie de vivre*, he said, "My congratulations, m'sieur."

The pathetic but noble words reached out and squeezed Royal's heart. He did not feel victorious, but rather stricken that he had stripped the Creole of everything he owned.

Jean-Louis toasted Royal with a glass of champagne. After draining the sparkling liquid, he ran his tongue over his lips, savoring the taste. Then, without warning, he pitched the glass across the room into the marble fireplace. The glass shattered into a thousand pieces, which flew in all directions, briefly catching the light of morning.

Jean-Louis smiled in reaction, then drew a small pistol from his breast pocket and aimed it at Royal. The assemblage gasped as one, and Royal froze as he heard the sharp click of the safety catch. Abruptly Jean-Louis turned the pistol away from Royal and raised it to his own eye level.

One of the whores cried out. Odalisque stood up and staggered toward the table. Lajeunesse tried to grab Jean-Louis's arm, but he was too late. The explosion was as sharp and loud as if the room had been struck by lightning. Jean-Louis pitched forward, his handsome face shattered by the ball of lead. His blood blended perfectly with the scarlet tabletop.

PART TWO

Chapter Four

A sudden wind whipped down the alleyway, causing some of the magnolia petals to fall from the branches like a spring snow. The air turned cool. A bank of rushing clouds swam across the sky and swallowed the jaundiced moon whole, plunging the countryside into darkness. Suddenly unsure of his footing, the horse slowed his pace. The whippoorwill renewed its call, and the annoying reiteration of the same notes grated on Royal's nerves. Why didn't it go on with the melody or alter a note or two?

The dark was finally pierced by a pair of lampposts stationed between two of the magnolia trees, thirty feet ahead and to the right. As he approached, Royal could just make out the ornate letters on a wrought-iron sign, painted white to be easily seen in the darkness. It read: HERITAGE.

Royal reined the horse to his right, and the wagon rolled onto the driveway. The moonlight returned, brighter than before. Royal could see the impressive edifice of Heritage looming ahead.

The builder of Heritage had been fortunate in his choice of architects. The big house was large and elegant, yet simple in design, with dozens of fluted columns forming a veranda that apparently extended around all four sides of the perfectly square structure. The building had been freshly painted a stark, gleaming white, and in the moonlight it resembled a gigantic wedding cake.

Royal caught his breath. The big house was more beautiful than he could have imagined—and it was his. But he did not take comfort from that thought. He was now faced with the problem he had avoided thinking about since the start of the trip to Magnolia Landing. How was he going to tell the widow? What words could he choose to help alleviate her suffering? Should he tell her everything at once, or wait until the shock of her husband's death had subsided? The horse moved faster, transporting him down the driveway toward the big house. Royal glanced uneasily about him and barely took note of the passing landscape.

As he neared the front entrance, the door was thrown open, revealing a golden-haired woman in a gown of emerald silk. "Jean-Louis," she called, "did you bring our ball gowns?"

She stopped short when she saw who was in the driver's seat, and what lay on the bed of the wagon. She took a step backward, her eyes wide with apprehension.

Royal pulled up the horses, quickly climbed out, and mounted the stairs to the veranda. The light from the open door silhouetted the young woman. When he saw how lovely she was, he was momentarily taken aback. Assuming this was Jean-Louis's wife, he hesitated.

"Who are you?" she demanded in French, her eyes fixed on the coffin.

"My name is Royal Brannigan. Do you understand English?" She gave a vehement nod. "Your husband, M'sieur Jourdain, has killed himself." He said it baldly, clumsily.

"You're lying," she said, her eyes still riveted to the oblong box.

"I wish I were."

She took a step toward him, crossing her arms in front of her breasts, as if protecting herself from assault. Her face drained of all color, and her eyes were unblinking. She looked down at his huge hands, and her eyes darted once again to the coffin, then back to him.

He knew what she was thinking. "I didn't touch him. He shot himself."

She shook her head slowly and, in a childlike voice, denied his words. "No, you're lying. No, no." She grabbed his arm with both hands and opened her mouth to scream, but no sound came forth, only a dull rasp constricting her throat. Her body began to waver. Then her eyes fluttered shut and she crumpled into his arms.

Royal gathered her up in a rustle of silk. She looked so pale that he pressed her chest against his own to ascertain her heartbeat. As he carried her into the house, he was uncomfortably aware of the soft contours of her body and the sweet womanly scent that exuded from her. He called to a slave lurking in the foyer. "Bring me a bottle of brandy. Do you understand? Brandy!" The slave nodded and rushed away.

Royal carried the young woman into the parlor and carefully laid her on the sofa. He knelt beside her, undid the pearl buttons on the bodice of her gown, and waited for the brandy to arrive. He stared at her, transfixed by her beauty.

Her skin was flawless and as white as ivory, and in repose she reminded him of a beautifully sculpted cameo.

The slave arrived with the brandy and a goblet, then ran away again. Royal uncorked the bottle with his teeth and poured a heavy dollop of the amber liquid into the glass. Tenderly he lifted the young woman's head and tilted the glass to her lips.

She came to, sputtering and coughing, and fixed her gaze on Royal. Hate spread over her face, like a blush she couldn't control. She sat up and began to flail Royal with her fists. He grabbed her wrists and held them fast. She threw back her head, agony sweeping over her until the scream finally came, an anguished and piercing sound that rent the silence.

The scream echoed throughout the big house. Suzanne Jourdain came rushing out of her room. She was wearing a gown of sapphire blue that almost matched the color of her eyes, and her skirts rustled as she hurried down the servants' stairs, which were closer than the grand staircase to the source of the cry. On the first-floor landing she was met by Zenobia, who was brandishing a large brass candlestick. "It come from de parlor, Miz Suzanne."

When they reached the parlor they saw Royal standing over Angélique, who was sobbing into her hands.

"What's happening?" Suzanne demanded in French. "What have you done to her?"

Royal put out his hands in a gesture of helplessness. "I don't understand French," he said. "I'm an American."

Suzanne repeated her questions in English.

"My name is Royal Brannigan," Royal began. "And I'm from New Orleans—"

"Yes, yes," Suzanne demanded impatiently.

"I'm afraid I had some bad news for Madame Jourdain."

Suzanne moved toward him, her body tense, her steps measured. "*I* am Madame Jourdain," she said. "What is this bad news that has upset my sister-in-law so greatly?"

Angélique flung herself face downward on the sofa and sobbed into the cushions, "Jean-Louis! Jean-Louis!"

"Sister-in-law," Royal repeated, now realizing his mistake. He looked Suzanne directly in the eye and was met by a hard gaze.

"I was with your husband at the hour of his death. We

were playing cards at Odalisque. He . . . he took his own life. I brought his body here to Magnolia Landing."

Zenobia groaned and dropped the candlestick.

"But that is impossible, m'sieur. My husband has lost at cards before. He would never do such a thing."

"I'm afraid his losses were very high, madame."

"Where is my husband?" she asked carefully.

"Outside," Royal replied. "In the back of the wagon. I took the—ah—liberty of selecting the casket."

Ghastly sounds issued from Angélique as she rocked backward and forward on the sofa, pushing her fists into her eyes.

Suzanne regarded Royal with incredulity, then walked swiftly to the French doors and peered outside. A patch of moonlight streamed through a live oak, clearly illuminating the coffin. When she turned around, she had an unreadable look on her face.

"He must have lost a great deal," she said in a hoarse, strangled voice.

"I'm afraid, madame, that he lost everything." Royal reached into his vest pocket, withdrew a paper, and handed it to Suzanne. He watched her as she read it. A sudden spasm ran through her body, and her right hand, which was holding the paper, began jerking uncontrollably.

Angélique got up from the sofa and ran to her sister-in-law. "What is it, Suzanne? What does it mean?"

Suzanne handed Angélique the paper. As Angélique read it, her face became even more stricken. When she finished, she flung the paper at Royal and screamed, "That's not my brother's handwriting!"

Royal bent over to retrieve the paper. "It most assuredly is, mademoiselle. It was witnessed by his factor, Corso Lajeunesse."

"But it was written under duress," countered Suzanne.

"It was self-imposed duress," replied Royal.

Angélique stumbled and fell against the sofa. Her coiffure was loosened, and her pale golden hair fell about her bowed head like a veil. "Jean-Louis! Jean-Louis!" she murmured over and over.

Suzanne stood stiffly for a long while. Then suddenly she came alive, as if the first shock had passed. She swung around and said, "Zenobia, have the coffin brought inside." The slave hesitated. "Bring it in!" Suzanne roared. "We must have proof that Jean-Louis lies inside."

"Please, madame, don't," Royal protested. "It has been two days since—"

She turned on him, her tone venomous. "You have nothing to say in this matter, m'sieur! I have not relinquished my authority in this house as yet! *Bring it in!*"

There was a long, awkward silence while Zenobia went off to carry out Suzanne's orders. Only Angélique's muffled sobs could be heard. A short time later two male slaves carried the casket into the parlor. Zenobia followed them with a hammer and a flattened bar of iron to use as a wedge. She was staring straight ahead, as if in a trance, her hooded eyes half closed. Suzanne pointed to a heavy credenza and said, "Place it on there."

Royal started to help. With a sharp gesture Suzanne waved him away. "Don't come near him!"

The coffin was placed in position, and the slaves stepped back, fear in their eyes.

"Zenobia, pry open the lid," Suzanne said quietly.

Angélique, horrified by her sister-in-law's order, ran to the coffin and clamped her body against it like a starfish, stretching out her arms as far as she could, as if to protect her brother. "Don't, Suzanne, don't!" Angélique pleaded. "He's, he's . . . not fresh."

Suzanne said softly, "The horror is that we die at all, not what happens to our bodies. Come away, Angélique. We have to know for certain." Suzanne gently pried her sister-in-law's hands from the lid and guided her back to the sofa.

"Madame, I beg you, don't do this!" said Royal, but Suzanne ignored his plea. Royal turned away from the scene that was about to take place. Despite the coolness of the evening, perspiration lay in a cold, sticky film on his skin.

Zenobia shoved the wedge between the top and the side of the coffin and, tears streaming from her dark eyes, sobbed, "Dear Lord, forgive me fo' disturbin' M'sieur Jean-Louis, but we just got to know fo' sure. Please, *please*, understand."

She slammed the hammer against the blunt edge of the wedge. At the sound, Royal, Angélique, and Suzanne stiffened visibly. Zenobia pried the coffin lid open an inch. The odor of putrefaction spun around the room. Zenobia took a deep breath and, working the lid to the right and left, managed to free it. Averting her gaze, she pulled the lid aside and propped it against the wall. Then, after a long pause, she looked into the casket.

Zenobia let out a scream. It was a horrible noise, high, continuous, and bestial. She beat her fists against her breasts and dropped to the floor on her hands and knees. Like a wounded animal, she began to circle on all fours, sobbing and wailing.

Angélique did not move. From her vantage point she could see part of her brother's body and recognized his suit. But Suzanne, seemingly oblivious of the corruption, moved deliberately to the side of the coffin. There she trailed her fingers among the ruined blossoms and stared dully at her husband's shattered face.

Then she crossed herself, stepped back, and ordered the coffin to be closed once again. "Take it to the conservatory."

Zenobia led away the servants bearing the coffin. Suzanne turned to face Royal and Angélique. Both were stunned by her cool manner. In a formal voice she said, "I must have my lawyer look at the deed, of course. But if it is in order, how much time do we have before you evict us?"

Royal stammered, "Why, you can take as much time as you wish. I'm not an unreasonable person."

"Aren't you?" Suzanne replied. "Will you be content in a guest room, M'sieur Brannigan, or do you wish the master bedroom?"

"A guest room will be more than satisfactory." He bit down on his lip and said, "I'm terribly sorry for your husband's death, but I was not responsible."

"Who is responsible, then, M'sieur Brannigan? Fate?"

He had no answer to give her; all he could offer was a weak shrug.

Angélique, tears staining her cheeks, said, "I can't believe you're taking this so calmly, Suzanne! Your husband, my brother, is dead, and this man is to blame! Why, you're treating him like a houseguest!"

"On the contrary, Angélique, it is we who are the houseguests. I think if M'sieur Brannigan so wished it, he could have put us off Heritage this very night."

"Jean-Louis is dead," Angélique wailed. "Isn't that enough?" She rushed to Royal and grabbed his arm. She was near hysteria. "You can't mean to hold us to the agreement! Where would we go? What would we do?"

"I told you, mademoiselle, both you and Madame Jourdain are welcome to stay as long as you wish."

"Welcome to stay as long as we wish," Angélique repeated

bitterly. "This is our home! My father built Heritage. My mother furnished it with taste and style." Her lip curled as she flung the words from her mouth. "What will the likes of you do here? Your very presence desecrates their memory." She spat on the floor in front of him.

Suzanne walked swiftly to her sister-in-law and put an arm around her shoulders. "Hush, Angélique," she crooned gently as she led her away from Royal, toward the open doors leading to the foyer.

They were met in the doorway by Zenobia. "When M'sieur Brannigan is ready," Suzanne said, "show him to the blue guest room and see to his needs." The slave nodded imperceptibly. "You'll excuse us, m'sieur." Zenobia helped Suzanne support Angélique, and the three women left the parlor.

Royal was about to pour himself a brandy from the bottle still sitting on the floor when Suzanne reappeared. She spoke in a cool, detached voice. "By the way, M'sieur Brannigan, we will be holding funeral services tomorrow afternoon. I hope you will have the good manners not to attend."

Alcée lifted the freestanding frame that held her macramé and carried it next to the bedroom window overlooking the gardens of Salle d'Or. She placed the chair from her dressing table next to the frame, sat down, and resumed work on her project. It was a portieré—a doorway curtain—for her mother's bedroom, and Alcée planned to give it to her as a Christmas present. Macramé was one of the few pursuits allowed young Creole ladies that Alcée actually enjoyed. Her fingers automatically worked the heavy string as her thoughts returned to her father.

His talk of eligible young men had left her depressed and rebellious. She vowed that no matter how much he pressured her, she would defy his wishes. Alcée believed she was as strong as her father—perhaps stronger. She knew she would need to be, for she could expect no help from her mother. Over the years, she had watched Henriette become the pathetic, ineffectual being that she was. And Philippe would give her no support. He was worse than her father, possessing all of the Duc's faults and none of his strengths. His only saving grace—if it could be called that—was his devotion to his father.

As she tied the knots, Alcée gazed anxiously at the open window, watching for the signal that she knew was forthcoming. Sure enough, a distant lantern, as bright and yellow as the eye of a tiger, began to flash. She stood up, her heart beating wildly.

For over six months now—no, longer than that—Alcée had been irretrievably in love. Maybe she had been in love for years, and just hadn't realized it. Whatever the case, she did not for a minute doubt her heart and she wished only that everyone could experience the same unbounded joy. Shivering with expectancy, she threw on a dark hooded cloak and quickly made her way out the French doors and down the back stairs.

The moon was full. It looked unnaturally large, as if there were a danger of it dropping from the heavens. The stars had appeared, and the sky resembled an endless canopy of spangled indigo. Moonlight spilled through the trees and fell about Alcée's feet, so bright and substantial that she fancied she could scoop it up in her hands. The air was drenched with the magic perfume of sweet olive and boxwood, and the stillness was broken only by the occasional lovesick outbursts of a night bird.

Alcée made her way down a gravel path framed by honeysuckle. She passed through a gate where the formal gardens ended and beyond which the guests of Salle d'Or rarely ventured. She hurried through a grove of sago palms. Here the land sloped downward, and Alcée quickened her pace, rushing headlong toward a small Chinese bridge that spanned a creek near an artificial lake. She paused halfway over, leaning against the railing to catch her breath. A pair of swans glided past, and Alcée felt her body shaking with her heartbeats.

She inhaled deeply, and when she lifted her head she looked directly at the summerhouse, just on the other side of the lake. Its angular lines were softened by wisteria vines, which, untrimmed and untended, clung to it like a desperate lover. Alcée saw the lantern flash again, and tossing propriety aside, she picked up her skirts and dashed across the bridge toward the summerhouse.

Blaise was waiting in the center of the building, holding the lantern in front of him. Alcée entered shyly, as if it were their first meeting.

"I didn't know if you'd be able to come," Blaise said in a husky voice.

"Don't you know that nothing could keep me away?" she

replied softly. Their fingers met before their eyes did. His large, finely sculpted hands folded over hers. Alcée reacted as if a shock had been sent through her body, and she wondered if Blaise felt it too. She glanced at him and knew that he had. They sat down next to each other without speaking or turning their heads. Only their hands and their hearts joined them.

Alcée was the first to break the silence. "Papa was more difficult than usual tonight."

"Yes, he was," Blaise agreed.

"I thought that the arrival of the chandelier would make Papa happy. And when he's happy, he's kinder to Mama. But that doesn't seem to work anymore. Must marriage always be such a battleground?"

"*I* would never hurt you, Alcée."

"Nor I you. But the simple fact of our being in love will eventually hurt us."

"Nothing is ever simple between colored and white."

She turned to him, and her words tumbled out in a rush. "We're no different, you and I. Being in love should be simple! Why, we've always been friends, so what could be more natural? I wish we could marry and stay here at the Landing—we could live at Villeneuve. Mama's promised it to me if I marry before Philippe, and—"

He touched a finger to her lips. "Hush, Alcée," he said gently. "That's just a sweet dream."

"I know. I know. But sometimes I think that if I repeat it often enough, it'll come true."

"Not here at Magnolia Landing. You know that someday we'll have to leave."

"I hate to think of leaving. No, that's not true. I just hate to leave Mama." She gulped in the night air. "I'm afraid, Blaise."

"I am too. Oh, why do we have to love each other?"

"You don't mean that. It's all we have. It's everything!"

"No, I don't mean it."

"We have to trust that our love will sustain us through everything we're going to have to face."

Their gazes lingered on each other for the first time, and they both wondered if they could ever escape the world of color lines, class distinctions, and arranged marriages. In an unvoiced gesture of frustration, Blaise threw out his hand and accidentally knocked over the lantern. The glass shattered.

He knelt and managed to right it before the flame went out, but he cut his finger on a shard.

Alcée cried, "You've hurt yourself!" She knelt beside him, took his hand, and pressed the bleeding finger to her lips; she held it there until the blood stopped flowing. "There," she said finally. "Now I am part colored too."

Overcome with emotion, Blaise seized Alcée in his arms and kissed her. It was not the usual tentative adolescent kiss, but one of fire and passion. Alcée felt her flesh burn with a sweet, hot fever. It coursed through her body, making her blood jump and her mind a network of flashing lights. Her body began to give in to its natural urges, and she could feel his body responding to hers.

They broke apart, gasping for breath and full of wonder at their own daring. They were frightened of the consequences, but they knew full well that they were unable to stop what was happening between them.

And there, in that secluded and shadowy place, they cast aside all convention and made love for the first time.

The conservatory was located on the east side of the house at Heritage so that it could enjoy the first rays of the morning sun. Originally it had been used as a music room for Jean-Louis and Angélique; she played the piano and he the cello. As youngsters Jean-Louis and Angélique had been considered prodigies and were always in demand to play their duets, both at Magnolia Landing and in New Orleans. Many of the gentry kept their pianos in tune solely in the hopes of cajoling the talented brother and sister to entertain at their social functions.

As Jean-Louis and Angélique had entered adolescence, however, they had turned to other pleasures. The piano and the cello, like outgrown toys, had been abandoned, and eventually the room was given over to exotic plants.

Now, only hours after Royal Brannigan's arrival, it served as a funeral parlor. The coffin had been propped up on a makeshift bier fashioned from four ballroom chairs. A bouquet of flowers that Zenobia had gathered by lamplight lay strewn across the lid. Flowering potted plants were banked around the sides, and the atmosphere was heavy with the odor of burning incense, candle wax, and putrefaction.

The three women—Suzanne, Angélique, and Zenobia—garbed in black for mourning, sat at the opposite end of the room from the bier. Although the French doors had been opened to let in the night air, Suzanne and Angélique pressed perfumed handkerchiefs over the lower half of their faces. The odor did not seem to affect Zenobia, who was busy making the *immortelle*, a funeral wreath of black linen flowers, to be placed on the front door of the big house.

Angélique's severe gown of black bombazine seemed to drain her skin of color. She stared at the coffin with shocked eyes. Suddenly, with a startled expression, she turned to Suzanne.

"What about the priest?" she cried.

Suzanne stared at her sister-in-law as if she were mad. "Priest! Jean-Louis committed suicide. No priest will officiate at the ceremony." Then in a gentler tone she added, "It doesn't matter. I'll read something. When the time comes I'll face God, and if there's any retribution to be exacted, then He can exact it from me." She reached out to touch Angélique's shoulder, but the other woman pulled away. Suzanne fumbled with the onyx buttons on her own black silk dress and sighed. Her face looked drawn and pinched, its severity heightened by the hairstyle she now wore. Gone were the cascades of raven side curls; she had flattened and pinned her hair into a chignon at the back of her neck.

She asked Zenobia, "You've shown him to the guest room and seen to his needs?"

"Yes, Miz Suzanne. He be asleep by now."

"Good."

"Good!" Angélique gasped. "What a thing to say! Nothing's good anymore, is it?"

Zenobia glanced at the two women through hooded eyes but said nothing. She clipped a length of wire with a pair of shears, then twisted it around a black linen flower and attached it to the wreath.

Angélique began crying once again, and Suzanne said, "Hush, now. We'll see our way through this."

Angélique dabbed her handkerchief to her eyes. "Jean-Louis's death is bad enough, but leaving us like this—it's too much to bear."

"We must bear it. We have no other choice. We need time. We need to stay on at Heritage until we can find a solution to our situation. Perhaps we can try to make ourselves useful to him until then."

"You're not suggesting that we . . . we ask for his charity?" said Angélique.

"No, of course not. But perhaps we could borrow some money on our crop."

"*Our* crop? It's his crop now." She glanced for an instant at Zenobia, then said to Suzanne, "He doesn't know how many slaves we have. We could sell some without his knowing it."

Suzanne shook her head. "No, we can't do that. Besides, that wouldn't bring enough money to buy back Heritage."

Angélique stood up. "I must get some air. It's stifling in here."

Suzanne grabbed her arm, restraining her. "No, we must talk. We must make plans for our future."

Angélique pulled away from her sister-in-law and replied sharply, "What future? I don't have a future. I have no money, no property." She rushed to the open French doors, threw back her head, and sucked in the night air. Without turning, she said bitterly, "How do you know he didn't kill Jean-Louis? How do you know?"

"We'll know for certain. I've sent Toby to New Orleans with a letter to our lawyer. If he rides all night he should reach Señor Mendoza by morning. He'll make inquiries into the matter. But . . . despite what we think of the American, I don't think he killed Jean-Louis."

Suzanne's gaze returned to the coffin. "Jean-Louis is gone, and there's nothing we can do about that. Now we've got to get through tonight and tomorrow. I've written notes to all of the residents of the Landing, letting them know that we're having the funeral services at two o'clock tomorrow afternoon. Seth will see that they're delivered first thing in the morning."

Angélique swung around, her eyes glowing like an animal's caught in a beam of a light. "You're not actually planning on asking people to Jean-Louis's funeral?" she cried. "They can't come! I won't be seen!"

She formed her fist into a ball and slammed it against one of the square panes in the French door. The glass splintered and broke. "Don't you understand? I won't have people feeling sorry for me!" Her fist shattered another pane. "I won't have them staring and . . . and . . . speculating!"

Suzanne rushed to her sister-in-law. "Please, Angélique. Please bear up. I don't have any more strength to give you."

Angélique clawed at her own cheeks, digging into them as

if to tear them off. Suzanne, frightened for her sister-in-law, finally took her wrists and forced them to her sides. Angélique opened her mouth to scream; the lips stretched taut over her teeth. But before a sound could erupt, Suzanne slapped her hard across both cheeks, grabbed her shoulders, and shook her with all her strength. "You mustn't let yourself fall apart, Angélique. You mustn't!" Then she whispered, as if to a child, "Come. Come back and sit down. Come with me." Angélique allowed herself to be led back to her chair, and the two women sat down.

Suzanne said as she wiped away Angélique's tears with her scented handkerchief, "I promise you that somehow, some way, I'll find a solution to all this. I love Heritage as much as you do, and I don't mean to give it up without a fight. We've got to go on, do you understand? We've got to go on until I say it's finished."

Zenobia picked up the shears and snipped another length of wire, then said, "Be de simplest thing in de world fo' me to go into dat room and kill him while he sleeps."

The white women searched each other's face, but neither could read the other's thoughts.

The kitchen door at Villeneuve opened a crack, but was stopped by the hook-and-eye latch that had been installed as a safety measure. A black leather riding crop was inserted between door and jamb several inches beneath the latch, and in one swift upward motion the lock was disengaged. The door opened wider and admitted the owner of the riding crop.

The man's heavy footsteps and labored breathing broke the stillness as he felt his way across the room, which was lit only by the red glow of the banked fire. He bumped into the kitchen table. The wood scraped against the floor. The man cursed.

Lilliane's eyes snapped open. Instinctively she looked across the bedroom to Azby. His breathing was deep and regular. He was still sleeping soundly.

She slid her hand under the pillow and retrieved a large butcher knife, the blade of which had been wrapped in a piece of cloth. She sat up and unwound the material from the sharp blade, her eyes focused on the bedroom door. Lilliane always slept with the knife under her pillow; in the past year there had been a lot of criminals—bandits, runaway slaves, vagabonds—prowling Magnolia Landing. Several people had been robbed and beaten, and one Negro girl had been brutally raped. Lilliane's only thought was to protect her son.

Clenching the weapon in her hand, she slipped out of the room. A chill scurried like a centipede along her spine as she started down the narrow hall toward the kitchen. There was no sound except for the harsh, ragged breathing of the intruder. Then it ceased.

Lilliane's heart stopped. She thought the breathing sound must have been her imagination. She waited for it to begin anew, but it did not.

Silently praying to her favorite voodoo gods and Catholic saints, she moved past the shelves of preserved food and reached the partly open door that led to the kitchen. She pressed herself flat against the wall and listened. At last, summoning all her courage, she eased the door further open with her foot and, holding the knife in a striking position, stepped into the kitchen. Her eyes strained against the darkness.

"Who's there?" she asked with false bravado.

There was no response, only utter silence. Lilliane was oddly aware of the scents that hovered about the kitchen. It was the lingering incense of Creole cuisine—filé powder, crayfish, chicory, and . . . something else. . . .

The riding crop cut through the air, striking her wrist, and the knife clattered to the floor. The man stepped out of the shadows.

"You wouldn't want to kill me, would you?" he said thickly.

Lilliane swung around. Philippe was grinning crookedly. His eyes were glassy but opaque, like those of a dead fish. His skin was damp, and a faint reek of sour sweat exuded from him.

Still gasping with fright, Lilliane muttered, "I thought you weren't coming tonight."

He lifted the hem of her night shift with the riding crop. "I'm here now."

Lilliane backed away from him until her buttocks pressed against the heavy table. Philippe slowly circled the table, poking at her breasts and abdomen with the tip of the crop.

"When are you going to tire of me?" she said, more to herself than to Philippe.

Philippe laughed, but it was a sound devoid of humor. He traced her jawline with the handle of the crop. Then forcibly raised her head, so that she was facing him. "I wouldn't be so anxious for that to happen, because when I'm tired of you, I'm going to sell you."

"Sell me? But what about Azby?"

"He's a strong boy. He'll make a good worker in the cane fields." He punctuated his remark by slamming the crop against the table edge.

Separated from her son! Never to see him again! It was a possibility that she had never even considered. The realization of what he was saying was worse than any nightmare she could imagine. Hate coiled within her, and her beautiful face was distorted with loathing.

Philippe struck her with the crop. A delicate thread of crimson trickled from the corner of Lilliane's lips, and a bad taste filled her mouth. It was the coppery taste of blood.

"Philippe, please don't." She rearranged her face into an approximation of passion. "I can be ready in a few minutes. I'll come to you in the big house."

Philippe shook his head, then made a grab for her. Lilliane sidestepped him, but he caught her sleeve and yanked her closer, ripping the front of her shift.

"You wouldn't deny your master his rights, would you, Lilliane?" Poking, then whipping with the riding crop, he backed her out of the kitchen, down the corridor toward her bedroom.

She held out her hands to ward off the stinging blows and pleaded, "No, not here! Azby's here."

But Philippe was too drunk to care. He pushed her into the bedroom and forced her onto the bed, then climbed on top of her and began tearing at the fabric of her shift. Lilliane did not fight him. But the commotion caused Azby to wake up.

"Mama, what's wrong?"

Lilliane ordered her son, "Azby, quick—go into the kitchen and wait there till I call you."

The little boy hesitated. "But he's hurting you."

"No, no, no he isn't." Philippe parted Lilliane's legs, and she screamed, "Azby, go!"

The little boy scrambled out of the bedroom, ran down the hall, and hid beneath the kitchen table. He held on to the table leg, and although the room was warm, he began to shiver. He clenched his eyes shut as he heard his mother's cries of shame and Philippe's grunts of passion. Azby crawled about on his hands and knees within the perimeters set by the table legs, like an animal in a self-imposed cage. His tiny hands came to rest upon the fallen knife. He picked it up and pressed the flat of the blade against his heaving chest and vowed that someday, when he was older and stronger, he would kill Philippe Duvallon.

The chill wind whipped around Royal, making his skin crawl. He was alone, standing in the center of the Promenade, not knowing how he got there. His breath floated on the night air like a puff of dandelion down. The crushed seashells cut into his bare feet like shards of glass. Why hadn't he worn his boots?

Against the black sky the moon hung grotesquely, like a swollen and rotting piece of fruit. Suddenly the sky-curtain was split apart by a forked tongue of lightning, and everything was illuminated.

The coffin stood upright in the center of the Promenade. Magnolia petals, bruised and decaying, fell around it like snow, settling in moldering drifts about the base. A smattering of applause broke the ominous quiet, then grew and grew in volume until it sounded like overhead thunder. At that moment the lid of the coffin swung open.

Jean-Louis Jourdain was hardly recognizable. His remaining hair was matted with dried blood. The bones of his shattered right cheek were visible. His lips had festered, and his teeth hung loosely from liver-colored gums. One of his eyes was missing; the other, hanging from its socket, was staring at Royal. Like a flirting coquette, the rotting hand opened a fan of seven cards.

Applause burst forth anew, and the corpse began to decompose before Royal's stunned eyes. The overripe flesh congealed and dropped in pieces from the rapidly disintegrating body. The features blended, merged, ran together like melted tallow. The corpse bowed as if to acknowledge the applause, and when it raised its skull, the cards had disappeared and the half-fleshed hand now clutched a pistol. The corpse raised the pistol slowly and aimed it directly at Royal. The applause grew in volume, and the pistol exploded.

Royal sat up in bed. A cold film of perspiration covered his nude body. He kicked off the clammy sheets and held his head in his hands, trying to shake off the hideous nightmare. The air in the room was oppressive. He staggered to the

French doors, parted the heavy drapes, and pushed both sides open wide. The moonlight streamed inside, staining everything with its fulgent rays.

As he regained his composure, Royal looked around the unfamiliar room. Although it was tastefully appointed, it was not a room that normally would have been given to an important visitor. He recalled how Zenobia, the plantation mammy, had "seen to his needs" herself. She had escorted him to this room, turned down the bed, unpacked his clothing and hung it in the wardrobe—and had taken some satisfaction, he thought, in pointing out the chamber pot beneath the wooden washstand.

Royal was greatly relieved to have the confrontation over. He wondered if he had made a mistake in telling the women they could stay on as long as they wished. Perhaps it would have been better to settle some amount on them and have them leave. He was also upset by their manner toward him. But then how could he expect them to react? He truly felt a measure of guilt over Jean-Louis's death and winning the plantation. But on the other hand, the Creole had goaded him into the game, and he had won it fair and square. Why then did he feel so bad?

And why did they both have to be so beautiful?

Royal knew that the nightmare, combined with the unaccustomed surroundings, would probably keep him from going back to sleep. He suddenly remembered the bottle of brandy in the parlor. He pulled on his trousers and boots, put on a black silk robe, and went in search of it.

The house was as quiet as a church. Royal hoped he remembered his way back to the parlor. He moved down a narrow hallway. The doors to a side room were open, and a faint, wavering light issued from within. Royal stopped at the threshold and looked inside. With a start he realized that this was the conservatory, and the unwelcome sight and smell of the coffin brought the nightmare back to him in a rush of terror.

Sitting between him and the bier were two women, their backs toward him. One was wearing a tignon, and Royal assumed she must be Zenobia. The other—probably Jean-Louis's widow, he thought—wore a black shawl draped over her head. Royal crossed himself and moved on. The parlor door was ajar. Without hesitation he went inside. A small lamp burning in the window cast furtive shadows around the room. He made his way to the sideboard and began feeling around for the bottle of brandy.

"Over here."

Startled, Royal swung around. Seated next to the fireplace in one of a pair of armchairs was Suzanne.

"I said it was over here." She was pointing at the bottle of brandy, which sat on a low table in front of her. "I assume this is what you are looking for."

Perhaps because of the gloom, the mourning clothes, and the severe hairstyle, Suzanne made a striking, almost unearthly, figure, and Royal was astonished all over again by her beauty. He gestured toward the brandy. "You don't mind?"

"How could I?" she replied bitterly, then sipped from a nearly empty snifter. "It's all yours now. The brandy, the glasses . . . everything."

Her words were slightly slurred, and Royal suspected that the glass of brandy she was holding had not been her first. He found another snifter on the sideboard, poured himself a heavy dollop of the liquor, and upon impulse sat down in the armchair opposite her.

"I assumed you were in the conservatory," he said.

"I was, but then I needed to be by myself."

He started to get up. "I'll leave you, then."

"No, sit back down. I need to know more about my husband's death. What was his state of mind?"

Royal thought for a moment before answering. "He had been drinking rather heavily."

"I assumed so," she said flatly. "But I meant other than that."

"He seemed intent on proving me the lesser man."

"And are you?" she asked with a wintry smile.

"How can I answer that? I didn't know your husband, not really. I'm sure I wasn't seeing him at his best. But I don't consider myself inferior to any man. I'm not ashamed of being American or a gambler."

Suzanne leaned forward to put down her glass. To Royal it seemed that she had an inborn grace, a way of moving that turned even the most common act into a brief piece of theater. She seemed to be unaware of her attractiveness, however, and to Royal that was perhaps her most arresting trait.

"Ah, yes, a gambler. I have never put much faith in chance."

Royal started to pour her another brandy. Suzanne snatched the bottle away, but not before their hands had touched.

"I'm sorry," Royal said.

"Don't say you're sorry. Everyone says they're sorry. And it doesn't matter a *damn* whether they're sorry or not." She poured herself some more brandy.

Attempting to change the subject, Royal said, "You speak English very fluently."

"I was brought up by my parents to be bilingual. My father always said that you can't know the enemy if you can't understand him."

"I don't expect you to be pleasant."

"I shan't be," Suzanne replied. "And please spare me your attempts at gallantry."

"Very well. After your husband suffered his first losses I didn't want to continue the game. But he goaded me on with his arrogance, and when he ran out of funds, he left the room with Lajeunesse and returned with the deed to the property. I was appalled by the proposal—everything I had won against Heritage."

"Appalled? That's an odd word to employ, M'sieur Brannigan. You weren't too appalled to collect your debt."

"I am a gambler, Madame Jourdain, and collecting debts is part of the game."

"And death is too?" She raised her voice, as if loudness would give her words more validity. "Everybody loved Jean-Louis. Everybody. Even the slaves loved him. He was that kind of man." She looked directly at Royal. "What kind of man are you, M'sieur Brannigan?"

"What do you mean?"

She stood up and walked around the side of the table to the fireplace. "Most men in your station wouldn't have bothered bringing home my husband's body, for instance."

Royal shifted in his chair. "I thought I was doing the honorable thing."

Suzanne crossed and stood next to him. "Honorable?" She shook her head and drew out the words. "No, I wouldn't call it that. You want me to give you absolution, don't you? Well, I won't. You were instrumental in my husband's death. I know you claim coercion because my husband insulted you; but wasn't it less his insults than your own vanity that caused you to participate in an event that could only have brought disastrous results? You may not have handed my husband the pistol, but you gave him your cooperation in a stupid masculine charade." She set her glass on the mantel and faced him. "I know what kind of man you are, M'sieur Brannigan. I cannot help but wonder what made you that way."

Royal stood up and looked directly into her eyes. "You'll have plenty of time to find out, Madame Jourdain."

They were standing less than a foot apart. For a moment Suzanne appeared as if she were going to faint, but she continued to return his stare, not retreating an inch.

Royal's temper was up, but he was distracted by her womanly scent. She did not hide behind perfume. She smelled of the wind and the rain and the sun and the shadows. Her skin had the look of ivory satin, soft and gleaming. He wondered how it would feel, how it would taste.

As if reading his thoughts, Suzanne took a step backward, glared through narrow eyes, then slapped him hard across the cheek.

Royal touched his hand to his smarting flesh. "I'll bid you good night, Madame Jourdain—and I'll take *my* brandy with me."

Without another word, he collected the bottle and left.

Chapter Five

Propped up on several cushions on an old chair, Seth sat at the chopping block in the Heritage kitchen, eating the special breakfast Zenobia had prepared for him: fried oysters, buttermilk biscuits, and an omelet filled with fresh cream and candied fruit, all of which Seth had drowned in a lake of molasses. Between bites he raised his head, screwed up his old man's face, and pronounced, "Yo' sure makes a good breakfas', Zenobia."

Zenobia scowled at the molasses-covered plate and said, "Yo' hurry up and finish dat mess. It almost six-thirty, and yo' got yo' responsibilities."

Seth's responsibilities were the four letters that Suzanne had written during the night, and which were now lying on the corner of the chopping block. The letters, addressed to the owners of Victoire, Salle d'Or, Taffarel, and Bellechasse plantations, informed them of Jean-Louis's death and the time of the funeral. It was not necessary to send one to Villeneuve, since it was owned by the Duvallons and there were no whites in permanent residence.

Seth asked, "What yo' 'spect dis here gambling man is going to do with us niggers? Yo' 'spect he's going to gamble us away like M'sieur Jean-Louis? Yo' 'spect—"

"Yo' can 'spect till yo' turn blue. Ain't no good in trying to guess what dat American is planning."

"Do I have to take one to Taffarel?" Seth asked plaintively. "Miz Julia won't come nohow."

Zenobia eyed him ruefully. "'Course yo' do. And don't go giving me any of dat ghost business. Ain't nobody whose word I trust done seen dat spook."

Seth finished his breakfast in silence, mopping up the excess molasses with a final biscuit. He jumped out of the chair and started to reach for the letters.

Zenobia slapped his hand with a large wooden spoon. "Don't yo' go touchin' dem letters with yo' greasy hands. Miz Suzanne done labored over dem half de night. Now, go wash yo'self up." While Seth followed her orders, Zenobia wrapped the letters in a clean white napkin. "Now, put dese inside yo' shirt, so yo' don't lose dem. And get movin'. I want yo' back real quick so yo' can give me some help with de funeral preparations." With an uncharacteristic display of affection, Zenobia hugged the little boy before ushering him out of the kitchen. "And leave dat banjo behind. People don't want no serenading dis early in de mornin'."

Seth hurried to the stables to get a mount. Suzanne had instructed him to take Arab, Jean-Louis's horse. The stunning white Arabian stallion was four years old and the swiftest horse on Heritage. Seth, despite his diminutive size, was the best horseman among the slaves; Jean-Louis had carefully trained him.

The horse acknowledged Seth with a whinny as the little boy put him in harness. Seth placed a wooden box next to the stallion, climbed up on the animal's bare back, gave him a gentle nudge in the ribs, and they were off.

When horse and rider reached the Promenade, Seth urged the stallion to the left, deciding to deliver the letter to Taffarel on his way back. By then the sun would be high, and there would be less chance of running into a ghost.

As Seth was passing the turnoff leading to Villeneuve, he heard a voice call, "Hey, boy!"

Seeing a rider approaching in a cloud of dust, he reined in. As the man neared, Seth realized it was Philippe Duvallon. The boy was not surprised to see him coming from Villeneuve, for Philippe's affair with Lilliane was common knowledge; he was surprised, however, to see the young Duvallon up and about at such an early hour.

"What are you doing with M'sieur Jourdain's horse, boy?"

Seth lowered his head and replied, "I'm from Heritage, m'sieur."

"Dammit! I know that, boy. What I'm asking is what are you doing with that horse? Did Jean-Louis give you permission to ride around the countryside? Or did you just decide you'd slip out early in the morning and show off in front of the other niggers? Well, answer me! Does he know you've got his horse?" Philippe raised his riding crop, threatening to strike the boy.

Seth lifted his head and arrogantly replied, "I'm on an assignment. I be delivering a letter to yo' papa, the Duc."

"Then give it to me. I'm going to Salle d'Or now. I'll see that he gets it."

Seth hesitated.

"I said give me the damned letter!"

Seth, who couldn't read, had to turn all the letters over to Philippe. The Creole selected the one addressed to his father and slapped the others back into Seth's waiting hands. Without hesitation he ripped open the letter, and his bleary eyes scanned the handwritten message. "Well, I'll be damned!" he exclaimed, and without another word spurred his horse hard and took off down the Promenade in full gallop.

Seth decided to be philosophical about the confrontation. "I don't mind if de white man does de nigger's work fo' him," he mumbled. "Now I gots only three to go."

He reached the turnoff to Victoire. The driveway leading to the big house was lined on both sides by sago palms that had been imported from Indonesia by the Beauchemins. Seth's eyes roamed over the goat-cropped lawn. A stately live oak well over a hundred feet tall dominated the surroundings and offered an extra measure of shade to the veranda. Its massive limbs supported three swings—one for each of the three children. Standing alone on the center swing was Denis. He and Seth were friendly rather than friends; the differences in their ages and social station separated them, plus Denis was usually in the company of his two younger sisters.

"Hey!" called Denis.

"Hey," returned Seth. He jumped off the horse and secured the reins to the base of one of the palms.

The two boys regarded each other for a moment with unconcealed interest before engaging in conversation.

"Where yo' sisters?" asked Seth.

"They always sleep late. I get up early and come out here so I can have some time to myself," Denis replied in a world-weary manner. "A man needs time to think . . ." He puffed out his narrow chest. "Unencumbered by females. You know what I mean."

"I surely does," replied Seth, nodding vigorously and admiring the maturity of the comment.

Denis glared at the horse and back at Seth. "What are you doing riding around so early?"

Seth pulled himself up to his full height and replied with great self-importance, "I'm delivering a special letter to yo' grandpapa."

Denis jumped off the swing and sauntered up to Seth. "You know what's in it?"

"Uh-huh. But it a secret."

Denis, bursting with curiosity, said, "Do you want to trade secrets?"

Seth nodded eagerly.

"So what's in the letter?"

Had Denis been colored, Seth would have held out to hear his secret first; but as it was, he merely hesitated a few seconds before answering the white boy's question. "M'sieur Jean-Louis done lost Heritage in a card game down in New Orleans. Den he killed hisself."

"Suicide!" Denis seemed to savor the word with a macabre relish. "I never knew anyone who committed suicide before."

"Me neither," Seth echoed proudly, and then went on. "De new owner is an American. He brung de body back last night. He's a big handsome fellow name of Royal Brannigan. Dat gambling man owns us all now. De big house, de cane fields, and all us niggers."

"How'd he do it? How'd he kill himself?"

"Shot hisself through de head. He was just a terrible sight," Seth added, implying that he'd seen the body. "De letter's all about de burying dis afternoon."

"You gonna get to keep the horse now that your master's gone and committed suicide?"

"I just might," replied Seth. "'Course, dat depend on M'sieur Royal. I guess I has to put it to him."

"What's going to happen to the ladies?" Denis asked, referring to Angélique and Suzanne.

"Don't know. Dey gonna stay on fo' a while. How long I don't know. Dey sure don't like dat American none."

"No, I guess not," replied Denis thoughtfully.

"Go on now," urged Seth. "What yo' secret?"

Denis put his arm around Seth's shoulders and drew him close. "Our slave Coffey saw the ghost."

"He saw it? He actually saw it? Where? When? What did it look like?"

"The night before last, around midnight, in the woods behind Heritage."

Seth shivered. "Heritage? He saw it on *our* plantation? What was it doing dere?"

"Just wandering through the woods. He had white skin, long straggly hair, and it was a he-ghost."

"In the woods behind Heritage," Seth repeated. Despite the warmth of the morning sun, the little boy shivered. He dug into the inside of his shirt and offered the remaining letters. "Here—yo' take your grandpapa's. I got to get going."

Denis picked out one of the letters, then the boys shook hands in a manly fashion and said goodbye. Seth ran across the lawn to where Arab was patiently waiting, and Denis bounded toward the big house, waving the letter in the air like a rare trophy.

There was no one in sight at Bellechasse, neither slave nor master. Seth paced back and forth on the veranda, trying to make up his mind whether or not to ring the front bell. It was an unlikely thing for a slave to do; still, he knew that the letter was of great import. He started to ring the bell when a voice behind him demanded, "Don't you dare ring that bell!" Startled, he swung around and found himself facing a disheveled Marguerite Martineau.

"Who are you? What are you doing here?" Her voice was so shrill and demanding that for a moment Seth was bereft of words. In any case, he barely recognized her in her present state. She was wearing a wrinkled dressing gown and looked as though she hadn't slept at all. Her hair was undone and hanging in lank coils, and the previous night's cosmetics were smeared across her dry flesh. Her manner was so disoriented that Seth thought maybe she had been in some kind of accident.

"Miz Marguerite, it's Seth from Heritage."

Marguerite drew nearer to the little boy and examined him through slitted eyes. "Why, so it is!" she exclaimed. Her manner became more affable. "What are you doing up at this hour of the morning, young Seth? Don't tell me that you didn't sleep either?"

"No, ma'am. I slept fine, but I had to get up early in order to deliver an important letter to M'sieur Léon."

Marguerite selected the correctly addressed letter and opened it without hesitation. Her bloodshot eyes scanned the page, and suddenly she burst into tears. "*Mon dieu!*" she cried. "He was so young. So very, very young."

Seth excused himself and hurried away from the distraught woman. He scrambled atop Arab and urged the stallion back down the Promenade at a steady canter.

The moist morning air enhanced the scent of the magnolias, and as Seth rode, the spicy perfume made him giddy, almost lightheaded. It was too nice a day for a funeral, he thought as he urged the stallion toward Taffarel. The sun was warm and comforting, and its rays, spilling through the tangled magnolia leaves, projected bright disks of light like scattered gold coins on the ground below. The sky was so blue that it almost hurt to look at it, and despite haunted houses, ghosts, and suicides, Seth knew that he would be young forever.

The scent of freshly brewing coffee drifted out of the kitchen and floated across the loggia. It wafted its way around the columns of the big house, stimulating anyone still slumbering at Heritage into wakefulness.

The pungent aroma entered the blue guest room and hovered over the sleeping form of Royal Brannigan. His nostrils twitched, and his eyelashes fluttered. Not yet fully conscious, Royal stretched his long frame, luxuriating in the caress of the silk sheets, which were as soft as a woman's flesh.

Somewhat disoriented and thinking that he was with someone, Royal rolled over and was surprised to find that he was alone. He opened his bloodshot eyes and stared at the unfamiliar surroundings. Suddenly remembering where he was, he kicked off the sheets and sat up—but he had moved too quickly, and his head throbbed painfully. He rubbed his temples until his vision came into focus. The first thing he noticed was the empty brandy bottle sitting on a bureau against the wall. His watch was next to it. He staggered across the room and picked it up. It was twenty past ten. Plenty of time to get out of the house before the funeral.

After putting on his robe, Royal opened the French doors and stepped out onto the veranda. The scent of the coffee—extra strong and chicory-laced—immediately lifted his spirits. Good Creole coffee was always his remedy for late nights; it was as stimulating as the first kiss of the morning from a beautiful woman. He heard the clatter of pans from the kitchen outbuilding and noted that the guest room was on the north side of the house, away from the morning sun. His suspicions of the previous night were reaffirmed; obviously this was not a room for a favored guest.

As Royal turned back inside, his foot touched something. He bent down to pick up a mysterious object that lay at his feet, then held it up for examination. It apparently was a dead hummingbird, plucked clean of its feathers and as dry as a wad of paper. He was about to throw it away when he noticed something had been crammed into its beak. He pulled it free. It was a tiny piece of fabric, and it appeared to have some writing on it. He dropped the bird into the pocket of his robe and held the cloth up to the daylight. Written in charcoal, in a scrawling hand, were his initials.

"They'll not frighten me away with their voodoo antics," Royal growled. He yanked on the bell pull.

Zenobia appeared almost immediately, her hooded eyes cold and impenetrable. Royal held out the cloth and the dried bird and asked, "What do you know about this?"

When the woman didn't respond, he asked, "Did you understand me?"

"I understand all Americans, m'sieur."

"Good. Then what can you tell me about this?"

A trace of a smile played on Zenobia's lips. "It's a voodoo gris-gris, m'sieur."

"Voodoo? Here at Magnolia Landing?"

"Voodoo is everywhere," she replied enigmatically and swept it out of his hands. "I get rid of it fo' yo'."

"I want hot water brought for my bath and something light for breakfast. Plenty of coffee, croissants, and some fresh fruit—I don't care what kind."

She gestured to a pitcher of water and a bowl on top of the commode.

"I like to bathe all over, if you don't mind."

Zenobia, without waiting to be dismissed, left to fulfill her duties.

Royal washed his face in the tepid water, then sat down in a chair between the two sets of French doors. His headache had subsided, and now he was fully able to comprehend his situation. As the new owner of Heritage, he didn't intend to stay confined to the guest room. But the prospect of dealing with Suzanne and Angélique was not a pleasant one.

A short time later Zenobia reappeared, carrying a tray. She was followed by a retinue of slaves bearing earthenware jugs and craning their necks to get a good look at Royal. Bringing up the rear was a wizened little boy weighted down with several cakes of soap, a soft brush, and a stack of towels.

The slaves carried the jugs into the bath and left, except for the boy. Propping the tray on her hip, Zenobia pulled a side table next to Royal, then set the tray down. It contained a silver pot of coffee, a cup and saucer, a plate of warm croissants, a small tub of butter, and a crystal bowl filled with a fruit compote. As she poured the coffee she announced, "This is Seth." The boy smiled at Royal. "He will pour yo' bathwater, scrub yo' if yo' likes it better, rinse yo' and dry yo'."

Royal nodded and started to compliment Zenobia on the coffee, but before he could, she said, "Miz Suzanne suggests dat yo' might go riding till . . . later."

"You mean until after the funeral? Yes, that would be fine."

"Seth will show yo' to de stables and help yo' select a horse."

Royal was relieved. Not only was it an excuse to get away from the house while the funeral was taking place, but it was also a chance to explore the grounds.

As she was leaving, Zenobia admonished, "Now, Seth, don't yo' let yo' chattering interfere with yo' duties."

Royal started to pour another cup of coffee when Seth hurried to the side of the table. "I'm supposed to do dat, m'sieur."

Royal, amused, let the boy serve him. He was fascinated by the lad's antique face. He pointed to the tray. "Would you like something, Seth?"

Seth shook his head. "No, m'sieur. I done ate my breakfas' at six-thirty dis morning."

"What an ungodly hour! What were you doing up so early?"

"I had to deliver de invitations to M'sieur Jean-Louis's funeral," he replied, with a touch of impudence.

"I imagine you were quite fond of your master, Seth."

The little boy looked at the floor. "Well, I did like him a lot, dat's fo' certain. He taught me to ride and to tend de horses. I liked him till almos' a year ago."

"What happened then?" Royal asked gently.

The little boy's eyes clouded over. "He got hisself married and he changed."

"In what way?" Royal was curious about the nature of the man whose suicide had served him so advantageously.

Seth glanced toward the door, then lowered his voice to a hoarse whisper. "He jes' stopped talking to anyone. He started drinking real hard and staying away from de plantation. And he didn't go jes' to New Orleans—sometimes he went upriver to Natchez or Memphis. In Memphis dere's dis bad part of town called de Gut. He liked dat. Zenobia said he developed hisself a taste for de gutter. When he come back he looked worse and worse all de time. Zenobia said it was a bad road he was traveling." His voice rose in volume. "I saw yo' coming in, and I saw de casket. And I figured who was in it."

"How did you know?"

"Zenobia always say dat de way M'sieur Jean-Louis acted up, someday dey gonna bring him back in a casket. And yo' did, and now yo' owns us. Are yo' going to stay around, or are yo' going to go back to gambling?"

"I'd like to stay around, Seth, but I don't know much about running a sugar plantation."

"I can help," Seth said brightly. "I know all about horses, cutting cane, and making de sugar."

Royal smiled. "Then I'll depend on you."

Seth looked directly at Royal and asked, "Yo' gonna kick Miz Suzanne and Miz Angélique off de place?"

"Of course not. Why do you ask?"

"I was sort of hoping dat Miz Angélique would be going."

"Don't you like her?"

The little boy shook his head. "Not anymore."

"And Miss Suzanne?" Royal added.

"Zenobia said she was de best thing dat ever happened to Heritage, but after de wedding she changed her mind. I never did, though." Seth seemed anxious not to continue the line of conversation. "Yo' better be getting yo' bath now, M'sieur Royal, befo' de water gets cold."

"Thanks for reminding me, Seth."

The bath adjoining the room was small but attractively designed. The ceiling and top half of the walls were plastered and painted a light blue. The rest of the room was covered with Italian tiles. The tub, typical of the kind provided in the better-class hotels, was made of copper and resembled a seashell. Seth started to lift one of the jars, and Royal said, "I'll do that, Seth. They're too heavy for you."

"I'm stronger dan I look," the little boy replied defiantly.

Royal shrugged his shoulders. "All right, if you're sure."

After the boy filled the tub, he picked up the bar of soap and scrub brush and stood at attention. Royal was amused and wondered if all of Heritage's guests received such personal service. He stripped out of his robe and stepped into the tub. Although his large frame was a bit cramped in the tub, which had been designed for a much shorter person, the water was soothing to his tired muscles.

"Seth, would you bring me my shaving kit from the top of the chest?"

Seth did as he was told, and when Royal began to lather up he asked, "Don't yo' want a mirror, m'sieur?"

"Well, I'll tell you, Seth. I've been in so many places where there weren't any mirrors available that I've learned to shave by touch. Wouldn't know how to do it any other way. Why don't you sit down over there, and we can continue our talk."

Seth climbed onto a cane chair and said impertinently, "What do you want to ask me?"

"I found something very strange outside my door this morning. Do you know anything about it?"

"Was it a dried hummingbird with a message in its beak?"

Royal dunked his head under the water and came up sputtering. "That's exactly what it was."

There was a long pause. Finally, Seth said, "I put it dere."

"You did? Why?"

"Dat's a voodoo fix to keep yo' from leaving. A bird dat can't fly can't go nowhere. I copied yo' 'nitials offen yo' luggage."

"I see," said Royal solemnly. "Did you kill the bird?"

"Oh, no. Dat's one of Zenobia's birds. She catches 'em and

wrings dere necks. Den she scalds de feathers off 'em and dries 'em in de oven. Later she dips 'em in honey and eats 'em whole. It her favorite treat. She say dey better dan anything."

Royal was glad that he hadn't heard the story before breakfast. Changing the subject, he asked, "Are you going to attend the funeral, Seth?"

"Of course. All us niggers is going. I'm going to play de banjo."

"Is that typical of a plantation owner's funeral?"

"Guess not. Miz Angélique don't like it much, having all us slaves attending and no priest in charge. But Miz Suzanne, she tell her dat dere are many ways to gloryland."

Royal finished bathing and pulled the plug. The tub drained through a pipe into one of the large metal vats hidden between the ground and the first floor of the plantation; the vats would be emptied later by slaves.

"All right, Seth, I'm ready for my rinse."

The little boy moved a stepstool next to the tub, and balancing one of the earthenware jugs on his hip, he climbed to the topmost step and emptied the warm water over Royal's head. "Another one, m'sieur?"

"Another one should do it, Seth."

The little boy repeated the action, and when Royal stepped out of the tub, Seth was waiting with an oversize bath towel. Royal wrapped it around his waist and, using another, began drying himself. "I feel like a new man, Seth."

The boy looked at him quizzically. "Yo' look de same to me, m'sieur."

Royal laughed. "That's just a figure of speech, son."

Royal put on a suit of clothes identical to the one he had worn on the trip upriver, though the vest he selected was cream colored and embroidered with blue vines and flowers.

Seth admired his new master, saying, "Yo' looks mighty good in dat outfit, M'sieur Royal. But I didn't think yo' were going to de funeral."

"I'm not wearing mourning, Seth. It's my trademark."

"Den it not practical fo' a ride. Lots of dust dis time of year."

"It'll have to do. It's all I've got. All my suits are exactly the same."

"How many suits yo' got?"

"Seven. One for each day of the week."

"Dat's a powerful lot of suits. But I bet M'sieur Jean-Louis has yo' beat. He had a whole roomful of clothes. Enough clothes, I spect, to outfit every male nigger on de plantation."

As Royal and Seth walked through the gardens, the little boy treated Royal to his own personal guided tour. The first thing Seth pointed out was the plantation bell, which hung from a ten-foot-high stone arch. He informed Royal that Henri Jourdain, the father of Jean-Louis and Angélique, had the foundry melt down over a thousand dollars' worth of golden eagles when they were casting the mold, believing that the gold would add a sweeter tone to the bell. Royal instinctively reached for the rope, but the little boy stopped him.

"Oh, no, m'sieur. De plantation bell's only rung when de most importantest things happen. Hurricanes, floods, fires, or—" He glanced uneasily at the ground. "—de death of de master."

"I'm sorry, Seth. I'll remember that. Shall we proceed?"

The little boy chattered incessantly, but Royal was so overwhelmed by the beauty of Heritage that he barely heard Seth's words. The boy informed him that the rose gardens of Heritage were famous throughout Louisiana. Indeed, there seemed to be roses everywhere, and of every conceivable variety, ranging in color from palest pink to fuchsia to crimson red, making it appear as if the earth were blushing.

Royal turned around to get a good look at the back of the big house in the daylight and from a distance, and what he saw pleased him. It certainly was a far cry from what he was accustomed to. It stood majestically, two stories high with a steeply pitched roof and a raised basement. The stately columns surrounded the entire structure, supporting the veranda and the galleries on all four sides. The stuccoed walls had been whitewashed until they shone. Royal was impressed with the house's dignity and fine proportion.

They reached a high hedge that served to hide the potting shed and greenhouse. Farther on was a broad crescent staircase of brick that had been built like an amphitheater into the side of a sloping hill. In the distance was an array of huge old sugar cane kettles sunk in the ground. Vines surrounded the rim of each, making them appear like wreaths that might have been discarded by some Roman emperor.

The kettles were now filled with rainwater and served as

oversized baths for large flocks of blackbirds. As Royal passed, he noticed that the bottoms of the sugar kettles glistened with coins that had been tossed there by wish-makers.

They arrived at a charming glen of bamboo and fern, where a series of miniature waterfalls spilled into pools ever increasing in size, formed by a series of artfully constructed rock terraces. The topmost pool was not more than several feet wide, while the one on the bottom was large enough for bathing. Seth explained that originally there had been thirteen terraces, thirteen pools, and thirteen waterfalls. But three times thirteen had dire foreboding in voodoo superstition, and the slaves would not come near the glen. The Jourdains had relented, and one terrace, one pool, and one waterfall had been removed.

Royal noticed a fat blacksnake sunning itself among an arrangement of white candles that had been placed upon the stones of the nearest pond. The candles had been burned halfway down, leaving ribbons of melted wax that made it appear as if the reptile had given birth to albino offspring.

Royal looked at Seth. "Voodoo?"

The boy nodded and shrugged his shoulders at the same time, his answer being the equivalent of "Yes, I don't know."

A staircase made of cypress rose from the glen to the crest of the hill, where the gardens stopped. Beyond were the fields of sugar cane. Endless rows with tasseled tops waved beneath the light currents of air. Windmills sprang out of the cane like lighthouses, ports of refuge in a rippling sea of green and yellow.

Royal drew in his breath and asked in a hushed voice, "Is all of this Heritage?"

"As far as de eye can see," Seth replied proudly.

Royal followed Seth to the stables, but his eyes remained riveted to the splendid view of the lands that were Heritage. Following Seth's advice, Royal selected a chestnut stallion named Alezan. After it was saddled, he left the boy and rode off in the direction of the cane fields.

As he approached the adjacent slave quarters, figures appeared in the doorways and faces at the windows. Royal now realized why the cane fields were empty of slaves; they would be attending their master's funeral that day. He rode slowly past, and the onlookers dropped their eyes in deference to their new master. Only the children, more curious than fearful, stole glances at him. Royal wanted to stop and reassure them all that nothing would change, that they would not be mistreated or sold, but he decided that the time was inappropriate.

He noticed they were all dressed in similar plain garments that almost looked like uniforms. The males wore loose-fitting shirts and drawstring pants of rough white cotton; the females wore white tignons and flowing white shifts. Everyone had a piece of black cloth tied around one arm.

Beyond the slave quarters were the buildings used for storing and processing the sugar cane, and sitting just apart from these was a small house. A man stepped out onto the front porch. He was dark and muscular, with a square, humorless face. He, too, was wearing white, but it was a suit that had been tailored to fit his beefy body. There was also a mourning band around his arm. He lifted his head and stared at Royal. His somber eyes resembled pieces of black shale, and beneath his flat nose and broad, flaring nostrils, a black mustache drooped around an unsmiling mouth. His expression did not change as he touched the brim of his hat. It was less a gesture of greeting than one of defiance. Royal nodded in return and urged the horse onward.

Royal continued on through the fields of cane, occasionally turning to look over his shoulder, trying to ascertain the distance he had covered. Heritage was far more extensive than he had imagined; why, it was almost as big as the entire town of Glassboro!

And everything was his—the big house, the outbuildings, the gardens, the cane fields, the slaves, the warehouses . . . everything. All on the turn of a card. He felt full of himself, exhilarated by the prospect of being the owner of such a plantation. The distasteful circumstances of his fabulous acquisition and the plight of Angélique and Suzanne were pushed from his mind. He could not—would not—allow himself to dwell upon the misfortunes of others.

Chapter Six

Death has its own way of altering the outlook of each person who survives the passing of a loved one. There are the expected reactions—a numbing grief, a sudden burst of tears, a disruption of routine, a loss of appetite or sleep—and there are the more unusual responses.

For Suzanne, the world seemed suddenly devoid of physical color. At first she thought something was wrong with her vision, for she began to perceive everything in muted tones. Not black, white, or gray, but murky representations of what she knew a color should be. It was as if someone had drawn an opaque curtain around her life, and she wondered if she would ever experience splendor again.

Suzanne adjusted the black lace veil and secured it with several hairpins, then stepped back and looked at herself in her bedroom mirror. The pattern on the veil made it appear as if a thousand shadowy spiders had suddenly spun their melancholy webs about the room. It couldn't be helped. The black veil and the black silk dress were the only things she owned suitable for a funeral. There had been no time to have anything made. When one was young, one simply didn't anticipate such events.

Yet she didn't feel young anymore, Suzanne thought as she sat down at her dressing table. She began searching the drawers for a pair of black gloves she had once worn to her Aunt Annette's funeral. She rummaged through one drawer after another, not discovering the gloves until opening the very last drawer. They were lying on top of a man's cravat, which Suzanne remembered was blue, the color of cobalt. She also remembered it had once been stained by the salt of her tears.

That had not been so very long ago. Then she had been Suzanne Delisle, a young woman who had lived all her life on a cotton plantation in Georgia and had come to New Orleans to visit her mother's sister, a wealthy widow named Annette Casaque.

Suzanne's mother and aunt had entered into a secret agreement that Annette would launch Suzanne into New Orleans society in the hope that the young woman might find a suitable husband. Suzanne's mother considered the young men of Georgia too coarse and uncosmopolitan for her favorite child.

It was during the whirl of festive events in New Orleans that Suzanne had met the dashing Jean-Louis Jourdain. He had a reputation as a rake, and at first Aunt Annette had tried to discourage the blooming relationship. But Jean-Louis was rich and socially acceptable, and Annette found it difficult not to at least tolerate his interest in her niece, particularly since Suzanne seemed to welcome his attentions.

Jean-Louis and Suzanne scrupulously attended to all the ritual details of a Creole courtship, but as October approached, the young man made plans to return to Magnolia Landing. He had to be at Heritage during the harvesting of the sugar crop. At any other season he would have invited Suzanne and her aunt to stay at the big house; but harvest was not the time to entertain guests.

Despite her aunt's protestations that it was "indelicate, my dear," Suzanne was determined to see Jean-Louis off on his journey upriver. Annette finally relented, but insisted that she come along as chaperone. The *Belle Créole* was scheduled to leave New Orleans at ten o'clock, but a faulty carriage wheel kept Suzanne and her aunt from quayside until the gangplank had been taken away. Suzanne jumped from the carriage and ran toward the edge of the wharf.

Jean-Louis had seen her at once. He had rushed to the edge of the railing and begun waving at her. On impulse, he untied his cravat and threw it across the narrow gap of water toward her. A sudden breeze from the river sent it spinning through the air like a satin bird, and it glided and dipped until it came to rest on the wharf in front of Suzanne. She reached down, picked it up, and held it against her cheek. Suddenly she was crying. The ship was pulling away from the dock, and she was sure she would never see Jean-Louis again. Using the cravat as an impromptu handkerchief, she dabbed at the tears that she could not keep from flowing.

When Jean-Louis saw that Suzanne was crying, he, too, began weeping. He ran along the deck of the departing ship, trying to remain as close to her as possible. Leaning over the railing, he shouted something above the din of the engines.

She couldn't understand him. He rushed to the stern of the

departing ship, and cupping his hands around his mouth, he roared, "I said, marry me, Suzanne!"

This time she heard him. The tears stopped flowing, and she burst into a dazzling smile. She nodded her head vigorously, blew him a most unladylike kiss, and shouted, "Yes! I say yes, M'sieur Jourdain!" She was completely oblivious of the applause, laughter, and catcalls of the dockworkers who had stopped their labors to watch the young lovers.

When she returned to the carriage, she was surprised to find Aunt Annette crouched on the floorboards, hiding beneath her parasol in mortification. "That was *really* indelicate, my dear," she had admonished.

Suzanne was smiling in remembrance of her aunt's comic consternation, when there was a knock at the door. Zenobia entered. "Yo' need any help, Miz Suzanne?"

Suzanne replied, "No, I'm quite ready, Zenobia. Would you ask Angélique to join me in the conservatory for prayers?"

After Zenobia closed the door, Suzanne looked down and saw that she was still holding the cravat. She began shedding fresh tears, and once again she used the satin tie as a handkerchief. She cried, "Oh, Jean-Louis, why was our love not enough?" as she drew on the gloves.

The children's room was located on the second floor of Heritage. Brightly lit by the noonday sun, it was a large, cheerful room, and although the children who once occupied it were now grown, it was still cleaned every week by the house slaves. The walls were a dusty shade of red, and dark cherry shelves rising halfway to the ceiling were filled with games, toys, stuffed animals, and dolls. Hanging in the center of the room was a chandelier fashioned to resemble a bird cage.

Sitting on the polished parquet floor directly beneath the chandelier was Angélique. She was wearing her black bombazine, and resting in her lap was a small bouquet of white violets she had picked earlier. Before her was a large dollhouse, an exact replica of the big house itself, down to the most minute detail, including carpets, furniture, and make-believe chandeliers. There were also dolls: several black dolls representing the house servants, and two well-worn white dolls—smaller than the others—representing Jean-Louis and Angélique as children. The dolls had delicate porcelain faces and real hair cut from the children's own heads. Angélique had taken delight in pretending that she and her brother lived alone at Heritage as master and mistress of the great plantation.

She wiped a strand of hair out of her eyes, leaned back on the palms of her hands, and reflected that things hadn't turned out the way she had planned.

The original owner of Heritage had been her father, Henri-Antoine Jourdain. An aristocrat, he had had the good sense to leave France before the Revolution and join his older brother Charles, who owned a sugar plantation on Santo Domingo. Forced to flee the island during the slave rebellion of 1791, the brothers resettled near New Orleans, where they prospered. They were hardworking men, too busy accumulating wealth to bother with whatever frivolities New Orleans society then had to offer.

Henri finally did marry in 1805, when he selected a ravishing young lady by the name of Lucie d'Auber. Lucie, who came from a family of modest means, was a determined social climber and would not rest until Henri bought into the land of her dreams—Magnolia Landing.

At that time, the huge tract adjoining Taffarel Plantation had lain fallow for many years, for Julia Taffarel, the owner, had neither the capital nor the labor to plant a crop. But for some reason she turned down the Jourdains' generous offer more than once, and without explanation.

During the successive years, however, Taffarel and the neighboring plantations were plagued by a recurrent sugar blight, which ruined all hope of profit. Nearly destitute, Julia finally agreed to sell the land, and by far the best offer she received was from the Jourdains.

The Jourdains built an extravagant new house, and Henri, hoping for a good many offspring, christened the plantation Heritage. To his disappointment, however, Lucie, claiming she did not want to spoil her figure, bore him only two children—Jean-Louis in 1807 and Angélique in 1810. Shortly after Angélique's birth, she abandoned her family and returned to the New Orleans social whirl.

In 1817 Lucie succumbed to a respiratory ailment and died. It was said that Henri did not miss her. Content to devote all his time to the plantation, he let Zenobia rear his children and did not look for another wife. In 1826 he was killed in a steamboat accident, and because he had not left a will, the entire estate went to his son. Angélique deeply resented this, though she kept it well concealed. Despite her beauty, the lack of a suitable dowry meant that her marriage prospects would be considerably lessened.

Jean-Louis reluctantly took over the reins and ran the plantation as best he could. But work ill suited him, and the plantation soon began to run into debt. Angélique urged him to hire a well-trained overseer, and he complied. The overseer—a man named Bastile—was somewhat harsh, but the operation was soon back in the black, and Jean-Louis could return to his favorite passions—drinking, gambling, and women. Everyone was surprised when he fell in love with Suzanne Delisle, proposed marriage, and was accepted. But soon after the wedding, he drifted back to his former ways. . . .

Angélique was shaken out of her reverie by a hard knock at the door. Before she could answer it, the door opened and Zenobia entered.

"Miz Angélique!" she exclaimed in disapproval. "I been looking all over fo' yo'. What yo' doing in here?"

"Why, I come here often when I want to be alone," Angélique replied with a toss of her head.

"Too often, if yo' asks me. Miz Suzanne wants yo' to join her in de conservatory fo' prayers."

Angélique frowned. "Tell her you couldn't find me. Tell her . . . no, tell her I'll be down in a moment." She looked sharply at the servant. "You needn't wait for me."

As Zenobia closed the door, Angélique retrieved the dolls representing herself and Jean-Louis. She placed the Angélique doll on a miniature chair in the old music room. Then, tenderly, she laid the Jean-Louis doll on the floor in front of her own image. Two tears appeared in the corners of her feverish green eyes as she scattered violets over her brother's body. Then she got up, smoothed the folds of her dress, and started for the door. As she crossed the room, she caught sight of her reflection in a mirror. Pausing to scrutinize herself, she decided that the black bombazine was definitely unflattering to her pale complexion.

"Perhaps a touch of rouge," she said as she flounced out of the room.

Royal reached a canebrake that concealed the beginnings of a swamp. The ground became marshy, and he dismounted. Presuming his horse was thirsty, he decided to enter the forbidding place in search of fresh water. The swamp was guarded by dark cypress trees growing at odd angles and festooned with Spanish moss. The air was heavy with the stench of decay.

Royal's footsteps were soundless on the damp carpet of moss as he led the horse through waist-high ferns and then a glade of saw grass. Lizards scurried to safety to avoid being stepped upon. He passed several pools of water, but they were wine-dark and looked undrinkable.

The dense overgrowth managed to blot out all but the most persistent rays of sun. A battery of dragonflies, their iridescent wings glistening in the half-light, hovered and darted over the undergrowth. The horse snorted and started to back up. "Easy, Alezan, easy," said Royal, calming the animal by stroking its neck.

Royal's search for fresh water was in vain, and he led the stallion toward the sunlight. They came out of the swamp into another field of sugar cane. When Royal remounted, he saw that the fields were being worked by slaves. They were not wearing black armbands, and he realized that he was no longer on his own land.

Trotting Alezan round the edge of a field, he noted that the crops here were hardy, although the outbuildings in the distance were ramshackle and in need of repair. He headed toward the buildings; perhaps the overseer would let him water his horse before returning to Heritage.

The cane fields ended, and a garden full of thriving vegetables began. He saw a woman in a large straw hat bent over pulling weeds, her back toward him.

"Pardon me, could you tell me where I am?"

The woman straightened up and turned around. Royal was surprised. She was not a slave but an elderly white woman.

"You're on my property, young man," the woman replied in perfect English.

"I'm sorry."

"Don't apologize. Get off your horse and let me take a look at you." Royal complied, and the old woman, hands on hips, executed a complete circle around him. "I heard you were good-looking, but they weren't right by half." She smiled. "So you're the man who won Heritage from that fool Jean-Louis."

"Why a fool?"

"He was foolish to bet you and more foolish to shoot

himself." She extended her hand. "I'm Julia Taffarel. Obviously I know who you are."

"I heard you were a recluse."

Julia's blue eyes twinkled, and her mouth curled into a puckish smile. "Only when I choose to be."

"But how do you know so much about me, Miss Taffarel?"

"The Negroes carry messages faster than lightning bugs." She called to one of them, "Lucien, take M'sieur Brannigan's horse and give him some water." She turned to Royal. "Come to the house and have a cold drink. You look like you can use one, and I feel like talking. Besides, I'm curious to see if I can still hold a conversation."

"Gladly. But aren't you going to the funeral?"

She removed her hat and fluffed up her hair. "I don't attend fools' funerals. Besides, I never did like that boy or his sister."

Royal followed the woman across an unkempt lawn to a row of silver-green willow trees. "These once served to screen the outbuildings, vegetable garden, and cane fields from the big house," Julia remarked. "Now it's the other way around."

As he stepped through the curtain of trailing branches, Royal was unprepared for what he saw. The big house, which had once been a testament to fabulous wealth, was now in an advanced state of decay. He noticed that a section of the second-floor gallery had collapsed and that part of the roof had been blown away during some long-ago storm. An attic shutter flapped in the breeze, making a lonely sound, like the applause of a single person.

Julia Taffarel spryly mounted the back steps to the veranda. Despite her age, she moved with the fluidity and grace of a well-finished adolescent girl.

"Watch that step, Mr. Brannigan—it's broken." She led him around to the front porch, to a pair of carved wooden chairs situated deep in the shade. "Take that one. It's stronger and much less likely to collapse." Royal sat down and glanced around; he noticed that the windows had all been boarded up and that the whitewash and plaster had scaled off the walls, making them look leprous.

Julia made no apology for the run-down surroundings or for her appearance. She was wearing an ancient day-dress so patched that it was hard to make out just what constituted the original material. A rolled-up pair of elbow-length gloves that had probably once belonged to a ball gown protected her hands from outdoor work. She also wore heavy men's shoes—the kind that laced to midcalf and had been out of style for several decades.

Julia called to an elderly slave who appeared from the house. "Ottile, make us two of your wonderful brandy cocktails, please."

Royal was surprised. A brandy cocktail was the most popular—and potent—drink in New Orleans, and one that he also favored. It was made with a touch of sugar, water, and bitters, plus a lot of brandy.

The old woman smiled at his reaction. "Despite my eccentricities, Mr. Brannigan, I try to keep in touch with civilization . . . from a distance, of course." She appraised him openly for a minute, then asked bluntly, "So what's to become of the Jourdain women?"

Royal was embarrassed by her direct question. "They'll stay on for a time," he said.

"I don't suppose you know a damn thing about raising sugar cane?"

"No, ma'am."

"Then you should make some sort of business arrangement with them so that they'll stay until after harvest time. I understand that Suzanne is adept at running a plantation, and Angélique knows as much about cane as a man. Take my advice—you can learn from them. It would be to your advantage. It would also cement your relationship with Rafe Bastile, the overseer at Heritage. He's difficult but the best around. He had to be, with that Jean-Louis as master of the house. Am I being too dictatorial?" She didn't wait for Royal's reply but plunged on. "Of course, there's the possibility that you might tire of plantation life and return to the gaming tables."

"No, ma'am. I've given that up for good."

Julia's tone was incredulous. "Because some poor fool shot himself? You may feel that way now, but mark my words"—she wagged a narrow finger at him—"gambling is like a fever in the blood. Once you get it, you have it forever."

Ottile arrived with the prepared drinks—two extremely tall glasses of golden brown liquid over ice and fragrant with lemon peel. "I'm afraid this is nearly the last of the ice," Julia sighed. "Captain Calabozo was kind enough to bring us a block downriver from the north. We've kept it in the root cellar, portioning it out as if it were diamonds." She noticed

Royal staring at the size of the glasses and explained, "Papa always said give your guests a good drink. Why waste the servants' time?" Julia lifted her glass and proposed a toast. "Here's to your new adventure, Mr. Brannigan. I sincerely hope it is successful."

"Thank you, Miss Taffarel," Royal replied. He sipped his drink, pronounced it excellent, and then asked, "Do you think I should offer the women a share in the profits of the crop as an incentive to stay?"

"I should say that it was an excellent idea."

"How much would you suggest?"

She replied without hesitation, "Twenty-five percent for the two of them."

"I only hope there is a profit."

"I hope so, too, Mr. Brannigan. It's the only thing that keeps Taffarel afloat. I—we—depend upon it as our sole means of support." She sighed, took a long drink, and gazed sideways at the house. Her eyes widened in surprise, as if she were seeing it for the first time. "Taffarel wasn't always like this, Mr. Brannigan."

"I assume not," Royal replied. Hoping he hadn't offended the old lady, he quickly added, "I mean, I've heard stories."

Julia smiled wistfully. "Stories. Stories are just stories, Mr. Brannigan. Usually they're not very accurate, and certainly never as exciting as the truth." She leaned forward in the chair and, as eager as a child, asked, "Would you care to hear a true story, Mr. Brannigan? A nice long tale to while away the morning? Full of triumph and tragedy, passion and privilege? Indeed, all the things that make up a good tale." She lowered her voice to a whisper, and her blue eyes shone like pieces of the sky. "Now, think carefully before you answer. For like any good tale, it must be told to its conclusion."

Royal answered without hesitation, "I would be honored, Miss Taffarel."

"Then draw your chair closer. I have only so many breaths left, and I don't want to waste them by having to strain my voice."

Julia was obviously pleased. She set her glass down, cleared her throat, and in a suddenly theatrical voice, full of shading and vibrato, announced, "I call it the tale of the pirate and his child bride!" She leaned back in the chair, rested her elbows on the arms, and, stroking the wood as if it were a talisman, began her story.

"Once upon a time, Taffarel was the only plantation to occupy the area now called Magnolia Landing. My father, Julius Taffarel, began its construction in 1769 as a tribute to his intended bride—my mother-to-be—Claudine Rivière. Long before the first sugar crop was ever harvested, Taffarel became the very heartbeat of New Orleans society. Here, behind these very columns, the rich, the powerful, and the notorious attended elaborate parties. People traveled immense distances to stroll across this veranda and wander through the tropical gardens. Young women flirted behind ivory fans, while gentlemen toasted their beauty. There were elderly ladies who boasted of bloodlines that reached back further than anyone could remember. At these gatherings, styles were set and gossip was elevated to an art. Government policy was drafted, and huge business deals were settled. The events that took place here affected every man, woman, and child, white or colored, French or Spanish, who lived within the Louisiana Territory."

"No Americans?" Royal asked.

"Most definitely not. And if you keep interrupting me, I'll never get to the good parts."

"I'm sorry—I won't do it again."

"Now, as I was saying—*everyone* who lived within the Louisiana Territory . . ."

As she sat opposite the newcomer to Magnolia Landing, Julia Taffarel could not help but wonder what he must think of her, of the life she now led. His expression was inscrutable as he patiently listened to her; yet she felt that he was a kindred spirit and, more than anyone, would appreciate the strange story of the Taffarels, which had begun with her father. . . .

Julius Taffarel had been born in the year 1711 to a peasant family in Lyons, France. He had been arrested at the age of fifteen for thievery but had escaped and boarded a ship for Louisiana and, hopefully, a better life. He had survived the arduous voyage and reached New Orleans late in 1726. From all accounts, he had been a good-looking, physically fit young man with great ambitions and few scruples. The brawling, vulgar new city must have suited his purposes just fine—though not as a resident, for no sooner had he arrived than he joined a band of river pirates who preyed upon local shipping.

Amazingly enough, the band was led by a female pirate

who called herself Betzy Boulotte. Betzy, a heavyset but nonetheless coarsely appealing woman, had a lusty appetite for handsome young men. Julius became Betzy's lover, and she taught him everything she knew about sailing and piracy. Less than two years later, Betzy was shot and killed boarding a Spanish ship, and at the age of eighteen Julius took control of the pirate band.

Mindful of Betzy's fate, and desiring some measure of respectability, Julius eventually began diverting his ill-gotten gains into a legitimate enterprise. He started a shipping business of his own, gave up piracy, and as his fortunes grew, he began looking around for a wife.

Through the ensuing years Julius met and romanced many beautiful women—not all of them strictly eligible for marriage—but his devotion was fleeting, and he never considered any of them as a possible mate until finally, in 1768, he met Claudine Rivière and fell hopelessly in love.

By this time Julius was fifty-eight years old, immensely rich, and still a handsome and vital man whose desire for feminine companionship had not diminished. Claudine, youngest of four daughters, was just fourteen and as pretty and delicate as a porcelain doll. Her father was a widowed New Orleans shopkeeper who made a moderate living. Pious and practical in his views of matrimony, he would not consider a union between Julius and Claudine until his three elder daughters were married and his youngest reached the age of sixteen.

Julius, already older than his future father-in-law, and every bit as practical, decided to hasten matters by presenting each of Claudine's sisters a handsome dowry, and in no time they were all happily married. Although Claudine was less than a third Julius's age and not exactly madly in love with him, she was genuinely fond of the older man and determined to be a good wife and mother to his children. The wedding was to take place on April 20, 1770—Claudine's sixteenth birthday.

Julius bought a huge tract of land thirty miles upriver from New Orleans. He intended to build a magnificent home, one that would serve as both a monument to his life's accomplishments and a tribute to his love for Claudine. An eminent French architect was imported from the Caribbean to design the house and the gardens. Julius wanted his home to emulate the regal magnificence of the French chateaux he recalled from his youth, yet his peasant's practical sense told him it should be built with an eye to the Louisiana weather and terrain.

Since it was planned that he and Claudine would be married on the premises, time was of the essence. Under the architect's direction a corps of carpenters, gardeners, and masons worked around the clock in three shifts. Completed in less than a year, the main house was sixty feet wide and twice as long, with a steep gable and wide veranda, and columns along all four sides. The main floor was well above the ground and supported on brick piers ten feet high. The elevation had two purposes—to protect the house from possible floodwaters, and to catch the passing breezes. Leading to the main entrance was a flight of marble stairs that gave the whole an imposing appearance.

As impressive as the house was for its day, the gardens of Taffarel were an even greater wonder. The only camphor trees in North America were here, imported from northeastern China; ships from Japan, Siam, Madagascar, India, and Brazil brought in an exotic assortment of subtropical vegetation; and as if this were not enough, Julius also shipped in rare species of birds and animals, including kangaroos, ostriches, gazelles, and peafowl. The result was pure fantasy, a private utopia that was destined to become legend.

The Promenade had been Claudine's idea. She was particularly fond of magnolias, and when she presented her plan to Julius—sixty mature trees (one for each year of Julius's life) to be planted thirty to a side, in two straight rows from the steamboat landing to the big house—Julius was delighted and flattered. Sixty sturdy young trees as uniform in size as possible were gathered from all over Louisiana. It took hundreds of workers and several weeks to transplant the deep-rooted trees.

As a finishing touch, the alley between the trees was covered with tons of crushed white seashells. As soon as the rough and tumble rivermen—many of them Americans—who ran the keelboats, flatboats, and rafts up and down the Mississippi caught sight of the two lines of trees, they dubbed the place Magnolia Landing. They were told again and again that the estate was Taffarel Plantation, but they shook their heads and quickly forgot. Eventually the river captains also adopted the title, and the area became irrevocably identified as Magnolia Landing.

The wedding of Julius Taffarel to Claudine Rivière took place as scheduled, witnessed by some two thousand guests, many of whom had traveled for days to attend this extravagant social event. And they were not disappointed.

The highlight of the festivities was, of course, the ceremony itself, which was held in the garden beneath an arbored walk. A cargo of spiders imported from China had been freed among the trellises days before, to spin a cloud of webs that the slaves had sprinkled with gold dust. Through this blazing corridor the bride made her way toward the rosewood altar, to the side of her husband-to-be. Julius was red-faced and appeared anxious in a white suit that was unflattering to his bulk; but Claudine was resplendent in a gown of white silk trimmed with *dentelle valenciennes*, the finest lace obtainable.

Despite the hospitality that Julius and his new bride extended to their guests, there were those, smarting with envy, who derided Taffarel and its owners. Snickering behind their fans and whispering over their brandy, they cruelly criticized the couple.

"Haven't you found him, well, a bit coarse?"

"Mercenary little bitch. She's after his fortune, that's for certain."

"He's old enough to be her grandfather. Shouldn't be surprised if he suffers a heart attack within a fortnight."

What conceit! What vulgar display! Why, there were slaves employed to do nothing more than fetch Julius's spectacles or wipe fingerprints from the stair rail or keep the flies off the sideboard. Who were they, anyway, to be so pretentious? Just an aging river pirate and his child bride!

To be sure they owned a huge tract of land and a mansion of unparalleled beauty. But what crop did they grow? Not cotton, not sugar, not tobacco, *not even indigo!* Instead the land lay idle, nothing more than a place of diversion for the rich. It was all too lush, too opulent—a veritable Garden of Eden. Well, the Lord had turned Adam and Eve out of Eden; surely the time would come when He in His wisdom would drive the Taffarels from their wicked paradise.

The doomsayers were proved right. For a short time Julius and Claudine enjoyed their idyllic existence, but soon it appeared that all the bitter feelings and bad wishes combined to bring down a run of ill luck on their house.

The first cause for alarm came disguised as a blessing. In the summer of 1770, Claudine discovered she was with child.

Though both she and Julius were elated, the pregnancy proved difficult, ending with a long and arduous labor. The baby was large—nearly eight pounds—and its entry into the world caused damage to the birth canal. The doctor advised Claudine that she should have no more children, insisting it would be very dangerous to her. The young woman pretended to heed his advice, but at the same time ordered him not to tell her husband. When Julius was allowed to enter her bedroom, Claudine said she was sorry she had disappointed him with a girl. But Julius beamed with pleasure as he picked up the baby. There was no need for forgiveness; he loved his *petite* Julia.

As soon as Claudine was healed, she welcomed her husband back to her bed. During the next two years Claudine suffered two miscarriages, but still she did not tell her husband about the doctor's warning. She was more determined than ever to give him a son.

Claudine finally completed another pregnancy in January of 1774. The baby arrived in a jackknife position, and Claudine's internal bleeding could not be stopped. Although she knew that she was dying, Claudine was happy and proud that she had given Julius a son. In her few years at Taffarel, she had come to love her husband very deeply.

A favored house servant ran through the slave quarters, weeping and grinning, bearing the sad and joyful news. Madame Claudine was dead, but a *petit garçon* had been delivered to Taffarel.

The two children were now motherless, and with a father more like a *grand-père*; yet only a few years later, at a time when others their age were still being dressed by their mammies, Julia and Claude were making their own decisions. This was largely due to the efforts of Julius, who knew that he might not be around to see his children reach their maturity. Arthritis had made him infirm, and he had come to depend upon alcohol to dull the pain.

Julia and Claude were nine and six respectively when Julius decided they each needed a personal slave. He bought a young Negro couple named Ottile and Cato to see to their needs. Fortunately the pair took well to the children, becoming a kind of surrogate father and mother.

Claude and Julia shed their childhood and entered adolescence with complete self-assurance. Both had typical Creole coloring—pale, flawless skin, and thick, dark, lustrous hair.

There was only one major difference—Claude had his mother's eyes, black and sparkling, while Julia took after her father, with eyes as blue as a summer morning. There was no rivalry between them as often existed between brother and sister; they were best friends and kept no secrets from each other. Indeed, they seemed closer than their years—as close as twins.

Over the past two decades Julius had poured much of his fortune into Taffarel Plantation, with virtually no monetary return. Now that he was nearing the end of his days, he wanted to provide for the future of his children. He decided, at his advanced age, to become a planter, and he began looking for a dependable staple crop. Others had tried tobacco, myrtle wax, indigo, and saffron, none of which were very successful. The ground was too damp for cotton, and not wet enough for rice.

Sugar cane had yet to become a commercial success in Louisiana, partly because sugar production required a sizable investment. Julius, however, was determined to succeed. A sugar mill would have to be built and machinery brought upriver from New Orleans, and more slaves would be needed to work the land. His total investment would easily exceed two hundred thousand dollars.

At first he failed, but he refused to become discouraged. Occasionally the sugar cane did survive the caprices of weather and crop disease, but for years Taffarel continued to operate at a deficit.

Julius's life came to a tragic end in the spring of 1789; he was killed by a bolt of lightning while working alongside the slaves in the fields during a thunderstorm.

Julia was eighteen and Claude fifteen when they buried their father next to their mother in the Taffarel family cemetery. The two young people had little time for grief; the plantation had been operating at a loss for a good many years, and pressing financial matters demanded attention. It had come to light that Julius's factor, who had been empowered to borrow large sums from a New Orleans bank to keep the plantation running, had been skimming off a sizable portion for himself. Upon hearing of Julius's death, the factor had quietly packed his bags and left New Orleans for points north. The bank now wanted to collect the monies due. In order to save Taffarel, Julia and Claude learned, they would have to sell a good part of their land to meet the debt.

Reluctantly they followed their lawyer's advice, deciding they would make the best of it and be very selective in their choice of neighbors. Many of the richest families wanted to buy into Magnolia Landing, but Julia and Claude turned them down. Finally they accepted the bid of Anatole Beauchemin, a wealthy French planter who had emigrated from the West Indies with his family. Beauchemin built a home not nearly as grand or as large as Taffarel, but attractive and functional for the Louisiana climate. He christened it with his own surname and went about the business of raising sugar cane.

The Beauchemins had three children. The oldest, a good-looking and well-mannered youth named Theophilus, was a year older than Julia. Theo, as he was affectionately called, became close friends with both the Taffarels, and as might be expected, Theo and Julia fell in love. Claude and the Beauchemins were delighted with the match, and a wedding date was set.

A month before the marriage was to take place, however, tragedy once again called on the Taffarels. Claude was stricken with a malady that the doctors seemed unable to diagnose. Postponing the wedding date indefinitely, Julia nursed her brother through the steamy months of summer. Then, in September, Julia sent Theo a letter telling him that Claude had passed away and that she could no longer honor his proposal; her grief would not allow her to accept happiness. She went into seclusion.

The gossips of New Orleans had a field day. Julia Taffarel loved her brother, to be sure, but to forfeit marriage to a wealthy, handsome young man because of grief? Nonsense! There must be other reasons. Some said that actually it was Theo who had broken the engagement and that the other story was circulated to save Julia's reputation. Others speculated that Julia had been afflicted by the same mysterious disease that had taken her brother. Still others whispered far crueler things, hinting that something more than friendship had existed between brother and sister.

In 1824 Julia freed her slaves, including her beloved Ottile and Cato. Many stayed on to work the plantation and were paid a modest wage. More than most, Julia and her servants were dependent upon the success of each year's sugar crop. Seldom was there money for extras, and repair and maintenance of the house and gardens had become impossible. In order to get through the leaner years, Julia continued selling off parts of Taffarel, until six plantations composed the community that had come to be called Magnolia Landing.

The ice had melted and the glasses were empty. Julia tilted her head toward Royal and lowered her voice to a whisper. "The superstitious stay away from Taffarel, Mr. Brannigan. They claim that a ghost wanders the grounds. Is it the spirit of my mother, who rages against fate for having lived such a brief time? Is it my father, returned to Taffarel to continue his work from the afterlife? Or is it Claude, who stalks the corridors of the ruined rose garden?" Briefly, a dark, troubled look touched her features, as if she, too, believed in ghosts. "No one seems to know for certain, but the stories continue to surface with astonishing regularity.

"But I ought to warn you, Mr. Brannigan: Should a stranger, curious as well as brave, choose to wander down the Promenade after dark, he might just see Taffarel as it was in its former days of glory. On certain magical nights, when the moon is thin and round, and the air heavy with the scent of magnolias, the plantation seems to undergo a transformation. The outlines of the columns grow brighter and the shadows fade; the tangled gardens become orderly. Somehow the glow of silver moonlight softens the ravages of time. On one of these nights, if the stranger stands very still and listens beyond the wind, he may hear the sound of violins coaxing the dancers back to the ballroom for another waltz. If he listens closely, too, he might just hear the whisper of fans and the sigh of silk as Creole ladies glide toward their partners.

"And if he's fortunate, he might see silhouetted in an upstairs window a lone figure beckoning him back to a gentler time, when the passing hours did not count unless they were happy. The stranger will probably shake his head and claim that it is just an illusion—and perhaps it is."

A mischievous expression suddenly transformed Julia's face, until it seemed to Royal that, sitting there in the softened shadows of the veranda, she almost looked young again. It was as if her face had been veiled and smoothed by candlelight. He fancied that he could see her as she once had been—beautiful, vibrant, and in love with life.

Julia said softly, "I've reached the conclusion, Mr. Brannigan; there's nothing more to say. The tale has been told."

"You're quite a storyteller, Miss Taffarel. And that's quite a story. But you're wrong about one thing."

"What is that, Mr. Brannigan?"

"You're still alive and appear to be in good health, so the story hasn't reached its conclusion yet."

Julia smiled sadly. "I'm afraid that it has, Mr. Brannigan. I'm the end of my line, and I'm very, very tired. Tired of the whole process of just trying to keep body and soul together—mine and the servants' and . . . I suppose you could say I'm just tired of living."

"Pardon my impertinence, Miss Taffarel, but you should get out more, be with people. I'd be glad to help you in any way I can."

Julia, shaking her head, seemed about to dismiss his advice, but then a curious look crossed her face.

"If you really mean that, Mr. Brannigan, then your timing is exquisite. The Duc Alexandre Duvallon, who owns Salle d'Or, one of the plantations here at the Landing, has been hounding me to attend his various social events. I always refuse, but nothing seems to discourage the man. His latest assault is to get me to come to his midsummer ball. That's a party he gives every summer when it's time for the sugar crop to be laid by."

"Laid by?"

"Oh, that simply means we let it be. It will do fine on its own until harvest time."

"You should go, Miss Taffarel."

"I wasn't planning on going, but I'm beginning to have second thoughts." She seemed to come to a decision. "Mr. Brannigan, if you'll be my escort, I'll attend the Duc's midsummer ball. You'd better say yes. It would provide you with an opportunity to meet the residents of Magnolia Landing. And I rather doubt, given that you're an American and a gambler—not to mention the usurper of the Jourdains' plantation—that you would otherwise be asked to attend."

Royal grinned. "You're very persuasive, Miss Taffarel. I'd be most delighted to be your escort."

"Besides," she sighed, "it would be nice to see Theo again after so long."

Royal was surprised. "You mean Theophilus Beauchemin, the man you almost married? He still lives here at the Landing?"

"Yes, he does."

They smiled at each other conspiratorially. Then Julia called to Ottile, who was standing in attendance not far away. "Ottile, two more brandy cocktails, please!"

An hour later, Royal left Taffarel by the front drive. As he rode past the vine-covered stone gateposts, he paused and looked over his shoulder. In the flickering afternoon light, something extraordinary happened—Taffarel and its grounds appeared to be undergoing a magical metamorphosis. He narrowed his eyes, and the transformation was complete. Spellbound, Royal held his breath and allowed the experience of seeing the plantation as it was in its halcyon days to wash over him in a wave of gold.

The sensation passed. Perhaps it had been Julia's stimulating words, or perhaps the brandy cocktails—a drink not meant for the middle of the day. More likely it was a little of each, Royal thought; yet he felt he had truly been transported backward in time to a place of dignity and enchantment—a place he was sure would never reassert itself in this modern century of fast-moving steamboats, iron railways, and instant fortunes for those who gambled everything and won.

Chapter Seven

A slave began tolling the plantation bell. Its clangorous sound signaled not only the passing of Jean-Louis Jourdain but also marked a day of succession for Heritage.

A flatbed wagon led the cortege. It was driven by a male house slave in a hand-me-down black suit and a top hat that was too large for his narrow head. The wagon was normally used to transport hogsheads of molasses, but in lieu of a funeral coach it had been decorated with black crepe and masses of flowers from the plantation gardens and now bore Jean-Louis's body to its final resting place. The coffin was covered by a blanket of dark red roses.

The temporary hearse made its way up the side of the hillock to the Jourdain cemetery, which overlooked the big house. It was followed by a line of carriages that wobbled from side to side on the narrow, rutted road. The first carriage was driven by Rafe Bastile, the overseer of Heritage, and transported Suzanne, Angélique, and Zenobia. The following three carriages carried mourners from the plantations of Salle d'Or, Victoire, and Bellechasse.

In sharp contrast to the somber line of black carriages were the Heritage slaves. Despite Angélique's protestations, Suzanne had decreed that they could say farewell in their own manner. Dressed all in white, their Sunday best, with mourning bands, they danced and strutted up the hillside while singing a heartfelt spiritual. Many of them carried tambourines or other homemade instruments, and a few of the dusty faces were streaked with tears as their late master was ushered to his final reward.

"We're a-marching to de grave,
We're a-marching to de grave, my Lord,
We're a-marching to de grave,
To lay dis body down."

The sky darkened, turning from a bright blue to a murky gray as the funeral procession reached the plateau of the hill. The carriages were left in a small, barren lot, and the assemblage waited while the coffin was removed from the wagon and delivered into the hands of the four pallbearers—the Duc, Philippe, Theo, and Léon. Struggling under the weight of the casket, the four men made their way toward a grove of dogwood trees and the open grave. The cemetery contained but two other graves—those of Henri and Lucie Jourdain. There were no headstones, and the only marker was an elaborate sculpture, over fifteen feet high, depicting in a romantic, almost sentimental style a kneeling angel with outstretched arms. At the time of its commission the statue had been called pretentious and even irreverent by the other residents of Magnolia Landing; they said it looked as if the angel had fallen to earth and was pleading to be transported back to heaven. But over the years the weather had worn away its stark newness, leaving a softer patina. The sight of the white angel atop the hillock had come to stand for a certain sense of continuity. The angel seemed to be praying for them all.

Once the casket was laid in position, the mourners gathered in a loose semicircle around the foot of the grave, the slaves taking their allotted places in the rear. The grave had been dug on an east-west axis because the slaves, as well as many of their masters, believed that the dead should be facing the east and not have to turn around when Gabriel blew his trumpet in the sunrise.

Suzanne, clutching her Catholic missal, stepped out of the uneven ranks, walked to the head of the coffin, and stood before the huge marble angel. She lifted her black lace veil. Her face was pale but composed, her eyes dry. She scanned the assembled mourners.

Zenobia was supporting Angélique, who looked as lifeless as the marble statue, her mouth slack and her eyes unblinking. The Duc stood apart from his family. Although his head was bowed, his attention appeared drawn to a ripped seam in his black gloves. Henriette and Alcée stood side by side, their faces not hiding their genuine grief. Philippe, staring at the mottled sky, seemed to be willing himself someplace else. Theo, his face a mask of tragedy, cradled the roly-poly Blanche in his arms; she appeared to have fallen asleep. Denis and Fleur stood on either side of their grandfather, their expressions properly solemn.

Léon was behind Michelle, his hands on her shoulders, his pelvis pressed against her backside. Both their faces bore a beatific expression. Marguerite stood apart, and she alone among the white assemblage was weeping. Her tears were ruining her cosmetics.

The slaves had become quiet, restraining their emotions in respect for the white tradition of burial. Suzanne opened her missal. Her voice was deep and clear as she read:

"O Lord, do not bring your servant to trial, for no man becomes holy in Your sight unless You grant him forgiveness for all his sins. We implore You, therefore, do not let the verdict of Your judgment go against him, whom the loyal prayer of Christian Faith is commending to Your mercy. Rather, by the help of Your grace, may he escape the sentence which he deserves, for during his earthly life he was signed with the seal of the Holy Trinity. You Who live and reign forever and ever. Amen."

Suzanne's final amen indicated that no response was expected from the assemblage, and to their surprise the service was over. Suzanne stepped back from the grave and nodded to the slaves to lower the casket.

Seth came forward, carrying his banjo. He crossed to the statue and seated himself at its base. He bowed his head, but the grief he felt was undisguised. The sounds his fingertips produced from the usually joyful instrument were doleful and struck the hearts of all who heard. He lifted his tear-stained face to the skies and in his wavering voice began to sing:

"Swing low, sweet chariot,
Coming fo' to carry me home . . ."

Suzanne walked slowly to the mound of dirt next to the grave. She scooped up a handful of damp earth and, standing by the edge of the grave, let it run through her fingers. As she did she made a silent promise to herself. No matter what trials lay before her, she would always try to remember the good about her husband and let her hurts and disappointments be buried with him.

"Swing low, sweet chariot,
Coming fo' to carry me home."

The other mourners lined up behind Suzanne, and as custom dictated, each dropped a handful of earth onto the coffin. When they had finished, they stood at the foot of the grave and, silhouetted against the gray backdrop of sky, listened as the Negroes joined Seth's vocal tribute to Jean-Louis.

"I looked over Jordan, and what did I see,
Coming fo' to carry me home?
A band of angels coming after me,
Coming fo' to carry me home."

And as if paying homage to the young Creole, the clouds opened up and the sky began to weep.

Royal had returned to Heritage a short time earlier and taken Alezan directly to the stables. He hadn't noticed the ceremony until he heard the spiritual. As he stood on the front veranda, he was struck once again by the song's simple beauty. He had heard it many times before, for it had been sung by the Negroes in prison. Back then it had seemed to him as much a cry for freedom and a plea to be released from the bonds of slavery as a desire to reach the promised land.

He sat on the top step and listened. Unconsciously he began to sing along. The wind picked up his ringing baritone and carried it up the hill, joining it with the other voices.

"A band of angels coming after me,
Coming fo' to carry me home."

The song ended, and in the distance the white congregation began walking to their carriages. Royal got up, brushed the dust from his suit, and noticed the *immortelle* on the front door. His fingers touched the black blooms, and he wondered who had created such a beautiful tribute.

He entered the big house, and his footsteps broke the ominous silence. No sound issued from the clock standing in the foyer. The hands had been set at the hour of Jean-Louis's death. Then he saw that the mirrors had been turned so that their faces were toward the wall. The sight of the funeral, the clock, and the mirrors depressed Royal. The wondrous feeling he had felt at meeting Julia Taffarel was destroyed by the presence of death.

Royal went to his room, sat down on the edge of the bed, and questioned his decision to stay at Heritage. He was an outsider, a man alone. There was no one to talk to, no one he could trust.

What was he doing here? Miss Julia was right. He didn't know a damn thing about raising sugar cane or running a plantation. Perhaps he was even being presumptuous to think the women would welcome his offer to stay. And even if they did, would he be able to bear their disdain? At that moment Royal felt that his life was as empty as the big house.

The family lawyer, a Spaniard named Gilberto Mendoza, arrived at Heritage shortly after the women returned from the cemetery. A house slave ushered him into the library. Suzanne held the letter of deed in her hand. Angélique carried a red rose, a souvenir from her brother's grave. The lawyer took his time drinking an iced lemonade, and the women watched him with anxious eyes. He finished the last of the lemonade, set down the glass, and daintily wiped his lips with a napkin.

"The events," he said at last, "recounted to you by the American are just as he reported. I checked each witness and have a sworn statement from Madame Odalisque herself. May I see the document in question?" Suzanne handed him the paper. Mendoza balanced a pair of pince-nez spectacles on the tip of his nose and read the letter several times before commenting. When he spoke, his tone was cold and accusative and belied his words.

"I am very sorry, ladies, but this letter of deed would stand up in a court of law."

Angélique crushed the rose in her hand and dropped the remnants to the floor. Suzanne nodded. Even though she had dared to hope, his words were expected.

Mendoza withdrew a paper from his coat pocket and said, "Additionally, there are certain debts acquired by M'sieur Jourdain against the holdings of the plantation that will have to be honored."

"What kind of debts?" asked Suzanne.

"Gambling, mostly. And others of a frivolous nature."

"Kindly keep your opinions to yourself, Señor Mendoza," said Suzanne. "I don't understand. I brought a considerable dowry to my marriage."

He regarded her with ill-concealed disdain. "A woman's dowry is never kept separate once the marriage has taken place, but is absorbed into the husband's holdings."

Angélique fixed a vacant stare upon the pattern in the carpet and, using the tip of her forefinger, copied it again and again on the arm of the chair.

There was a long silence; finally Suzanne spoke. "Then we are not only completely without funds, but it appears that monies are owed against the coming harvest."

""That is correct, madame."

The women both looked to Mendoza, hoping for his suggestions, but none was forthcoming. His contemptuous manner made it clear that neither he nor his firm had any further interest in them.

"Now that our business is concluded, I must be going. I have a long ride back to New Orleans."

The women did not offer Mendoza any of the usual hospitalities—a meal, a room for the night, a change of horses. Indeed, they did not even offer to show him out.

After Mendoza was gone, Suzanne stood up. "What an odious little man. The sooner we have a talk with M'sieur Brannigan, the better."

Angélique was aghast. "You can't mean to see him this afternoon! We've just buried Jean-Louis."

"We must determine our position as soon as possible."

"Can't you ask your parents for money?"

Suzanne shook her head. "Papa's made some bad investments. I don't mean that he and Mama are poor; they just have to be careful for a while. And I don't want to worry them."

"What about your sisters? They all married, didn't they?"

"Not well, I'm afraid."

"I thought your aunt left you something."

"Just some pieces of jewelry. Aunt Annette believed in having her kingdom on earth, and I'm afraid she had to pay for it. We have but one hope, Angélique . . . that M'sieur Brannigan turns out to be a gentleman."

Angélique sniffed. "And *that* is highly unlikely."

Suzanne yanked the bell pull, and a short time later Zenobia answered the call. "Zenobia, has M'sieur Brannigan returned yet?"

"Yes, Miz Suzanne. He been back fo' some time now. He in de guest room."

"Would you ask him to come to the library?"

Zenobia left to do Suzanne's bidding. Suzanne turned to her sister-in-law. "Angélique, I'd appreciate it if you'd let me do the talking. I've a proposal to make to M'sieur Brannigan. I just hope he doesn't refuse."

"Are we going to throw ourselves on his mercy?" Angélique asked bitterly.

"Not in the least. He's a gambling man, isn't he? Well, I'm going to bluff him. We're not going to let him know that we're totally without funds; I don't want to give him any more of an advantage than he already has. Now, compose yourself. You're both a Creole and a Jourdain. He's just an American and a nobody." She snatched the list of debts from the table and held it up. "He might as well start assuming responsibility right now."

Royal, wearing a fresh suit of clothing and with his boots polished, followed Zenobia to the library. She rapped on the door, opened it, and stepped aside to allow him entrance.

Without looking at him, Suzanne said, "Please be seated, M'sieur Brannigan. We have some things to discuss with you."

He took a chair, then sat gazing at Suzanne. Her appearance of ease, he thought, was deceptive, and he found himself half irritated, half amused by her superior tone. Despite the circumstances, she was still acting as mistress of the house.

He turned toward Angélique, who was sitting in front of the French doors that overlooked the hill where her brother was now buried.

"Has the rain stopped, Mademoiselle Jourdain?"

Angélique replied strangely, "The world shines after good men are buried. Their souls rise up and wash the sky clean—"

Suzanne, visibly embarrassed for her sister-in-law, interrupted. "M'sieur Brannigan, if I may have your attention, I have outlined a plan for our working and living arrangements that I think you will find suitable. . . ."

Suzanne proposed that she and Angélique stay on until after the harvest, so that they could instruct him in the rudiments of operating a sugar cane plantation. During the morning hours she would familiarize him with all that was involved in running the big house, and in the afternoons Angélique would help him get acquainted with the plantation—the overseer, the slaves, and the process of raising the valuable crop. She further proposed that he occupy a suite of rooms on the first floor, that she and Angélique keep their rooms on the second floor, and that they take their meals separately and avoid socializing in any other way.

Royal listened patiently, but he found his thoughts drifting. It was difficult for him not to regard the women in a physical sense. Despite the uncomfortable predicament in which he found himself, he could not help but admire their beauty. Although their coloring was in sharp contrast, and Angélique's features were perhaps at first glance more striking, the two women were nearly the same height and weight, affected a similar hairstyle, and were about the same build. They were even wearing mourning dresses of the same cut. He looked at Angélique, admiring her exquisite silver-blond hair, startling green eyes, and delicate complexion. Then he looked back at Suzanne. Her raven hair seemed to reflect a light that was not in the room, and her blue-gray eyes were dazzling, almost hypnotic. . . . Royal became aware that she was speaking to him.

"I'm sorry, Madame Jourdain, you were saying?"

Her mouth pinched with irritation, Suzanne repeated the question, "I was asking you, M'sieur Brannigan, if the proposal is to your liking."

He straightened up in his chair. "The agreement suits me, madame, but I feel that you should be paid in some way for educating a poor American in the ways of plantation life."

Suzanne's eyes flashed with anger, but she said nothing.

"I was thinking perhaps a share in the profits of the harvest. Say twenty-five percent for you and Mademoiselle Jourdain."

Suzanne replied, "That seems fair, m'sieur." Angélique didn't respond.

Royal was irritated. Neither of them expressed anything like gratitude; but had he really expected them to?

"By the way, M'sieur Brannigan," Suzanne said, "here's a list of debts currently owed by Heritage. I thought that as the new owner you'd wish to see them immediately."

Royal took the sheet without looking at it, then stood up. Obviously the conversation was at an end. "Good afternoon, madame and mademoiselle."

On his way out, Suzanne remarked, "M'sieur, I suggest that if you're going to be working on a sugar plantation, black is an impractical color—except, of course, for mourning."

Royal nodded curtly and left the library. Later, when he was alone in his room, he looked over the list of debts. The total amount, combined with his rough estimate of what it would take to support the household, equaled the bulk of his savings. His future and the future of others depended upon a successful sugar cane harvest, and he wondered if his luck would hold out.

Chapter Eight

The month of June settled in, and almost overnight the countryside underwent a subtle metamorphosis. Dawn came earlier, wearing a cloak of warm, fragrant air, and when the sun rose it sent a shower of golden needles spinning through the treetops. Shrubs and lawns blazed a brighter green, richer and more vibrant than any green in memory. The flowers appeared larger, more profuse than before. Tassels exploded on the sugar cane, and the sword-shaped leaves became tinged with yellow. Summer was coming earlier than expected to Magnolia Landing and was planning a long, hot stay.

* * *

Suzanne buttoned the bodice of one of the mourning dresses that had been made up for her in New Orleans. It was dark gray, loose-fitting, and unbecoming. She covered her hair with a triangular scarf, which she tied at the back of her head. Painfully aware of Royal's attraction to her, she was determined to make herself look as plain as possible.

It was obscene, really, she thought—the man responsible for her husband's death lusting after her. Well, he had destroyed her dream, and she intended to hold him accountable for it. But she mustn't think of that now. She had a duty to perform. She was positive that Royal would tire of plantation life. Eventually he'd want to sell out and would return to the gaming tables and to the women.

"Just like Jean-Louis," she murmured bitterly.

Suzanne caught sight of herself in the freestanding brass mirror and gasped. She looked washed out, lifeless, and, yes, old. She closed her eyes and a year melted away. She could smell orange blossoms and feel soft silk against her flesh. She could actually taste her happiness. Suzanne blinked, and in that instant the past overlapped the present like a superimposed image, and she saw herself as she was on her wedding day. She was young, she was beautiful, and everything was perfect. Even the wedding cake had arrived from New Orleans undamaged. Yes, everything was perfect except . . .

Darling, please don't drink so much. You won't be able to enjoy the party. . . . Jean-Louis, I don't think you can hold another glass of champagne . . . please, somebody help him!

Suzanne blinked her eyes again, and the present returned. She traced her fingers over the mirror, out lining her reflection. Had she ever been so young, so innocent, so full of trust in the future? A tiny tear escaped from her right eye. Suzanne, surprised she had any tears left, roughly wiped it away with the back of her hand. Then she thrust out her chin and hurried down the back stairs to keep her appointment with Royal Brannigan.

Suzanne rapped loudly on the door. He's probably not even up yet, she thought.

The door swung open. "Please come in, Madame Jourdain," said Royal. "I'll be with you in a minute."

Suzanne stepped inside. Royal was wearing a dress shirt of white cotton with a ruffled front and cuffs, and snug-fitting beige breeches.

"I took your advice and dug out a shirt and trousers that

weren't black. They'll have to do for now. I'll order more suitable clothing from New Orleans."

Suzanne could not help but notice that the light weight clothing did nothing to disguise the pronounced strength of his body. Indeed, it served to emphasize his powerful physique. Royal sat down on the chair, raised a leg, and began pulling on one of his boots. The beige material stretched taut against his calves, thighs, and buttocks, so that it almost appeared to Suzanne he was nude from the waist down. She quickly looked away.

"You've had your breakfast, M'sieur Brannigan?"

"Yes, and very good too. The meals are as fine as any I've eaten anywhere in my travels."

Suzanne realized that she knew nothing about Royal Brannigan, but although she was curious, she refrained from asking.

Royal stood up and stretched. "There. All ready for my morning's instruction."

Suzanne thought that he was treating her too casually. He must realize that this wasn't easy for her, being demoted from mistress of the house to virtually the status of a servant, all in a matter of days.

Royal went to the chest of drawers and took out something he had wrapped in a handkerchief. "I wanted you to have these," he said awkwardly as he handed her the packet. "I have no use for them."

Suzanne unwrapped the fabric. Inside were Jean-Louis's rings and watch. She looked at Royal in surprise.

"I won them from your husband."

"But I can't accept—"

"Please, take them. They're much too fancy for me, and I wouldn't feel right wearing them. I should have given them to you sooner. You might have wanted to bury them with him."

"No, I wouldn't have done that. Graves have been robbed for less."

"Here? At Magnolia Landing?"

"It's a rich community. The desperate prey on the rich, just as the rich prey on the desperate." She dropped the packet into her pocket. "Very well. I accept them. Now, I thought I'd start off by giving you a complete tour of the house; then I'll take you into my office and show you the books that record the expenditures of running the big house and the grounds. It's not all parties, you know. My mama always said it was the hardest job a woman can have."

"Your mother taught you all these things?"

"Yes," replied Suzanne, but she didn't elaborate. "I'll also introduce you to the house slaves. You must be patient with them. They're confused now, and their loyalties are divided. But I'll call them together and have a talk with them."

"Thank you," said Royal. "Madame Jourdain, I know we can't be friends, but let's try not to be enemies. It'll be easier on both of us." Before she could answer, Royal said, "I've taken the liberty of planning my living accommodations. I don't want to be confined to one room. The rooms on either side of me, what are they used for?"

"They are generally only put to use after large dinner parties. On the right is a sitting room for the ladies, and on the left a smoking room for the gentlemen."

"I'd like to turn the smoking room into an office, and the sitting room can serve as my dining room."

"That will be fine, providing you're not planning to do any entertaining."

"I have no one to entertain," Royal replied.

She was tempted to ask about his friends and family but again restrained herself. She was determined not to become intimate with the American. "I should ring for Zenobia and let her hear this; she can instruct the slaves to take away the furniture you don't want and add whatever you do." She pulled the bell cord and, when the slave arrived, explained what Royal wanted done. From time to time Zenobia would glance at the American with her strange hooded eyes and nod.

When Suzanne was finished, Royal said, "One thing more. These drapes. They're heavy and oppressive. I'd like to get rid of them."

Suzanne looked embarrassed. "Ah, well, I'm sure some material could be ordered and new ones made, M'sieur Brannigan, but in the meantime the French doors must have some sort of covering. My sister-in-law and I often stroll along the veranda, as do the female slaves."

"I don't understand," said Royal.

Zenobia interceded, "She mean dat dey ain't anxious to see yo' buck-ass naked."

"Zenobia!" gasped Suzanne.

Royal suppressed a grin. "I see what you mean, madame.

Very well, they can certainly stay until we can have something else put in their place."

Suzanne gestured toward the door. "Then shall we begin the tour?"

The Duc Duvallon was resplendently attired, perhaps in honor of the coming summer, in a suit of yellow linen with white accessories, including the inevitable gloves. Out of deference to the beautiful morning he ordered breakfast served in the garden. Instantly the house slaves were set into a frenzy. Not only did this mean cleaning the garden furniture, but the food would have to be kept warm yet not overcooked on the longer trip from the kitchen. It also meant keeping flies and other insects well away from the table and from the Duc in particular, in order to ensure a breakfast free from catastrophe. The nervous state into which his orders put the slaves pleased the Duc immensely. He was a man who needed the security of wielding power over others.

The dining area selected by the Duc was often used in the summer and was a particular favorite of his. It was a patch of ground, twenty by twenty feet, covered with bricks and mortar and enclosed on three sides by a tall hedge, which had been tortured by gardeners into a rigid geometric design of unattractive proportions. A pair of live oaks grew on both sides and offered shade as well as privacy. At one time the lower branches had grown together, rather like clasping hands, but the Duc, who was annoyed by falling leaves, had ordered them cut back. Now the trees had a dolorous appearance, like parted lovers, and were referred to by the servants as *les tristes*, or "the sad ones."

While servants scrubbed the table and chairs, the Duc walked among his gardens, scrutinizing everything he saw. Although the gardens were the most elaborate in Louisiana, the Duc's taste for precision had rendered them peculiarly unattractive. Here nature was forced into conformity; there was no room for inspiration. Every plant was arranged to form severe patterns. Azalea edged the walkways in sharply defined borders. Docile roses bowed their heads in submission. Towering over all were hollyhocks planted in perfect lines and resembling so many soldiers at inspection. Prior to social gatherings, any flowering plants not up to the Duc's expectations would be wired with artificial blooms fashioned from silk, to create what the Duc redundantly referred to as *"la perfection parfaite."*

The Duc subconsciously noted and recorded what needed to be done. An azalea hovering over the walkway—cut it back! A dying rosebush—*alors*, replace it! A pink hollyhock in a row of red—uproot it! His immediate thoughts, however, were elsewhere. This morning the Duc reflected, as often he did, upon what he secretly called his supreme design—his plan to completely control Magnolia Landing. He had intended to achieve that aim through his children—Alcée and Philippe. His dream was that they would marry the son and daughter of neighboring planters and thus create an extended clan over which he, as monarch, would hold sway.

At one time the Duc had envisioned Philippe marrying Angélique Jourdain, but those plans had been thwarted by the older Jourdain's leaving everything to Jean-Louis, as well as the young man's subsequent marriage to Suzanne Delisle. Of course Philippe showed no signs of wanting to be tied down to a wife as yet. Perhaps, the Duc thought, just perhaps he could make Philippe wait until Theo Beauchemin's oldest granddaughter, Fleur, came of age. But that was several years away. The Duc spied a ladybug contaminating his walkway and crushed it with the heel of his boot.

It remained a sore point that Jean-Louis Jourdain had met and married Suzanne Delisle. The Duc had hoped to match his dear Alcée to the capricious Creole. After Jean-Louis and Suzanne's marriage, he had begun pushing Alcée toward Léon Martineau, but Léon had discovered Michelle de Ventura. Now there were no young men left at the Landing, unless he considered Theo's grandchild Denis; and because of the difference in age, even that match was out of the question. The Duc was now decided that Alcée should marry Gilbert Gadobert. Although the couple would be given Villeneuve as a wedding present, the Gadoberts, who were wealthy and pretentious, would not rest until they, too, had acquired property at Magnolia Landing, and the Duc was more than willing to help them get their wish. In the meantime, he was determined to make friends with Julia Taffarel. She was old, constantly in debt, and had no offspring. He planned to get control of Taffarel upon her demise by any means he could.

The Duc pursed his lips in meditation. If his marriage plans for Philippe and Fleur did not work out, he would have to think of an alternative course of action. And Bellechasse was another matter. He knew that Léon and Michelle were dissatisfied with "rural living," as they termed it, and longed to move to Europe. At some point in the future the Duc was sure he could buy them out.

Heritage remained a problem. But Jean-Louis's suicide and subsequent loss of the plantation could work to his advantage. The American knew nothing about growing sugar cane. Probably he would fail, thereby placing himself in a precarious financial position. The Duc planned to be there with ready monies to buy him out.

The Duc continued his walk through his gardens. Yes, he thought, he would use his children's marriages to get what he wanted . . . just as he himself had done. He had married Henriette for one reason and one reason only—she was the heiress to Villeneuve.

Taking care not to dirty his boots, the Duc stepped into a flower bed and plucked several dead blooms from their bushes. He examined his gloves for stains and said aloud, "I should have had more children. But what could I do? I never could abide that woman."

Still grumbling over the flower beds, the Duc marched back to the breakfast table, his boots tapping a sharp cadence against the brick walkways. After sending a message to the gardeners that he wished to see them directly after the meal, he began badgering the slaves. "How long can it take to set up out here? *Vite! Vite!* Breakfast is already ten minutes late! Where is my family? Go and get them at once." He ran a white glove over the table and, satisfied that it had been properly cleaned, sat down. A jittery slave served him coffee.

As usual, Alcée was the first to arrive. She gave the impression of serene loveliness. She kissed her father on the cheek and took a seat to his left. "What a lovely idea having breakfast in the garden, Father. It's a delightful morning."

"Yes, yes," he replied sharply, though his bad temper was softened somewhat by his daughter's attentions. "Where are Philippe and your mother, Alcée? I distinctly told them that I had things to discuss this morning."

"They'll be here shortly," Alcée replied. "I rapped on Philippe's door. He was up. I called to Mother. She said she'd be down momentarily." She glanced at the slaves. "Where's Blaise?" she asked casually.

"Blaise? He's helping put up the chandelier." He eyed his

daughter suspiciously. "Why? Can't you eat breakfast unless a particular nigger serves you?"

"No—I thought he might be ill or something. That's all."

Alcée was saved further inquiries by the appearance of her brother. Philippe lurched across the lawn, his eyes puffy and caked with sleep. "Sorry, Papa, sorry."

The Duc glowered. "Sit down. Now, where is Madame Duvallon?" A mean twitch played on his tightly pressed lips.

The three looked toward the big house. Henriette burst through the doors and rushed across the lawn toward them, coming obediently to her husband's side. The Duc wrinkled his nose with distaste; as usual, she had a faint odor of incense and candle wax clinging to her.

The Duc stood up. "Ah, the good Henriette. You mustn't dash about, my dear. It's so unbecoming." He clasped her hand and squeezed so hard she blanched. He shoved her toward her chair and sat back down.

"Finally!" The Duc gazed expansively at those seated around the table and smiled. "*Ma famille*." Then in a cool, carefully modulated voice he said, "I wanted us all to have breakfast together because I wish to discuss the midsummer's ball, which is less than a month away."

Before she could think, Henriette blurted, "You're still planning to go ahead with the ball, Alexandre?"

"Go ahead with it? What do you mean?"

Henriette lowered her head, her voice almost a whisper. "Well, I just thought that with the death of the Jourdain boy and all the changes at Heritage that . . ."

"What does that have to do with us?"

"Yes," echoed Philippe. "Why should Papa cancel his plans just because Jean-Louis was stupid enough to lose a card game and take his own life as well?"

Alcée could bear no more. "I think you're both being very callous. What about the Jourdain women—Angélique and Suzanne?"

"I wouldn't think of excluding them just because of their altered positions," the Duc said sweetly. "Now, I expect all of you to give me your best efforts. We must make this the best-planned and most spectacular of all the midsummer balls." He looked toward Alcée. "After all, it may be the most important one we've had so far."

Alcée rolled her eyes toward heaven and asked, "What do you want me to do, Papa?"

"You can assist me in planning the menu. Have you ordered your gown yet?"

"No, Papa."

He gazed hard at his wife as he unfolded and refolded his napkin. "Henriette, do you think you could tear yourself away from your saints long enough to see to our daughter's needs?"

"The dressmaker was—is coming tomorrow, Alexandre. And she's bringing a wide selection of fabrics and patterns."

The Duc, irritated because his wife was able to meet one of his demands, said, "Well, I want to see the sketches when they're finished."

"Yes, Alexandre."

"Henriette, you will write notes to the other plantations and engage extra carriages and servants. "Philippe—" The young man straightened up in his chair. "I want you to make sure that we have the most spectacular fireworks display that this area has ever seen."

"I can go to New Orleans?" Philippe asked anxiously.

"No, I'll need you here. Send for Señor Vargas and plan the extravaganza from here. Also, I want you to select the strongest field slaves to act as guards. I won't have my guests attacked by marauding criminals."

"Yes, Papa," Philippe replied with a pout.

The Duc expanded his chest and announced, "Of course, I have planned the decor."

Henriette pursed her lips, and Alcée barely stifled a giggle. The Duc Duvallon's "taste" was the subject of much ridicule up and down the Mississippi. Still, his wife and daughter knew better than to voice their opinions or in any way criticize him.

"I have an errand for you, my dear," he said to Henriette. "I'll discuss it after breakfast. From now on, I'll be checking with each of you daily at this time. Kindly write down your progress and be ready to report to me." A line of slaves bearing silver-domed servers marched from the kitchen to the table and awaited the Duc's signal. "I will not tolerate any incompetence from any of you. Do I make myself clear?" The three nodded. "Good! Now, let's eat!"

Although the sun was in the center of the sky, Léon and Michelle Martineau were promenading through the gardens at Bellechasse, still wearing their nightclothes—she in a confection of silk and lace and he in a white batiste cotton nightshirt.

They had decided not to get dressed. Their decision was in reaction to a remark made by Marguerite the previous evening. She had scolded the young people for various reasons and had ended by calling them pretentious.

"We'll show Aunt Marguerite that we're not *pretentious*," smirked Léon. "How can we be *pretentious* if we aren't even bothering to dress for the day?"

"Well, if we are pretentious," sniffed Michelle, "at least we're pretentious about the *right* things." She looked toward the big house. "I wonder where she is? Probably lurking about the gallery, spying on us."

"I'll give her something to see!" Léon executed a somersault and in so doing revealed his backside.

Michelle clapped her hands together and laughed.

"I've an idea, darling. Let's go on a picnic!"

"A picnic? How gauche."

Léon stepped behind his wife, cupped his hands over her breasts, and whispered, "Not where I'm planning to take you."

Her face brightened. "The maze?"

"Yes. And if you're extra nice to me, I just might teach you the combination."

Michelle turned, threw her arms around his neck, and kissed him. "You're too, too delicious."

"Let's go to the kitchen. We'll have Uncle Prosper and Jolie make us up a basket. I'm sure there's still a couple of bottles of cold champagne if the ice hasn't all melted. We'll spend the afternoon avoiding Aunt Marguerite."

"Doesn't she know how to get into the maze?"

"She did once, but I'm sure she's forgotten the combination, what with all that laudanum she takes to get to sleep at night."

"And she criticizes us. Why, she's practically addicted to it."

A little while later, with a picnic basket laden with champagne and foodstuffs, the young couple hurried out of the kitchen. After a mad dash across the garden, which Michelle won, they stood panting at the entrance to the maze.

Léon said, "It's really very easy. Just use your head." He teasingly smacked her across the rear. "The secret of finding the way to the center is right turn, left turn, right turn, left turn, then two rights, two lefts, and then repeat."

"If you begin right then you can't go wrong," giggled Michelle.

The rose maze, which had been designed by Léon's mother, was the focal point of the Bellechasse gardens, and over the years had been a source of delight to the many guests of the plantation. The well-trimmed hedges were now over seven feet high, and the roses, which were in full bloom, were the color of the inside of a conch shell.

Laughing all the while, Léon and Michelle threaded their way to their destination. The center of the maze was a visual treat for those who managed to find it. A perfectly green lawn surrounded a sparkling pool of water, in the middle of which stood a marble fountain that had been imported from Spain. The fountain's center piece comprised four erotically-posed nymphs, each holding an urn from which poured an endless stream of water.

Léon set the picnic basket out of the sun and with a cry of exultation tore off his nightshirt. Michelle squealed with delight. She loved her husband's young, firm body, and the sight of it always excited her. Léon jumped up on the edge of the pool, tested the temperature, then stepped in. Apparently the water had not yet been warmed by the morning sun, for Léon, submerged to his waist, tried to keep from shivering as he urged his wife to join him.

"Come in, Michelle. It's won-won-wonderful."

Michelle laughed. "So why are you breaking out with goosebumps? Besides, I couldn't. Someone's liable to see me."

"No one can see us in here. Come on, I dare you."

Michelle never refused Léon's dares. She turned toward him and very, very slowly removed her nightgown. Despite the coolness of the water, Léon began to get aroused.

Undulating her hips and running her tongue over her lips, Michelle walked to the edge of the fountain.

"*Mon Dieu*, Michelle," Léon said. "If anything ever happened to me, you could surely find work at Odalisque."

Michelle looked shocked and pleased at the same time. "You mean work in a whorehouse?" she said with pretended outrage. "What would I do there?"

"Come closer and I'll show you."

Sitting on the edge of the fountain, Michelle dangled her feet in the water. "Ohhhh, it's cold!"

Léon positioned himself between Michelle's legs. "If you come in, I promise I'll make you warm."

She snuggled closer to him, pressing her breasts against his chest and tightening her thighs around his waist. He pulled her over into the water. They came up sputtering and squealing and holding on to each other. Michelle slipped her hand down between their tingling bodies and guided him toward her, and they were joined together as man and woman.

In his newly appointed dining room, Royal ate his lunch in solitude. An oval Chippendale table with four straight-backed chairs and a matching sideboard were the only pieces of furniture that remained. The other chairs and small tables had been removed to different parts of the big house. The room was pleasantly decorated with striped wallpaper of maroon and cream, a Turkish rug, and a brass and etched-glass chandelier that had not been made at Brannigan Glassworks. In fact, none of the chandeliers, lamps, or glassware in the house was his father's. Suzanne had informed him that the Jourdains had imported almost everything, except for a few items that had been purchased from a local concern run by French Creoles.

The food was delicious and well served by a young female slave named Nicey. Royal assumed that Zenobia was busy tending to her mistresses. Nicey, unlike Seth, was reticent and performed her duties with downcast eyes. Royal surmised that she was either afraid of him or still grieving for her late master.

It was a lonely meal. He reflected that the atmosphere had been more convivial in strange hotels in strange cities. When he had finished, Royal glanced at his pocket watch. It was nearly two. He hurried out of his dining room in order to keep his appointment with Angélique. By prearrangement they were to meet at the stables for a tour of the grounds and the sugar refinery.

Royal arrived a few minutes late and somewhat out of breath. Angélique was tapping her foot impatiently. Her eyes were hard and piercing beneath the veiled black hat that she wore to shield her fair skin from the sun. "You're late, M'sieur Brannigan," she said in a voice totally devoid of warmth.

Royal, annoyed by her manner, was tempted to ask her

how she knew the time, with all the clocks at Heritage left unwound after the master's death.

Seth popped up, and his presence alleviated Royal's sudden hostility. "Good day to yo', M'sieur Royal. Do yo' wants to ride Alezan dis afternoon?"

"Yes, thank you, Seth."

"And I'll take Arab," Angélique said. She stared at Royal defiantly. "My brother's horse."

"Yes, Miz Angélique. How abouts if I comes with yo', M'sieur Royal?"

Before Royal could answer, Angélique snapped, "No! Don't you have work to do? Cleaning the stables or something?"

"Why not let him come?" interceded Royal.

"M'sieur, this is to be a period of instruction. I do not intend to be constantly interrupted by his never-ending gibberish."

Royal looked at the little boy apologetically. "We'll get together later, son."

While Seth and two other stableboys saddled the horses, Angélique took Royal on a tour of the stables. All the while she kept up a running commentary, although she did not look at him once. She told him in precise detail the number and kind of horses, the number of slaves needed to care for the horses and the stable, the amount of feed consumed each year, and various other facts. Her monologue was totally lacking in enthusiasm, color, or humor.

They mounted the horses and rode to the cane fields. Angélique resumed her lecture. "Heritage encompasses nearly five hundred acres. Approximately twenty acres of that is occupied by the big house, the gardens, the various outbuildings, the slave quarters, and so forth. The rest is farmland. At present we have two hundred and sixty slaves, the majority of whom are field hands. They are divided into teams, each of which is headed by a driver, who is also a slave. The drivers are, in turn, responsible to our overseer, a man named Rafe Bastile."

"Any on the way?" asked Royal.

"I beg your pardon?"

"How many female slaves are pregnant?"

Without batting an eyelash, Angélique replied, "Twenty-three."

"I assume these twenty-three newborn children will also be the property of Heritage?"

"Some of them. There is a high mortality rate among slave children. If they survive the first two years, then we count them as ours."

"Who attends the slaves? Do you have a doctor?"

"We have midwives for the birthing, and the Landing shares a communal doctor who makes his residence at Salle d'Or."

"Why there?"

Angélique looked askance. "The Duc owns more slaves than the rest of us." She hesitated a moment. "And apparently requires more use of the doctor's time."

"Do you beat your slaves, too, mademoiselle?" Royal's implication was clear.

"I don't personally. We have drivers for that. When punishment is necessary."

"And is that often?"

Angélique looked at Royal directly. "We aren't monsters, M'sieur Brannigan. But discipline must be maintained."

"I don't believe in flogging fellow human beings."

Angélique uttered a harsh laugh. "Fellow human beings? You put them on the level of whites? Well, m'sieur, that's a matter you'll have to take up with Rafe Bastile."

She nudged her horse in the ribs and took off through the fields of cane. Angélique was an excellent horsewoman, and Royal had difficulty keeping up with her.

As they rode through the waving fields, slaves momentarily stopped their hoeing and weed-pulling and raised their heads to get a better look at their new master. Angélique did not acknowledge them in any way but continued to ride at top speed down the rows. Some of the older slaves who weren't as alert as the others had to jump or be pulled out of her way.

Royal followed, but at a much slower pace. He found her dismounted, waiting for him under some trees near the sugar refinery.

She raised her veil and said, "Having trouble keeping up with me, M'sieur Brannigan?"

"I consider it uneconomical to trample *my* slaves, mademoiselle."

" 'My slaves?' You're quick to adapt, aren't you? Despite your high-minded words."

As Royal dismounted he replied, "I can't change the structure of your society, but I intend to do things my own way.

At least I can make sure that they're properly clothed and housed."

"Oh, really, M'sieur Brannigan! Do they not look well fed? And I can assure you their other basic needs are more than adequately met. I would even venture to say that our slaves are better off than your free laborers of the North."

Royal was skeptical. "But they seem subdued, as if they're afraid of something."

Angélique laughed. "They're afraid of you, m'sieur. You're an American—a barbarian, by all accounts. Some of them probably think you're going to eat their children."

"Then you must correct that impression."

"No, m'sieur. I leave that to you. I agreed to instruct you in the ways of running a sugar plantation, not to convince the slaves that you're not a barbarian. How could I? I share their opinion. Now, do you want to learn about the process of producing sugar or not?"

"Of course," he replied with an aggressive smile.

She led him toward a large building, talking as she went. "Sugar cane, M'sieur Brannigan, is a tropical plant, though in Louisiana we have a semi tropical climate. The cane's natural growing season is over twelve months; here it is nine. Many of the early planters failed because they could not develop a process for making sugar from immature cane. Jean Étienne Boré, a planter and the first mayor of New Orleans after the Louisiana Purchase, was the first to crystallize sugar successfully from cane grown in this area."

"When does the planting season start?" asked Royal.

"About mid-January. We dig shallow furrows, and stalks of seed cane are laid flat and buried. We use ribbon cane—it's sturdier than the other strains. By spring the new plants appear from each joint of the seed cane. The crop is laid by around the beginning of July."

Royal could not resist repeating what Julia had told him. "You mean left to grow on its own?"

If Angélique was surprised by his knowledge she did not show it. "Just because the plants can be left unattended doesn't mean a vacation for everybody. We generally give the slaves some time off, then put them to work gathering driftwood or cutting wood in the swamps, to provide the fuel for sugar making."

"When is harvest?"

"The harvest and actual sugar making, which we refer to as

the 'grinding,' take place in October or November. This is the hardest time for everybody on the plantation. There is no rest for slave or master. Work has to continue around the clock, although of course the actual cutting of the cane is restricted to daylight hours. On Heritage we work the slaves in eight-hour shifts. The adults work two such shifts, the young slaves, one."

Angélique had paused at the door. "We call this building the sugar house. Wait here, m'sieur." She stepped inside and reappeared a few moments later holding a cane knife. The knife resembled a machete except that it had a hook at the end. "This is what the cutters use."

She walked to the edge of the field and expertly cut the cane blades away from the stalk, stretched high to lop off the top of the stalk, then severed it from the roots at ground level. She did the job efficiently, with little wasted motion.

She turned toward Royal and tossed the knife at him. He caught it smoothly by the handle. "Would you like to try it? After all, the master of a great plantation should know how to do everything."

Royal could not resist asking, "Did your brother?"

"Jean-Louis was an expert at everything," she replied.

Royal repeated her actions, and although he was a novice, he felt he made a good showing of himself.

"Not bad," she conceded, "for a first try." He threw the knife back to her. She caught it and in turn tossed it to a passing slave. "Once the cane is cut, it is brought here to the sugar house, where it's fed into a steam-powered mill and the juice is extracted. We don't waste anything. What's left of the cane is what we call *bagasse*. It is dried and then used forfuel."

For some reason Royal found himself watching the throb of her pulse along the column of her neck. "How is the sugar actually made?" he asked.

"It's a very intricate process. But in essence, it consists of boiling off the water from the juice. That leaves a higher sugar content in the remaining syrup. From that we crystallize the sugar."

"How do you get molasses?"

"Molasses is a residue, but, of course, a salable by-product. If you'll follow me." She took him into the sugar house and pointed to stacks of large wooden barrels. "The sugar is loaded into these hogsheads and then shipped downriver to New Orleans."

"How much do the barrels hold?"

"About a thousand pounds each—and they're hogsheads, not barrels. In case you're interested, the current market rate in New Orleans is fifty-one dollars per hogshead of average-grade sugar."

Royal whistled. "And after all this is over, do the slaves get some time off?"

"We all do. The slaves are treated to a huge party—plenty of drink and food as a reward for their efforts."

A man emerged from the shadows of the building. Royal had seen him the day before, standing on the porch of his house.

"There's Rafe—M'sieur Bastile, our overseer."

The swarthy man came forward to meet the new owner of Heritage. Angélique's introductions were as smooth and emotionless as if she were at a party introducing two people she didn't like.

After the men shook hands, Royal said, "Mademoiselle Jourdain has been explaining the process of the grinding to me."

Openly staring at Angélique, Rafe replied, "She knows the business better than any woman I've ever worked for."

Angélique did not thank him for the compliment but said, "M'sieur Brannigan does not hold with the flogging of slaves."

The overseer stared at Royal, but his eyes betrayed nothing. "Doesn't he?"

"Rafe, the cane in the north field appears to need water."

"That's because the higher ground drains off faster."

"I know that," she replied impatiently. "Just take care of it!"

Rafe nodded imperceptibly and walked away. Royal surmised that the two of them didn't care much for each other.

When Rafe had gone, Angélique said more to herself than to Royal, "He's impudent, but he's the best overseer in Louisiana." She added abruptly, "I'm tired. We'll continue tomorrow." She started to walk out of the sugar house.

Royal, angry at this curt dismissal, caught up with her as she reached the horses. "Wait a minute, mademoiselle. We're not finished."

"Yes we are."

Angélique climbed upon Arab and looked down at Royal

with intense scorn. "You may own the plantation, M'sieur Brannigan, but you don't own me." Then she rode off, urging the horse to a fast gallop.

Royal stared after her, wondering which he preferred—Suzanne's condescension or Angélique's out-and-out hostility.

Chapter Nine

Julia set aside the pen and sighed with profound relief. "There, that's finished," she remarked to Ottile, who was sitting nearby mending.

"It sure took yo' long enough, Miz Julia," Ottile said, not unkindly.

Julia's eyes scanned the page she had just so painstakingly written. "Hmmm . . . looks like a lot of bird tracks to me. Of course I haven't written anything except figures on a balance sheet in Lord knows how many years. I just hope my spelling is correct. I don't want to give the Duc any reason to return my acceptance note."

Ottile giggled. "I wonder what he going to say 'bout yo' bringing dat American to his persnickety party?"

"Well, he wouldn't dare refuse us entrance. One never refuses a Taffarel! Or at least they didn't. Oh, I don't expect there'll be any problem. He's anxious enough for me to come. He's got his eye on my property, you know."

"I knows dat. Cato and I seen him often enough, riding around, eyeing de place from de Promenade." Ottile became suddenly concerned. "Yo' wouldn't sell to dat man, would yo', Miz Julia?"

"Never. But perhaps when the time is right I might consider selling to someone else."

"Yo' means dat American? Yo' liked him, didn't yo', Miz Julia?"

Julia smiled. She did like Royal Brannigan, perhaps in part because both of them had created their own persona. She replied, "I've always admired handsome, virile men, Ottile. Now, don't scold. We're neither of us so decrepit that we can't remember physical attraction."

Ottile fanned her face and laughed. "I remembers."

Julia rolled the sheet of paper into a tight cylinder and tied it with a length of red ribbon. She dripped a bit of melted candle wax onto the ribbon and then stamped it with the Taffarel seal—a large *T* superimposed on a fleur-de-lis. "I'm sure the Duc will appreciate my ostentation."

Julia leaned back in her chair and gazed at the room. Water stains made the ceiling resemble a huge map of some mythical world. The wallpaper, now faded and yellowed, hung in strips like loose bandages. And the once beautiful amber velvet drapes were so weighted down with mildew and rot that no one dared touch them, for fear they might crumble.

"This used to be Mama's writing room."

"Yes, I remembers, Miz Julia."

"I used to come here as a child and watch her by the hour writing and answering invitations. She taught me how to write, you know. The first letters of the alphabet I learned were R.S.V.P. Mama said that was fine because they were the most important letters of the alphabet. In a way I suppose they are, if only people could apply them to everyday life."

Ottile didn't understand her mistress, but she nodded as she went on sewing.

"Yes, it will be good when it comes time to sell. This was once a happy house. A house like this needs people and children, dinner parties and soirées. It's a sad house now, lived in by an old woman who has lost her interest in life." Julia stood up and with a sudden burst of energy cried, "Ottile, come with me!"

The puzzled servant followed Julia out onto the veranda. They passed a stack of broken ballroom chairs now being used for firewood. On one of the seats lay a forgotten slipper. The silver leather shoe, tarnished by the elements, had become a cozy nest for field mice.

Julia stopped abruptly and eyed the slipper. "I wonder where the other one's gotten to? Ottile, we must go through my wardrobes and trunks to find something suitable to wear to the ball."

"After all dis time, Miz Julia?"

"Mama always said that beautiful things never go out of style."

They reached the front entrance, which was no longer in use. Julia gazed critically at the huge oak door. Once it had been brilliant white; now a few scabs of dull, grayed paint were all that remained. "That door needs repainting, Ottile. How are we going to entertain properly if the guests have to come in the back way?"

"Yo' means de American?"

"Whoever," Julia replied airily.

Ottile indicated the front stoop. "How dey gonna get up dem steps?"

The steps had been stripped of their marble. Through the years it had been carried off to mark the graves of favorite slaves. On the remaining, underlying stones huge spiders had laced extravagant webs, which now sparkled with drops of early morning dew. One of the spiders, frightened by the sudden intrusion, scurried across the porch. Ottile started to step on it.

"No, don't, Ottile. If you kill a spider it'll bring rain for sure. Besides," Julia added wistfully, "it just might be a descendant of one of those Papa imported from China for his and Mama's wedding. Have Cato chase them away, but gently. They'll find another place to decorate."

Not wanting to disturb the spiders by using the steps, Julia sat down on the edge of the veranda and jumped onto the lawn. Ottile followed. As the black woman dusted herself off, Julia cast a critical eye over the front gardens of Taffarel. The lawn had surrendered to the encroaching vegetation, and the flower beds, untended for a generation, were overgrown with weeds.

"I hadn't realized just how I've let things go, Ottile."

"Yo' can't do everything, Miz Julia."

"Remember the exotic birds and animals Papa imported from all over the world?"

"I remembers."

"Parrots, gazelles, kangaroos . . . all gone. A prey to old age or the climate, I imagine. What happened to the peacocks, Ottile?"

"We ate them, Miz Julia. After one of de times when de crops didn't come in."

"Oh, yes. As I recall they made better ornaments than stew."

The old woman wandered across the grass to where a bronze sundial lay on its side. It was at such an angle that the morning sun could not reach its face.

"Ottile, come here. Help me lift this." Together the two women righted the sundial so that it caught the rays and informed them that it was approximately eight o'clock. "There," Julia announced in a loud voice. "Time is no longer at a standstill at Taffarel."

The frequent afternoon rains kept the foliage dark green and lush, and the magnolia trees seemed to be weighted down with their leaves. The Promenade opened before Henriette's gig in a ribbon of dazzling white.

She held the reins tightly, keeping the horse at a slow canter. As always, Henriette approached Villeneuve with reluctance. Returning to the home of her youth never failed to fill her with a bittersweet emotion, happiness diluted by remorse. She brushed away her thoughts. Old memories were tenacious, and she couldn't afford to dwell on the past. There was no time now for regrets. Even though Henriette believed that the pattern of her own life was determined, she was committed to changing the course that her husband had charted for Alcée.

She realized that the midsummer ball was the first step in the Duc's scheme to control their daughter's life. He intended to use the event as a virtual slave auction, with Alcée as the prize. Not even an auction, for the Duc had already selected the buyer—Gilbert Gadobert. Henriette couldn't abide the odd-looking young man or his parents. They were typical of the new breed of New Orleanians—grasping social climbers. Her own parents, God rest their souls, would never have entertained their like at Villeneuve, any more than they would have approved of Alexandre, had they lived to meet him.

Henriette crossed herself as she recalled her parents' untimely deaths from yellow fever. She had been left so alone, so desperately afraid that she was going to become a spinster. It had not taken her long to start believing the Duc's promises of "eternal adoration," as he had put it. *Adoration! Assassination* would be a better word, she thought solemnly. Yes, that was the word—assassination. Only slowly. A slow, painful death brought on by his malicious remarks, his denigrating cruelty and, worst of all, his complete disregard for her basic human rights. "Assassination," she murmured, turning the word over in her mouth like a piece of sour candy.

Well, she would do what he asked concerning the ball, and even perform with a modicum of enthusiasm, because she intended to upset his plan. It was a matter of survival—her daughter's. She *would* triumph. After all, her beloved saints were on her side—Saint Denis, Saint Anthony, Saint Peter, and of course, her favorite, Saint Roch, the saint of impossible tasks. Henriette often found herself envying the martyred saints—tortured and killed for their beliefs. She would gladly offer herself on the altar of God if she could save her daughter.

Despite her morbid thoughts, Henriette was smiling. She was pleased that she had surprised and thereby disappointed the Duc by her "efficiency" concerning Alcée's ball gown. She was learning that the best way to irritate him was to give him little or no cause for complaint.

Henriette turned into the driveway of Villeneuve and, despite the warm weather, shivered. There were other reasons why she avoided the place. The rumors concerning Philippe and Lilliane had long since reached her ears. There was also talk of a child. Henriette knew that Lilliane had a little boy, but she could not bring herself to believe that Philippe was consorting with a woman of color or that he had fathered her child. Henriette had been brought up to believe that intermingling of races was a sin. She accepted Philippe's explanation that he often went to Villeneuve and occasionally spent the night to keep an eye on the house and grounds and make sure the slaves were doing what was expected of them.

It *couldn't* be true, she thought. Alexandre wouldn't send her on an errand to deal with a woman who was supposedly Philippe's mistress. His taste for cruelty didn't extend that far.

Despite her apprehension, Henriette was overcome with nostalgia as she approached the big house. Villeneuve was a jewel of architectural design. One of the most felicitous of Louisiana's pseudo-Greek temples, it stood two stories high and was fronted by a large veranda and a row of Doric columns. Despite the structure's massive size, everything was simple, and the lack of ornamentation set an austere, masculine tone. Even though the big house was mostly unoccupied, it was kept in perfect order. In fact, both house and grounds were immaculate. That was one of the few things upon which she and the Duc agreed. Henriette vowed that Villeneuve should be preserved for her daughter and the man *she* chose to marry.

She reined the horse to a stop in front of the entrance, which was framed by two huge clumps of Spanish dagger belligerently guarding their white blossoms. As she climbed out of the gig, a little boy rounded the corner of the house at top speed. "Let me help you, Madame Henriette," he called.

Henriette stiffened. She recognized him as Lilliane's son. "I'm sorry," the little boy apologized, taking the horse's bridle. "I didn't hear you coming." He looked directly at her, not lowering his head as did most slaves. Henriette had not seen the youngster for nearly a year, and never at such close range. She quickly looked away from him.

"That's all right," she replied stiffly. "I'm arriving quite unannounced. I'm here to see Lilliane."

"That's my mama. She's in her room. Should I bring her out here?" Azby continued to stare at her, as if trying to memorize her face.

"No, no, no. I'll go to her," Henriette replied, focusing her vision somewhere above the boy's face. "I—uh—have some packages in the back of the carriage, some bolts of fabric. Perhaps you ought to call someone. . . ."

"I can carry them," Azby said, and retrieved the bolts of fabric before she could protest.

"Why aren't you off playing somewhere?" Henriette asked irritably.

Azby came to her side, the bolts tucked under his arms. "I don't play much," he replied. "The other children don't like me."

Although Henriette did not ask why, he proceeded to tell her anyway as she walked toward the kitchen. He announced in a loud, bright voice, "Nobody plays with me because my skin's too light and I talk too white. But I don't care. I don't like any of them, either. Someday I'm going to go away from here, and I don't want any of them to come see me, because I won't let them. Ha ha." Azby picked up a singsong rhythm and began chanting over and over, "My skin's too light and I talk too white. My skin's too light and I talk too white."

Henriette could stand no more. "Stop that, do you hear? Stop that, whatever your name is!"

He replied with a crooked smile, "It's Azby. What did you think it was, Madame Henriette?"

Lilliane appeared in the doorway of the kitchen. "Madame Duvallon! Is Azby bothering you?"

"No, no." She grabbed the bolts of material from the little boy and lunged into the kitchen.

Lilliane said in a hard, even voice, "Azby, go do something."

Azby scowled at his mother. There was a strain of embarrassment on the young woman's face, as if she were afraid to confront her own son. Henriette could feel the tension between them, and it made her even more uncomfortable.

Azby finally disappeared, and Lilliane joined Henriette in the kitchen. "Would you like a cold drink, Madame Duvallon?"

"Yes—yes, I would. Water would be fine."

Henriette let the bolts of fabric drop on the kitchen table and sank into a chair as Lilliane poured her a tumbler of water. "He's not coming in, is he?"

"No, he'll stay away. I'm sorry for his behavior. He's not used to being around—" She paused. "Around white folks."

Henriette took the offered glass and drank. "Ah, that's better. I should have had someone accompany me."

"You should have, madame. The roads can be dangerous. Even here. Even in the afternoon."

Henriette set the glass down and fumbled nervously with the fabric. Always uncomfortable giving orders to slaves, she was even more so in this case. She spoke elaborately, as if her words had been memorized. "I was sent by the Duc. As you know, he is holding his annual midsummer ball this year on Saturday, July the third. In view of your talents as a seamstress, the Duc requested that you make the outfits for the Negrilions. There will be six in all. The boys have been selected from both Salle d'Or and Villeneuve. My husband, being a man of precision, wanted them to be of a similar size. He hoped that your son would be one of them."

"Of course, madame."

"I have here two bolts of fabric—one of gold satin, one of green silk. That is the color scheme of the ball. My husband has drawn up the sketch of how he wants the uniforms to appear." She produced a sketch, which had been pinned to one of the bolts, and handed it to the slave. Lilliane studied it for a moment and handed it back.

"These should not be difficult, madame, but I'll need the boys to come by for measurements."

"I'll see that they come to you as quickly as possible."

"Good. In the meantime I can start with Azby."

"If you please the Duc, rest assured that there will be a reward for you."

"Don't you worry. The Duc will be pleased."

"Very well. Then I suppose I'd better be on my way."

"Aren't you going to visit your home?"

"No, no, I can't," Henriette stammered. "I just can't." She stood up and left the kitchen without a further word.

Henriette's footsteps were measured and heavy; she felt as if she were carrying a tremendous weight upon her back. As she rounded the house, she could hear Azby's chanting. "My skin's too light and I talk too white." She lowered her eyes and walked directly toward the carriage.

When Azby saw her, he stopped chanting and dutifully grabbed the bridle. Henriette climbed back onto the seat. Upon impulse she looked down at him. He was standing very stiffly and staring at her with huge gray eyes, as if challenging her to love him. Henriette cracked the whip in the air, and the gig pulled away, leaving Azby in a cloud of dust.

The clock in Theo's study struck eight, and the old man awoke with a start. He had nodded off at his desk while working on his memoirs of the War of 1812, which were unimaginatively entitled "The Battle of New Orleans, A Personal Account by Field Commander Theophilus S. Beauchemin." He rubbed his eyes and stared at the striking clock, which sat on his desk. He yawned and told himself, *I must be getting old. Or perhaps my account is more boring than I thought*. He put his papers in order for the next day's work and wearily eased himself out of the straight-backed chair. It was time to say his good-nights to his grandchildren.

He hoped they didn't require a story; he didn't feel up to it tonight. He had been in a depressed state of mind ever since Jean-Louis's funeral. Not that he'd been that close to the young man—he hadn't. It was just that the event brought back many unhappy memories. He had attended too many funerals in his time. Theo vowed he would only attend one more—his own.

As he climbed the stairs that led to the second floor of the big house, Theo thought of Cédonie Debro, the woman he had married after Julia retired from public life. Cédonie had been a faithful, loving wife, and she had borne him a fine son, one whom he had been proud of. Matthieu would have been only thirty-seven now, if he had lived, and his wife, Lynette, would have been . . . Theo shook his head, telling himself he must set aside past sorrows and concentrate on the happiness that now existed on the plantation.

He paused on the top step and caught his breath. "I'm out of shape. I've got to stop being so sedentary. Instead of riding, I'll start taking long walks. Perhaps I'll visit the Jourdain women and see if they're in need of anything." He stroked his beard and admonished himself. "Besides, I've been lax in meeting my social obligations. A visit to Heritage would afford me an excellent opportunity of meeting the American."

Unlike many of his Creole contemporaries, Theo was not prejudiced against the Americans. After all, he had fought side by side with many of them in the Battle of New Orleans, and had even renamed his plantation in honor of that splendid victory. And hadn't he always tried to judge men on their individual merits?

Theo walked slowly down the hall and, unnoticed, paused before the open door of Denis's bedroom. All three children were inside, sitting on the floor, totally absorbed in their play. As Theo watched, he was struck by how small and vulnerable they appeared. They were working some of the puppets he had made for them. He believed that puppetry was a healthy diversion, particularly on rainy days. Certainly his grandchildren had taken to it. Denis wrote elaborate scripts, while Fleur made the costumes and Blanche provided sound effects. They all were adept at manipulating the puppets, in this case in a Creolized version of Aesop's fable of greed and deception, the Fox and the Grapes. Denis was working the fox, Fleur the crow, and Blanche the bunch of grapes, which was complete with eyes and mouth.

"Almost ready for a production?" asked Theo.

The trio looked around at their grandfather, and Denis said, "It's coming along fine, Grandpapa. When we're perfect, we'll treat you to a show."

"I'm perfect now," announced Fleur.

"I had an idea for another play, Grandpapa," said Denis. "A ghost story."

"Oh?" replied Theo, cocking his head to one side. "I wonder what inspired that?"

Denis was crestfallen. "Aw, you guessed. Anyway, I thought I'd write a play about the ghost of Magnolia Landing. Would you do a ghost puppet for us, Grandpapa?"

"Yes! Yes!" squealed Blanche.

"Well, now, I don't know. I like to be authentic. How can we know for sure that Coffey's description was accurate?"

"I see what you mean," replied Denis. "But maybe we'll get to see it ourselves."

"I want to see the ghost! Now!" demanded Blanche.

"Now, no more talk of ghosts," Theo said. "I think it's time for you to get into your nightclothes before Aunt Lolly comes to tuck you in."

"Are you going to tell us a story, Grandpapa?" asked Fleur.

"Not tonight, sweetheart. I'm a little tired."

"There's nothing wrong with you, is there, Grandpapa?" asked Denis, the breaking pitch of his voice heightened by his alarm.

Theo knew that he was remembering his parents' deaths. He quickly replied, "No, I'm fine. It's just old age."

After kissing his granddaughters good night, Theo left the lamps burning, for Aunt Lolly would be along any minute to tuck the children in. Aunt Lolly had held the family together during the terrible cholera epidemic of 1824, which had taken the life of Theo's wife, his only son, and his son's wife. Theo had been left in a state of shock for a long period, unable to concern himself with his grandchildren. Aunt Lolly had seen to his needs and taken care of the children as though they were her own.

When Theo reentered Denis's room, the little boy was already in bed, awaiting a good-night kiss on the forehead. Theo sat down on the edge of the bed and put his arm around Denis's narrow shoulders. "Denis, promise me you'll always watch out for your sisters."

"I will, Grandpapa."

With unabashed affection the old man hugged him tightly for a long time before leaving.

The clocks at Victoire struck the hour twice more, but there was no one awake to note the passing of time. Then, when they chimed eleven, a light appeared in Denis's bedroom. The boy tiptoed across the floor and changed from his nightshirt into his play clothes. As he was crossing back to fetch his shoes, his sisters, whom he had thought were asleep, appeared in the doorway between their rooms.

"Denis," scolded Blanche. "It's still dark. What are you getting up for?"

"Shh! You'll wake Grandpapa and spoil everything."

"*I* know what he's getting up for," whispered Fleur.

"Well, somebody's got to do it," Denis said. "Before it's too late."

"You're not going to the graveyard?" gasped Blanche.

"Of course I am. You heard what Aunt Lolly said—the only

way you can attract a ghost is to carry around dirt in your pockets from a freshly dug grave. So I'm going to go get some."

"From M'sieur Jean-Louis's grave?" asked Fleur. "That doesn't seem neighborly."

"Denis, take me too. Me too!" Blanche pleaded

"You're much too little to go," said Fleur. "Besides, there's going to be a storm."

"How do *you* know?" challenged Denis.

"Because the bullfrogs were singing loud and clear."

"That's just superstition," argued Denis.

"So's graveyard dirt," replied Fleur with a toss of her head.

A sudden flash of heat lightning caused the panes in the French doors to light up like a hundred staring eyes. All three children shivered, and when the thunder started rumbling, Blanche ran back to her bed.

"I'll wear my oilskin," said Denis bravely. "The pockets are deep."

"Don't you want me to come with you?" Fleur asked faithfully, though without enthusiasm.

Denis struck a stalwart pose and replied, "This is man's work."

He slipped out of the room and down the back staircase. In the cloakroom he lit a lantern and found his oilskin.

He kept the light shuttered as he ran down the driveway toward the Promenade. Denis was in excellent physical condition and a swift runner. He made good time, and soon he was sprinting down the alley of magnolias toward the turnoff for Heritage.

By now the sky was supercharged with violent lightning flashes, and the thunderclaps were so loud that Denis let the lantern slide to the crook of his arm and covered his ears with both hands. The wind encircled him like a questing beast, and as he ran, Denis glanced at the sky to see if it would rain. A full moon, floating on a swell of thunderclouds, was traveling westerly like a solitary ship on a dark sea. He had seen storms like this before—all noise and fireworks but no rain. Denis reached the entrance to Heritage slightly out of breath and, pacing himself, decided to walk the length of the driveway.

A short time later he was at the bottom of the rutted road that climbed the hillside to the graveyard. The air was filled with the metallic smell of electricity, and the thunder was so powerful that it seemed to shake the earth on which he stood.

The storm clouds claimed the moon as its victim, and the lightning momentarily subsided. Denis could not see the top of the hill. He unshuttered the lantern. From this point of view the road seemed to stretch toward infinity. For the first time since he had started his journey, Denis was frightened.

Still, his determination was stronger than his fright, and placing one foot in front of the other, he started up the hill. The night was so dark that he had to hold the light at arm's length to see the rutted road ahead. The wind knocked the lantern from left to right as he climbed. Keeping his eyes straight ahead, he tried not to examine his surroundings too closely. In the darkness the vegetation took on strange humped shapes, their outlines undefined and menacing.

He felt a clammy perspiration crawl across his skin. His head was buzzing, and he was having trouble keeping his eyes in focus. He was halfway there when he thought he heard a movement in the nearby underbrush. He turned and held up the light against the clump of vegetation. The leaves were shivering. Was it the wind or something else? He took several steps backward and then bolted up the road to the hilltop.

Suddenly the clouds parted and the moon appeared. The air smelled hot and rotten, of death and decay. The hilltop was quiet. No insect, bird, or animal stirred. The wind had dropped. It was as if the entire world were holding its breath. As Denis slowed to a walk, the cemetery's wrought-iron gate—possibly prompted by a vagrant breeze—swung open, then continued to creak back and forth in slow motion.

Denis stopped in his tracks and stared at the moving gate. Abruptly it stopped, remaining in an open position. It seemed to be daring him to enter.

Denis ran through the gate and walked over the dry grass toward the fresh grave. As he approached, the sky was suddenly filled with an unearthly glow, unlike anything he had seen before. Something compelled him to look upward into the face of the marble angel. The finely carved eyes seemed to be staring at him, and the wings appeared to flutter and vibrate in the glow, as if ready to take flight.

Denis clapped his hand over his mouth and jerked his head away. When at last he forced himself to look back, the statue was still there, unmoving. He set the lantern on the grave and almost laughed with relief. He fell to his knees and began scooping up handfuls of the dirt, jamming them into the pockets of his oilskin. He was trying to ignore the thoughts that were screaming in his mind. *You are in a graveyard! You are in a place of the dead! What if one of these graves holds the ghost of Magnolia Landing?*

When his pockets were more than half full, Denis decided that he had more than enough graveyard dirt. He was just about to stand and leave when the earth near the center of the mound began to move. Small fissures appeared as the dirt buckled and crumbled. Something was digging its way out of the grave.

His mind exploded. He was paralyzed by terror. He couldn't move. He couldn't even cry out. His eyes were riveted to the undulating ground.

"I'm imagining this," he told himself. "I'm dreaming." But he knew in the depths of his soul that what he was seeing was real.

Denis did not move a single muscle. He was choking with the effort to hold back his breathing so that he wouldn't attract the attention of the thing in the grave. How long he stayed like that, totally immobile and completely terror-stricken, he could not tell. It might have been ten seconds, it might have been ten minutes. Then a sudden, furious movement of the thing beneath the earth brought him out of his trance. Denis threw back his head and screamed. He lurched away from the opening grave, stumbled through the gate, and ran directly into a pair of clutching arms. He screamed again as he struggled to break free from his captor.

"Relax, son, relax. I'm not going to hurt you," said Royal.

"I don't know you!" cried Denis.

"I'm Royal Brannigan. I now own Heritage."

Denis nodded and gulped. "We've got to get out of here! He's digging his way out of the grave! He's coming after me!"

Still holding on to the struggling boy, Royal looked across the field to the mound of dirt that was highlighted by Denis's forgotten lantern. A section of earth was indeed moving. Royal caught his breath, when suddenly the ground broke open. What emerged was not the rotting hand of a dead man, but a rather large, brown mole. The creature poked out a flat, pointed head, blinked at its surroundings with small, blind eyes, then began burrowing yet another tunnel in its unending search for earthworms and grubs.

Royal forcibly turned the boy's head toward the grave. "Look, son—it's a mole. That's all, just a mole."

Denis almost collapsed with relief. Royal knelt down in front of the boy. "Are you all right?" Denis nodded. "I thought you were a grave robber. The thunder woke me up. I was having a cigar on the veranda when I saw the lantern up here. So if you're not a grave robber, who are you, and what are you doing here?"

"I'm Denis Beauchemin. I live with my grandpapa and sisters at Victoire."

"Shouldn't you be in bed by now?"

"I was but, but . . . " Denis was reluctant to tell Royal the reason for his nocturnal visit to the graveyard.

"What have you been doing? Your hands are all dirty."

"I needed some graveyard dirt," he blurted out. "Aunt Lolly—that's our mammy—told me that if you get dirt from a fresh grave and carry it around in your pockets, then a ghost will be attracted to you. And I want to see the ghost of Magnolia Landing."

Royal suppressed a smile. "Well, now, I guess you're a lot braver than I was at your age. I don't suppose your grandfather knows you're out alone at this time of night?"

"Oh, no, he doesn't. Please, M'sieur Brannigan, don't tell him."

"I guess there's no harm done. Come on, I'll walk you back down the hill. Then I'll get a horse and take you home."

"You—you won't tell him?" Denis was incredulous. Most adults, he had found, displayed little loyalty to children and their secrets.

Royal stepped away from the boy, crossed his heart, and spat on the ground. "I promise it will be our secret."

Chapter Ten

The excitement generated by the Duc Duvallon's approaching midsummer ball spread like a fever downriver to New Orleans. Everyone in the Crescent City was infected by the color and the glamour of the event, and there appeared to be no cure.

The Duc divided the invitations into three sets, according to the importance of the persons receiving them. The first set, which was sent out six weeks in advance, went to those of the greatest importance—the governor and select political officials, the doyens of high society, and the wealthiest and most influential planters. At four weeks prior to the ball, the second set was sent. These were received by persons of only slightly lesser distinction and social standing, including other plantation owners and members of established Creole families. The third set was begrudgingly delivered a mere two weeks before the event. These were allotted to merchants, shopkeepers, and businessmen whose social status or antecedents were questionable, but with whom the Duc nonetheless was obliged to curry favor. The lateness of the third set made it clear to the recipients that whether or not they attended the ball was a matter of little concern to the Duc.

Of course no Americans were included on any of the three lists.

The Duc's tactless rating system delighted the snobs, particularly if they were among the first to be invited. Those on the second list received their summons with gratitude and pleasure for the most part, but many who were delegated to the third parcel of invitations suffered great humiliation. Still, no one declined; to do so might mean elimination from future lists.

The gossips (and who in New Orleans was not?) gathered in the cafés, the gambling houses, and on shaded patios to speculate and trade stories about the affair. Plantation families sat on their verandas and spoke in hushed tones concerning the serious matter of what they should wear. At the French Market, rumors were examined with the same zeal as a prospective purchase. The subject was on everyone's lips, and even those who wouldn't even dream of being invited—whores, dockworkers, thieves, pirates, and other social outcasts—chattered endlessly about what promised to be the social event of the season.

Just as the subject was beginning to lose ground, a startling rumor added grist to the mill. An article appeared in the gossip column of the *Louisiana Gazette*, an English-language newspaper, which stated with gleeful malice that Royal Brannigan, the *American* who now owned Heritage plantation at Magnolia Landing, would be attending the Duvallons' midsummer ball. *And* he was to be the escort of the legendary Julia Taffarel. The madwoman was coming out of seclusion!

The item created a delicious scandal. Creoles, pretending

outrage, spoke of nothing else. The tragedy of Jean-Louis Jourdain's suicide was all but forgotten, and the prospect of meeting and inspecting Royal Brannigan was on everyone's mind. They were intrigued by the brashness of this American gambler who was the usurper of Creole tradition, of which Magnolia Landing represented the absolute bastion. If they were outraged, they were also delighted, and nothing short of a yellow fever epidemic would keep them from attending the ball.

As the night of the ball drew nearer, Salle d'Or became a madhouse of activity and lost tempers. The Duc reduced nearly everyone to tears by his demands, complaints, and fits of anger. Henriette bore the brunt of his wrath. But her decision to thwart her husband's plans for her daughter had given her courage, and she found that she was able to endure his cruelty with greater equanimity.

Although Philippe usually enjoyed lavish parties—the food, the drinking, the dancing—he was not looking forward to the ball with any great enthusiasm. To his mind, it had been too long since he had been allowed to go to New Orleans, or to enjoy the company of any woman except Lilliane. Philippe lusted after a new adventure. The young Creole women who would be attending the ball, all prospective mates, were too wholesome to interest him.

Alcée was even less enthusiastic than her brother. Not that she didn't like balls. She adored dancing in particular, but she wanted to be dancing with the young man of her choice. She wished that she and Blaise could run away together, but what would happen to her mother if Alcée were not there to intercede on her behalf? Her father and brother would surely drive the poor woman to her grave.

The Duc was fuming. Someone had sent him a copy of an American newspaper, with the gossip column item circled. The Duc had flown into a rage and immediately called his family together in the ballroom to berate them, as if somehow they were the cause of his embarrassment.

Henriette, Philippe, and Alcée stood silently with their heads bowed as he marched back and forth like a general dressing down his troops. "How did they find out? *How?* It must have come from one of you. When I received Julia Taffarel's acceptance note stating—not *asking*, mind you—

that the American was to be her escort, I told you that I wanted it kept quiet. My invited guests number over three hundred—everybody of note in New Orleans. Including Governor Dupré. I've engaged three steamships to transport these guests to Magnolia Landing. The total cost of the food, drink, and decorations is staggering. I am not about to have the affair disrupted by an American gambler!"

Henriette surprised everybody by speaking up. "Why don't you simply cancel Miss Julia's invitation, Alexandre? You could write her a note and express your displeasure to her rather than to us."

The Duc narrowed his eyes and took several steps toward his wife. "Of course I cannot cancel the invitation, Henriette. It would be discourteous." He clenched his gloved hands into fists and looked about to strike Henriette, when Alcée interceded.

"Papa, admit the truth. You don't care a whit about courtesy. If you told Miss Julia not to come, it might hamper your plans. We all know your real reasons for asking her. You want control of Taffarel."

"Be that as it may," the Duc sputtered, "how did the item get in the newspaper? I swore the three of you to secrecy. After all, there was always the possibility the American wouldn't come or Miss Julia might change her mind."

Henriette silently prayed to her saints that Royal would not come. She didn't want the Duc to know that she and Marguerite had already met him.

"Well, I'm sure *I* didn't tell anyone, Papa," Alcée continued. "And neither did Mama. Why don't you ask Philippe?"

The Duc marched up to his son and stood so close to him that the tips of their boots touched. "Well, Philippe?" His voice was a low, throaty growl, like the warning of a guard dog. "Whom did you tell?"

"Nobody, Papa. I swear, I . . ." Philippe suddenly remembered something. "I might have mentioned it to Señor Vargas when we were planning the fireworks display."

The Duc stepped back. "Ah, yes, of course, Señor Vargas."

"I didn't think," Philippe stammered, and then, asserting himself, added, "You can be sure when I go to New Orleans to pick up the order that I'll make my displeasure known."

"You'll not be going to New Orleans. We'll make other arrangements."

"But, Papa—"

"Shut up! The matter is closed. Now, I'm sure each of you has duties to perform, so I won't keep you any longer."

They were relieved to be dismissed. Alcée hung back, hoping to assuage her father's anger. "Really, Papa," she said, "what can it matter? People will be too curious to stay away. Besides, I think it adds a bit of notoriety to the proceedings. To tell you the truth, I'm anxious to meet Royal Brannigan myself." She kissed his clenched cheek and left.

Snorting in frustration, the Duc glared across the ballroom at a group of slaves working on the decorations. He was not mollified by Alcée's words, even though he thought that her reasoning was probably correct. Turning his anger on the slaves, he subjected them to a tantrum that surpassed all his previous fits of pique. He felt justified, since his rage was in proportion to the scope of the event.

Royal settled into the routine prescribed by Suzanne. He spent the mornings in her company, quickly coming to admire her expertise in management. He was continually astonished by the endless details of running the household. Of course someday he would have a housekeeper or perhaps a wife to fulfill such duties, but in the meantime he needed to learn everything for himself.

As planned, his afternoons were spent with Angélique, who continued to instruct him in the workings of a sugar plantation. He became acquainted with the key slaves and was given a tour of their quarters by Rafe Bastile. The houses were small, but clean and decently furnished. To his credit, Bastile believed in supplying the slaves with proper food, clothing, and shelter—if only to get a better day's work out of them. Royal ordered that flogging no longer be used as punishment, and although Bastile didn't like it, he agreed.

This period of instruction with the two women was difficult for Royal. He was naturally outgoing, and his inclination was to befriend them, but obviously this would not do. Suzanne continued to be polite but cool, and Angélique sustained her bitter hostility. More and more, Royal missed the intimate company of women. His strong physical attraction to both Angélique and Suzanne did not help matters.

Seth alone seemed to be pleased that Royal was the new owner of Heritage. One evening, as Royal was seated just outside his rooms, on a section of the veranda that had been designated as his, he asked Seth to join him for a drink. Royal was relaxing with a whiskey and water. Seth, emulating his idol, drank from a glass of lemonade whenever he saw Royal take a sip. They had turned their chairs so that they could enjoy the setting sun. The display was awe-inspiring. Golden flames burned up the whole western sky, then slowly faded, transforming the heavens into a canopy of bluish-purple that gradually became dappled with stars.

Seth was the first to speak. "Dat's sure a pretty sight, M'sieur Royal."

"One of the prettiest I've ever seen," Royal agreed.

"I bet dat old Duc wishes he could buy de sunset, wrap it up, and save it for de night of his party."

"There are some things that can't be bought, Seth. Not even by the Duc."

The boy turned his elderly face toward Royal and asked, "M'sieur Royal, are yo' really going to de party with Miz Julia?"

"She asked me to be her escort, and I accepted her invitation. That's the only way I could get there."

"Dat's for sure. Dey don't like Americans much round here."

"Seth, I would take it kindly if you'd drop the 'monsieur.' It's too Frenchified for my taste."

"But I can't call yo' by yo' first name."

"Then how about Mr. Royal?"

"Dat suits me."

Royal took a long swallow of his drink. So did Seth.

"I'm going, too, Mr. Royal. I'm going to be one of the Negrilions."

"What's that, Seth?"

"We helps de guests out of dere carriages when dey arrive."

"You don't sound too pleased."

"I gots to wear dis sissy-looking outfit dat Miz Lilliane over at Villeneuve is making fo' us boys. What yo' gonna wear?"

"I haven't given it much thought. I'm glad you reminded me. I'd better send a note off to my tailor in New Orleans and have him come up here with some fabric." Royal held up his arm. It was burnished by the sun. "A white suit would be flattering. Perhaps a green or gold vest to satisfy the Duc's color scheme."

Seth stuck out his lower lip in a pronounced pout. "Dat sounds a lot better dan what I'm wearing."

Royal said, "How about this, Seth—I'll have the tailor

bring along enough fabric so that he can make a suit of clothes for you, just like mine."

Seth jumped up from the chair. "Dat would be tremendous, M'sieur . . . I mean Mr. Royal. Jes' tremendous!" In a burst of emotion, the little boy hugged his new master. Royal hugged him in return. It was the first real display of affection anyone had shown him since his coming to Magnolia Landing.

Julia and Ottile managed to push open the door that led to an attic storage room. The windows had been boarded up, and the air was stale and hot. They moved about the cramped room, piling and unpiling trunks and wooden boxes, trying to ascertain what clothes had been stored where. Their footfalls were muffled by the dust, which had been gathering for decades.

With a great effort Julia pulled open a pair of wardrobe doors. Her hand flew to her mouth and she gasped. The rows of ball gowns, which had been so carefully put away more than a generation ago, looked as if they had fallen prey to some dreadful disease. They were hanging in shreds, rotted by mildew.

"Ottile, I can't wear these. They're completely ruined."

"Dat's what I tried to tell yo', Miz Julia. After all dese years yo' can't 'spect dem to stay de same. Nothing ever does."

Julia knelt and examined the matching pairs of shoes that had been carefully placed beneath each gown. The silks were faded, the leathers cracked.

"What could I have been thinking of?" Julia muttered. "Even if a pair remained intact, my feet have become broad and callused from years of wearing men's boots. I guess I thought only people and houses grew old."

She began opening trunks and boxes. She moaned with dismay and didn't bother repacking anything.

"Ottile, I can't go to the ball. I'll have to tell M'sieur Brannigan that I'm not well."

"Why don't yo' tell him de truth, Miz Julia?"

"I couldn't admit my dire situation to my new friend. I simply can't go—that's all there is to it."

Julia stood before the final trunk to be opened. "Bring the lamp over here, Ottile. This one's been labeled, but I can't make out what it says."

Ottile held the light as Julia wiped the grime from the

label. "Ottile! This one contains the material we were going to use for my wedding dress."

"Now, yo' don't needs to see dat, Miz Julia."

But Julia had already opened the lid and peered inside. The bolt of white satin was water-stained and flecked with rot. She pulled at the end of the material, hoping that the inside layers had remained intact, but the fabric crumbled like stale pastry.

Julia was close to tears. She picked up the round conc form that was to have held her wedding bouquet of white orchids. The lace and ribbons disintegrated in the air. Julia was about to replace it when she noticed one more thing in the trunk. It was a white leather box, now yellowed and split.

"Ottile! My pearls!"

"What pearls yo' talking about, Miz Julia?"

"Don't you remember the beautiful rope of pearls that Claude gave me in honor of my betrothal?"

"I thought dey had been sold off like everything else."

"No, I put them away along with my wedding things and forced myself to forget about them. In the back of my mind I knew they were there, of course, but I always promised that no matter how difficult things became, I would not sell them. I held on to my pearls because they represented a life I once knew." She looked at her servant in near panic. "Oh, my God, Ottile. Pearls don't rot, do they?"

"Dere's only one way to find out."

With trembling hands Julia retrieved the case and opened it. The strand of one hundred perfectly matched pearls was lusterless and in need of a cleaning, but otherwise intact.

"Ottile, look. Look! They're all right."

Ottile inspected the treasure. "Dey jes' need a good washing in some hot, soapy water, and I better restring dem fo' yo."

Julia sat back on her haunches and laughed. "Ha! What I wouldn't give to see the Duc's expression if I showed up at the ball with those wrapped around my neck!"

Theo stood before the full-length mirror in his bedroom. Stroking his beard, he regarded himself with satisfaction. Once again he had managed to get into his dress uniform, which had served for every noteworthy social event since he had first worn it on the night of the ball to celebrate General Andrew Jackson's victory at the Battle of New Orleans. He still looked impressive in his red field jacket, snug white breeches, and knee-high black boots. Gold epaulets and a red sash signified his grade as field commander. He struck a pose, and then laughed self-consciously at his own vanity.

There was a knock at the door, and Aunt Lolly came into the room. Hands on hips, she stepped back and scrutinized him, not with a critic's eye, but with one of pride in the master of the house. "I hears dat dis thing is supposed to be all green and gold costumes."

"My epaulets are gold. That will serve as my concession to the Duc's silly color scheme."

"Uh-huh. Well, if yo' plans to do any sitting down, dem breeches need letting out."

Theo asked, "You don't think I look ridiculous, do you, Aunt Lolly?"

" 'Course yo' don't! Yo' looks mighty distinguished. Why, yo' gonna put all dem younger Creole fops to shame." She laid her hand on his arm. "Yo' jes' nervous 'cause Miz Julia's comin' to de ball, ain't yo'?" Theo nodded. "I reckon time didn't do no standing still fo' her neither."

Theo smiled wistfully. "You should have seen her then, Aunt Lolly. She was the most beautiful creature that God ever created. She dazzled the eye. Looking at her was like looking into the sun."

"It don't seem right somehow dat two people living so close couldn't remain friends."

"It was her choice, Aunt Lolly, and I respected her wishes. You couldn't do otherwise with Julia Taffarel." He asked, "Are the children asleep?"

"Dey should be by now. I tucked dem in a little bit ago." On her way out, Aunt Lolly said, "If yo' plans on dancing in dem boots, den yo' better leaves dem outside de door to-night. I get Coffey to soften dem up with some saddle soap."

"Thank you, Aunt Lolly . . . for everything."

Theo stood in the center of the room, his arms hanging limply at his side. A melody from times past began playing inside his head—the lilting strains of a waltz, a new dance from Germany wherein men and women actually touched each other. It had been popular the summer of his first courtship.

Theo shook off his memories. It was forty years later. The waltz was no longer a novelty, and he was no longer young. Only the mystery remained. He collapsed into a chair and moaned. "Julia, why did you send me away?"

* * *

Denis, Fleur, and Blanche were also making their plans for the night of the fancy dress ball. They were seated beneath a tent of their own devising in the middle of Denis's bed. The tent—a cotton sheet—was pushed high by the pyramidal frame of an artist's easel. A small lantern illuminated the interior. This subterfuge was necessary so that the light would not show under the door and thereby alert Aunt Lolly to their nocturnal shenanigans.

They sat in a circle around the base of the easel, hands joined and eyes closed. Hanging from the neck of each of them was a chamois bag not unlike Aunt Lolly's wish bag; but instead of containing foul-smelling herbs, these bags had been filled with a portion of the graveyard dirt Denis had retrieved from the Jourdain cemetery.

The three of them were chanting quietly but intensely in an attempt to draw the ghost of Magnolia Landing from the realms of the supernatural. "Come-to-*us!*" They repeated the three-word entreaty, with the emphasis on the final word, over and over. "Come-to-*us!* Come-to-*us!*"

Blanche, who was about a half a beat behind, interrupted the proceedings by whining, "I'm hungry!"

"Hush, Blanche!" scolded Fleur. "Ghosts don't like to hear talk about food."

"That's enough chanting, anyway," said Denis in a voice that sounded like ice cracking. "Besides, the ball is still a week away. If everything goes as planned, I don't think we'll have any trouble getting out of the house. Aunt Lolly will be helping out in the kitchen at Salle d'Or, and we'll be looked after by Vermillion."

"Mama would not have approved," sniffed Fleur. "Vermillion takes her duties far too casually."

"Nonetheless, that works to our advantage. Now, as we know, the ghost has most often been sighted on the nights of large social events. This is our big chance. And with the graveyard dirt to guide him to us, we're sure to see him."

"What precautions have you taken for our safety, Denis?" asked Fleur. "After all, she may be dangerous."

"He," corrected Denis.

"She," persisted Fleur.

"He-she, he-she, he-she," Blanche chanted, until Fleur shushed her.

"I'm going to carry one of Grandpapa's carving knives,"

Denis said, "and we'll dress in dark colors, which will keep us from being seen by highwaymen. Maybe you two shouldn't come along after all. It's a huge responsibility, even though I am a man."

"Denis, you have to take us. You promised. And I'll keep Blanche quiet."

Denis glanced at his younger sister, as though not quite convinced. "We'll position ourselves in the gardens at Salle d'Or. We'll have to be careful not to be discovered by the guests."

"Can we sneak in and get some food?" Blanche asked. "Sometimes they serve food in the garden."

"Blanche, would you rather stay home and eat than see the ghost?" Fleur asked sternly.

Blanche thought for a moment and then shook her bright yellow curls. "No," she said with childish resolution. "I want to see the ghost."

"Good," said Denis. "Then if we're all in agreement, let's join hands and continue our chant."

"Come-to-*us!* Come-to-*us!* Come-to-*us!*"

Angélique and Suzanne were in a quandary. Their official period of mourning was far from over, yet the Duc, who was less than understanding of the plight of others, would certainly be offended if they did not attend the ball.

Suzanne, acknowledging the Duc's power, influence, and wealth, offered her opinion to her sister-in-law as they sat doing their needlework. "Angélique, I feel that we should put aside our personal feelings and attend." Angélique started to protest, but Suzanne held up her hand. "We're in a precarious position, and the Duc's always been fond of us. One day we might need to call upon him for a favor. And if our sugar crop is particularly good this year—and it looks like it's going to be—he might even consider lending us the money to buy back Heritage from M'sieur Brannigan."

Angélique parted her thin, petulant lips and replied, "Suzanne, the Duc doesn't grant favors without getting something in return. I certainly don't intend to offer myself up as collateral."

"Angélique, be serious."

Angélique executed another stitch and replied with a self-contained, catlike smile, "I was."

Suzanne sighed and looked over at her sister-in-law's needlepoint. Her representation of the avenging angel was almost finished. Suzanne found the design vaguely disturbing. "You work so much faster than I," she said, examining her own work, which was only half finished.

"I'm the impatient one," Angélique said, "so I use larger stitches."

"We still haven't come to a decision. I think we should go as a matter of pride. M'sieur Brannigan will be attending, and we should go too. We shouldn't let that riverboat gambler rob us of our dignity as he robbed us of our plantation."

"I suppose you're right," Angélique conceded in a silky voice. "Particularly since the ball gowns have arrived and the bills have been duly presented to M'sieur Brannigan. I suppose it's only divine justice to make use of them."

The women looked at each other and burst into laughter. The unexpected sound of their merriment startled them both.

Suzanne said, "I should ring for Zenobia and have her lay out our gowns."

"No, let's do it ourselves. I'm not interested in her opinion. Besides, we include her in our affairs too much. It's not as if she were a member of the family."

Suzanne was slightly shocked by her sister-in-law's words but said nothing.

Angélique went on, "What does an old black thing like her know about fashion, anyway? I'm not in the mood for her disapproval. You know perfectly well she'll be against our attending the ball and we'll get a lecture."

"I suppose you're right. But she'll have to know sooner or later."

"Later, then. And you tell her. You have a better way with her than I do. I'm sure you understand that just now I don't want any more disapproval."

"I understand, Angélique." She got up. "Now, come—I know you're going to look just stunning in your gown. That particular shade of green will be exquisite with your coloring."

"I'm sure it will," Angélique replied, as she jabbed the needle into the eye of the angel.

Marguerite spent an hour each morning at her writing desk, composing long letters to every relation, no matter how distant, and to every friend she still heard from. The letters were filled with cheerful anecdotes about herself—most of which she had manufactured—and solicitous inquiries regarding health and offspring. The effort of writing sentiments she didn't feel to people she didn't care about exhausted her.

She sat staring at the stack of letters and wondered at her own inventions. When had lying become so easy for her?

Marguerite got up and wandered around her room in agitation. Every surface was cluttered with souvenirs she had gathered on her visits to homes of friends and relatives throughout the years—a bottle of cloudy water from Saratoga Springs; a bowl full of shells she had lovingly selected on the Maryland shore; a piece of pottery crafted by Pueblo Indians; a menu from Delmonico's restaurant in New York City.

There were a hundred other things worthless to anyone but herself, and yet these objects represented the sum total of her life.

She ran her fingers through her dry and brittle hair and suddenly remembered that she had to touch up the roots sometime before the night of the ball. With the social event on her mind, Marguerite took one of her three ball gowns out of the closet and laid it across the bed. It was made of heavy satin and was the milky-green color of absinthe. Even though Michelle and Léon were being newly outfitted from head to foot, Marguerite had stubbornly refused to have another gown made for the Duc's ball. She would just remove the black trim from this old one. In any case, she had been invited only because of her position at Bellechasse. How many invitations would be forthcoming in the future? she wondered.

Marguerite walked the length of her room to the French doors. She loved her room. It caught the first rays of the sun each morning. Unfortunately, she had been getting up later and later, often too late to take notice of the sun at all. Natural sleep seemed to elude her. Instead of spending the night tossing on her bed and worrying about the future, she had begun taking more and more laudanum just to get a bit of rest. And she usually slept through the morning like a person more dead than alive. It took endless cups of coffee to awaken her fully.

Marguerite was afraid she was becoming addicted to the drug. Who would want her then? An old woman—rigid, without humor, and addicted to drugs. Tonight, she promised, she would try to get through the night without taking any. But she knew even as she promised herself that she would not keep her word. Whatever was to become of her?

Time was running out. In a few months Léon would reach

his twenty-first birthday and she would relinquish her role as controller of the estate of Bellechasse. Marguerite knew too well of the young couple's desire to live in Europe. She also knew that they would hardly want her trailing along. What would happen to her? A small pension? Living first with one relative and then another? Would she have to become somebody's paid companion? It was unlikely that anyone would pay for her company. She realized that she was not lovable, perhaps not even easy to like. Still, she had her standards, and she must preserve them, even if they didn't make her popular. Somebody, she assured herself with steely defiance, had to remember the genteel ways and live by them.

"I don't want to leave Bellechasse!" she suddenly cried. "I'm too old to make such changes in my life."

She stepped out onto the veranda. The view of the gardens always lifted her spirits. Marguerite pressed her cheek against a column and absentmindedly began counting the blooms on her favorite rosebush. Michelle and Léon came bounding into sight. She watched them as they played tag across the lawn, finally disappearing into a grove of bamboo at the edge of the garden.

"Tag! How appropriate," she murmured with disdain. "A children's game for children." A sudden thought seized her. *If only Michelle were to become pregnant*. That would make a difference. Then an aunt would be needed at Bellechasse.

Alcée, her skirts gathered high, her feet barely touching the ground, hurried down the brick-covered walk. The walk was flanked by planter boxes of white azalea bushes, which were being shaped by diligent slaves into uniform height and fullness.

"Ambrose, have you seen Blaise?" she asked one of the slaves.

"Yes, Miz Alcée. He working in de carriage house."

Alcée turned onto the walk that would lead her to her lover. Peacocks folded their tails and shrieked as she rushed by.

The carriage house was located next to the stables. It was a large, low building of brick and cypress, shaded by ancient pecan trees. In late fall, the slaves would wait until there were no whites around, then shake the tree limbs, causing the ripe pecans to fall onto the roof with a clatter like a shower of hail; then they would hungrily eat them. Alcée knew this because Blaise had told her.

She pushed open the doors. The interior was redolent of oil and leather, a pungent aroma that she found oddly appealing. Sunlight slanting through the high, narrow windows highlighted motes of dust dancing around the cypress columns supporting the roof beams.

"Blaise," she called softly.

"Over here."

The griffe wiped his hands on a rag and walked down the aisle between the carriages to meet Alcée. The smiles they offered each other were guarded.

Blaise said, "You make me so happy every time I see you. I wish I had a present to give you."

"You've given me your love; that's enough." She touched his cheek, then reluctantly drew her hand away. "What's Papa got you doing now?"

"I'm oiling the harnesses on all the carriages to make sure they're ready to roll with no squeaks."

"Goodness, there's so much work going into this affair. Papa's driving everyone to distraction. Why, we'll all be too tired to enjoy the ball."

"Do you expect to enjoy it?" Blaise asked as he rubbed the back of his hand over Alcée's silky black hair.

"No, but I'll have to endure it. Oh, I wish that we could be going together."

"Dreaming again," Blaise said tenderly.

"No, not dreaming—wishing. They're two different things." She climbed into the nearest carriage, a smart barouche recently painted and polished to perfection. "Come up, Blaise." He stepped up into the seat next to her. "Remember what we used to play? Let's drive away to a mythical kingdom where everybody's the same color."

"We have no horses," he chided.

"Mythical horses for a mythical kingdom!" Alcée stood in the carriage. "Giddyup," she cried fervently. "Giddyup!"

Blaise looked up at her. She was very still, as if expecting a sudden movement. A crescent rim of tears suddenly appeared on her eyelashes. "We're standing still," she said softly. He took her hand and pulled her down beside him. He kissed the tears from her lashes and brushed his lips across hers. "We're not going anywhere, Blaise," she said with a catch in her throat.

Before he could console her, two slaves appeared in the door. The couple quickly parted, Alcée climbing out of the carriage on one side, Blaise jumping out on the other. Alcée marched around the carriage and said in a too-loud voice, "It looks very fit, Blaise. I'm sure the Duc will be pleased." Dropping her voice, she whispered, "Come to my room tonight, but be careful. Please!"

Alcée ran from the carriage house and hurried through the gardens. As she was approaching the big house, a slave called from the veranda, "Miz Alcée, Miz Alcée, I been looking fo' yo' everywhere. De dressmaker's here with de ball gown. Yo' papa wants yo' to try it on fo' his approval."

"He does, does he?" Alcée replied. "Well, you tell Papa that he can wait like everybody else to see it the night of the ball."

"Oh, Miz Alcée, I can't deliver dat message. He in a extra bad temper, and he whip me fo' sure."

Climbing the steps to the veranda, Alcée replied solemnly, "Then I shall deliver the message myself."

Lilliane was in a state of anxiety. Her period was several days late, and she prayed that she was not pregnant. She couldn't have another child. Philippe wouldn't like it, and it would certainly be too much of a burden to her. She sat on the edge of her bed, counting her money. The bills and coins, most of them from New Orleans, included francs, crowns, ducats, livres, sous, shillings, and one precious Louis d'Or. Not satisfied with the total, she counted the money again. The sum was disappointing. Despite all her efforts, she had managed to save only the equivalent of two hundred and thirty-eight American dollars and change. The amount was a very long away from what she needed to buy Azby's freedom.

There couldn't be another child. There just *couldn't*!

Lilliane realized that she had been deluding herself into a false sense of security. Philippe's threats that he would sell her when he had tired of her were very real. She knew that he was not the kind of man to just put her to work in the fields. He would have to get rid of her so that she wouldn't be around to remind him of his indiscretions. What about Azby? He would sell him as well, of course. It was unlikely that they would be sold together.

Lilliane clenched her fists, threw back her head, and groaned with frustration. She shut her eyes and could feel them filling with stinging tears. Azby on an auction block? She would die before she would let that happen.

Lilliane recalled the slave market all too vividly. She remembered being separated from her mother, who had been auctioned off as a house servant. But Lilliane, then fourteen, had been of pleasing color and a virgin. She was sent to the "fancy-girl" market, a place where planters and wealthy Creoles purchased attractive young female slaves for their own pleasure or the pleasure of their unmarried sons. Fancy-girls brought twice, sometimes three times the amount of a first-class blacksmith or prime field hand.

Lilliane remembered the heat of that blistering afternoon, felt her fear and her shame. She saw the leering faces of the white men and heard the terrible words that had determined her future.

"Going once, going twice—sold to the Duc Duvallon for thirty-five hundred dollars!"

Lilliane broke out in a cold sweat. Her stomach went sour, and bile began rising in her throat. She lurched out of the bedroom and ran into the yard, where she fell on her knees and vomited. "Oh, dear God," she cried. "Don't let me be pregnant. Please, sweet Jesus, don't let me."

After washing her face in some cool water, Lilliane went back to her work. The six uniforms were folded neatly on the kitchen table. The boys had been duly measured, and the outfits were finished except for the detail work. Lilliane sat down, threaded a needle, and began working on her son's coat. She hoped that Henriette remembered her promise of a reward for work well done. She would add the money to her special fund. Lilliane believed that she would remember and that Henriette would be more than generous. It would be guilt money she was paying. Guilt because she would not even acknowledge her own grandson.

As she worked, Lilliane could not help but think of all the money the Duc was spending on his party. It could probably buy the freedom of more than one hundred slaves.

Azby appeared at the door and asked shyly, "Mama, can I have a piece of bread and honey?"

"Since when do you have to ask? You know you can."

He walked by without looking at her, and Lilliane sighed. She wondered when they would be friends again. She watched him cut himself a slice of bread and slather it with swamp honey. She knew that he was going to take it outside to eat it.

"Azby, before you have your treat, I want you to do me a favor and try on your costume. Come on—it will only take a minute."

The little boy reluctantly stripped out of his clothes and put on the costume. The breeches and jacket were snug-fitting and made of bright gold satin. Extravagant ruffles of jade green silk surrounded the neck and cuffs. "Stand up straight. Turn around. It looks very good on you."

"I feel silly."

"Well, you don't look silly. You look very handsome."

He raised his eyes to his mother. "If I look so handsome, then why does everybody act so ashamed of me?"

Lilliane drew back as if she had been struck. How could she explain the cruelty of people to her child? "Baby, they're not ashamed of you. They're ashamed of their own selves."

She knelt down in front of her son, and for the first time since the terrible night when Philippe had attacked her, he allowed her to embrace him. He stood stiffly for a moment as she hugged him tightly and kissed his face, and then suddenly he was hugging and kissing her in return.

"Mama," he said. "You're crying on my costume."

The breach was finally sealed.

Royal had just finished his supper when one of the house slaves informed him that he had a caller: "It dat Ottile from over at Taffarel."

Royal was alarmed. His first thought was that something was wrong with Julia. "Show her into my office, and I'll be there right away," he told the slave.

When he entered the room, he was sure that his fears were confirmed. Ottile looked greatly distressed.

"Ottile, what is it? There's nothing wrong with Miss Julia?"

"Oh, no, m'sieur. She's in good health."

"Then what's the matter?"

Ottile twisted her hands together and stammered, "Maybe I shouldn't have come, m'sieur, but I was concerned 'bout her."

"Tell me," urged Royal.

Ottile, embarrassed, looked at the floor. "Miz Julia ain't got nothing to wear."

"I don't understand."

"She's got nothing to wear to de ball. She dragged out some old dresses, but, M'sieur Royal, dey was older dan yo', and . . . and . . ." Ottile burst into tears. "Oh, m'sieur, since yo' been coming over, everything's changed fo' her. She got real perky thinking about going to de ball, and she no longer talk about dying."

"I've noticed the changes."

"She's too proud to let yo' know dat she got nothing to wear to de ball and no money to buy anything. And I just took it upon myself to come over here and tell yo' all about it. She's going to say she's not feeling well, and . . . oh, m'sieur, she's just got to go! If she doesn't she'll just go back to being de way she was, all sad and living in de past."

"Of course Miss Julia's going to the ball, Ottile. I'll have something made for her. My tailor's coming to Magnolia Landing the day after tomorrow. I'll write him a letter and have one of the slaves take it downriver to New Orleans. I'll have him engage the best seamstress in the city."

"What 'bout shoes? She got to have shoes."

"I'll send for a shoemaker too."

"But dere's only a week left befo' de ball, m'sieur. All dem people are engaged in making other people's outfits."

"Don't worry, Ottile." Royal grinned. "Money will make the difference. I'll just outbid them."

Overcome with gratitude, Ottile knelt in front of Royal and kissed his hand. Royal was embarrassed as well as touched by her show of emotion. He took her hand and pulled her to her feet. "You were right to come to me, Ottile. Any time that Miss Julia's in need I want you to come to me."

"Yo' a good man, M'sieur Brannigan. Yo' may not have de fancy airs of dem hereabouts, but to my way of thinking yo' much more of a gentleman dan any of dem, fo' all dere uppity manners."

"That's the nicest compliment I've ever had, Ottile. Now, it's getting dark out. How did you come here?"

"I walked, m'sieur."

"I'll call Seth and have him take you back in a carriage." He took her hand. "Now, don't worry about a thing, Ottile. I can assure you that Miss Julia and I are going to be the best-looking couple at the ball."

After seeing that Ottile was safely in the carriage, Royal returned to his room. The coffee was still warm, and he poured himself another cup. Even as he had said it, Royal realized that he probably couldn't afford the expense of outfitting Julia; but there was no question of his not doing it.

Perhaps there was no cause to worry. Bastile had told him that the sugar crop looked particularly good, and barring any calamities, a bountiful harvest would make everything right.

Royal was looking forward to going to the ball. It would give him a chance to meet his neighbors and perhaps overcome their prejudices against him. Seth had told him that Angélique and Suzanne had decided to attend. Royal believed that they were going only in order to show him up, and perversely that made him all the more determined to attend.

PART THREE

Chapter Eleven

The setting sun was a curious shade of yellow, soft yet piercing, turning the river into a sheet of hammered gold. The warmth of the afternoon slowly dissipated as dusk approached Magnolia Landing. Swarms of mosquitoes danced in lazy clouds over the surface of the water, seeming to keep time with the German brass band that was practicing on the wharf. The band had been engaged by the Duc to greet the guests arriving for his midsummer ball.

Soon the first steamship pulled into view. It was the *Belle Créole*, transporting those persons of greatest consequence, notably the governor of Louisiana and the mayor of New Orleans and their wives. Most of the passengers were on the Duc's premier list and would be staying at Salle d'Or for several days following the ball.

The ship had been decorated with swags of laurel, honeysuckle, and ribbon. Green and gold banners stretched from the garlanded smokestacks to both ends of the steamship. Ostrich plumes dyed to match the party colors exploded from every crevice.

Captain Calabozo was in command, and he prided himself on giving the prestigious group a smooth ride up the Mississippi—so smooth, he asserted, that not a glass of champagne had been spilled. He strutted about the decks wearing a brand-new uniform of gaudy green satin that he had commissioned at his own expense. His short, hefty frame was so tightly encased and the suit so lavishly trimmed that he resembled a buffoon from a comic opera.

Captain Calabozo, too, was invited to the midsummer ball. He was invited every year, although he was always on the third list. Actually he was included only to ensure his best performance aboard ship, but in the taverns and gambling houses of New Orleans, Calabozo always bragged that he was among the first invited. After all, who could dispute him?

As the ship glided toward the dock, the captain hurried to the hurricane deck to ingratiate himself with the most prominent guests on board, in hopes of being asked to share a carriage to Salle d'Or. The group included Governor Jacques Dupré and his wife, Aimée, Mayor Denis Prieur and his wife, Lisette, and the indomitable Verbena Chevereaux, a widow and the undisputed leader of New Orleans society, who, as usual, was at the center of the group directing the conversation. The others were unimportant to Calabozo. They were merely sycophants and hangers-on, who, like himself, were fascinated by persons of celebrity. It was taken for granted that every New Orleanian was a dedicated celebrity-chaser.

The captain wedged his way into the periphery of the crowd, straining to catch the gist of the conversation, which seemed variously concerned with genealogy, politics, and the problems of dealing with slaves. The discussion was punctuated by snide comments about the pretentiousness of the Duc and his annual ball. There was also a good deal of speculation about the American gambler, Royal Brannigan.

As Calabozo edged nearer, Verbena Chevereaux declared in a honeyed voice, "If anyone has the temerity to introduce me to this American, I, for one, shall snub him. I say let them remain outside our society."

"I hear he's terribly good-looking, Verbena," teased Lisette, the mayor's wife.

Verbena offered the governor and mayor a generous smile. "Sweet saints, we have two of the best-looking men in the state of Louisiana right here, and you ladies know it! A Creole woman needn't go looking for Americans to find visual gratification in the masculine gender. Certainly not *this* poor old widow."

Governor Dupré chuckled good-naturedly. Indeed, he was quite handsome, with typical Gallic features, including dark hair, deep-set brown eyes, a long, tapering nose, and pointed chin. He was wearing a practical, dark-green suit that looked several years old.

His wife, Aimée, was a petite and pretty brunette. She had the habit of moving her head in a pecking manner as she spoke, like a little bird, and indeed it was said that her husband's nickname for her was *ma pie*, "my magpie." She was wearing a gown of parrot-green chambray with huge, winglike sleeves. The couple held no particular affection for the Duc Duvallon but viewed their presence at the ball as politically advantageous.

Mayor Prieur wore a suit of gold silk. Unlike the governor,

he was a small and undistinguished-looking man with a tiny mustache and unmemorable features. His wife, Lisette, was short and stout but not unattractive in her simple moss-green dress. She and her husband did not openly criticize the Duc, though they seemed to enjoy the witty comments the others—especially Verbena—made at their host's expense.

Verbena Chevereaux was by far the most striking and fashionable woman on board. A brilliant mass of jet-black hair crowned a face whose features were so sharply defined that they looked as if they might have been outlined in pen. Her complexion was pure, creamy, and her eyes were a clear blue-violet and heavily lashed. Her mouth, in stark contrast, was loose and moist and very red, the mouth of a voluptuary.

Verbena was popular with men—especially with the Duc, who had always been attracted to her—while women trod near her with caution. She was twenty-seven years old and extremely wealthy. Her much older husband, Oliver, had died two years ago of a heart attack, rumored to have been sustained during sexual intercourse with his wife. Their union had produced five children, yet Verbena still retained her trim figure and looked splendid in a gown of iridescent green silk. The clinging fabric was cut in the Empire style, a fashion that still lingered in New Orleans. She wore jade earrings and a matching pendant, which drew the eye to the ample swell of her breasts.

"It looks as though Alex had his way with nature," Verbena said. "The sunset has gilded everything in sight. I wonder if that funny little wife of his would look better dipped in gold? Sweet saints forgive me, but I cannot think of her name. Hortense? Honorée?"

"Henriette," Captain Calabozo supplied, poking his head over someone's shoulder.

"Whatever!" snapped Verbena. She paused to collect her laughs and went on. Rolling her eyes, she said, "Why, they've gotten this ship up to look like the Whore of Babylon. I couldn't believe it when I got the invitation. Green and gold! My two very worst colors." As usual, Verbena's self-derision elicited nothing but compliments.

"Nonsense—you look ravishing."

"I beg to differ."

"Green is your color."

"Most flattering."

She bowed her head slightly. "You are all so very kind.

Last year it was black and white—too funereal. I'm going to tell Alex once and for all that next year it must be red. Scandalous, I know, the color of tarts, but it just so happens to be my best color. Besides, I so rarely get a chance to wear my rubies. And I just *know* that the two of you would look lovely in shades of red. Aimée, I can see you in rose. And Lisette, carmine, dark and seductive. I'm sure if the three of us get together we can convince Alex. If not, next year I'll simply take to my bed and not emerge until the whole thing is over."

"There, there, Verbena," said the governor, "I'm sure Aimée and Lisette will do their best."

"Of course I will," Aimée said, not entirely convincingly.

"I will too!" bubbled Lisette. "I'll draw up a petition," she promised, though they all promptly forgot the subject as the ship bumped gently against the wharf.

As the mooring lines were secured, three things happened simultaneously on shore: Hundreds of white doves were released and the birds began circling the waterfront; the German brass band began to play a lively march; and a brace of cannon boomed from Salle d'Or to welcome the first arrivals. The doves were so frightened by the noise that they decorated the sweating German band with unusual precision.

"Sweet saints!" shrieked Verbena. "He's firing on us!" She cupped her hand around her mouth and shouted, "I take back what I said about the color scheme, Alex!"

Captain Calabozo hurried below and stationed himself on the end of the gangplank, striking his customary figurehead pose. The passengers, the cream of New Orleans society, disembarked quickly, rushing pell-mell toward the carriages lined up at the base of the windmill. Drivers in full livery were standing next to each team of horses, calming the animals, which were fearful of the cannons' repeated booms.

According to protocol, however, all the carriages had to wait until the governor and his wife occupied the first vehicle in line, the mayor and his wife the second, and Verbena the third. After these luminaries were carefully ensconced, the entire parade of carriages began rolling down the Promenade.

At regular intervals along the drive, male slaves were stationed to act as guards. They were armed with machetes, which glinted menacingly in the half light. Their faces were impassive and unsmiling as they watched the carriages pass.

The governor's carriage reached the turnoff, and the procession veered left down the driveway leading to Salle d'Or. On each side of the drive were marble statues sculpted more or less in the classical style and supposedly representing various gods and goddesses, though they all looked strangely alike. Between the figures were oblong flower beds as regular as well-tended graves. The roadway turned and rose to slightly higher ground, and Salle d'Or greeted the guests in a blaze of light.

The big house was an aberration, a Gothic monstrosity that looked as though it had been constructed from the leftovers of a half-dozen odd palaces. The design was primarily the Duc's and was ornate to excess. Along the front a narrow veranda hid behind an ungainly colonnade of alternating thick and thin pillars that supported a massive gallery and a red tile roof. At either end of the house squatted a huge turret, at the base of which stood a cannon. The walls behind the colonnade were painted to simulate white marble, though a hodgepodge of recesses, cornices, and unlikely protuberances conspired against any monumental effects. In fact, despite the abundance of architectural detail, the house looked curiously unfinished, as though the architect could not decide what to do next.

Verbena was heard to exclaim, "My God, just see what horrors money can buy! Alex has the cannons aimed in the wrong direction!"

The Negrilions stood in an exact line down the marble stairs leading to the big house, looking princely in their gold and green uniforms. One at a time they advanced down the steps to open the doors of the arriving carriages. Then they retreated to the end of the line and reassumed their positions.

The Duc and his family were waiting on the veranda. On any other occasion he would have greeted his guests in his own good time, but in deference to those at the head of the first list, Alexandre had gathered Henriette, Alcée, and Philippe together in a show of hospitality.

After a brief exchange of fawning greetings, the Duc ushered the occupants of the first three carriages into the house and directly down the wide arched hall that led from the foyer into the ballroom. He wanted to treat them to the spectacle that awaited within before they dispersed to the assigned suites to ready themselves for the evening. Verbena protested, but the Duc prodded her and the others along like a sheepdog herding his flock. The brass-plated doors swung open before them, and as the Duc had expected, the sight of the interior of the ballroom drew a series of delighted exclamations.

In keeping with the sugar cane theme, the room had been elaborately decorated in green and gold. The walls were covered with watered gold taffeta, and the woodwork and ceiling had been recently repainted white with green ornamentation. The floor was perfectly matched squares of white Italian marble, and five huge crystal chandeliers infused the room with a festive amber glow.

At the far end of the floor a full orchestra, hired for an exorbitant fee from the Théâtre d'Orléans, was playing light selections from a French opera. In the center of the ballroom, a marble fountain gushed an endless supply of champagne. Servants bearing trays of food moved among the early arrivals, their black countenances contrasting sharply with the gleaming white uniforms that duplicated, in a finer fabric, the clothes they wore in the cane fields.

Standing between the French doors and at both ends of the ballroom were the Duc's *pièces de résistance.* Fake stalks of sugar cane, fashioned of wood, wire, fabric, and paint, rose majestically from the floor to the eighteen-foot-high ceilings. Oil lamps, concealed and shuttered at careful angles, made the stalks appear almost real and gave viewers the impression that they had suddenly become children once again, left to play in a magical field of sugar cane. Even the governor and the mayor and their wives were dazzled by the spectacle and tempted to "oooh" and "ahhh" in admiration. Verbena, however, loudly remarked, "This is all very nice, Alex, but when do we get to meet the American?"

As Marguerite walked along the gallery to the master bedroom, she was uncomfortably aware that she did not look her best. When she had removed the black trim from her absinthe-green ball gown, her hands had been shaking so badly that she had cut the material in several places, and she had repaired it hurriedly. Her green-feathered fan was molting, and she would have to employ it with caution. She had dyed her hair with coffee the day before and had arranged it in a topknot with side curls, but it looked as dry and stringy as Spanish moss. Her sallow complexion reflected the color of the gown, making her skin appear green and tainted. To compensate, she had rubbed pink rouge over her entire face—but that made her look sunburned, and now the skin on her neck and arms did not match. As she walked, she noticed that the heel of her left shoe was coming loose. She would have to favor it without appearing to limp.

Marguerite reached the entrance to Léon and Michelle's room. The shutters were closed across the French doors. She rapped on a louver and noticed that her glove was grease-stained. There was no answer, and in frustration she rapped harder.

Finally Michelle responded in a dreamy voice, "What is it?"

"What is it?" Marguerite repeated. "It's time to go to the ball! Aren't you two ready yet?"

"We'll be a little while longer, Aunt Marguerite," called Léon. "Why don't you go on without us?"

"We've lent out all the carriages except one," Marguerite cried in exasperation. "How do you expect me to go? By dogcart?"

"Use the coach and then send it back."

"No, I won't go alone." She pressed her head against the shutter and whispered to herself, *"I can't."*

"Then you'll just have to wait for us," said Léon irritably. "We'll try not to be too long."

"I'll be in the foyer," replied Marguerite, and limped away.

Léon and Michelle were lying nude on the carpeted floor of their dressing room. Between them, on a tray alongside a nearly empty bottle of wine, lay a still-smoldering pipe containing opium.

"Can you feel it yet?" asked Léon.

"Oh, yes!" Michelle turned toward her husband and gazed at him provocatively through lowered lids. He smiled back in appreciation of her feline prettiness. Then he languidly brushed his lips over her forearm.

"I feel like I'm caught up in a dream," she giggled. "Everything's so soft and lovely and just a little bit out of focus. There are no hard edges to life anymore."

"I knew you'd like it. It will help us through the tiresome ball."

"Where did you get it, Léon?"

"Where everyone gets it—from the one-armed Chinaman. He gets it straight from Hong Kong."

"It's not addictive, is it?" she asked in a childlike voice.

"Only if you do it all the time—and we never do the same thing twice." They laughed in unison. Léon took a mouthful of wine, pressed his lips against his wife's, and let the liquid flow inside her mouth. Michelle was delighted by the sensation, and he continued until the bottle was empty. He tossed the bottle aside and then pressed his firm body against her yielding flesh. He traced his tongue along the line of her jaw, opened his mouth, and took her chin inside and began sucking on it.

"Léon," she protested weakly, "we can't now. Aunt Marguerite's waiting for us, and we're not even dressed."

"To hell with Aunt Marguerite," he replied as he teased her throat with his active tongue.

Michelle gently pushed him away. "Léon, she's an old lady; we can't disappoint her like this."

Léon was surprised and slightly disgruntled. Rarely did Michelle deny him his marital rights. He assumed that she was more anxious to attend the ball than she admitted.

"All right," he grumbled. I'll get dressed. But I'm not wearing undergarments."

Michelle squealed in mock consternation. "You aren't?" He shook his head. "Then I shan't either."

Their costumes were made of the same fabric—a tissue-weight muslin interwoven with gold metallic thread. Léon wiggled into his trousers and worked his arms into the matching jacket, which in lieu of a shirt had a froth of ruffles at the neck and the cuffs. Moving very carefully, he sat down and eased on his knee-high white calfskin boots, then stood up to allow his wife to admire him.

"Léon, you look beautiful. If I squint, you look very nearly naked."

Michelle's gown was in the Empire style, with the back cut almost to the waist. Perilously thin straps held in place a bodice that was indiscreetly lower than fashion dictated. A snug belt of the same insubstantial fabric was cinched beneath her bosom and helped draw attention to her ample breasts. The skirt fell in a smooth line to the current ankle length.

Léon stared at his wife with unabashed lechery. The lamp behind her shone through the fabric so that the lower half of her body was outlined in silhouette.

He wet his lips, his eyes smoldering. "Are you sure you want to go to the ball?"

There was another knock at the door, and Marguerite called plaintively, "Aren't the two of you ready yet?"

"We'll be right there, Aunt Marguerite," called Michelle.

They hurried to their closets to retrieve the matching cloaks. Knowing that their costumes would create a scandal, they had decided to keep themselves covered until arriving at the ball. They put the cloaks on, tied the bow under each other's chin, and opened the door. Marguerite nearly fell inside. She gaped at Léon and Michelle with disapproval. Her nostrils wrinkled, and her nose began to twitch.

"What is that dreadful odor?" she demanded.

Léon lied. "We've been enjoying a cigarette, Aunt Marguerite. They're the latest rage."

"Both of you?" Marguerite's tone was condemnatory. "Well, they make a terrible stench. If you ask me, they'll never become popular."

Theo drove himself to Salle d'Or. He had lent his usual driver to the Duc, to help man the carriages ferrying guests from dockside to the big house. In truth, the old man hadn't acted in a self-sacrificing manner; he simply liked to drive. He was nervous and excited about the prospect of seeing Julia Taffarel, and perhaps that had prompted him to arrive at the ball earlier than planned.

When he reached the front entrance, the Negrilions snapped to attention and vied with one another for the privilege of opening his carriage door. All of them knew Theo and were appreciative of the attention he paid them whenever their paths happened to cross. Theo complimented the six boys on their efficiency and presented each with a coin.

As he crossed the veranda, he nodded and smiled at those people who looked familiar—faces seen just once or twice a year at the Duc's functions. He knew he had been invited only as a neighborly gesture, for he and the Duc did not socialize. They had nothing in common except that they both owned plantations at Magnolia Landing. Theo was sweating profusely as a result of his anxieties. He wiped his hands on the back of his trousers and wished that he had worn gloves.

The doors were opened by two uniformed slaves, and Theo entered into the glamorous world of the socially elite of New Orleans.

In spite of his lack of warm feelings toward the Duc and his disapproval of the man's extravagances, Theo was as impressed as the other guests with the fantastic decor of the ballroom. He was looking for the host and hostess when he was confronted by a strange-looking couple wearing half masks.

"Theophilus Beauchemin, I'll bet you can't guess who we are?"

Theo sighed to himself. "Good evening, M'sieur and Madame Gadobert." He stiffly bowed and thought that there was no mistaking those receding chins.

The Gadoberts removed their masks. "You guessed," cried Madame Gadobert.

Theo winced. He certainly didn't want to be saddled with the Gadoberts for long. He was well acquainted with Emile from the Sugar Exchange and had met Emeraude and their son Gilbert many times—too many—at social functions related to the sugar industry. The *nouveau riche* Gadoberts owned a great deal of land near Lake Pontchartrain that produced an amazingly successful crop every year. Theo found them grasping, gauche, and essentially dull.

"We thought it was going to be a masquerade," said Emeraude, who continually blinked as she talked.

It should have been, Theo mentally responded, observing her tic with fascination, a smile frozen upon his face.

It was not easy for Theo to get away. Both Emile and Emeraude were short, animated people, and as pesky as terriers who had latched on to a trouser cuff. They both had crinkled brown hair, light green eyes that resembled unripe gooseberries, slightly off-center noses, and of course those distinctive chins—or lack of them. Theo strongly suspected they were first cousins, which would explain their son Gilbert.

"We came up on the *Belle Créole*" Emeraude announced. Theo figured it was her way of telling him they were on the Duc's first list.

"You know our son Gilbert?" said Emile.

"Indeed I do," Theo replied, nodding in the direction of their offspring. Gilbert stood a good foot taller than his parents and was considerably better-looking. He had a head of straight brown hair—now partially covered with the mask he had pushed up from his face—large, limpid green eyes, and a nose that stayed on course. Unfortunately, he was the recipient of the Gadobert chin. Theo thought him good-natured, if a bit slow-witted. He wondered why the Duc had put the Gadoberts on the first list this year.

"You haven't seen Alcée, have you, Theo?" Emeraude

asked, blinking rapidly. The Gadoberts persisted in calling everyone by their Christian names.

Theo slowly shook his head. "No, I haven't, Madame Gadobert. I've just arrived myself." Now he knew the reason for their invitation. Most likely the Duc was planning a match between Alcée and the heir to the Gadobert fortune. Poor Alcée.

He looked the Gadoberts over with new interest. All three were wearing vaguely Oriental costumes of the same cloth, which, Theo thought, could best be described as bladder green. The necks and cuffs were trimmed with a profusion of emeralds, which glittered in a blaze of green fire. Plus buttons and rings for the men, earrings, bracelets, and pins for Emeraude. Oh, well, Theo thought uncharitably, they need all the sparkle they can get.

"We were reluctant to come up by steamboat," Emile explained. "Even if the boilers don't blow, there are sandbars, fallen tree limbs, irregular channels, snags—"

Theo interrupted Emile's possibly endless list of dangers. "Please excuse me. I see our host and hostess, and I must compliment them on their . . ." He fumbled for a word. "Imagination."

As he crossed the ballroom floor, he heard Emeraude's voice trailing after him. "Don't forget—if you see Alcée, tell her that Gilbert . . ."

Given the Duc's reputation as something of a mountebank, Theo was not surprised to find him perched on a dais as if he were royalty. Also on the raised platform were Henriette and five other people, all of whom Theo recognized—the governor of Louisiana and his wife, the mayor of New Orleans and his wife, and the inevitable Verbena Chevereaux. The Duc, Theo noted, looked quite dapper in a suit of gold, complete with large diamond buttons. Henriette was wearing a magnificent mint-green gown embroidered with gold fleurs-de-lis. She seemed embarrassed, like a maid who had been caught trying on her mistress's clothes.

Theo reached the dais and bowed to the glittering assemblage. He exchanged brief greetings with all and chatted with Verbena. The widow tapped him on the shoulder with her fan and said, "Theo, you look divine in your uniform. Look how it fits after all these years! Well, you're simply a magnificent specimen, and that's all there is to it. If you were only a bit younger . . ."

Theo fell in with her banter. "I'm not looking for a wife, Verbena."

Verbena's eyes sparkled with mischief. "And I'm not looking for a husband, Theo."

A sudden hush fell over the noisy throng, and all heads turned toward the entrance to the ballroom. Even the orchestra faltered for an instant. Léon and Michelle Martineau had arrived, and everyone was staring at Michelle, who had just removed her cloak. While Marguerite still hovered in the background, Léon, with a grandiose gesture like a toreador, swept off his own cloak. A series of gasps rippled through the company. Most of the men gaped openmouthed. Creole matrons looked away, or else blocked out the offending sight with their fans. A dull thud resounded to Theo's left, and he suspected that somewhere one of the dowagers had fainted.

Eyes sparkling with self-importance, the young Martineaus made their way across the center of the ballroom floor directly toward the dais.

Verbena pressed her cheek against Theo's whiskers and said, "Sweet saints, that dress is cut so low that you can see her nipples! And he looks as if he has been dipped nude in whitewash."

Theo stepped off the dais, saying, "Verbena, you must excuse me, I'm in need of champagne." But she didn't answer; her eyes were riveted to Léon's approaching crotch.

As Theo made his way through the titillated throng, he thought that he hadn't seen such a turnout since the victory ball after the Battle of New Orleans. But here a different mood prevailed. The people attending that earlier ball had been celebrating their own and their commander's courage and perseverance. What, he wondered, were the people celebrating here? Wealth? Power? A rigid set of social rules concocted by themselves to be broken at will? Theo found the whole spectacle suddenly disheartening and repellent. He left the ballroom, crossed the back veranda, and went into the gardens. He spotted Blaise Christophe carrying a trayful of glasses.

"Blaise, I'll have one of those." Seizing a champagne glass, Theo drained it immediately.

"You look like you could stand another, M'sieur Theo."

The old man agreed. He accepted another glass of champagne and went farther into the garden, hoping to escape the self-indulgent crowd and the frivolous music.

* * *

Philippe Duvallon, attired in a suit of nubby chartreuse silk, excused himself from a knot of attractive young Creole women on the back veranda. They hardly seemed to miss him, for they were too intent on watching Blaise Christophe walk across the neatly cropped lawn to the outdoor bar to replenish his tray. Philippe cursed under his breath as he heard the women giggle, and he watched their eyes follow the handsome griffe.

When the bartender had arranged and filled another dozen glasses on the tray, Blaise, instead of staying at his assigned post in the garden, climbed the steps to the other end of the veranda and began winding his way through the crowd. He stopped in front of a pair of open French doors and craned his neck, as if hoping to catch a glimpse of someone.

Philippe came up behind him and caught him by the arm. He could barely control his temper. "What are you doing here on the veranda, damn you? You're supposed to be serving in the garden!"

"I heard somebody call for champagne, M'sieur Philippe." His tone was not apologetic.

"There are enough slaves up here to serve them. They don't need your help."

The young griffe did not reply.

"Get back to your post—now!"

Blaise withdrew. Philippe glowered after him. He didn't like Blaise. His outfit fit him too well. It was too flattering. And he was arrogant and far too good-looking for a slave. The Duc had been wrong in assigning him to such a highly visible position.

Philippe quickly forgot his anger when he saw Michelle step onto the veranda. He sucked in his breath when he saw what she was wearing, and he noticed that she was alone. If only she wasn't married, he thought; but married or not, she looked as if she might like a little something extra. To bolster his courage, Philippe called for more champagne. "Blaise, here!"

The griffe hurried back to the veranda, and Philippe grabbed a glass and drank it down. "Don't stare at me, you yellow bastard. Keep your eyes down like the rest of the niggers." Blaise moved away.

Philippe's head was swimming from the champagne, and at first he fancied that Michelle's dress was completely transparent. She was smiling at him. There was no mistaking that expression—he had seen it before on so many young women; it was most certainly an invitation.

Philippe absently handed his glass to a passing servant and walked toward Michelle.

"Welcome to Salle d'Or, Michelle. You look . . ." His eyes dropped to her breasts, and he paused and wiped his mouth with the back of his hand. ". . . wonderful."

Michelle's response was restrained as she acknowledged the compliment. He knew that she was playing the game in case anyone was listening.

"Would you care for another glass of champagne?"he asked.

Her eyes narrowed, and the reply was tart. "No, thank you."

He could not keep his hands off her. As if moving of their own volition, they enclosed each narrow wrist in a viselike grip. "Come, I'll show you the garden."

"I've seen the garden, Philippe." She tried to pull away from him—but that was all part of the game, he told himself.

Philippe shook his head so that his hair shadowed one eye. He puckered his lips and lowered his lashes seductively. His "look" had been well practiced in front of his mirror; it seldom failed to bend the will of the most obstinate female. He traced his tongue over his lips and said in a low, wet voice, "You haven't seen everything. There are secret places in the garden that only I know about."

With a gasp, she pulled her hands free and replied through clenched teeth, "Then I suggest you find one of them and compose yourself. I don't appreciate your compromising words."

She's playing it too realistically, he thought. "Michelle," he stammered, "I know you want me as much as I want you."

Her expression suddenly changed, and her smile mocked him. "I'm very surprised by your interest in me, Philippe," she said sweetly and loudly. "I was given to understand that your taste ran to women of a somewhat darker hue."

The young women behind Philippe giggled. He turned and shot them an angry glance, and when he turned back, Michelle was gone.

Philippe was confused. He was certain he hadn't misread her emotions. But why had she left him? Alcoholic reason took over. "She's afraid," he mumbled. "After all, she's married." He hiked up his pants and decided to circulate. She would probably seek him out later, and when she did, he would take her to the far edge of the garden to the wax room—a small building where the fruit of the wax trees was made into candles. There, beneath the hanging lines of fragrantly scented tapers, he'd find out just what, if anything, she was wearing beneath her gown.

Chapter Twelve

A miniature railroad made its way along a set of tracks laid out in an elongated oval. The tiny steam locomotive was precise in every detail and pulled a dozen flatbed cars, each bearing one tray, from the kitchen at Salle d'Or to the big house. The food arrived quickly and still warm from the oven or pot, and leftovers and dirty dishes were ferried back on return trips. The train was the Duc's newest plaything and had been installed just a week prior to the midsummer ball.

The railroad fascinated the slave children. Despite the efforts of the house servants and kitchen help to keep them away, the youngsters were drawn back to the mechanical marvel again and again, like metal shavings to a magnet. The tiny transport wasn't all that intrigued them, however. There were the heaping platters of food.

A half-dozen wide-eyed faces peered around the hedge as the last tray was being loaded from the kitchen. Seeing that the flatcars were momentarily unguarded, the children bounded across the lawn and crouched in the shadows of a tulip tree, gaping at the arrayed delicacies. The train lurched suddenly, its locomotive slowly gaining headway, and the children, unable to control their hunger, darted toward the tracks and thrust a dozen grasping hands into the cargo.

Ambrose, chef of Salle d'Or, appeared at the kitchen doorway. "Yo' chillun get away from dere, or I gets one of de guards to slice yo' into little bits!"

Cramming fistfuls of purloined food into their mouths, the children scampered away. Ambrose looked around and muttered, "Where are de guards? If de Duc catches dem chillun stealin' food, he have me whopped fo' sure."

Ambrose was a tall, bent old man with blue-black skin and

a circle of curly white hair around his moon-shaped head. His eyes were frightened and continually moving from left to right, as if he expected to find someone hovering over his shoulder. He caught sight of a muscular guard ambling across the lawn. "Yo' dere, Tooker!" The guard stopped and waited as Ambrose hurried to his side. "Another bunch of chillun was here stealin' de food. Yo' gots to keep dem chased off."

In a voice as rough as a cornhusk, the guard replied, "My job is to guard de white people, not dere food." He withdrew his machete, and for a moment Ambrose thought he was going to be cut down. The guard stretched out his long arm, speared a chicken breast from the last car of the departing train, and took a formidable bite. "I says one thing fo' yo', Ambrose—yo' sure knows how to cook."

Muttering with frustration, Ambrose trudged back to the kitchen. He began snapping at his helpers, who tonight included Zenobia, Aunt Lolly, and Lilliane from the other plantations. Uncle Prosper had been requested but was absent; he refused to be lent to the Duc and had informed Léon that if he were, he would run away.

Ambrose marched around the kitchen, spouting orders and in general creating a disturbance. Aunt Lolly, who was seated at a table, busy stuffing patty shells with snipes' tongues—a Creole delicacy—pointed a cautioning finger. "Yo' better simmer down dere, Ambrose, or yo' have a blood rush."

Ambrose turned on her. "Yo' hold yo' tongue!"

The rotund mammy threw back her head and laughed heartily. "Dat's jes' what I'm doin' brother, dat's jes' what I'm doin'!"

Aunt Lolly's good humor restored Ambrose's naturally gentle temperament. "I's sorry, sister," he apologized. "But de chillun was stealin' food from de train again."

"Doesn't the Duc feed his slaves properly?" Lilliane asked innocently.

Ambrose snorted. "Yo' jes' lucky cause yo' down at Villeneuve, and bein' a kitchen slave like me, yo' gets to steal all yo' wants."

Lilliane responded, "I don't have to steal food."

"Well, here dey does. Most of the field niggers gots to sneak out of dere shacks at night to trap animals and birds and frogs to fill out dere bellies."

Zenobia said, "Dat jes' don't make good sense. De field

hands work better if dey got full bellies, and dey don't get sick so much."

Ambrose shrugged his shoulders. "If dey don't work good or get sick here, dey get sold real quick. Sometimes dey makes de mistake of stealing from de Duc's private stock. De Duc don't hold with dat. If he catches yo', why yo' is just as good as dead. Yo' gets fifty lashes at least."

Lilliane looked around in exasperation. "But what about all this food? Surely there's going to be plenty of leftovers?"

Ambrose shook his head. "Only fo' de house slaves. De rest goes to de hogs. De Duc don't like spoilin' his field niggers with de taste of fancy food."

One of the slaves remarked, "I's glad I ain't a field hand. Bein' house slave is much better."

"Dat's all yo' know," Zenobia grunted. "House slaves is on call 'round de clock. Dere ain't no quittin' time fo' us. And yo' gots to keep dem white folks happy. Yo' gots to be careful what yo' says and even of de look on yo' face. A nigger's jes' a mirror fo' de white man—yo' gots to remember dat. Yo' gots to be always on guard not to let dem know what yo' is thinking."

"But yo' part of de family," another slave said. "Particularly if yo' de mammy."

Zenobia's dark eyes became opaque and her words a litany. "If yo' don't know nothin', sister, den don't say nothin'. Yo' take to dem like dey was yo' own; yo' suckles dem; yo' wipes dey butts; yo' dresses dem; and when dey big enough yo' covers up dere follies from dere parents. All dat effort and dey grow up, take a good look at yo', and some part of dem hates yo' 'cause yo' is a nigger. And ain't nothin' gonna change dat. Dat's de way de white folks thinks."

Aunt Lolly protested. "Not my chillun."

"Dey ain't yo' chillun', sister, and yo' always gots to remember dat."

Lilliane spoke up. "I'm lucky. Azby's my own natural born. He'll never turn against me."

Zenobia shook her head. "He one-half white, sister. Dat's a tough row to hoe. Nobody gonna accept him. He ain't all yo's. He's half his papa's."

"He's mine!" Lilliane protested. "And nobody—not the Lord God himself—is ever going to take him from me."

Zenobia, softening, reached out and patted Lilliane's hand. "I hopes not, sister. I sincerely hopes not."

Ambrose said, "I better check on dat train. If dem chillun steal dem vittles again an' de Duc catches dem, it's my hide dat gets whopped." He scratched his head. "Since de Duc just put in dat contraption, I don't rightly know how many lashes dat amounts to."

"What yo' mean?" Zenobia asked, narrowing her hooded eyes.

"I mean de Duc got my punishments all figured out science-tific. Ten lashes if somethin' cold. Fifteen if it burn. And twenty—"

"Is yo' tellin' de truth?" Zenobia interrupted. "De Duc really whips yo' fo' all dem little things?"

"He don't do it hisself," Ambrose explained. "M'sieur Philippe, dat's his pleasure. He meaner dan any slave driver. I 'members once, three years ago, dere was a light-colored little gal eight months gone, I reckon. Well, I don't know what she did to make him so crazy wild, but one night when he was jes' about as drunk as I'se ever seen him, he dragged dat little gal—Annie was her name—out to de stables so dat he could whip her away from de house. Dat way Madame Henriette don't hear nothing."

Lilliane turned toward Ambrose. Her shoulders began to quake, and a drop of perspiration crawled down the side of her head.

" 'Cause she was so swollen with the baby, he made her dig a hole in de ground fo' de belly. Den he made her lay down in it, and he starts whipping her. One of de slave drivers even offered to take her whipping for her, but M'sieur Philippe, he says no, and he whipped her and whipped her until dat baby was born right in dat hole in de dirt. Of course it come out dead."

The slaves were quiet, even the ones who had heard the story before. They continued their work but did not look at one another or speak. It was a bitter tale for them to digest, but there was no reason not to believe it, given what they knew of Philippe Duvallon.

Lilliane was afraid she was going to be sick. She pressed her legs tightly together and lowered her head. The others didn't notice her, for their attention was still focused on the ghastly story.

"And Annie, did she live?" Zenobia asked finally.

"Oh, yes, she live, but she never right in de head after losing dat baby. One night she mix herself up a dose of jimson weed and went to bed. In de morning she just never woke up. Dat M'sieur Philippe wouldn't let us bury her proper. He took her hisself down to de swamps, and I 'spects he fed her to de 'gators."

A convulsive spasm racked Lilliane. She pitched from the stool as if pushed by an invisible force and thudded to the floor, her body twitching. The women jumped up to attend her. Lilliane felt a wetness begin to flow between her legs. Her period had arrived. An odd smile formed on her ashen face.

"What is it, sister?" asked Aunt Lolly.

Lilliane lifted her head and whispered, "My period. It finally came."

Zenobia said to Ambrose, "We gots to send her home. She's in no condition to be working."

"No," protested Lilliane, "I'm not going until Azby is through with his duties. I'll be fine. Really I will."

"Where can she rest?" Zenobia asked. The chef looked over his shoulder before answering.

"Sometimes I lays down in de storage room." In spite of the situation he smiled. "Dat only five lashes."

Zenobia and Aunt Lolly helped Lilliane to the store room, which was attached to the kitchen but far enough away from the heat and the noise.

While Zenobia supported Lilliane, Aunt Lolly unrolled a worn quilt and spread it across some burlap bags that were filled with rice. "Dere, little sister, yo' rest now."

"Could I have a pan of water and some cloth?" asked Lilliane. "I'd like to clean myself."

"I brings dem right away," said Zenobia.

Lilliane lay back on the makeshift bed and closed her eyes. It was cool in the storage room, and the mixed aroma of grain and spices was somehow comforting. "Thank you, dear God, sweet Jesus, Papa Legba," Lilliane murmured. She took the coming of her period as a sign. The gods would show her the way to save herself and Azby.

The Duc leaned over to Henriette and, without moving his lips, said, "Gilbert is looking for Alcée, and she is nowhere to be found. Find her. And for God's sake stop fumbling with that cross! Tuck it in the bodice of your dress; it looks sacrilegious."

"How can a cross be sacrilegious?" Henriette murmured.

The Duc jabbed her in the ribs with his knuckles. "Find her!"

Whimpering, Henriette hurried away from the dais. As she circled the veranda in search of Alcée, guests tossed random compliments at her, like scattered flowers before a conquering hero. *Why are they complimenting me?* she wondered. *This isn't my party, and most of them don't even remember my name*.

Henriette caught sight of her daughter in the north gardens. She was alone on a bench, almost completely hidden beneath a camellia tree.

As Henriette approached, her spirits were lifted by the pride she felt for her daughter. Alcée looked so beautiful. Her raven black hair was arranged in an upsweep, with a cascade of curls spilling from the crown down the back of her neck. On either side of her head she wore a magnolia bloom of pale yellow silk. Her gown was flattering both for her age and her coloring. It was of sheer silk the color of topaz and had a scooped neck, small puffed sleeves, a fitted waist, and a full-blown skirt that fell to her ankles. The bodice was trimmed with a gathering of fine eyelet lace a shade lighter than the gown.

"Alcée, why are you sitting here alone?"

Alcée lifted her head in surprise. "Mama, come sit down. You must be exhausted, having to perch on that throne and smile at a lot of people you barely know."

Henriette joined her daughter on the bench. "No, I'm enjoying myself," she lied. "And you? Why aren't you dancing with some handsome young man?"

"The handsome young man I want to dance with isn't able to, Mama."

Henriette looked alarmed. "What's the matter, is he hurt? Has be been injured?"

Alcée regarded her mother with affection. "Hurt, yes. Injured, yes. He's both of those things."

"Alcée, are you in love with someone I don't know about?"

Alcée crossed her fingers and replied, "No, Mama, I was just being dramatic." She put her arm around her mother's shoulder and said wearily, "I suppose Gilbert is stalking the corridors of Salle d'Or, looking for me."

Her mother giggled in spite of herself. "Yes, he is. Your father sent me to find you, but I decided to warn you instead."

"You're a dear, but I suppose I'll have to do my duty and dance with him at least once."

"He's not so bad," offered Henriette.

"He's vain and stupid, not to mention chinless—but not so bad." Alcée released a long sigh. "You might as well go back inside, Mama—I'll be right in. But if I'm going to dance with Gilbert, I'll have to fortify myself with another glass of champagne."

As soon as Henriette left, Alcée got up and hurried past several slaves bearing trays of champagne, but she did not stop them. She was looking for Blaise.

She found him a few minutes later, at the other end of the garden. He was watching one of the spider monkeys that the Duc had imported from South America especially for the ball. The poor animal, frightened by the noise of the cannon and disoriented by the strange surroundings, was tethered by a chain, its arms clutching a tree trunk as it shivered with terror. The monkeys had been leashed at the Duc's orders so that they couldn't get into the food, bother the guests, or run away. And they had not been fed: the Duc didn't want them defecating during the party.

Alcée watched as Blaise took a piece of fruit from a passing tray and tossed it to the furry little animal. The monkey caught the fruit, sniffed it suspiciously, then bit into it. As it chewed, it favored Blaise with what Alcée interpreted as a smile of appreciation.

Alcée was so filled with pride for the man she loved that she could hardly keep from crying. She slipped up behind him and, her heart in her throat, asked, "Could I have a glass of champagne, please?"

The griffe turned and, smiling broadly, lowered the tray. As Alcée lifted the glass to her lips, she said softly, "I want us to be together tonight."

"Yes, my Alcée," he whispered in response.

Her dark eyes sparkling in anticipation, Alcée finished the champagne and hurried away. As she reached the veranda, a score of young Creoles, vying for her favors, surrounded her like hunters trapping their prey.

The cannons boomed again. Suzanne, reacting quickly, pulled the reins taut to keep the horses from bolting. "A stupid and dangerous pretension," she muttered, and pulled harder on the reins. The horses resisted, and the leather was yanked through her hand, burning her palm.

When she complained, Angélique said, "You should have had one of the slaves drive us, Suzanne. How do you suppose it's going to look, arriving in a driverless carriage?"

Suzanne replied lightly, "Everybody knows we're broke; there's no need for subterfuge. Besides, I prefer Seth as driver, and since he's unavailable, I'd rather do it myself. And we'll need the space if we're going to bring Seth and Zenobia back with us."

"I don't know why they have to ride with us, Suzanne. I'm sure the Duc's made some provision for returning our slaves."

"It's just more practical this way." She changed the subject. "We should have started earlier."

"Yes," agreed Angélique. "Everyone will think that we're among the second group to be invited."

The horses, now calm, pulled the carriage at a steady pace down the Promenade, and the two women were quiet, each lost in her own thoughts. Both Angélique and Suzanne were usually prompt—it was one of the few traits they had in common—yet they had dawdled over their makeup, fiddled with their ball gowns, and fussed with their hair. The reason for their procrastination, however, was painfully apparent to both of them.

Heritage was no longer theirs; they were living off the charity of a stranger. The prospect of attending the ball under such circumstances was not attractive. How were they going to fend off impertinent questions and deal with expressions of sympathy? They both knew the evening was going to be an ordeal.

With a touch of malice Angélique asked, "I wonder how M'sieur Brannigan is going to get to the ball? All our carriages are lent out to the Duc except this one."

"I'm sure he's made other arrangements. If he had need of a carriage, he would have told me. I imagine he's going to ride over to Miss Julia's and accompany her in her carriage. I've never seen her, you know, and I must say I'm curious."

"I'm curious too. I haven't seen her for at least eight years." She laughed derisively. "She was quite a sight, I can tell you. Wearing an old patched dress and men's boots and her hair flying. She scared us half to death."

"Us?"

"Jean-Louis and me. When we were young, we use to

sneak over to her place and steal the feathers that her peacocks had dropped about the grounds. We didn't have any here—Papa couldn't stand their squawking. Anyway, one time I wanted to gather enough to cover the bodice of a ball gown, and after we had collected a dozen or so, Miss Julia suddenly appeared around the corner of the house, brandishing a hoe and shrieking like a harpy. Naturally we were frightened off. Looking back on it, I imagine that she actually enjoyed herself."

The story caused Suzanne to become wistful. "I don't suppose I shall ever get over my initial impression of the Promenade. When Jean-Louis brought me here the first time, I thought we had entered the land of fairy tales—that such a place actually existed. I thought that somehow life was going to be as simple and uncomplicated as those nursery stories led us to believe."

"You must have hated Jean-Louis," Angélique said passionately.

"Sometimes I did. He'd promise to change, and then do it all over again. But he was my husband, and I had to have faith. I had to believe that eventually he would change his ways."

"You should have given up."

"That's what Jean-Louis said."

"Do you hate him now?"

"No," Suzanne replied. "At first I did. But not now."

"You should never have come to Magnolia Landing."

"But I did, and I intend to stay and make the best of it. It is my rightful home, and I shall not be turned out of it. And I won't let you be turned out either."

"God damn Jean-Louis for placing us in such a dreadful position."

"I don't believe that God damns people for being weak. You mustn't allow yourself to become bitter, Angélique. Bitterness is harder to live with than forgiveness. Besides, I think I can turn around our situation."

"How do you expect to do that?" Angélique demanded.

"Let's just say I have a plan."

Angélique was about to question her sister-in-law further, but just then they approached the turnoff leading to Salle d'Or and came upon a long line of carriages stretching back in the direction of the Landing. A Negro driver stopped his carriage and allowed Angélique and Suzanne to take their place in the procession winding its way toward the big house.

Suzanne brought the carriage to a halt. The line moved slowly, and the two women's nervousness grew with each forward progress. Suzanne willed herself to act calm, at least, but the sound of Angélique's labored breathing did not help reassure her. "Take deep breaths, sister-in-law," she said. "And with each breath remember my promise. I will get Heritage back. *I will!*"

As Suzanne pulled to a stop at the front entrance, Seth jockeyed positions with the other Negrilions so that he could open the door of his mistresses' carriage. His aged face burst into a proud smile.

"Miz Suzanne, Miz Angélique, yo' looks mighty pretty," he said as he helped them alight. "I 'spect yo' going to be the most beautiful ladies here."

"Thank you, Seth," Suzanne said gratefully. The boy's presence and words bolstered her courage. She and Angélique might be penniless, she reminded herself, but at least they didn't look that way. Their coiffures, exactly the same, were the latest in fashion, with a part in the center and long curls falling over the ears. Their gowns were also similar in style, tight-waisted and ankle-length with gently ballooning skirts. Suzanne's was fashioned from burnished gold taffeta and had huge puffed sleeves and a round décolletage. The sleeves of Angélique's gown were capped and the neckline square. It was made of green-and-white ribbon-striped silk with an overskirt of sheer white net.

Taking each other's hand, they climbed the stairs and crossed the veranda. The main doors to the ballroom were open, their brass reflecting the candlelight from within.

Angélique stopped abruptly and gazed at Suzanne in terror. "Come on," urged Suzanne. "Let's get it over with." Angélique took a tentative step forward.

"I think I'm going to faint."

"No, you're not. Only weak people faint."

They paused at the threshold to take in the Duc's spectacular decorations, but when Suzanne looked at the crowd, the first thing she noticed was that everyone was watching her. The gossip was spreading in waves of murmurs. Suzanne took her sister-in-law's arm.

Angélique said between her teeth, "Haven't they anything better to do than enjoy other people's misfortune?"

"Perhaps they are staring at us for other reasons, Angélique. We probably look better than most of the women here."

Angélique seemed slightly heartened by these words, and Suzanne, much to her own relief, saw the Duc coming toward them, apparently to escort them in.

"What now?" Angélique whispered nervously.

The Duc kissed first Angélique and then Suzanne on both cheeks. "The Jourdain women," he gushed effusively. "The humble decor of my little fête is overwhelmed by your duplicate beauty."

"How kind you are, Alexandre," Suzanne replied, "but Angélique and I beg to disagree. We were just saying that you've outdone yourself again this year."

The Duc positioned himself between the two women, took their arms, and guided them across the floor toward the dais. He called for two more chairs and champagne for the women, then introduced them to the governor and the mayor and their wives, whom they didn't know, and to Verbena, whom they knew only too well.

Verbena grudgingly complimented Suzanne and Angélique on their gowns, adding, "They look brand new, and *so* expensive." Her implication was clear, and Suzanne bridled.

Angélique, however, had evidently overcome her nervousness, for she smiled cold-bloodedly and replied, "I daresay when one is young and attractive, one can wear anything."

Verbena drew back sputtering, and was saved from having to come up with a retort by the appearance of a handsome young Creole, who asked her if she would care to dance.

"Would I?" She snatched the young man's arm and made a hasty retreat.

"What an odious woman," Angélique said under her breath.

Suzanne settled back in her chair, sipped her drink, and told herself that the worst was over.

"Thank God for champagne," she whispered to Angélique. "I believe my fingers have actually stopped trembling."

Angélique opened her ivory fan and said, "I wonder if M'sieur Brannigan and Miss Taffarel are here yet?"

"I don't think so. But I'm glad they're coming. It will take some of the onus from us."

"What a combination! Ha! You must be aware of the way he looks at us. I have to admit it gives me pleasure to know he'd rather have our company than that of crazy old Julia Taffarel."

Suzanne said, "It could have been worse, Angélique."

"What do you mean? What could have been worse?"

"Somebody worse could have gambled with Jean-Louis. Somebody worse could now own Heritage."

"You speak as if you're defending that American."

"No, not defending him—but I do think he's trying to do his best to make us as comfortable as possible."

Angélique laughed. It was a bitter sound. "You happen to believe in people, Suzanne, and the more common they are the more you believe in them. Well, I've seen their dark side, and I know what people are capable of."

Suzanne settled back in the chair and sorted through her own thoughts. Yes, he was common, and he was probably capable of unimaginable things. Yet he was attracted to her, and she was counting on that.

Not bothering to dispute her sister-in-law, Suzanne smiled as she fanned herself, presenting the appearance of greatest ease.

Marguerite crept around the edge of the ballroom. She was glad that Léon and Michelle had gone off somewhere, yet she felt alone and discomforted. She wanted to approach the dais and talk to her friend Henriette, but looking as she did, she could not bring herself to be seen at close range by such luminaries as the governor, the mayor, and their wives—and certainly not by Verbena Chevereaux, whose caustic wit could be as devastating as a bludgeon. The Creole women of Marguerite's own age—self-satisfied, stout matrons for the most part, with husbands, social position, and wealth—were sitting in a line, watching the dancers and gossiping behind fans. They had asked her to join them, but Marguerite could not bring herself to do it. Their efforts to draw her into the conversation had been patently condescending; they knew she was an unwanted spinster who would probably soon be turned out of her home.

Overcome with self-pity, Marguerite began to cry. She quickly opened her fan and covered her face. Bits of green feather fell to the floor. She edged her way toward a pair of open doors to find a place where she could suffer her disgrace in private.

The food kept coming, with scores of slaves bearing trays of hot meats, cold meats, terrapin, shrimp, and crab. She saw platters of snipe and quail, vegetable salads, fresh fruit, wines, and liquor carried into the huge room. The sight of so much food nauseated her. She stumbled out onto the veranda and made her way through a group of jubilant young people; as she descended the steps toward the gardens, their laughter seemed to mock her. Half blinded by tears, she ran across a lawn and finally found a deserted area. She did not stay on the pathways but tripped through the rose beds, oblivious of the damage she was creating and of the harm the thorns were doing to her gown. She stumbled down a flight of stone steps, breaking off the loose heel of her shoe. Her chest heaving with her sobs, she reached a grove of mimosa and leaned against the trunk of one of the trees, fighting for breath. The gardens, glittering with flowers and peacocks, reeled around her.

She turned, and something blocked her line of vision. A spider monkey hung limply from a chain attached to its neck. Marguerite, her heart hammering against her rib cage as if it were going to burst from her chest, stared in fascinated horror. A light breeze stirred the horrible object, and it turned around slowly, as if twisted by a living hand. Her lips stretched taut over her teeth, and a wordless scream of anguish escaped her throat. Then her eyes went blank and she fell limply to the ground.

Having found no kindred soul to talk to, and having consumed more champagne than he thought wise, Theo decided to return to the ballroom and partake of some food.

As he passed through a set of French doors, he noticed that several of the panes were cracked. Knowing of the Duc's penchant for perfection, he was surprised. A moment later, he nearly collided with the Duc himself, who was prancing about in a state of advanced agitation.

"The third steamboat is delayed! Now, I ask you, Theo, how can I plan a proper midnight supper with people not arriving on time?" Without awaiting an answer, the Duc hastened off in the direction of the kitchen.

Theo ignored him; he was busy debating whether or not he should leave now, before Julia arrived. He wondered if it were wise to reexpose himself to a grief that was so old, so intimate, it had become almost an appendage of himself. He decided to stay.

On his way to the buffet table, he had to pass the seated

group of Creole matrons and could not help overhearing their conversation.

". . . happy? What does it matter if she's happy? He buys her everything she wants . . ."

". . . I heard that Verbena Chevereaux and the governor . . ."

". . . Creole, my foot! Her father was a fur trapper and her mother a Choctaw squaw . . ."

". . . the Jourdain women don't seem like they're grieving to me . . ."

". . . imagine, appearing half nude! Those Martineaus are as nervy as gnats!"

". . . no, he's not here yet. Of course he's coming with that mad Julia Taffarel. He's probably having trouble getting her out of the attic!"

When he reached the buffet table, Theo helped himself to a plate of peppered shrimp. As he bit into one, his gaze settled on Angélique Jourdain, who was standing in a group a few yards away. As always, she was extraordinarily beautiful—but for the first time Theo noticed a slight twitch playing at the corner of her mouth. Her green eyes seemed to brim with an uncontrolled panic, like those of a trapped animal.

Theo felt sorry for her. He could understand her predicament. Of course it was Suzanne who had lost a husband, but Theo knew that she had a moderately well-to-do family in Georgia. Angélique, on the other hand, had nothing except her beauty. And although it was undeniable that her beauty attracted men, it also inhibited them and frightened them off. Her beauty was too daunting, too overpowering. What man could possess her? On the contrary, her beauty would possess him. Was any man willing to give up that much of himself?

The orchestra was playing a saraband, a slow, stately Spanish dance in triple time. Theo noted that Governor Dupré was dancing with Lisette Prieur and that the governor's wife was dancing with the mayor. Perhaps a bit of political collusion? Philippe wandered through the ballroom, looking, Theo thought, like a hound in heat. He would not find any loose women of easy virtue here, except perhaps for Verbena Chevereaux.

As he followed Philippe's progress, he caught sight of the young exhibitionists, Léon and Michelle. The initial sensation that they had created had worn off, and now they looked bored. He pitied them just a bit. Young, rich, attractive, and obviously in love, yet so determined not to enter the adult world. He wondered what would become of them.

Someone bumped into him, and he quickly caught his fork before it clattered to the floor. He turned and found himself looking into the red face of Captain Calabozo.

"Excuse me, M'sieur Beauchemin." The captain smiled crookedly. "Why is it that my uniform doesn't look as good as yours?"

"I think your uniform is very handsome, sir. Why don't you have something to eat? The food is excellent."

"I'm as good as anyone here," Calabozo announced in a loud, thick voice.

"Of course you are. Now, why don't you try some of the—?"

Calabozo lurched away, heading toward the fountain of champagne.

As Theo was biting into a pastry—it was filled with snipes' tongues, he discovered—he spotted the Gadoberts bearing down upon him.

"Look, look," barked Emeraude. "Gilbert's found Alcée!"

"They're dancing together." Emile jabbed his arm across Theo's plate, pointing in the direction of the dancing couple. Theo noticed that one of the snipes' tongues stuck to Emile's sleeve, but he did not mention it.

"Don't they make a lovely couple?" gushed Emeraude.

Theo looked at Alcée. Her face was that of a weary madonna who had answered a mortal's prayers but who was now having second thoughts about it.

The Gadoberts began waving and calling to Alcée and Gilbert. Blushing in embarrassment for the young woman, Theo took advantage of Emile and Emeraude's inattention to him and quietly disappeared into the crowd.

Alcée waved back to the Gaboberts, all the while thinking that if she married Gilbert, her children would look exactly like him and his parents . . . squat little gnomes with foreshortened faces. She looked up at her dancing partner. He had pleasant manners, at least, and he danced well, as did all young men in her world. It was not his grace or manners, however—or even his nonexistent chin—that drove her to distraction. It was his conversation. Gilbert's favorite subject was himself.

The dance ended, and Alcée almost applauded with relief.

Gilbert stood preening in front of her and finally said, "I dance the saraband quite well, don't I?"

Alcée could have screamed. Didn't he know how to begin a sentence without an "I?" Smiling sweetly, she said through clenched teeth, "*I* don't feel like dancing anymore, Gilbert. Why don't we meet in the garden, later?" She fluttered her lashes as a further enticement. "I'll meet you at the rose hedge."

"Why can't we go there together?" he complained.

"That would be quite compromising. Besides, I want to get a wrap. The wind is up and the night air has grown cooler." She started to leave.

"How will I find the rose hedge?"

"Just ask Philippe—he'll give you directions. And bring some champagne."

"But—"

"Now, don't disappoint me."

As she crossed the ballroom, Alcée was stopped again and again by male admirers asking for a dance. She muttered apologies and moved on quickly, aware of her father's disapproving looks. She was unsure of her direction. All she knew was that she had to get away from Gilbert. She stepped onto the front veranda and stood in the shadows, hoping to avoid attention. She wondered why so many people had come to the affair. Didn't they have anything better to do with their time?

People passed by without noticing her hovering in the darkness like a fugitive. Alcée thought about going back into the garden and looking for Blaise but quickly dismissed the idea. They would not even be able to acknowledge each other by name. She would have liked to shut herself in her room, bolt the door, and work on her macramé, but she knew her father would never forgive her.

She was just about to go back inside when a strange apparition appeared on the front drive. It was a carriage at least fifty years out of date. Although the cab had recently been painted, and the farm horses that pulled it had been groomed to a fare-thee-well, the efforts served only to make the final effect more bizarre.

Fascinated, Alcée moved closer to the stairs. The Negrilions were pop-eyed and openmouthed as an ancient Negro driver wearing a threadbare uniform jumped down from his perch. He spurned the help of the nearest Negrilion and himself opened the door for his passengers. The man whom she took to be the American gambler got out first, then helped Julia Taffarel step down. His back was turned, and she could not see his face—only his impressive physique, tightly encased in a suit of dazzling white linen. She was astounded when Julia stepped into the light. Alcée had seen her many times from a distance; as a child she had thought her a frightening witch, but later had realized she was just a sad old woman. Now that same old woman was marvelously transformed, her hair arranged in soft white waves that seemed to add dignity to a gown of pale green taffeta with an overskirt of white lace and a soft, draped neckline and fitted sleeves. A rope of pearls wrapped tightly around her throat formed a collar of exquisite luster.

Alcée pressed her hand over her mouth and murmured, "I can't believe it. She looks like a queen!"

Then the man turned around, and Alcée caught her breath. She stared at the tall, dark-haired American gambler and decided then and there that Royal Brannigan was the handsomest man she had ever beheld. Even in the half-light, his deep-set eyes were the most remarkable blue, reminding Alcée of shimmering diamonds. His nose was a trifle broad by conventional standards of good looks, but his full mouth, humorous and sensual at the same time, was one to set Creole women dreaming of forbidden kisses. Underneath the white suit he wore a vest of burnished green and gold, which looked as if it had been hammered from metal and fit his expansive chest and narrow waist to perfection.

They both stood still for a moment, as if posing for a painting. Alcée was struck by what a peculiarly well-suited couple they made. A handsome dowager aunt with her favorite nephew.

She overheard the young man say to Julia, "We seem to be among the last to arrive."

Julia replied, "We are late on purpose. I planned to let them suffer in suspense. Do you realize that you're probably the biggest cause for gossip since the Americans took over New Orleans in 1803? And I wouldn't be surprised if you take over Magnolia Landing before you're done."

Royal laughed. "You're a treasure, Miss Julia, a goddamn treasure!"

As they started up the steps, Alcée emerged from the

shadows and greeted them. "Miss Julia," she said tenatively, "I'm Alcée Duvallon, and I'm so delighted you could come."

"Thank you, Alcée. You're quite lovely."

"And this can be none other than Royal Brannigan." She offered her hand, and as Royal took it, she added, "Welcome to Salle d'Or, M'sieur Brannigan."

"I think you mean that, mademoiselle."

Alcée grinned wickedly. "I do. I do."

Then, in what she knew would be interpreted as an act of rebellion against her father, Alcée escorted Royal and Julia into the ballroom.

As they entered, the nearest couples stopped dancing and stumbled against one another, as if the music had suddenly run out. Conversations ended in midsentence. With uncanny speed, the reaction spread, until every couple was speechless and motionless. Even the musicians were distracted. The conductor turned around, and the hand holding the baton fell limply to his side. Violins slid off course, clarinets spouted off-key notes, and cellos grumbled like unfed stomachs. Finally the orchestra ceased playing.

Standing behind the arrivals, Alcée glanced around the ballroom. Her father, seated at the dais, registered shock and indignation, and he was nervously yanking at the fingers of his gloves. Alcée caught his attention and frowned at him, and he managed to rearrange his face into a semblance of courtesy—but his eyes remained hard, and his mouth was having difficulty holding its smile.

Beside him, Henriette was slouched down in her chair, her face mottled with fear. She was pressing her scented handkerchief to her mouth and appeared to be having difficulty breathing.

Verbena's reaction was the least surprising. She parted her wet, devouring lips, revealing sharp, very white teeth. Her blue-violet eyes narrowed with a predatory gleam; it was obvious what she was thinking.

Repelled, Alcée looked away, and her gaze fell upon Suzanne. Anger and resentment dominated the young widow's face, yet Alcée detected a trace of something else, though she was not sure what.

Alcée glanced next at Angélique, and what she saw startled her. Angélique's face was almost ugly. Her eyes were stony and her lips drawn and set. An emotion frightening in its intensity seemed to freeze her face, and that emotion could only be called hate. Alcée shivered and looked away.

The room was quiet except for the gurgle of the fountain; the entire company seemed to be holding its breath. Suddenly Alcée remembered Theo, and she wondered what he was feeling. Like everyone else at Magnolia Landing, she knew the story of Theo's and Julia's unrequited love. She spotted him on the far side of the champagne fountain. His eyes were riveted to Julia. His face, like Angélique's, was frozen in intense emotion, but Alcée was certain it was not hate.

The Duc suddenly stood up and looked around, as if surprised to find himself standing. He stepped off the dais and started toward Royal and Julia. Alcée could imagine his thoughts: For years to come the gossips would forget his pageant, forget the coup of getting the governor and his wife to attend; all they would remember was the appearance of Royal and Julia.

As the Duc approached the newcomers, Alcée stepped aside. The Duc was just a yard away, his mouth already forming a greeting, when suddenly the cannons boomed. The third ship had arrived.

Tension was so high and the cannon fire so unexpected that the crowd gasped as one. The prisms of the chandeliers rattled, and the already cracked and weakened panes of glass in the French doors began to fall to the floor and shatter. Women screamed, men cried out, and people crowded away from the doors in a panic as shards of glass flew in all directions.

The cannon fire ended, and the last piece of glass fell to the floor. There was a pause, then everyone grew quiet and turned back to the interrupted scene.

Julia was the first to speak. "I should get out more often, M'sieur Duvallon. That was indeed an inventive reception."

Everyone laughed; the tension was released. The Duc had no choice but to laugh with them, and he welcomed Julia and Royal with all the effusion he could muster. But he neither kissed Julia's hand nor shook Royal's. Then he quickly excused himself and began issuing orders at the slaves to clean up the glass. Pausing before the bandstand, he roared, "Play something! What do you think I'm paying you for!"

The orchestra struck up a lilting waltz. Alcée watched from a discreet distance as Royal took Julia's hand and guided her to the dance floor. How beautifully they danced together! Sweeping and gliding, they circled the fountain with a grace and élan surpassing anything Alcée had seen before. For a few measures, Royal and Julia were the only ones dancing; then little by little other couples joined them, until the entire ballroom was filled with the soft, measured thread of gliding feet and the rustle of skirts.

Chapter Thirteen

The waltz ended and Theo walked onto the dance floor. He introduced himself, then asked Royal, "M'sieur, may I have your permission to dance with the most beautiful lady at the ball?"

"Of course, M'sieur Beauchemin. You'll find that she is as light as a feather."

"I remember," Theo replied.

Royal stepped back. Neither Julia nor Theo spoke at first; they just gazed raptly into the other's eyes. Then the music began again. It was another waltz. Theo put his hand around Julia's waist, and, looking younger than their years, the two of them danced away.

Someone tapped Royal on the shoulder.

"Quickly, m'sieur, dance with me." He turned around and was pleased to find that the request had come from Alcée Duvallon. "That is, if you don't mind."

"It would be my pleasure, mademoiselle." He took her in his arms and started to waltz her around the floor.

"No, no, not in that direction. There's someone I'm trying to avoid. You see that young man over there? Standing in the doorway?"

"The one clutching a bottle of champagne and sweating profusely?"

"Yes," Alcée responded gaily. "He looks as though he's been running, doesn't he? Probably summoned by the cannon fire."

"A suitor?"

Alcée frowned and nodded.

"But he hasn't any chin!" Royal said.

The bottle that Gilbert was holding suddenly exploded, and he was bathed with champagne and foam. Alcée began laughing uncontrollably.

"You'll have to excuse me, m'sieur." She clamped her hands over her mouth and ran in the opposite direction from the damp young man.

Royal went in search of a drink. He found a waiter, took a glass of champagne, and watched a pair of nervous slaves sweeping up the last of the shattered glass from the French doors. The incident of the breaking panes had unnerved him and revived memories best forgotten—the night following his mother's funeral, when he had smashed everything in the display room of his father's glassworks, and . . . Royal drained his drink. And the morning, many years later, when Jean-Louis Jourdain had hurled his final glass of champagne into the fireplace at Odalisque.

Royal was startled out of his reverie by the gruff sound of the Duc's voice. "Ah, M'sieur Brannigan, I'm so pleased that you are availing yourself of my hospitality."

The American scrutinized his host. The Duc's hospitality was indeed generous, but Royal suspected that his motives were not. "An excellent champagne, m'sieur."

"I demand the best . . . of everything," the Duc replied. His dark eyes moved restlessly as he spoke, and although his voice remained congenial, his smile was gone. "I trust you are settled in at Heritage?"

Royal nodded.

"And you are getting along with the lovely Jourdain women?"

"Ours is a business arrangement, m'sieur."

The Duc obviously expected Royal to elaborate and looked disappointed when he did not.

"You've got an excellent piece of property there, M'sieur Brannigan. No doubt you will do well with it."

"I intend to. My overseer tells me that we have a promising crop this year."

"If you should need any advice, I shall gladly make myself available to you."

"Thank you."

"Ah, I have yet to introduce you to my wife and our guests of honor."

As the Duc guided him toward the dais, Royal was acutely aware of the stares and whispers accompanying their progress. He wondered why his host was bothering with such a formality. Was it to show everyone how magnanimous he was?

At the platform, the political couples greeted Royal with feigned courtesy. Royal remembered the Duc's wife from his trip upriver and thought that she looked about to faint as he kissed her hand.

"Of course you know the Jourdain women," said the Duc with unconcealed relish.

Royal wondered whom the Duc was trying to embarrass—him, or Angélique and Suzanne.

Suzanne nodded imperceptibly. "Of course."

Angélique did not acknowledge Royal; instead, she suddenly stood up and walked from the dais. Royal noticed that the Duc's smile had returned.

"And," the Duc continued, "the ever-enchanting Madame Verbena Chevereaux."

Verbena leaned forward and extended her hand. In doing so she treated Royal to an unimpeded view of her breasts—an action, he suspected, that was not accidental.

"Your reputation, as they say, has preceded you, M'sieur Brannigan," she breathed.

Royal was amused. "My reputation, madame?"

She let her hand slide under his and stroked his palm with her sharp fingernails. "Your reputation as a man who plays the game and wins."

Royal frowned in response to her tasteless comment. He was sure Suzanne had overheard it. Perhaps Verbena had meant her to. To avoid any further embarrassment to Suzanne, Royal said, "Would you care to dance, Madame Chevereaux?"

"But of course. I thought that was your reason for coming to the dais."

Royal clutched Verbena's narrow waist and spun her across the floor.

"You have remarkable hands, m'sieur," she murmured. "So large and yet *so* well formed. The hands of an artist, I should say."

"In some circles gambling is considered an art."

"I don't travel in those circles, m'sieur."

"There are gambling places in New Orleans where ladies are welcome."

"Sweet saints, I wouldn't be caught dead in one of those prissy little parlors where doddering old ladies drink lemonade and place penny bets on a roulette wheel. That's not my idea of excitement."

"And what is your idea of excitement, Madame Chevereaux?" Royal mentally counted the ways she could answer the question, but knew that whatever her response, it would have but one meaning.

"I should like to watch you . . . *play*, M'sieur Brannigan."

"I don't play anymore, madame."

"Thc odds arc on your side, m'sieur."

Royal smiled wryly at his dancing partner. He was not surprised at her behavior. Her flawless beauty and bawdy sense of humor were much discussed in New Orleans. But there were other things said about her, things spoken only in whispers between men. Stories of perversity and debauchery that he had not believed at the time of the telling, but now, gazing upon the bewitching Verbena, he reconsidered.

The music ended, and the passengers from the third steamboat began to stream into the ballroom. They were boisterous and eagerly began to gorge themselves on the Duc's food and drink, as if intent on making up lost time.

Verbena shuddered. "The common people have arrived."

"Then we should both feel more comfortable."

Royal could tell that his remark surprised her, but she dismissed it with a shrug and turned her back to the new arrivals.

Royal gave her his arm and guided her through the surge of humanity back to the dais. He noticed that the chair on which Suzanne had been sitting was now empty. Verbena resumed her own seat, smiled sweetly, and said, "Both of your tenants seem to have disappeared."

"They're not my tenants."

She looked at him quizzically. "But you are the master of Heritage, are you not?"

"I'm merely the owner. It takes time to become the master of the house."

She stretched out her elegant arm and took his hand. There was a hint of alarm in both her grasp and her voice. "I'll see you at the midnight supper, won't I?"

"I'm escorting Miss Taffarel."

"But it's gauche to dine with one's escort," she said with a vehemence that surprised him.

"Then we'll see," Royal replied. He bowed, then turned away, to be quickly swallowed up by the motley crowd.

Why had he been so unwilling to respond to such blatant flirtation, Royal asked himself as he shouldered his way toward the champagne fountain. But he knew the answer to his own question. The Jourdain women—*they* inhibited him.

The situation was impossible. Jean-Louis's death had created a gulf too wide to be bridged. They both scorned him, and they revealed it with every word and action.

Royal scanned the room for a sight of Julia. He went to the back veranda and spotted her and Theo strolling in the gardens along the geometric flower beds. Royal was infused with empathy for the older couple. He hoped that they would be able to reestablish their friendship. If that was the only good to come of this ball, then he would consider all of the Duc's extravagance worthwhile.

Royal returned to the ballroom filled with optimism. He decided to take advantage of his notoriety and become acquainted with some of the young women in attendance. He would use his good looks and outgoing personality to full advantage and do his best to charm every last one of them.

A few minutes later, as he was dancing with a pretty brunette, Royal noticed a familiar-looking young man standing at the edge of the crowd, glaring at him. He asked his partner who the man was and was told it was Philippe Duvallon, the Duc's son. Royal wondered what he had done to make the young Creole dislike him so intensely.

Royal was with his third partner when the Duc, clapping his hands for attention, moved through the dancers, instructing them in a slightly hectoring voice to move into the gardens so that the slaves could prepare the ballroom for the midnight supper. The throng drifted slowly toward the open doors. They were delighted to find the gardens alive with entertainers—the Duc's promised *divertissements*. There were mimes, clowns, acrobats, puppeteers, jugglers, and strolling minstrels with mandolins, guitars, and flutes, who together easily seduced the pleasure-seeking throng onto the verdant lawns.

Marguerite, shocked into consciousness by the noise of the cannons, did not immediately get up. She lay in a stupor beneath the mimosa tree, not knowing whether she was awake or in a laudanum-induced trance. Then suddenly the evening came rushing back, bringing with it her dissatisfaction with her appearance, her feelings of humiliation. Finally, as her eyes focused on a shadow hovering above her, the image of the dead monkey came back to her. Quickly averting her eyes from the hideous dangling object, she got to her feet, retreated a safe distance, then began to brush off her skirts. The fabric was grass-stained and damp from the moisture of the earth. She steadied herself against the base of a tree. She felt sick and miserable. She couldn't return to the ball. Well, she thought, she would show them. She would go home. *Show whom?* an inner voice echoed. No one would even notice her absence.

Marguerite stumbled across the grass, unsure of her direction. All she knew was that she wanted to go home, take an extra heavy draft of laudanum, and find blissful oblivion from all of the pain she had suffered. "I'll walk home," she suddenly announced, to no one but herself. "They'll be worried when it's time for them to leave and I'm nowhere to be found."

She looked about, unsure what part of the garden she was in, for the surrounding trees blotted out any sight of the big house. She could hear faint music, but it dissipated quickly in the wind, and she couldn't be sure from which direction it was coming. With a sinking heart she realized she was lost. She vaguely remembered crossing some rose beds and running down a flight of stone steps. She couldn't have come too far. She would find her way back.

Her jaw set, Marguerite took a deep breath and, limping in her broken shoe, started off in what she hoped was the right direction.

With glass in hand, Royal wandered over the lawn. He stopped to watch the various performers the Duc had engaged. Onlookers were roaring with laughter at the antics of a melancholy patchwork clown as he put his troupe of trained dogs through their paces. The dogs, hairless and with protruding pink eyes, were dressed in ruffled skirts trimmed with bells and would not follow the man's commands, which, of course, was part of the act.

Royal heard Julia speak his name, and he turned around. She looked absolutely radiant. It was as if she were shedding years as the party progressed.

"You must forgive me, Royal. I didn't mean to disappear completely and leave you on your own."

"There's no apology necessary, Miss Julia. I couldn't be

more pleased that you've met up with M'sieur Beauchemin again."

"He's asked me to sit next to him at supper."

"By all means, do so. In any case," he added with a wink, "I'm not entirely on my own; there are quite a few attractive women here besides you. And if you get an offer to be driven home, take it. I'll use your carriage and return it tomorrow."

Her hand touched his cheek. "Royal, I think you're quite the kindest young man I've ever met. I'm so glad we came, and I thank you again for the wonderful gift of my ball gown." She placed her lips where her hand had been and whispered, "Wish me luck, Royal."

Royal watched her hurry back to Theo, who was waiting beneath a grape arbor. Royal smiled to himself and moved on to the next performer. This was a clown of a different sort, however, and Royal's smile vanished. He was a large, clumsily built man with a painted-on expression of inordinate stupidity. He was wearing a ragged suit of red, white, and blue stripes and apparently was supposed to represent the popular view of an American—that of a bumbling barbarian. As he executed his pratfalls, he farted to the tune of "Yankee Doodle Dandy." The crowd, delighted by his crude antics, cast nervous sidelong glances at Royal as he made his way through their midst. If they were expecting an angry reaction, they were disappointed. Royal dismissed the clown with a stony gaze.

Suddenly a loud, belligerent voice said, "You can always spot an American no matter how he's dressed." Royal turned around. Several feet away was Philippe Duvallon. He smiled, raised his champagne glass in a mock toast to Royal, then emptied it on the lawn. Royal started to walk away when Philippe grabbed his arm. "Have you nothing to say, American?"

"Not here, not now," Royal replied evenly. "I'm a guest in your father's house."

"You're not a guest," sneered Philippe. "Nobody wanted you. Nobody invited you. You're only here because you're Julia Taffarel's pet."

Royal took a step toward Philippe, and the people nearby grew quiet. "Not all pets can be trained, M'sieur Duvallon." With that Royal pulled out the waistband of Philippe's pants and emptied his champagne into the gap. He stepped back, and Philippe stared down at his pants in horror. The laughter grew until Philippe, burning with anger and embarrassment, ran to the big house.

Royal knew that he now had an enemy at Magnolia Landing, but with luck there would be no more such incidents this evening.

In another part of the garden he stopped to admire the muscular grace of a trio of acrobats dressed in skin-tight harlequin costumes. They elicited gasps from the onlookers as they spun through the air.

"They have magnificent bodies, don't they?" Verbena whispered hotly in his ear. She was standing so close to him that he could feel her hard nipples pressing into his back.

"Yes, they do, Madame Chevereaux. Interesting that you should notice."

"Why don't you call me Verbena?"

"Very well . . . Verbena."

"I've arranged everything," she said, blowing on the back of his neck.

Royal turned to face her. "What have you arranged, Verbena?"

"You're sitting next to me at supper."

"How did you manage that?"

"I have my ways," she replied, sliding her arm through his. "Shall we stroll?"

Dressed in dark clothes and stocking caps, Denis, Fleur, and Blanche crept across the gardens of Victoire. Around their necks they wore the chamois bags of graveyard dirt, and they had smeared lampblack on their faces for extra concealment. Denis carried one of his grandfather's carving knives for protection. Fleur, to his consternation, affected a large parasol. Blanche had stuffed a piece of honey cake into her pocket, but the honey had melted, effectively gluing the pocket shut, and hunger and frustration were causing her to whimper.

"Hush, Blanche," admonished Fleur. "One does not whimper when one is on a ghost hunt. Now, hurry up."

Denis glared at the parasol Fleur was twirling. "I don't know why you had to bring that silly thing along."

"I will not," she announced, "become moonstruck. Neither of you must let the moon get on your face. If you let that happen, you'll go crazy, just like ole Miss Julia."

The three children glanced nervously at the sky. The gibbous moon, framed by clouds shredded by the wind, took on the semblance of a hideous face with long, streaming hair.

The trio shivered and hurried on their way. When they reached the end of the driveway, Denis said, "We can't go down the Promenade. Grandpapa told me that the Duc was posting guards there.

"But won't the guards scare away the ghost?" Fleur asked.

"Ghosts don't scare. It's their business to scare people."

"I'm going to be scared," Blanche gurgled with anticipation.

The children made their way along the grounds that bordered the Promenade. Victoire ended, and the land belonging to Bellechasse began.

"It won't be much farther now," Denis whispered. "From here there's to be no talking. You two keep behind me, and Fleur, you've got to keep Blanche quiet." His tone became deadly serious. "Our lives may depend upon it."

"Our very lives," Blanche repeated, until she was shushed by Fleur.

The children continued at a steady pace. As they moved along they could see the guards standing watch. Then Fleur's parasol caught on a low hanging branch. She cried out in alarm, and Denis ordered, "Everybody down!"

The children flattened themselves on the ground. The parasol swung back and forth lazily from the branch, then dropped beside them.

Denis raised his head. The sound had alerted the guards. They stepped around the trees with their machetes poised, their alert eyes scanning the darkness. Then, after what seemed to the children an eternity, they resumed their posts, satisfied that the sound had been caused by a small animal.

Despite her reluctance to do so, Fleur collapsed the parasol, and holding it tightly against her body, she crawled along behind Denis and Blanche through the high grass. They reached an area just across from the driveway that led to Salle d'Or, and Denis suddenly realized that he hadn't planned for everything.

"Fleur," he moaned, "how are we going to get across the Promenade without the guards seeing us?"

Fleur, taking charge, considered the predicament for a moment, then replied, "We'll simply wait for the clouds to cover the moon, and when they do, we'll run across."

"But what if the moon comes out while we're on the Promenade? Surely they'll see us."

"My parasol," she said suddenly. "We'll open it up, stick some leaves and twigs into the lace, and hide beneath it. If the moon comes out, it will simply look like a bush uprooted by the wind."

"It's not big enough for all of us," Blanche put in.

"Then we'll make two trips," Denis pronounced. "I'll take you across one at a time."

It was decided. As quietly as possible, Fleur and Denis gathered handfuls of leaves, grass, and small twigs and worked them into the lace until they were satisfied with their handiwork. Then they waited and prayed. Finally a ragged bank of clouds drifted across the moon. Denis grabbed Blanche's pudgy hand and, crouching low beneath the parasol, scampered with her across the Promenade. He deposited her beneath a clump of laurel and, warning her to be quiet, slipped back across the road to get Fleur. As he and Fleur were crossing, the moon suddenly reappeared, stronger and brighter than before. They fell to the ground, clutching the large parasol before them like a miniature canopy. Dust whipped up by the wind spun around them like angry spirits.

They heard one of the guards cry out, "What dat?"

Another called back, "It ain't nothin', brother, jes' a bush dat's done blowed across de road. Let one of dem uppity drivers clear it away."

Scarcely daring to breathe, Denis and Fleur prayed that Blanche would remain quiet as they waited for the moon to disappear. The Promenade was plunged into darkness once again, and they scurried to the other side.

When she saw them, Blanche whined, "I'm hungry."

Fleur sighed, shook her head, then produced a handful of candied violets, which Blanche jammed into her mouth. They stripped the foliage from the parasol and folded it up, then continued on their way.

Summoned by the dinner bell, Verbena and Royal reentered the ballroom to find it transformed into an elegant restaurant. The chandeliers had been extinguished, and the only light now was a rosy glow emitted by the crystal globe lamps in the center of each round table. Punkahs—rectangular fans of stiff white linen—had been suspended from the ceiling over each table, and Negro boys stood in attendance to tug at the ropes and cool the air in Oriental fashion. One table, oval and larger than the rest, stood apart from the others at the far end of the ballroom. Verbena took Royal's hand and led him to it.

The lace-covered table was laid with silver implements that looked heavy enough to be dangerous. Freshly cut flowers were massed around clusters of silver candelabras. The china was Sèvres, and each dinner plate shone as brightly as a fallen moon. The imported wineglasses at each place setting were of cut crystal. Royal doubted if kings and queens dined in better style.

Verbena and Royal found their seats, which were designated by hand-lettered place cards and facing the ballroom. Royal could not help but congratulate Verbena on her resourcefulness. He noticed that the other guests favored by the Duc, besides his family, included the governor and the mayor and their wives, the young man over whom the champagne had exploded, and five others unknown to Royal.

Verbena whispered into his ear, "What on earth can they be doing at our table?" He followed her gaze. "Those three—the Gadoberts. The chinless wonders of New Orleans."

"Perhaps it's because their son has an eye for Alcée."

"Well, she could do worse. He's very rich and not too bad looking, if you can overlook his chin." She put her hand in front of her face and severed Gilbert's chin with her finger. "Hmmm . . . perhaps a goatee—a full one—would help."

The Duc stood up. Everyone turned toward the host. He raised himself on tiptoes, and when the ball room was quiet, he said in a clear, ringing baritone, "I'm happy to welcome you to Salle d'Or. I hope you have enjoyed my little party thus far. At the conclusion of our meal I have an important announcement to make, then we will all retire once again to the garden for the fireworks display. *Bon appétit.*"

He nodded toward the expected applause. The procession of food began with steaming bowls of spicy gumbo. Verbena wet her lips, pressed her thigh against Royal's, and said, "The Duc serves the best gumbo I've ever eaten, but he won't give even me the recipe."

Royal looked across the table at an empty chair and remarked, "Someone didn't show up."

"Someone didn't hear the dinner bell."

Royal ate slowly, savoring the rich flavor of the extraordinary dish. The table conversation centered exclusively on food and drink. Royal noticed that Verbena went at her food as eagerly as she pursued her other interests. Her right hand was busy above the table while the left was active beneath it. As she ate and talked vociferously, her fingers stroked and massaged his inner thigh. Royal felt his leg growing moist with perspiration under her touch. He kept glancing at the other guests to see if they were aware of what was going on, but they seemed to be totally involved with their meal.

Royal was nearly finished with the gumbo when he happened to look up and see Captain Calabozo stagger into the ballroom. The man's eyes were unfocused, and his face so red that it appeared as if blood were oozing from the pores. He tottered toward the Duc's table, making for the empty place setting. He grabbed the back of the chair for support and announced loudly, in a voice hoarse from alcohol, "You started without me." There was an embarrassed silence as he pulled out the chair. "My place is here with the elite. I'm as good as anybody." He sank into the chair and began slurping the gumbo. After several noisy spoonfuls he pitched forward, facedown, into the bowl. Those who were seated beside him jumped up and edged away in disgust.

Henriette cried, "Somebody pull him out—he'll drown!"

Philippe growled, "Let him drown. Let the sodden son-of-a-bitch die!"

No one made a move to help the captain. Suddenly Royal got to his feet, ran around the table, and yanked Calabozo's head out of the bowl. Henriette appeared at Royal's side and began wiping the man's face clean with her napkin.

"He's not dead, is he, M'sieur Brannigan?"

"No, just passed out. He needs some air."

"Will you please help me take him into the garden?"

They lifted the limp captain and supported him under the arms.

"Henriette, sit down!" the Duc ordered.

"I'm attending to our guest, Alexandre," she replied quietly. "Please proceed without me."

As she and Royal were leaving the ballroom with their burden, they heard the Duc scream, "Next course!"

Although Calabozo remained unconscious, his feet moved as if by reflex, lessening his helpers' burden. On the veranda Henriette said, "Let's carry the good captain into the garden, someplace that's out of sight of the other guests. There's a fountain not far from here. It's hidden by a hedge. If you would be so kind, m'sieur."

"Of course, Madame Henriette."

Henriette turned to Royal in amazement, "You remembered my name, m'sieur. I want to thank you for not mentioning our previous meeting to my husband. It would have upset him."

"Your husband seems to upset easily."

"It's one of his pleasures. Just a little bit farther, m'sieur. We're almost there. It's behind those hedges."

They deposited the captain on a curved stone bench that surrounded the fountain. Henriette soaked her handkerchief in the cold water and began applying it to his forehead.

"We've known each other for a good many years, M'sieur Brannigan. I knew Bartolomé even before I was married to the Duc."

The captain was stirred by her ministrations but did not return to consciousness. "I believe that at one time he would have liked to be a suitor. Unfortunately, he was a riverman and I was Henriette Villeneuve, and my social position kept him from approaching me." She sighed. "And so I met and married the Duc, and I thought I was going to be happy for the rest of my life." She paused and rewet her handkerchief. "I did love Alexandre, you see. Well, I can manage from here, m'sieur. I'll stay with Bartolomé so that he will not be alone when he—how do you say?—comes to. Go back to the supper and enjoy the food."

"Are you sure you'll be all right?"

"Yes, and thank you, m'sieur, for being kindhearted. I hope that you will be happy here at Magnolia Landing." Almost as an afterthought, she added, "So few of us are."

Royal returned to the party in time for the next course, which was a whole wild duckling, stuffed with mushrooms, rice, and fruit. A sparkling glass of dry rosé wine accompanied it. Royal noted that Verbena's attitude toward him had changed.

"You should have stayed out of it," she said as she bit into the leg of her duck.

"But Madame Henriette was right. He could have drowned."

"It's of no consequence. The Duc is furious with you. You've made an enemy."

"That's two this evening," replied Royal. "Perhaps I should try for three."

The supper progressed through a half-dozen more courses, and at the end of the feast, the Duc stood once again and called for silence. He cast a conspiratorial look at the Gadoberts, who smiled proudly in return, basking in his reflected glory. "My dear friends," he said, his voice rising over the heads of scores of attentive guests, "it is my pleasure to announce . . ."

Royal anticipated the Duc's words. He quickly looked across the table at Alcée, who seemed transfixed.

". . . the betrothal of my daughter, Alcée, to Gilbert Gadobert. I am sure you will all join me in a toast to the young—"

Alcée pushed herself to her feet. Her eyes were burning with outrage, her voice tremulous. "Papa—you—never—even—asked—me!" She burst into tears and started from the table. Gilbert stood up and grabbed her arm. She stared at him in loathing, scooped up a charlotte russe, and screamed, "Never!" as she smashed it into his face.

There was a stunned silence, and Verbena, never able to resist a good line, loudly remarked, "Alex, I thought the fireworks were in the garden!"

Chapter Fourteen

Salle d'Or looked enormous and sinister with its hulking turrets darkly silhouetted against the night sky. The dim light that emanated from the first floor made the big house appear as if it were the entrance to some weird subterranean realm.

The children slowly made their way toward the rear of the house, avoiding the driveway and keeping to the underbrush. They managed to elude the guards and reached the outer gardens.

"Listen—you can hear the music," Fleur whispered.

The soft, lilting sounds of the orchestra drifted across the dark grounds.

"It makes me feel romancy all over. . . ."

Suddenly Blanche started moving toward the big house. Head up and nose twitching, she walked forward as if in a trance.

"What on earth is she doing?" asked Denis.

"I knew it! She's been moonstruck!" exclaimed Fleur.

Denis rushed after her and caught her by the arm. "Blanche, what is it? What's wrong?"

"I smell food," she replied in the singsong voice of the hypnotized.

Denis and Fleur looked at each other in exasperation. "Blanche, we're on a ghost hunt!" cried Fleur.

"I can't hunt ghosts without nourishment."

"I'm hungry too," admitted Denis. "Let's get closer. Maybe we can snitch something."

"All right," conceded Fleur. "But nothing heavy. A gentlewoman never eats heavy foods at night."

"We'll go by the Duc's kitchen," Denis said. "Perhaps we can get something there."

They reached the Salle d'Or kitchens and were stunned by the sight of the miniature train.

"Well, will you look at that!" said Denis.

"What is it?" asked Blanche.

"A railroad train," explained Fleur. "You saw one when Grandpapa took us to New Orleans. Only this one is smaller and carries food."

"Mmmm. I like this one better," said Blanche.

The children crawled under the elevated tracks and chose a secluded spot where they could examine the leftovers that were chugging by on their way to the kitchen.

"Where are we going to put what we take?" Denis asked suddenly. "I don't have any pockets."

Fleur calmly opened her parasol and set it upside-down on the ground. "We'll fill up the parasol," she said. "Blanche, you hold it steady. You're too short to reach the train anyway."

They waited until the next trainload approached from the house, then Fleur and Denis darted out and grabbed indiscriminately at the leftovers, tossing handful after handful of food into the parasol. Just then Ambrose appeared at the kitchen door and saw them. Because of their soot-smeared faces, he mistook them for slave children.

"Yo' chillun get back to yo' quarters befo' I calls fo' Tooker! He gives yo' a whoopin' like yo' never felt!"

Denis and Fleur grabbed the parasol—now nearly filled with food—and, supporting it between them, hurried off, with Blanche trailing behind, gobbling at a piece of mango.

The children ran away from the big house, toward the less formal gardens and the cane fields beyond. They ran until they were out of breath, and when they stopped, they found themselves next to a bamboo grove. They sat down at the edge of the grove and tipped the parasol toward them. By now the food was thoroughly mixed together.

Blanche picked a shrimp out of a glob of charlotte russe, bit into it, and pronounced, "Mmmm, it's good with icing."

Overhead the wind rustled through the leaves of the bamboo. The tall grass surrounding the grove bent and turned in wild swirls, and suddenly a loud crashing sound told the children they were not alone. They moved closer to one another and looked about them, tense and wary. The food was momentarily forgotten.

A dark figure outlined by the light of the moon abruptly stumbled into their midst. The children cried out as one and scooted backward until they were stopped by the wall of bamboo. The food in their mouths remained unchewed as they stared at the specter. Its face, bleached by the moonlight, was nearly covered by loose tendrils of hair.

Blanche swallowed a chunk of cake whole and asked timidly, "Are you the ghost?"

Fleur said triumphantly, "I told you! I told you! It's a woman!"

Denis relaxed. "That's no ghost. That's Miss Marguerite. How are you, Miss Marguerite? What are you doing in such a state?"

"State? State?" cried Marguerite. "I'm still in Louisiana, surely?"

"Of course you are, Miss Marguerite," replied Fleur. "You must have been lost."

Marguerite, shoeless and disoriented, stared at the children for a long time before her mind registered their identities. "You're Theo's grandchildren, aren't you? Why on earth are you disguised as minstrels?"

"I'll explain later, Miss Marguerite," said Denis. "Why don't you join us for something to eat? We're having a picnic."

Marguerite, who hadn't eaten anything since breakfast, needed no urging. She sat down and arranged her torn skirts. Then, daintily, she pulled a wing from a partially eaten squab and said, "Maybe I'll have just a bite."

Half an hour later, after Marguerite and the children had eaten their fill, Marguerite emitted a tiny ladylike burp and said, "What a nice idea! No plates, no napkins, and nothing to clean up." She licked her fingers, then wiped them on her dress. "I feel ever so much better. Now, tell me, what are you three doing out here in the wilds?"

Denis explained to Marguerite their desire to see the ghost of Magnolia Landing, how he had obtained the graveyard dirt, and the reports that the ghost was generally sighted on nights of large social functions.

"That's all very interesting," said Marguerite. "But why have you blackened your faces?"

"To hide from the guards," said Fleur, rolling up her parasol.

"Oh, I see. Very clever."

Denis asked, "You won't tell Grandpapa, will you, Miss Marguerite?"

"I'm not an informer, Denis. But I'm afraid that you're going to be disappointed. There are no such things as ghosts. If people report them after social affairs, that's because they've indulged in too many spirits." She laughed at her own unintentional joke.

Suddenly the dark sky burst into shimmering light. The four scrambled to their feet and stared in amazement as a shower of phosphorescence began to fall.

"Fireworks!" Denis exclaimed.

"It's beautiful!" Fleur gasped.

"It's Christmas!" Blanche squealed.

Marguerite's laugh was a peal of spontaneous joy, as innocent and infectious as a child's.

She and the children joined hands and, bathed in the aura of the light, they walked toward the lights.

The opening pyrotechnic display had been meant to dazzle and command the attention of the sluggish guests, but now Philippe was working toward his planned tribute to his father. The crowd standing in the east gardens endured a rambling speech by the younger Duvallon as his assistants prepared the next demonstration. A lightweight frame, tethered to guide wires suspended from two towering oaks, would be propelled into the air by rockets. Then the design on the frame would burst into green and gold flames and spell out:

Salle d'Or
Midsummer Ball
1830

Philippe's recitation, muddled by champagne, dragged on and on, at last concluding with "and now a glittering tribute to my father, the Duc Alexandre Duvallon!"

The crowd obediently applauded as Philippe himself lit the fuse to the rockets that would carry the frame to the skies. The rockets caught and, roaring and spewing a trail of sparks, pushed the frame some fifty feet into the air. The letters of colored sulfur, however, had been dampened by the fog and failed to ignite fully. They sputtered noisily for a few seconds, then fizzled out. An instant later the rockets ran out of power, and the entire framework crashed to the ground. Philippe turned toward his father, his hands outstretched in a gesture of helplessness.

The Duc glared at him in disgust. His anger was supreme. The entire evening hadn't gone according to plan. First there had been the scene-stealing appearance of Royal Brannigan and Julia Taffarel, then Alcée's outrageous behavior at the dinner table. And now this. He snarled, "Light something else, you ass!"

The guests murmured and shifted their feet in embarrassment. Titters erupted from unruly lips, but in the darkened garden the Duc could not tell from where they had come. Philippe quickly lit another fuse.

This time everything went as planned, and the rocket, undamaged by the damp, flew into the air and exploded in a brilliant barrage of man-made comets, meteors, and shooting stars. A spectacular red, white, and blue galaxy dominated the skies.

Verbena stepped in front of Royal. Her voice was petulant. "I've been looking everywhere for you. Why stay here? You look like the kind of man who makes his own fireworks."

"I seem to be better at making enemies, Verbena, and I'm just about to make my third of the evening."

She went on as if she hadn't heard him or had chosen not to weigh the meaning of his words. "As a special guest, I have my own suite in the big house. I've given my maid orders to spray the rooms with perfume and to remake the bed with my own sheets. They are of the softest silk that ever caressed your flesh."

There was something in her face that Royal didn't like. It was a look of conquest. "Verbena, I can't be with you tonight."

"Can't or won't?" she asked, her sultry voice turning sour.

"Won't," Royal conceded.

"You bastard!" she spat. "Leading me on. Toying with my affections."

"On the contrary, Verbena—you were toying with mine all

through supper. You don't have to be alone tonight. There are any number of men—"

She reached out for him with both hands, her nails bared to tear the flesh from his cheeks. Royal caught her wrists, held them fast, and finally forced them to her sides. "Verbena, you'd better learn when to cut your losses." When he let her go, she pulled back and slapped him hard across the mouth. Royal could taste blood mixing with his saliva.

"No man," she growled, "turns his back on Verbena Chevereaux!"

Livid, Verbena turned and rushed away. She was only a few yards off when she ran into the Duc, who was also leaving the exhibition.

"Have you seen Henriette?" he asked.

"Who?"

"My wife."

"Never mind about her. Come, Alex, let's have some champagne." She glared back at Royal, then grabbed the Duc's arm and pulled him toward the house.

Another fireworks display exploded in the skies over Salle d'Or, but the silence that greeted it indicated that the spectators were beginning to tire of the spectacle. Michelle blinked against the onslaught of primary colors and turned her head toward her husband. He looked as bored as she felt. She ran the flat of her hand down over the strong curve of his back, outlined his backside, and let her palm come to rest on the indentation in the buttock nearest her.

"This is giving me a headache," she complained.

Léon's voice was full of concern. "Can I get you something to drink?"

"I've had enough to drink. Let's go for a walk and get away from all this noise, glare, and smoke."

"All right—but we better not let the Duc see us or he'll be offended."

"The Duc's already slipped away with Verbena Chevereaux," Michelle said.

"Really?" Léon replied with raised eyebrows. "That's an obvious combination, but one I wouldn't have thought of."

"Do you suppose Aunt Marguerite got home safely?"

"Of course. She's probably been in bed for hours."

The young couple walked along the brick pathway till they reached the back lawns, which were deserted save for a few slaves who were collecting left-behind glasses. They joined hands and ran to the outer reaches of the formal gardens. The air was heavy with the scent of flowers. Léon plucked a rose and handed it to Michelle.

"Léon, make love to me," she said.

"All right. Shall we go, then?"

"No, here. I want to do it here. It's dark. Everybody's watching the fireworks. No one can see us."

They found a glade inhabited only by peacocks. After undressing, they knelt on the soft grass, facing each other. Clumps of fern sprayed shadows all around them, and overhead a palm spread a canopy of fronds.

Léon wrapped his arms around Michelle, and their two shadows merged into one. He kissed her hard, forcing her lips apart and tracing the outline of her teeth with his tongue. When they broke apart, Michelle lay back on the ground, her hair spreading outward like an ebony fan. The grass was dewy, and she shivered.

Léon bent over her and glided a hand across her warm, soft flesh. Michelle reached up and lovingly stroked his face. Suddenly she pulled herself up toward him, her lips hungrily covering his with a warm, damp pressure. He took her buttocks in one hand and held her to him so tightly that the breath was forced out of her lungs.

"Hurry," she gasped.

Léon nodded wordlessly. He lowered her gently, trailing his lips down her flesh from her throat to one of her breasts. His tongue flicked out, and a soft cry escaped Michelle's lips. He felt the nipple slide into his mouth and gently sucked on it. He moved downward over her flat stomach until his chin brushed against her downy pubic hair. He lifted his head, letting his warm breath caress the lower part of her stomach, then put his hands on her thighs as he stimulated her with quick touches of his tongue.

"Please, Léon, *please!*" Michelle pleaded.

Unable to resist any longer, Léon lay down on top of her and grew inside her like a night-blooming flower. And there, under the watchful eyes of the peacocks, they made love.

Angélique covered her ears against the deafening explosions. Ribbons of scarlet smoke unwound themselves in the sky and sprinkled molten glitter over the treetops. The air was filled with the tang of sulfur and the grumblings of guests who thought the spectacle had gone on long enough.

Angélique was disgruntled. "Everyone's been treating us as if we were lepers," she complained to Suzanne. "And to think how many times we've entertained the very same people at Heritage."

"They're just embarrassed, Angélique. I don't suppose that even the most blue-blooded Creole has a social code for the treatment of women in our position."

"No one has even expressed sorrow for Jean-Louis's death."

"Suicides are hard on all good Catholics," Suzanne replied, with a trace of sarcasm.

"And the young men! They're not shy about staring at us, but not one of them has asked us to dance."

"I suppose they're only being discreet. I wouldn't accept if they did."

"I would," Angélique said sharply.

"I think you should. I don't believe there would be anything wrong with it."

"I wasn't asking for your permission, Suzanne."

"I know, and I wasn't giving it."

"Not one independent mind among them," muttered Angélique. "They'll allow their parents to arrange a marriage for them to some socially acceptable little lump. They'll have children, she'll get fat, and he'll take a colored mistress and visit her house on the Ramparts every night. It's such a farce. Poor Alcée was certainly shocked by the Duc's announcement."

"Can you blame her?" asked Suzanne.

"No, but for the Gadobert fortune I believe I could overlook what Gilbert's Maker already has. Particularly considering my position."

"Angélique, you must believe me—all that will change. I'll get Heritage back in a year or so, and you'll have suitors by the score."

Another explosion of fireworks lit the sky. After a while, Suzanne said, "Do you feel like going home, Angélique?"

"Home?" she repeated, staring blankly at Suzanne. "I don't have a home." She turned and stalked toward the house.

Slaves were clearing the ballroom.

"We'll go somewhere else," said the Duc, his dark eyes fastened on Verbena's abundant bosom. "I'll get the champagne; you get the glasses." He called for a slave to bring three of the coldest bottles. In the meantime Verbena selected two very large crystal goblets.

"And what are *you* going to drink, Alex?"

Laughing, the Duc led Verbena down the back veranda to the library. He took a key from his pocket and unlocked the door.

"In here," he said. His voice was husky with excitement.

Verbena ran her long fingernails through his widow's peak and said, "Alex, after all this time!"

He ushered her inside. After lighting a small lamp he bolted the door. "I don't like guests coming into my library," he explained. "I have quite an extensive—and expensive—collection of books."

She wandered around the room, admiring its unabashed luxury. Louis Treize ebony-and-copper bookcases were filled with volumes bound in leathers of various rich shades, their titles tooled in gold leaf. The huge Persian rug, a brilliant red and beige, covered most of the parquet floor. The Duc's marquetry desk sat between two sets of French doors hung with dark blue velvet draperies. On the wall above was a huge painting depicting a voluptuous shepherdess tending her flocks.

"This is beautiful, Alex. Why have you never shown me this room before?" She spun around and cupped the champagne glasses over her breasts. The Duc was seated behind his desk. He began twirling a bottle of champagne between the palms of his hands. "Bring the glasses over here," he breathed.

Verbena glided toward him, turning the glasses around her globular breasts, as if polishing them. She set the goblets down on the desk directly in front of the Duc, whose breathing was now coming in short, ragged gasps. Holding a bottle with both hands, he clamped his strong white teeth around the cork and worked his head back and forth until the cork popped. He filled each glass nearly to the brim. Verbena started to reach for one.

"No," he said. "First I want to see your breasts."

"Really?" Verbena asked with a mocking smile.

"Yes, yes," the Duc hissed through clenched teeth. "Let me see them!"

Slowly, Verbena removed the fichu of lace that covered her bosom and dropped it on the floor. Then she pulled the brief bodice downward, and her breasts bounced free. They were as large and swollen as a nursing mother's. The large nipples resembled copper coins and stood out in sharp contrast against the smooth, lightly-veined contours of the flesh. The Duc sucked in his breath.

"Do you propose to make love to me here, Alex?"

"Alas, I can no longer indulge in that particular activity," he replied without apology or embarrassment.

"Oh, Alex, were you injured?"

"The doctor doesn't know why." He glanced down to his crotch and shook his head. "The soldier is willing, but he cannot salute. Unfortunately, my desire is still very active!"

Verbena pressed her pelvis against the side of the desk and bent over. Her breasts were poised above the champagne glasses. Perspiration broke out in tiny beads on the Duc's face. She lowered her chest until the tips of her nipples touched the cold champagne. "Ohhhh," she shivered, and let more of her flesh submerge in the golden liquid. Then she moved her breasts, first to the left and then to the right. Some of the champagne splashed onto the desk top.

The Duc licked his dry lips and leaned forward until his tongue was poised on the rim of one of the glasses.

"Drink, Alex," Verbena crooned. "Drink, *drink*!"

Philippe decided to turn over the running of the fireworks display to his Negro assistants. He pushed his way through the crowd. The incandescent explosions lit up their faces, bleaching out features into a mannequin sameness. From time to time he would stop to stare openly and rudely into the face of a pretty Creole girl. Then he would move on, grunting with exasperation. These corseted Catholic virgins had nothing to offer him.

Occasionally he would stop and whisper something into one of their perfect, petallike ears. They would back away, looking shocked or frightened. Unable to persuade any of them to be indiscreet, and too drunk to go downriver to New Orleans, Philippe went looking for Lilliane.

When he reached the kitchen, Ambrose was standing in the doorway, watching the fireworks. The slave flinched involuntarily and cried, "I's watching dat de chillun don't steal no food."

Philippe pushed him aside and staggered inside. He blinked against the sudden light. The Salle d'Or slaves quickly looked away from their young master, turning to their duties with an extra spurt of energy prompted by fear. Zenobia and Aunt Lolly were seated at the table, drying freshly washed silverware. They stood up and glanced nervously toward the pantry door.

Philippe caught their glance and asked almost pleasantly, "Where's Lilliane?"

"She not here, M'sieur Philippe," said Aunt Lolly as she rose and stepped to one side, covering part of the door with her bulk.

Zenobia spoke up. "She left early. She not feeling so good."

Philippe teasingly asked, "What did she do? Call for her carriage to take her home?" He slammed his fist on the table and screamed, "Get out! All of you! Go on—get out of the kitchen!"

Zenobia raised a heavy silver salver behind Philippe. Aunt Lolly quickly moved around to her side and made her put it back on the table. Stone-faced, they left with the others.

Lilliane was awake and waiting for him. A malicious smile crossed her face as he stepped through the doorway and glared at her. "Why didn't you answer me?" he growled.

"I didn't hear yo', massa," she replied.

"Don't mock me, nigger." His head bumped onto the overhanging lantern and threw his shadow black and sharp across Lilliane's prone form on the makeshift pallet. He reached down and yanked her to her feet.

"Stand up when I come into the room!"

"I's standing, massa."

"Take off your clothes."

"Yes, massa." Lilliane stepped out of her shift and dropped it to the floor. Philippe grabbed her. His expression changed from lust to anger.

"You're in your period. Why didn't you tell me?"

"Yo' didn't ask me, massa."

Philippe, furious at Lilliane's unclean state, backhanded her, sending her spinning across the small room. Lilliane fell against a wall of shelving, the breath knocked out of her. Philippe lunged forward and dug his strong fingers into the flesh of her throat. "Slut!" he roared. "Filthy slut!"

He held her down with one hand, drew back his fist, and rammed it against her jaw. "Filthy slut!"

Lilliane crawled backward along the wall, trying to get to the door. Philippe stepped in front of her. The whites of his eyes were red, and his pupils were dilated. He kicked her squarely on the chin, knocking her out. He kicked her several more times in the ribs and abdomen, and when she would not come to, he gave up. He stormed out of the kitchen and staggered toward the slave quarters in search of a sexual partner.

Henriette sat quietly on the stone bench. She had seen her husband and Verbena go into the library together, but she neither felt nor thought anything about it. Her husband's infidelities had long since ceased to hurt her. Besides, she had other things on her mind. She had overheard the gossip and knew of her husband's announcement and of Alcée's reaction.

Captain Calabozo was on his knees beside her. He was conscious and sober, and was half muttering, half crying, "I'm as good as anybody."

Henriette said, "You are better, Bartolomé. Their standards are false. Money, power, and position are their only interests. They have graven these things upon their hearts, and there is no space left for kindness. You are a kind man, Bartolomé. You are better than they."

The captain rested his head on Henriette's lap, and she let her arm fall around his shoulder. For the moment she forgot the dampness, the Duc's anger, even Alcée's betrothal, and was aware only of the warmth and comfort of being close to another human being. She smiled to herself, content to be exactly where she was, and that contentment stimulated past memories.

She recalled the young Alexandre Duvallon and how differently he had treated her before they were married. "I remember love," she whispered. Her voice held both surprise and wonderment. As the repressed feelings, long buried in the recesses of her soul, came to the surface, Henriette felt herself drawing new strength, almost as if she were once again young and able to hope.

Oblivious of the fireworks crisscrossing the sky above, she cradled the captain's head in her lap and murmured the soothing words over and over. "Yes, I remember love."

Blue and yellow and gold flashes pierced the night sky. Rockets hissed and broke, tumbling in cascades of sparks. The garden was filled with the acrid stench of gunpowder.

Julia glanced at Theo. His gaze was averted from the display. "Why, Theo, you don't seem to be having a good time."

"I'm not, Julia. They remind me too keenly of the battlefield."

"Then we won't stay. Shall we take a walk in the garden?"

"Yes, I'd enjoy that very much."

The couple passed through the formal gardens and reached the Chinese bridge spanning the artificial lake. They stopped in the middle, content with the serenity of their surroundings. A light wind rippled the surface of the water. Theo put his arm around Julia's shoulders.

"That's much better," Julia said. "It's gotten cooler. I'm glad we're friends again, Theo."

"We were never not friends, Julia. We just didn't see each other."

"Has your life been happy, Theo?"

The old man thought for a moment. "Yes, it's been happy, for the most part. And you, Julia?"

"I made certain choices, and lived my life the best I could. I suppose there's nothing more to say. I'm so sorry, Theo. If I could somehow go back and change things, I would."

"Julia, that's all in the past. And it's dangerous at our age to have regrets. You still look beautiful, you know."

Julia smiled. "We've both aged well, haven't we? That's what they call character, I suppose—it comes from surviving misfortune. But I didn't know how much of it I had until I got dressed for the ball. My gown was a gift from Royal Brannigan, you know."

"No, I didn't."

"You must get to know him. He's a charming young man."

"Should I be jealous?"

"If we were both younger, I might give you cause."

Julia shivered and moved closer to Theo. He kissed her lightly on the lips. Julia said, "Thank you, Theo. I've been waiting all evening for you to do that."

"Oh, I've been waiting much longer than that," Theo replied. "Much, *much* longer."

Suzanne saw Royal coming toward her. "Are you enjoying the spectacle, Madame Jourdain?"

"Yes, thank you. The fireworks are very beautiful, but they

make me a little bit homesick. You see, we always had fireworks at Christmas. It's a Creole tradition, even in Georgia."

"I didn't know where you were from."

They began strolling together, and it seemed natural.

"I'm from Glassboro, Pennsylvania," Royal said.

"Where they make the glass? Yes, of course—the Brannigan Glassworks. My family has chandeliers and glassware from there. You must be very proud."

Royal did not answer immediately. "Not exactly proud, madame. But that's all part of my past."

"And you don't wish to talk about it?"

"Let's just say that the past is like another country and that I do not choose to travel there."

They had reached the veranda and were standing before a set of open French doors. The tables inside had been cleared away, and the orchestra was tuning up. Royal said, "I'm going to be leaving soon. Would you like me to escort you and Mademoiselle Jourdain back to Heritage?"

"No, thank you, m'sieur. Angélique and I will probably stay until the last dance. Creole parties go on until dawn." She extended her hand toward him. Royal took it and held it for a moment before bending to kiss it with his lips. Suzanne looked over Royal's shoulder at the fireworks. The sky seemed to rush at her in a whirl of color. She suddenly realized that she was seeing colors properly again. In delighted confusion she looked at Royal and saw that his eyes reflected the exploding colors in miniature. And as she gazed into his eyes, she knew that he was thinking the same thing—that this was the first time they had touched on purpose.

Chapter Fifteen

After the incident with Gilbert and the charlotte russe, Alcée had locked herself in her room and changed from her ball gown into a plain dress. The fireworks were exploding in a crashing finale when she slipped out the back way, across the darkened veranda, and down the stairs to the almost deserted gardens. She stopped to watch Blaise at work collecting glasses that had been scattered over the lawn. He carried them back to the bar, then paused to feed the monkey tethered to the tree. Her heart was so filled with love for him that she could barely breathe.

When Blaise saw her approaching across the lawn, he looked troubled. Alcée could guess the reason.

They moved into the shadows where they would not be seen.

"I heard the announcement," he said quietly.

"Don't let it upset you, Blaise. At first I was upset, but then I realized there is absolutely nothing Papa can do to make me marry Gilbert—" She put a finger to her mouth in warning, and they both fell silent. A few moments later, Alcée whispered, "Speaking of Gilbert, he just wandered by. He's cleaned himself up, but I noticed a glob of charlotte russe still in his ear." She giggled. "I suppose that's how I'll always remember him."

"When is the wedding planned?" asked Blaise.

"I don't know. But it wouldn't be until after harvest. We'll be gone by then."

"How? We don't even have the money for steamship passage."

"I'll get it. I'll steal something and sell it. Papa has a lot of valuable things lying around."

"He'll never let us get away, Alcée. I've seen a side of your father that I know you haven't. Neither he nor Philippe will rest until we're brought back to Louisiana."

"They can't touch us in Canada, Blaise. Besides, Mama will help."

Blaise looked alarmed. "You haven't told her?"

"No, not yet. And I know what you're thinking—that she's completely under my father's yoke. But something's happened to her, Blaise. She's changed. She's beginning to stand up for herself. And she loves me very much. I know we can trust her, and that if at all possible she will find a way to help us."

Blaise shook his head. "If you were in love with a white man perhaps she would, but she will never accept me."

"You're wrong. She will. My mother may have been brought up among slaveholders, but she's different. You see how kindly she treats the slaves."

"Kindness is one thing, Alcée, love is another. But you do what you think is right. Maybe your mother won't give us away—but she'll never approve of me as your husband."

The spider monkey, straining its leash in their direction, began squawking for more food.

"You've made a friend," Alcée said. Blaise stretched his arm out and let the monkey pick some nut meats from his hand.

"Yes, we've grown quite fond of each other," he replied. "We're in a similar position here at Salle d'Or."

"Blaise," Alcée said suddenly, "let's turn him loose."

"What?"

"Let's turn him loose. Let's turn them all loose!"

"What about your papa?"

"I'll deal with Papa." She took his hand. Blaise glanced around nervously, but there were no whites to be seen back in the garden.

"But I can't leave my post."

"Of course you can. Everyone's getting drunk. The party's on its last legs. Come on, Blaise—no one will see us."

"All right . . . yes," he said, getting caught up in Alcée's enthusiasm. "At least they'll have a chance at surviving. There are plenty of fruit and nut trees on the plantation."

He reached out and undid the collar around the monkey's neck. The animal immediately jumped onto its benefactor's shoulder.

"I told you you'd made a friend," Alcée said.

"What shall I do with him?"

"Bring him with us."

"He should have a name. What shall I call him, Alcée?"

"Call him . . . Freedom." Then, in a gruff imitation of her father, she urged, "*Vite! Vite!*"

"I's comin', massa," said Blaise. "By the way, why did you change your dress? You looked so pretty in it."

"It had charlotte russe on it."

Laughing, they darted into the gardens and went from tree to tree, releasing the monkeys. Some of the animals scurried off, others followed the young couple. Silhouetted against the moonlit sky, Alcée and Blaise ran, jumped, and skipped across the deserted grounds, like pied pipers leading a parade of happy monkeys. From a distance they resembled figures in a shadow box, paper cutouts whose movements were controlled by invisible hands.

The fireworks were over. Marguerite and the children sighed deeply. Entranced by the spectacle, they had ventured as close as they dared to the big house but had not taken notice of their immediate surroundings. Now, with only the feeble rays of the three-quarter moon to illumine the darkness, they became uncomfortably aware of the strange place in which they were standing.

Le jardin des bêtes—the garden of beasts—was a topiary garden. Enormous boxwood shrubs had been trained and trimmed into unnatural shapes . . . a bizarre menagerie of beasts. The garden was laid out in the form of a huge clock face with twelve different animals representing the hours of the day. The original designer, a so-called tree barber, had fashioned the animal shapes, but he and the Duc had had a falling out over money, and the Duc had fired him. The chore of trimming the hedges had since fallen to the Negro gardeners, who seemed to have no anatomical knowledge of animals. Over the years, the lion's mouth had expanded to enormous proportions, the bear's snout had lengthened so that it seemed part elephant's trunk, and the wolf's ears had grown until they appeared more like misplaced legs. Paws had become knobby, distorted; unnatural appendages had been added apparently at whim. The animals had acquired such fantastical shapes that now not one of them seemed to represent a known form of animal life. The Duc, in any case, had long since lost interest in the garden, and the few guests at Salle d'Or who knew about it avoided it, finding it unsettling, even frightening.

While the three children and Marguerite had been watching the fireworks exhibition, the breeze had died down and a damp mist had risen. Now a thick fog lay around the base of each animal, so that they seemed to be floating, freed, as it were, from their earthbound roots.

Blanche, her eyes wide and staring, was the first to put in words the uneasiness they all felt. "I think I'd like to go home now."

"I'm rather tired myself," Fleur said, unsuccessful at keeping the tremor out of her voice.

"But we haven't seen the ghost yet," Denis complained.

"There are no ghosts," Marguerite stated gently. "But I think we should go. You children should be in bed. I'll walk you home."

Denis looked at her with disappointment. Marguerite's easy acceptance of them and their adventure had thus far made her seem almost a contemporary—but now she was reverting to an adult role and taking charge. Denis wasn't about to relinquish his authority.

"No," he said. "We'll walk *you* home, Miss Marguerite. There are three of us, and we've got protection." He displayed the sharp knife that he carried with him. Marguerite shuddered but did not argue.

"Next time I'll come by myself," he said in a disgruntled voice. "Now, let's see, which way is it to the Promenade?" Everybody made a different guess. Glancing at the position of the moon, Denis pronounced, "That way," and began leading them through the waist-high mist toward one of the exits in the hedge. The lawn underfoot was slippery with wet leaves. "Watch your step," he cautioned.

"Can't see, can't see," complained Blanche. Sighing loudly, Denis stopped and picked her up, positioning her in a piggyback fashion; then he resumed his way toward the gap between two of the loathsome leafy sculptures. One looked like a dog sitting on its haunches, its misshapen back about to sprout monstrous wings; the other could have been a cat, its head oversized and misshapen, its graceless body ready to spring.

Remnants of shredded clouds high above moved across the moon, causing shadows to leap from place to place. Fleur and Marguerite joined hands. Denis glanced back once, and the animal forms appeared to turn, flexing their deformed bodies in preparation for the chase. He quickened his pace and wished that somehow he could be transported out of this hellish place home safely to his bed.

Finally they reached a path and could hear gravel crunching beneath their feet. The sound was heartening to all of them. Marguerite expelled her breath, Fleur hummed an off-key melody, and Blanche nudged her chin against Denis's back. The pathway soon ended, however, and the reassuring gravel again became sodden leaves and grass. "It's that way," Denis announced, pointing to a long tunnel of low trees that resembled a huge, wet, open mouth. "We came through there."

Fleur nodded and gulped.

"Yes, I remember it," confirmed Marguerite.

As they started marching toward the tunnel, Blanche suddenly began squeezing Denis's neck so hard that it nearly choked him.

"Blanche—"

"Oh, oh, oh, oh!" She swallowed, kicking her feet against his ribs in an unconscious effort to run. Finally she managed to gasp out, "There's the ghost!"

She held out a pudgy arm to point but could not unclutch her fingers. All three turned in the direction of Blanche's balled fist.

Denis stopped in his tracks. Standing about twelve yards away beneath a magnolia tree, framed by billowing Spanish moss and lit by a patch of moonlight, was the unmistakable figure of a man. He seemed to be swaying in the wind, and was staring into space through eyes as luminous as stars. His grayish-white garment looked fashioned of spiderwebs, his face was ashen, glowing faintly, and his long, flowing hair was completely without color.

A breeze suddenly swept away the fog that floated around them, and the figure saw his audience for the first time. He turned his head and looked at them. His expression was sad, beseeching. He stretched out his arms toward them, and his mouth opened and closed wordlessly, as if he were trying to speak but had forgotten how.

The four remained motionless. Denis felt a numbing cold envelop him, as if it were deepest winter. The specter took a step forward. Denis broke their trance by shouting, "Let's get the hell out of here!"

They took off running. Blanche's little feet ran in place against Denis's ribs.

"Stay together!" Denis warned. "Don't look back!"

They ran for their lives without even thinking whether what they saw had been real or imagined. Pell-mell they rushed toward the yawning mouth of trees and raced down its slippery tongue. The fallen leaves that covered the path seemed as slimy as slugs, and Denis, off-balance because of Blanche's weight, slid and almost toppled with every step. He had the odd sensation that he was stationary and that the shadowy tunnel of trees was moving swiftly past them.

One of the ribs of Fleur's parasol caught on a branch and she was yanked backward. "My parasol!" she cried.

"Leave it!" screamed Denis.

"No!"

Denis swung Blanche off his back and shoved her at Marguerite, who clasped the little girl tightly against her bosom. Then he ran back and tugged at the parasol; but the strips of lace had become enmeshed in the branches. Using the carving knife, he cut through the lace and freed the parasol, but fumbled and dropped the knife among the wet leaves. He grabbed for it in the darkness, struck the handle, but felt it slip away from him again.

"Hurry," cried Fleur. "Hurry!"

No one had dared look behind them until now. As if compelled, Denis and Fleur turned toward the entrance of the leafy tunnel. The ghost was standing there, bracketed by the trees. The breeze behind him twisted his hair into waving tendrils so that it resembled writhing white serpents.

"Oh, God," moaned Denis.

"Forget the knife!" cried Fleur.

"Catch up! Catch up!" shrieked Blanche.

As Denis and Fleur scrambled to make up ground, Marguerite and Blanche reached a rise obscured by fog. Marguerite lost her footing, and she and Blanche slid backward down the dark passage. They slammed into Fleur and Denis, who could not stop or move aside in time. The four of them collapsed and sprawled ungracefully like puppets whose strings had been cut, a desperate tangle of arms and legs and parasol.

Before leaving, Royal went in search of his hosts to thank them for their hospitality. But none of the Duvallons was to be found. He hadn't really expected to find Alcée, and thought it just as well he hadn't run across Philippe.

He saw Verbena teetering along the veranda. He stepped back into the shadows, and she passed within a foot of him without noticing he was there. From her walk and the glazed expression in her eyes he could tell that she was drunk. She no longer looked beautiful, or even young.

Fascinated, he watched her progress. She traipsed across the lawn in the direction of the canvas tents that had been set up to accommodate the performers. She walked into the center of the small encampment, kicked at the remains of the fire, and appeared to be waiting for something to happen. She hadn't long to wait. One of the acrobats, dressed only in his support, stepped out of one of the tents. He didn't see her, but walked around the side of the tent and relieved himself. When he walked back into the light, Verbena was waiting, staring at him with a lascivious expression that transformed her face into a mask of carnality. Royal had to turn away. When he looked back a lamp had been lit inside the tent, and the silhouettes of the three muscular acrobats were cast against the canvas wall. Verbena walked toward the tent. A muscular arm threw open the flap for her to enter. The three male forms surrounded the slenderer form of the new arrival, then the lamp went out.

Royal decided that the rumors he had heard about Verbena Cheveraux were true after all.

Finding no one else to whom he could express his appreciation, Royal thanked each of the Negrilions as he descended the stairs to await his carriage. The Negro boys were having a hard time staying awake. Seth, more exhausted than the others, was actually asleep on his feet. Royal placed his hand on the boy's shoulder. Seth's eyes snapped open. Royal said, "Come on, son, the party's over for you."

"But I can't go yet, Mr. Royal. The Duc ain't give us leave."

"You were only sent here on loan, not forever. Come on, it's way past your bedtime." He picked the boy up in his arms and cradled him over his shoulder. Seth immediately fell asleep once again.

The ancient carriage and the turned-out farm horses were delivered. Royal laid Seth across the back seat, then climbed up front. Soon the carriage was rolling at a leisurely pace away from Salle d'Or.

As the carriage reached the Promenade, Royal glanced over his shoulder to check on the sleeping form of Seth. He turned back around just in time to see something dash in front of the horses. "What the hell!" He yanked hard on the reins and applied the foot brake.

The team came to an abrupt halt, the carriage jolted to a stop, and Seth was tossed onto the floor. "Hey, what's going on?"

Marguerite and the children scrambled into the carriage without waiting to be asked. Everyone was talking at once. Royal stared at Denis. The mist had washed away most of the lampblack from his face. "Denis, is that you?"

"Yes, M'sieur Brannigan. We saw the ghost!"

"We did! We did!" echoed Blanche.

Seth rubbed his eyes and complained, "Why is I always asleep when something's going on?"

"All of you? I take it these are your sisters?"

"Just the younger two," replied Denis. "That's Blanche and that's Fleur. This here's Miss Marguerite from Bellechasse."

Marguerite nodded coldly at Royal. "We've met before," she mumbled.

"It was a man after all," Fleur said. "We actually saw him quite clearly. But I was the only one who thought to take note of the pertinent facts. He was about five feet, eight inches tall, had fine-textured white hair that fell way past his shoulders. And he was very thin." She glanced at Blanche. "I guess ghosts don't eat. His skin was so white, and he was wearing a shroud. His eyes . . . they were wide and staring, and he looked like he was in pain. Ghosts sometimes don't know how to get to heaven. Isn't that right, m'sieur?"

"I don't know," replied Royal. Sensing, however, that the little girl's loquaciousness was a result of genuine fright, he looked to Marguerite.

"We saw something," she conceded. "But I believe the fireworks must have affected our eyesight. And it *was* quite foggy out there. No, I don't believe we actually saw a ghost."

The children looked at one another, as though hurt by Marguerite's breach of loyalty. Fleur said, "He looked lost and confused, like he wanted to go home."

"I want to go home!" wailed Blanche.

"I'd better drive you all home," said Royal. "Miss Marguerite, I'll take you first."

The carriage reached Bellechasse, and Marguerite kissed the three children. "I had a very exciting time. Thank you all for becoming my friends." Her voice was high and sharp, like the twang of a violin string.

Royal held the carriage until the front door was opened by a servant. Marguerite, smiling sadly, turned and waved at the children. She looked reluctant to enter the house.

Royal snapped the reins and asked Denis, "All right, young man, what are you doing out again at this time of night and with your sisters in tow? I don't know what you saw out there, but it must be three in the morning, and all of you should have been in bed long ago. I think it's about time I had a talk with your grandfather."

"Oh, M'sieur Brannigan, please don't tell Grandpapa. We'll tell him in our own way."

"Will you, Denis?"

"I promise."

"Very well—but no more nightly adventures. You've seen the ghost. Now it's time to settle down and start staying in nights."

"I promise that too," said Denis. "But we saw it, M'sieur Brannigan. We really saw it."

"It was better than food," said Blanche.

Fleur, twirling an incredibly dirty and tattered parasol, added, "It's been such a boring summer . . . until tonight."

Royal took a bottle of champagne to bed with him. Stripped of his clothes, he lay on top of the sheets and reviewed the evening. Despite his encounter with Philippe, getting on the wrong side of the Duc, and the episode with Verbena, he had to consider that the night had been more of a success than a failure. He had met so many people he liked and who seemed to like him in return. He had befriended both Alcée and Henriette Duvallon. Theo and Julia had gotten together after such a long, long separation. And Suzanne had let down her guard and been friendly for the first time since their difficult meeting. Royal hoped that in time he might win over Angélique too.

He wanted to say to them, *Don't you understand? I have to be here. After seeing what I've seen, I can't return.* Perhaps at some future date he could explain it to them, but not now. Neither of them would understand. They had been raised in pampered luxury, with all their needs attended to . . . at least until now.

"Yeah, Charlie, I hear you. You gotta know when to fold. You gotta know when to cut your losses."

Royal was lonely. Maybe he should have gone with Verbena. No! Despite his physical attraction to her, he didn't like her. He remembered the absence of feeling when she smiled. There was no life or warmth in those blue-violet eyes. Somebody once said that desire blinded the soul. "But not half as well as champagne," he added ruefully, and took another swallow.

As he drank, Royal listened for the sound of the women's carriage returning. His natural masculine instinct made him feel protective toward them, even though they had every reason to wish him dead. As he took another long swallow of champagne, he watched the room as it moved in and out of focus. Royal realized that he was getting drunk, and that knowledge gave him a sense of false security. He felt safe. He was in his bedroom at Heritage. He was home. He savored the purity of the word. *Home.* Royal reflected that he had never felt at home anywhere. In Glassboro he and his mother, between them, had fashioned a kind of uneasy existence, a protective shell against his father and brothers—but that could hardly have been called home. In prison his alliance with Charlie Hazard had established a similar kind of existence—two outcasts joining together in order to survive. Prison could be called home only by those who had known no other, or by those who had forgotten how to dream.

He started to get out of bed to open the stifling draperies, but the floor tipped up to meet him. It was no good. He couldn't stand. Royal fell back in bed. "I'm too drunk," he murmured happily. "Too goddamn drunk."

He finished the champagne and dropped the empty bottle to the floor. Then stretched out his arm and turned out the lamp. "Heritage," he breathed. "Home." The word was so comforting that he rolled up in it like a blanket and went to sleep.

Some time later Royal was awakened by the sensation that he was not alone. How long he had been asleep he couldn't tell. It could have been ten minutes, or it could have been two hours. One thing was certain, however—it was still night. There were no faint bands of light outlining the heavy draperies.

Royal was attuned to quick, sudden awakenings—a habit first acquired from his father's beatings and perfected in prison and later in the hotels and steamships frequented by unscrupulous gamblers, robbers, or worse. He shifted his head slightly, ears cocking like an animal's, and listened hard to make certain the sound that had awakened him was real and not imagined, not part of some now-forgotten dream.

He heard his own breathing. It had to be his own. But it sounded as if someone were breathing along with him, in a rhythm that wasn't quite synchronized. The heavy air stirred, causing the hairs on the back of his neck to quiver. He strained his eyes, trying to see across the room, but the blackness was not the mere absence of light, but a tangible force. His eyes seemed to play tricks on him. The darkness seemed to move and shift and form itself into shapes.

Royal sensed danger. *Dammit*, he thought—if he only had a weapon. He remembered the empty champagne bottle, and slowly, hardly daring to breathe, he eased himself to the edge of the bed. He stretched out his arm and abruptly stopped. A warmth ignited his hand . . . body heat!

He drew back his arm as if he had touched something

burning. Fear pricked his mind. He knew that he didn't have time to fumble for the bottle in the dark. His body grew tense, ready to spring. . . .

But what had he to fear at Heritage? This was his home, he reminded himself, not prison. He reached out once again, and touched naked flesh. It was smooth, soft, and unmistakably feminine. The flesh was real, of that much he was certain. But he had the strangest feeling that if he lighted the lamp, its wearer would cast no shadow.

Royal became confused, disoriented. He was suddenly unsure if he was indeed at Heritage. He thought that he was back at his rooms at the Plantation Hotel in New Orleans and in the company of one of his lady friends. He put out his hand again, palm flat, and felt the heated flesh of a woman's abdomen. She was standing against the bed. He moved his hand upward, and his fingertips touched a woman's breast. He began caressing it, and as he did, the reality of the situation became clear to him. He *was* in his bedroom at Heritage, and the woman standing next to his bed was either the wife or the sister of the man he had seen commit suicide. In a voice quavering with confusion as well as desire, he asked, "Angélique?" There was no response. "Suzanne?" Still no response, but he could feel the heartbeat growing faster beneath the ribs and flesh.

He was about to get up and pull open the drapes when the intruder climbed into his bed. Bewildered by the strange if pleasing situation, Royal ran his hands through the woman's hair in the hopes of identifying her, but his fingers could not tell color. They could only tell him that this hair was silken to the touch.

Royal was no stranger to the complexities of love making, but guided by his nocturnal visitor, he now embarked upon a voyage of sexual passion that heretofore had existed only in his dreams. It was like traveling to a different country—one that he knew must be real but had never been discovered. It was a country of cruel, reckless beauty where the traveler must surrender all principles, conventions, and pride before becoming initiated into a pagan ceremony that celebrated the senses and the senses only.

Chapter Sixteen

Dawn arrived over Magnolia Landing at exactly five twenty-seven. Coming quickly on the heels of departing night, it manifested itself not with a cool, gray, comfortable light, but as a hard and brilliant blue that spread across the countryside like a contagion, wilting the flowers, searing the lawns, drying up the creeks, and prodding summer pests into action.

The Duc marched back and forth on the gallery like a sentry on guard duty. He had slept very little—less than two hours, in fact—but he required no more, and indeed scorned nocturnal inactivity. He looked upon sleep as a kind of death and engaged in it as infrequently as possible.

From his vantage point, the Duc watched his slaves at work in the gardens, clearing away the debris of the previous night and setting up tables under a yellow-and-white striped marquee. In the kitchen, preparations were being made to serve a buffet-style breakfast to the guests staying at Salle d'Or, as well as to those who had spent the night on the steamships. The Duc knew that the slaves were aware he was watching them. They did not look in his direction, not one of them, not once. That was good. It kept them on their toes.

The Duc had dressed in a muslin morning coat of poisonous green, which suited his mood. His family—every member—had angered him to such a degree that he knew he would be hard put to fulfill his role as host. Worst of all had been Alcée's defiance of his wishes, and in such a blatant manner. Where had she learned such rude behavior? It had cost him more than a little embarrassment to convince the Gadoberts that she was young, overexcited by the prospect of marriage, and had drunk a touch too much champagne. But he had convinced them, just as he would convince Alcée of her filial duty.

Henriette was another matter. No one had paid very much attention to her when she had gone to the aid of Captain Calabozo. She had simply made a fool of herself, as had the American. But she *was* acting strangely of late. Perhaps she was going through that time of life that drove middle-age women insane. The Duc briefly smiled at the thought—but the smile vanished as he contemplated his son. There had been the problem with the fireworks. Of course, in retrospect, he supposed he couldn't put the blame entirely on Philippe. Señor Vargas and his assistants had improperly insulated the missiles against the damp. But Philippe had later become drunk and abusive to several of the young female guests. And finally there had been the unpleasant incident with the quadroon woman, Lilliane. Fortunately she had not been hurt that badly. And he had been able to hush it up. Philippe was high-spirited, and sometimes his temper got out of control. The Duc, always willing to excuse his son's peccadilloes, blamed himself for that. He shouldn't have kept Philippe at Salle d'Or for so long. The boy needed to go to New Orleans regularly to blow off steam. Still, the incident could have been ugly if word had gotten around.

As he paced the gallery, the Duc wondered vaguely why Philippe hadn't yet tired of the quadroon woman. True, she was handsome and well proportioned—but after so many years! Well, it was just a matter of time before he did. The Duc's lips twisted into a sour grimace. Imagine, abusing a birthday gift! After all, Lilliane had cost thirty-five hundred dollars. He planned to recoup most of his original investment, of course—if not from the woman alone, then from the woman and her son.

No matter that his family had defied his wishes. They would soon come around. What else could they do? They were financially dependent upon him, and he knew that that fact alone gave him all the power he needed.

The Duc narrowed his eyes and smiled crookedly as he recalled the episode in the library with Verbena Chevereaux. *Ah,* he thought to himself, *that's the kind of woman I should have married*. Beautiful, wealthy, witty, and a sexual reprobate. Their encounter had served to remind him of how exciting sex could be. And even if he was unable to reach orgasm, there was a particular satisfaction in pleasing her by engaging in an act that he had never before committed.

The Duc's thoughts of Verbena lightened his mood. He plucked a yellow rose from a marble urn and checked it for imperfections. Satisfied with the bloom, he fixed it in the buttonhole of his lapel. He drew himself up on tiptoe, took several deep breaths, and headed toward the staircase. He was feeling much better. He would go down to the gardens and be there to greet his guests. Until they arrived, he would have plenty of time to harass the slaves. It was going to be a fine morning after all.

Henriette breathed a sigh of relief as her husband's footsteps passed the closed door of her bedroom. She sat back on her haunches and directed a thankful gaze toward her plaster saints, arranged like so many chess pieces on the lace-covered altar. The flickering votive candles infused the tiny painted faces with life, and they seemed to be dispensing benevolent smiles on her. She quickly resumed her prayerful position, and her fearful expression was replaced by one of confident determination.

Henriette crossed herself and wearily got to her feet. She was exhausted from lack of sleep. She had stayed with Captain Calabozo for a good part of the night. When she had felt he was in control of himself, she had directed one of the slaves to drive him back to the *Belle Créole*. Then she had sat in a chair the rest of the night, pondering the question for which she had no answer—how was she going to keep Alcée from marrying Gilbert Gadobert?

Toward dawn she had realized that there was only one solution to the problem—but that required money. More than anything, money kept her and Alcée tied to the Duc. They had to go to him for money, no matter how minor the purchase, and they had to account for every penny. If she had some money of her own, then she and Alcée could go away. Henriette knew that her daughter was no happier at Salle d'Or than she was. Alcée was a simple girl, who disliked pretension and waste. If they had money, they could run away. But where would they go? Certainly they couldn't stay in the vicinity. No, they would have to find a secret place, so that *he* couldn't come after them and compel them to return. They could even change their names if they had to.

In finding such a simple solution, Henriette created a new problem, one that seemed insurmountable: How was she going to obtain such a large amount of money? It was ludicrous, really. At one time she had been the wealthiest heiress in Louisiana. But upon her marriage she had surrendered all her monies and properties to her loving husband, including the deed to Villeneuve. She couldn't even sell her jewelry, for the Duc kept the most precious pieces locked away in a strongbox, to which only he knew the combination.

Sighing, Henriette unbuttoned and unlaced the ball gown that the Duc had picked out for her. She stepped out of it and left it lying on the floor. She knew it made her look ridiculous. She didn't have the flair for such a costume.

"I'm not going down there and play hostess to a lot of people who can't even remember my name," she proclaimed.

She rang for a maid, and when the young woman appeared, she said, "Lucinda, please inform the Duc that I am sleeping in this morning and that I am not to be disturbed under any circumstances."

"De Duc ain't gonna like it if yo' don't come down to breakfast, Miz Henriette."

Henriette drew back her covers and climbed into bed. "I say to hell with the Duc," she replied, evoking a gasp from the servant. "Let him take Verbena Chevereaux to breakfast." She crossed herself and quickly fell asleep.

The relentless sun worked its way through the louvered doors and cast brilliant bands of light across the bedroom. The pattern eventually reached the four-poster. Alcée was awake. Propped up on one elbow, she was staring at the sunbeams stretching across Blaise's back. They reminded her uncomfortably of the bars of a prison. Using her forefinger, she followed one of the yellow stripes. Blaise stirred and turned over but did not wake up.

For a moment Alcée pushed from her mind the problems that threatened their relationship and concentrated on the man she loved. His light brown hair was burnished red-gold by the sun's rays, and his lips were slightly parted, his breathing as gentle as his nature. His skin was so smooth and golden that it looked as if his veins flowed with honey instead of blood. The contours of his body, forceful yet tempered with grace, might have been fashioned by a master sculptor. Alcée felt her heart leap in her chest. How could anyone not call him beautiful?

She sighed contentedly and glanced across the room at the beehive clock on the mantelpiece. She was surprised to find the hour was only six-thirty. Oddly enough, she wasn't tired. Rather she felt eager to face the challenge of the new day—and a challenge it would be. She would have to deal with her father, probably Philippe, and perhaps even Gilbert. But she could handle them. It was strange how easy everything became when one made up one's mind. She was not going to marry Gilbert, and there was nothing more to be said about it.

Just then Freedom, the spider monkey, jabbered his good morning from the hat rack, where he had slept the night. He swung himself to the brass chandelier and dangled there by one arm and his tail.

"Well, good morning to you," Alcée laughed. "I guess you're hungry. Well, so am I." She got out of bed and yanked on the bell cord.

The monkey jumped from the chandelier and landed in front of her. He looked up at her with affection. She stroked his head, then motioned for him to climb upon her shoulder.

When Alcée's personal slave announced herself at the door, Alcée opened it but a crack. "Saisie, would you bring some breakfast, please? Lots of coffee, a big, big bowl of fruit, some hot rolls and butter, and . . . are there any nuts about?"

"Nuts, Miz Alcée?" The young slave was puzzled by her mistress's request. "I think dere's pecans and walnuts. Maybe some cashews."

"Then bring me a dish of each, please." She eased around the door so that Saisie could see the monkey perched on her shoulder. "I have a new friend, and he's hungry too."

"I brings it right away, Miz Alcée."

"And, Saisie, if my father should ask, tell him that I'm not up yet." The slave nodded and hurried off.

Alcée closed the door and leaned against it. Saisie—what a sad name for such a dear person. The name meant seizure. Saisie was subject to fits. She had been bought at the age of twelve by the Duc to act as a personal servant to Alcée, who was of the same age. When the Duc found out that the girl was epileptic, he had wanted to sell her, but by that time Alcée had grown fond of her and refused to let him do so. He had acceded to her wishes, but had warned Alcée to keep the slave out of his sight. Alcée knew that Saisie was devoted to her and that the time would probably come when she would have to test the girl's loyalty.

Alcée climbed back into bed and kissed Blaise's eyelids until he woke up.

"What time is it?" he murmured.

"Just six-thirty. You won't be missed yet. I ordered the three of us some breakfast."

Blaise noticed the monkey and grinned. "I forgot about

Freedom. The kitchen slaves are going to think you're eating an awful lot."

"No one's going to complain. Papa has always urged me to eat more."

"So what are you going to do with the little beast?"

"Well, *you* can't keep him. Papa wouldn't allow it. I'll just tell him that instead of taking a husband, I've taken a pet."

Blaise kissed Alcée on the tip of the nose. "I'd better go wash up now. It wouldn't do for Saisie to see me here."

"You underestimate her, Blaise. She would never give us away."

Blaise smiled indulgently. "Don't be too sure of a slave's loyalty, Alcée. You don't know what they might do if your brother gets hold of them."

"Blaise, what do you mean?"

He was saved from answering by a knock at door. "There she is now. I'd better get out of sight."

Alcée opened the door halfway. "I'll take the tray, Saisie."

"Yo' Papa was asking about yo', but I tells him yo' still asleep."

"Thank you, Saisie."

A half hour later, after they had eaten, Alcée walked Blaise to the French doors. "I'll check to see if anybody's watching." She stepped onto the veranda and looked in both directions. "It's safe." Blaise slipped out of the room and hurried down the back stairs without being seen. Alcée closed the door, sat down, and poured herself another cup of coffee. Freedom was sitting in Blaise's chair, picking the meats from a pecan that he had cracked open with his teeth.

"Well, friend," Alcée sighed, "I'm going to have to house-train you." The monkey offered Alcée a toothy grin.

Philippe had roused himself to close his shutters against the piercing sun and morning sounds when he saw Blaise pass along the veranda. He was about to call out and order the slave to do something when instinct stopped him. What on earth was Blaise doing on the veranda at this hour, and in last night's clothes? Where was he coming from?

Even though he had drunk far too much champagne and had only a few hours' sleep, Philippe was alert. There was only one guest suite between his and Alcée's rooms. Philippe muttered in astonishment. "That bastard must be coming from Verbena's!"

He scratched his head in perplexity. He had heard the many stories circulated about Verbena Chevereaux and knew that some of them were undoubtedly true. But in all those lurid bits of gossip, not once had it been rumored that she had ever been involved with a man of color.

Not once! But Blaise had to be coming from Verbena's room. The only other place . . . No, that was ridiculous.

Still, Alcée had always been very fond of the griffe, and when they were younger they had been play mates. He shook his head. No—not his sister. Not with a slave. The situation was unthinkable.

But he'd better keep an eye on Blaise, Philippe decided as he stripped out of the clothes in which he had slept. The alcohol was beginning to wear off, leaving his nerves raw, his senses too acute.

There was a rap at the door, and Philippe's personal slave brought in his customary post-party breakfast, which consisted of a bottle of cold champagne and a half-dozen raw eggs. After curtly dismissing the young man, Philippe broke an egg into a glass, stirred it with a fork, then added champagne and gulped the mixture down. He repeated this action four more times, belching noisily after each ingestion. But curing his hangover was secondary to his curiosity concerning Blaise's whereabouts. He would have liked to return to bed and contemplate the puzzle, but he didn't dare. Philippe knew that his behavior at the ball had angered his father.

After leaving Lilliane unconscious, Philippe had gone to the slave quarters in search of a sexual partner. He had visited several cabins before selecting two pubescent girls—sisters of eleven and thirteen. After ordering their parents out of the cabin, he had forced the youngsters to have sexual relations with him. They hadn't been satisfactory—they were completely without experience and badly frightened. He had finally left them, vowing to come back soon to train them in the ways of pleasing a white man.

Philippe cracked the final egg into the glass, poured the rest of the champagne, and carried the concoction out onto the veranda. He heard his father's voice booming in the distance. "Move that table back a few feet. There isn't enough room to get through! Don't bring the cream out yet, you fool! It will spoil. What's that spot on the canvas? There! Wipe it off! *Vite! Vite!*"

Philippe could not help but smile. As usual, the Duc was

causing havoc among the slaves. He peered over the railing and spotted his father marching about, overseeing every detail of the breakfast. Philippe admired his father for many reasons, not the least of them being the Duc's ability to get things done to his exacting specifications.

Philippe was beginning to feel better. The champagne had raised the alcohol level in his bloodstream, and the eggs had calmed his rumbling stomach. Seeking to please his father, particularly after the previous evening's misfortunes, and knowing full well that the Duc was angry with his mother and his sister, Philippe shouted a cheerful greeting. "Good morning, Papa. Do you need some help?"

The Duc swung around on his high heels, and his stern expression softened.

"No, son—but I would enjoy your company, since it seems that your mother and sister will not be favoring me with the benefit of theirs."

"I'll be right down, as soon as I get dressed."

Philippe drained his glass and emitted a loud, hollow burp. "I wonder," he asked himself, "if Papa has any idea who entertained that high yellow nigger last night?"

Julia Taffarel's front parlor had undergone a change. The boards had been removed from the windows, and in lieu of glass, which was very costly, Cato had installed greased paper. Ottile had removed the sheets from the remaining furniture, and the floor and shelves had been thoroughly cleared of the decades of dust. Indeed, the oppressive atmosphere that had once filled the room seemed to have vanished overnight.

This morning, in between bites of breakfast, Julia related everything concerning the ball in colorful detail. She and Ottile and Cato were gathered at the small dining table beneath the portrait of Julia's brother. The faithful servants listened with spellbound attention as their mistress, a born raconteur, recalled in word and gesture what she had seen and experienced the previous evening.

The old woman's eyes sparkled with mischief as she spoke of Verbena Chevereaux. "You would not have believed the woman! A more predatory female I've never seen. Why, not a man at the ball was safe from her wiles." Julia fluttered her eyelashes, stuck out her lower lip, pushed her bosom forward, and launched into a devastating imitation of Verbena.

"Sweet saints," she breathed, "I just *love* the sweet aroma of your cigar, sir. I think a cigar is so becoming to a gentleman. An extension of his personality, if you will." Julia laughed. "Really, men are such fools not to see through women like Verbena."

"Oh, I think dey sees through her, all right," said Ottile.

Cato chuckled. "Did Miz Alcée really hit dat boy in de face with a charlotte russe?"

Julia howled and slapped the arm of the chair. "Yes! You should have seen his expression. It was priceless!"

"What about M'sieur Royal?" asked Cato. "Did dem Creole ladies take to him?"

"Well, if a man can be called the beau of the ball, then Royal certainly was it. Even those women who held a good deal of prejudice against Americans seemed taken by Royal's appearance and manner. Every time I saw him he was dancing with a different young lady."

"Did he dance with Miz Angélique or Miz Suzanne?" asked Ottile.

Julia thought for a moment. "No, I'm sure he didn't. But I did notice some hard glances. There's bad feeling between them, of course. But if I'm not mistaken, I did observe something else. I believe that Royal is in love with one of them—though I suspect he doesn't know which one. Not yet. It certainly would be a blessing to both women if he married one of them. I must say I favor Suzanne. I've never liked Angélique, you see, and it's not just because she and her brother used to sneak around here when they were children. There's something about her." She shrugged her shoulders. "Perhaps it's only an old lady's fancy. She *is* an extraordinarily beautiful woman."

Ottile said, "Tell us, Miz Julia, how was it seeing M'sieur Theo after all dese years?"

Julia glanced up at the portrait, then turned slightly away from it, as if its presence made her uncomfortable. "The years have been good to him. He's still handsome, and age has given him a certain stature that was not there in his youth. But . . . it's not so much like reviving an old friendship, Ottile, as it is making a completely new friend. Similar to the pleasure I felt when I met Royal Brannigan—and yet different."

"Yo' still loves him, don't yo', Miz Julia?" said Ottile.

"Yes," Julia conceded, "I still do. And I believe he still

loves me." Her voice grew wistful, and for a moment her attention seemed to wander, as it used to do so often. "What a wondrous thing love is. You can put it in a box, wrap it in paper, tie it with twine, and hide it away somewhere in the attic of your memory. Then one day you discover it again quite by chance. The paper is crumbled, the twine is rotted, the box is warped and mildewed with age. But that precious emotion is just as shiny and new as the day you stored it away."

"What will happen now, Miz Julia?" Cato asked carefully.

Lines of worry altered the old woman's face. "We'll see each other again, of course. Theo wants me to meet his grandchildren. Beyond that I cannot say. I do know this—that once having found Theo again, I do not intend to cast him aside as I once did."

"You had a reason, Miz Julia," said Ottile. "A good reason."

"It seemed so at the time, Ottile. Now I am not so sure. Maybe it was all a mistake."

There was a long, uneasy silence in the room.

"Well, if it was a mistake," Julia said finally, "it was *my* mistake, and I must learn to live with it. I hope I'm strong enough to do that."

"Yo' strong, Miz Julia. Yo' de strongest person I'll ever know," said Ottile.

"No, I'm not strong, Ottile. I'm not now, and I wasn't then. If I had been, I would have lived my life quite differently."

Ottile glanced at her mistress's tray. "Is dat all de breakfast yo' goin' to eat, Miz Julia?"

"I'm afraid I'm not very hungry, Ottile. I'm too full of last night to think about food. Forgive me. Everything was delicious."

Ottile collected the tray. "We leaves yo', den, Miz Julia. I guess yo' gots lots of things to think about."

After the servants had gone, Julia turned to the portrait of her brother. "I wonder if I'm going to be able to accept the burden of happiness, Claude?" She gazed into the unblinking eyes. "Forgive me, Claude, but you must let me go. I have to be selfish now. I have to think of myself. It's not too late for me to have a bit of happiness."

But Claude did not respond.

Chapter Seventeen

In earlier days, when Victoire had been host to many visitors, the plantation buildings had included a *garçonnière* to house male guests. But as the children were growing up, Theo had put the *garçonnière* to a different use. He had ordered the interior walls torn down, so that only a single large room remained. One end he set aside for his woodworking equipment, and another area, partitioned off by louvres, contained a desk and files and was used as a plantation office. The rest was given over to the children as a combination playroom and puppet theater.

Because the *garçonnière* had become a favorite retreat for Theo as well as for his grandchildren, they had dubbed it the *cercle*, or clubhouse. "Cleaning the *cercle*" was the punishment Theo customarily administered when his grandchildren misbehaved.

Theo was in his work clothes. Wood shavings and sawdust had collected in his beard like monochromatic confetti. He had replaced a section of the puppet-stage proscenium that had become wet and warped because of a leak in the roof. After tacking it into place, Theo stepped away from the stage and admired his own work. Then, beginning to feel the strain of the late night, he sat down. Seeing Julia again had upset his peace of mind. The reunion had brought home to him the singular and painful fact that he had not allowed himself to admit until now: He was lonely.

He loved his grandchildren and had a great affection for Aunt Lolly, but since his terrible losses, he had cut himself off from contact with everyone outside the perimeter of Victoire. He had simply been using up time, trying to live each day as it came, but no more. Even writing his memoirs was more a chore than anything else. Theo knew that it was a plodding work, which, if ever finished, would probably be read by no one. He had finally come to realize that he had a desperate craving to be close to someone his own age. He wanted to be with Julia, the woman he had loved for over forty years. But he knew that he would have to tread carefully, for both their sakes.

He looked up to see Denis, Fleur, and Blanche coming through the door. He noticed the absence of their usual perky good-mornings. Something obviously was bothering them.

Theo stood up, folded his arms, and said, "Well, good morning to you too. And what seems to be so serious that you've forgotten to embrace your old Grandpapa?"

Denis took a step forward. His Adam's apple bobbed up and down as he attempted to work the words out of his mouth. He started to speak, but nothing came out but a squawk. The girls giggled nervously, and Denis shot them a stern glance. Fleur, looking contrite, asked, "Would you rather I tell it, Denis?"

"No, I'll tell it. I'm the oldest. It's my responsibility."

"This sounds serious," said Theo. He turned one of the theater chairs around and sat down again so that he could be closer to their height.

Denis, his voice alternating from a boy's to a man's, launched into a full confession of the trio's nocturnal activities, including his securing of the graveyard dirt and the encounter with Royal Brannigan, how he and his sisters had deceived Vermillion and sneaked out of the house, their bumping into Marguerite, seeing the ghost, the lost knife, and their deliverance back home by Royal Brannigan and the promise he had exacted from them.

During the entire recitation, Theo said nothing, but his eyes narrowed in disapproval, and when at last he spoke, his voice was unusually stern. "It appears I owe M'sieur Brannigan a debt of gratitude—not only for saving your collective hides, but for urging you to tell me the truth."

"But we did see the ghost," Denis offered lamely.

"We did! We did!" the girls exclaimed.

Theo held up his hands for quiet. "Children, I appreciate that you have come to me with the truth, but I am still greatly disturbed by your disobedience. Sit down, all of you."

The children collected chairs and arranged them in a semicircle in front of their grandfather. "First of all, I must censure myself. Obviously I have not been strong enough in expressing my warnings concerning your being out alone at night. I want to emphasize what could have happened to you out there. You could have been injured, bitten by a water moccasin, fallen into one of the quicksand bogs. But even worse, there have been robberies and attacks upon residents, guests, and slaves here by marauding criminals. We do not live in a perfect world, and since Magnolia Landing is known to be a very wealthy community, that element will continue to come here and see what they can take from us. And I'm not talking only of possessions, but your lives. Why, it's amazing to me that one of the guards didn't lose his head and harm you in some way." He sat back and pulled at his beard. "Since I have always urged you to think for yourself, I ask you to consider what I've said and then select your own punishment."

Fleur was the first to stand. "Grandpapa, I give up the thing that is most precious to me—my parasol." Theo nodded.

Next, Blanche got to her chubby legs. She twisted her face into a grimace and groaned as she said, "I'll give up desserts for a week, Grandpapa." Theo, suppressing a smile, nodded again.

Finally, Denis rose and said solemnly, "Grandpapa, first of all I promise that I—that we—will never do it again. I wasn't thinking clearly. Besides, we've seen the ghost now, and I think that's enough excitement to last us the entire summer. And as for my punishment, I can't think of anything that is befitting, but I offer you this: I'll buy you a new carving knife out of my own savings, and I'll clean the *cercle* until you're satisfied that I've fulfilled my punishment."

After reflecting a moment, Theo stood up and said, "I think you have selected your punishments well and fairly. Now, why don't you go in to breakfast. Tell Aunt Lolly that I will be there momentarily."

"But don't you want to hear about the ghost, Grandpapa?" asked Blanche.

"Not now. Perhaps later, when my present mood has been softened by Aunt Lolly's cooking."

Each of the children kissed him on the cheek and hurried off. As they were leaving, Theo heard Blanche announce, "I'm going to eat a very, very large breakfast. How else can I make up for no desserts at dinner?"

Fleur admonished, "Real ladies do not stuff themselves at the table."

Denis called over his shoulder, "I'm really sorry, Grandpapa."

"I understand, Denis."

* * *

Lilliane moved slowly around the kitchen at Villeneuve. Every movement caused her pain, but she could not remain in bed. Although she was still exhausted from the work she had done preparatory to the ball, the beating Philippe had given her had prevented her from resting in comfort. Aunt Lolly had found Monsieur Pradel, the plantation doctor, and he had treated her as best he could. He had bound her rib cage tightly with strips of linen, and although he had assured her that nothing was broken, he had warned that the discomfort would be with her for some time. Her neck was marked by Philippe's fingerprints, her jaw and chin were bruised and swollen, and her abdomen burned with a fire that could not be quenched. There was a ringing in her ears, and her eyesight was worse than ever. It was as if something had split inside her head and she had to think above a terrible roar. Lilliane had fixed herself a small breakfast, but found that she had no appetite and took nothing but coffee.

The Duc had been all bluster when he had discovered what Philippe had done. He had made her and the kitchen slaves promise that they would say nothing about the "unfortunate incident," and had pressed a packet of money into her hand to ensure her silence. She and Azby had been driven home, and Lilliane had been thankful her son was so sleepy that he did not notice her injuries. She didn't know what she was going to say to him when he woke up.

Lilliane gingerly made her way down the hall to their bedroom. To her relief, Azby was still sleeping soundly. Suddenly she remembered the money that the Duc had given her. She took it from under her pillow. Silently she returned to the kitchen, then sat down at the table and counted the bank notes in the bright morning light.

She was astounded by the amount—nearly seventy-five American dollars. That would go toward her secret fund. Knowing she was physically unable to put it away in her hiding place beneath the bed, she tucked the money into a bag of rice, then sat down at the table to drink the coffee she had prepared for herself. The bitter brew sharpened her senses, and she contemplated her precarious situation. More than ever, she had to do something desperate if she was going to make any kind of change in Azby's life. She now realized how dangerous Philippe was. The ghastly story that Ambrose had told in the kitchen, later reinforced by her beating at Philippe's hands, made it clear to her that he might not sell her after all. He might kill her instead. And if she were dead, she could not protect her son.

Earlier the previous evening, Aunt Lolly had been extolling the virtues of Dr. Jacques, the leading voodoo priest in New Orleans. She had heard of him, of course. The slaves spoke of him as if he were their savior. According to Aunt Lolly, he was a man who helped his own people through the power of voodoo. Lilliane made up her mind that she was going to obtain permission from the Duc to go to New Orleans on some pretext or other. She smiled wryly to herself. He would give it to her to ensure her silence. And if Dr. Jacques was everything that the others said, then the beating would have been worth it.

Yes, tomorrow she would go to the Duc for the written pass, and she would ask Aunt Lolly to care for Azby in her absence. Lilliane was frightened. She had never been to New Orleans before. She was also afraid to get her hopes up. Pressing the coffee mug against her forehead, she murmured, "Dr. Jacques, you've got to help me. Somebody's got to."

Upon arising, Marguerite quarreled with everyone with whom she came in contact. First it had been her personal maid, who had taken too long to lay out her mistress's clothes and draw her bath. Marguerite so belittled the poor girl's efforts that the maid ran crying from the room. Later, breakfast had been delivered by Jolie, Uncle Prosper's corpulent wife. When Marguerite sat down at the table, she complained that the food smelled sour and fetid. Jolie huffed away, looking more morose than ever.

A short time afterward, Uncle Prosper, the feisty chef, came knocking at her door. When Marguerite opened it, he pranced inside, snorting and sputtering. How dare she imply his food was spoiled? He had prepared her breakfast himself, with his very own hands!

Marguerite, intimidated by the little man, quickly apologized, whereupon he demanded to know *exactly* what she wanted for breakfast. Marguerite, who wasn't hungry at this point, asked only for a boiled egg and another pot of coffee. Somewhat mollified, Uncle Prosper left to fulfill her order.

Marguerite cradled the coffee cup in her hands and, like some clairvoyant, stared into the brown liquid, examining the dregs for the key to her future. But nothing was revealed to her, except that her hands were shaking and she was exhausted. She had slept very poorly. The cuts, scrapes, and scratches that criss crossed her arms and legs had been left untended. They itched incessantly, and although she knew she must wash the wounds and disinfect them with alcohol, she had not done so. When she had returned home, she had been horrified to discover that she had only a small draft of laudanum left—an acceptable portion for a person unused to the drug, but not nearly enough to put her to sleep. She would have to make a trip that afternoon to Salle d'Or and hope that Dr. Pradel had a supply on hand. Perhaps she could persuade him to give her two bottles this time.

That meant she would have to go by herself, and the prospect of driving a carriage and team made her nervous. But if she had a servant drive her, she would have to check with Léon or Michelle, and they might ask where she was going and why, and she didn't want to explain. But she couldn't hold out for another day. Already she had begun to dread the oncoming evening and the nightmares it might bring.

Marguerite shuddered and put down the cup of coffee. Toward dawn she had fallen into a fitful sleep and dreamed that she was alone in a swirling fog. She had sensed that she was in danger, but hadn't immediately known the source of her fear. Then she had seen it floating toward her, through a sea of mist, like the figurehead of a phantom ship. It was the ghost! But its face was not a face at all, but rather the ill-formed visage of an unborn fetus.

She had turned in an attempt to flee from the ghastly specter, but her shoes had became stuck in the mire, and try as she might, she could not release her self. She could feel the wraith coming closer, its icy breath chilling her back as she struggled with the buckles and straps of her shoes. But her fingers had turned to putty, and the straps held fast. Against her will, her head shot up, and once again she had found herself staring into that face, only this time its features were not formless. They were distinct and identifiable. They were her own!

She had awakened screaming. . . .

Marguerite stared at the runny yolk in the eggcup and pushed the saucer away with a gasp of revulsion. She got up from the table and began pacing the room. Memories of the nightmare forced her to think back on the frightening events of the previous evening. "It couldn't have been a ghost," she told herself. "There is no such thing."

She tried to recall how much champagne she had drunk before fleeing into the garden. Several glasses, at least. And then there had been the fireworks, the night, the mist, and the strange setting in which they had found themselves. Without a doubt, all these things had contributed to her imagination. But why would all four of them have seen exactly the same thing? Their descriptions of the ghost had been precisely alike. Wouldn't they each have seen it differently?

Marguerite knew that she had disappointed the children in her denial of the ghost's existence, but she could not do otherwise. She simply did not believe in ghosts. They could not possibly exist, and that was that.

As Marguerite paced back and forth, she noticed that the maid had placed three letters for her on the dressing table. Hoping against all logic that one of them might contain an invitation or an offer of some future position, she snatched up the letters and rushed back to the breakfast table. Using the knife stained with yolk, she tore open the envelopes.

The first letter was from a distant cousin in Biloxi who had fallen on hard times and was asking *her* for money. Marguerite folded the letter and returned it to its envelope. The second was a short, rambling note from somebody she had considered a friend at one time. Apparently the person did not remember her and was making inquiries as to why Marguerite had written her. The third envelope contained nothing. Puzzled, she turned it over. Scrawled across the envelope in heavy black ink was the message: "Addressee deceased, please return to sender." Blood beat in her head, and the words swam before her eyes. The relative or friend of the person she had written to hadn't even had the decency to compose a short letter explaining the circumstances of her friend's death. The younger generation were all like that. They simply didn't care.

Didn't care!

Marguerite pulled herself to her feet and began pacing once again. She caught sight of herself in the mirror and gasped. Her dull, coffee-colored hair hung limply about her shoulders and resembled that of a drowned woman. Her face, still stained with vestiges of last night's makeup, looked ridiculous—a pathetic clown, made up for a show that had long since closed. She unscrewed the lid of a jar of cleansing cream, stabbed her fingers inside, and gathered a glob of the white paste. She rubbed it into her skin viciously, then, using a hand towel, roughly wiped her face clean of cosmetics.

She combed her fingers through her hair, pulled it back taut, and wound its length into a bun, which she fixed with pins at the nape of her neck. When she had finished, she gazed at herself in the mirror. A cold, hard face, sharply lined and disapproving, stared back at her. She put her hand up to the mirror and blotted out the unfamiliar image. "I *am* old," she said. "And I'll never be anything but old . . . and alone."

The words coiled and died in the heavy air, and Marguerite knew as she spoke them that she was coming to the end of her tether.

Léon and Michelle were wrapped in each other's arms and a tangle of twisted sheets. Their costumes from the ball were scattered on the floor in a trail starting from the bedroom door and leading to the bed. The couple would have slept the entire day, had it not been for the heat. As it was, the bedclothes had become sodden with perspiration and their flesh was clammy. They broke apart, panting and uncomfortable. Léon reached for the bellpull automatically, and a house servant named Marie appeared very shortly. "Marie, open the shutters and bring us some breakfast."

As Marie made her way across the room, she picked up the discarded garments and laid them across a chair, to be hung up later. She opened the louvers, and Léon groaned, "My God, it's as hot as August. Marie, is there any ice left?"

"I thinks so, M'sieur Léon."

"Then bring a big bowl of it." He cast a wicked glance at his wife. "We'll take turns rubbing each other down."

Marie, a plain, unmarried, and sheltered house servant, clamped her hands over her mouth and twittered like a little bird as she hurried from the room.

While awaiting their breakfast, Michelle and Léon discussed the ball, dwelling on the more scandalous happenings of the evening. They were still laughing over Alcée's response to the Duc's announcement when Marie reappeared.

"We'll have breakfast in bed, Marie," said Léon. "Just bring the tray over here."

They covered themselves haphazardly with sheets, and the embarrassed maid slid the large tray to the middle of the bed. While Léon and Michelle were eating, she drew their baths, hung up their clothes, then quickly departed.

Léon set the tray on the floor, save for the bowl of melting ice. "Ladies first," he grinned. Michelle stretched out face up, and Léon took a piece of ice and began running it over her warm flesh.

"Ooooh, that feels wonderful." She shuddered.

"I was thinking, Michelle. Aren't you getting a little bored with the Landing? There's going to be nothing to do around here now that the Duc's soirée is over. Why don't we take a trip downriver to New Orleans?"

"Do you suppose it's any cooler down there?"

"I doubt it. But at least there'll be something to do. I hear there's a new clothier opened on Royal Street who carries all the latest Paris fashions."

"Speaking of Royal . . . what did you think of M'sieur Brannigan?"

Léon shrugged. "I didn't get to talk to him, but he seemed pleasant enough, for an American. He was certainly well turned out."

"And handsome," Michelle giggled. "Very handsome."

Léon's jaw tightened, and his words came out clipped. "Yes—I suppose he was. If you like that type."

"You needn't be jealous, Léon. I was only making an observation. I was probably the only young woman at the party who didn't dance with him."

"Other than the Jourdain women," Léon replied, his jealousy evaporating as quickly as the ice.

"What about that Verbena Cheveraux? She's absolutely outrageous. I do believe she was stroking M'sieur Brannigan all during supper."

"How do you know?

"I noticed she was eating with only one hand, and she certainly wasn't searching for *her* napkin in *his* lap."

"She's a stunning woman."

"Do you think so?"

Léon laughed. "Now who's jealous? Turn over. Let me do your back."

"How soon can we leave?"

"The sooner, the better. And as I said, Michelle, there's nothing to keep us here."

"What about Aunt Marguerite?"

"What about her?"

"Shouldn't we bring her with us?"

Léon scowled. "Of course not. I wouldn't want her hanging around, making a nuisance of herself with her endless fault-finding."

"But what will she do here all alone?"

"I, for one, don't care what she does."

"I can't help but feel sorry for her."

"Fine, Michelle, you feel sorry for her. I can't. After my parents died and unwisely left control of the estate in her tight hands, I had to endure her moral judgments and condescension until I really thought I might strangle the old bitch."

"Oh, Léon, you don't mean that!"

"I do. And I might have, if it hadn't been for meeting you." Léon bent over and kissed his wife on the small mole that decorated the upper curve of her left buttock. "You see, Michelle, you not only saved me from marrying some prissy, frightened-to-death-of-sex ingenue, but you probably saved me from becoming a cold-blooded murderer as well." He slipped the piece of ice between her legs.

Michelle squealed with delight and reached for a piece of ice, saying, "It's your turn now!"

They were so immersed in their pleasure that they failed to notice the shadow behind the French doors; nor did they hear Marguerite's footsteps quietly retreating down the veranda.

The air inside the unventilated bedroom was as heavy and oppressive as a damp blanket. In his sleep Royal thrust out his arms to push it away, but the atmosphere remained stifling, like the interior of a sealed tomb. Perspiration slid down his forehead and came to rest in the sockets of his closed eyes. Royal blinked them open and awoke coughing and sputtering.

He swung out of bed and stood up. His right foot sent the empty champagne bottle clattering across the floor. He clutched his head and muttered, "Dear God, my brain feels scrambled." In a daze, he staggered across the floor to the French doors and yanked the heavy draperies open. Needles of golden light pierced his eyes, and Royal staggered backward, shielding his face with his arm and cursing under his breath.

Keeping his eyes covered, he managed to open the French doors, forgetting for the moment that he was nude. He awkwardly repeated his action with the other set of doors and hurried back to his bed, where he flung himself down, pressing his face into the pillow. He flexed his pelvis against the mattress. His thighs ached, and his penis felt chafed. He groaned in pleasure, sensing rather than recalling that an overindulgence in sex was the cause of his condition. Royal rolled over. A silly smile rendered his handsome face foolish.

Suddenly the smile evaporated, and he quickly sat up. "Son of a bitch. Which one was it?" He shook his head and ran his fingers roughly through his hair as he recalled pieces of the scene. Did it really happen, or had it been a dream brought on by an excess of champagne and wishful thinking? He grabbed the sheet and buried his face in its silken folds. It smelled of sex—the acrid mixture of sweat and body secretions. "Yes." He breathed into the fabric. "Yes, oh, yes."

But which one was it? She was not a virgin—that much was certain. Besides, she was too skillful, too imaginative, too delightfully perverse in the art of lovemaking to be a virgin. He drew his legs up and rested his chin on his knees. "It had to be Suzanne."

Despite her cold, officious manner, Royal sensed that she was a woman of passion. And whatever else he felt about Jean-Louis Jourdain, his instincts told him that the gambler had been a man who had possessed a certain sexual finesse, a man who enjoyed his pleasure with women.

"Could it have been Angélique?"

Young Creole women were supposed to retain their virginity until marriage. But wasn't there something lurking behind those sparkling green eyes? Was it a promise of potential delights? And if it was Angélique, then to whom had she given herself before him?

Royal jumped out of bed and smacked his fist against the palm of his hand. Of course! He would be able to tell who it was when he saw her again. She—be it Angélique or Suzanne—would be unable to conceal what had passed between them. He tapped his forefinger on his lower lip and frowned. "Wouldn't she?"

Royal smelled the sheets once again. They told him nothing except that they retained a rich, womanly scent.

He put on his robe and rang for his breakfast. The mystery stimulated him. He was both fascinated and annoyed by the deception. Perhaps it had not been meant to be one. Perhaps the late-night caller had ventured into his room unaware that the drapes had been drawn. "Damn those drapes," he muttered, and was half tempted to pull them down.

There was a knock at the door and Zenobia entered, glaring at Royal through her strange, hooded eyes. Royal asked, "Where's Nicey? Where's Seth?"

"Dey done work demselves to a frazzle at de Duc's ball, so I lets dem sleep in."

Royal waited for the formidable slave to ask him what he wanted. When she didn't, he said, "Bring me some breakfast, Zenobia, and lots of hot water for my bath."

Zenobia replied, "I brings yo' de breakfast and de hot water, but I don't scrub no man's back. Huh-uh!" Without awaiting his reply, she left.

"As if I would let her," grumbled Royal. "Damn it, that woman irritates me!"

While he was waiting for his breakfast, Royal sat down at the table and pondered the riddle. He could not recall every detail of the sexual act. Instead he was left with an overall impression of their union—a distinctly pleasurable impression.

When Zenobia arrived with his breakfast, she slammed the tray down on the table and started to leave.

"Are Mademoiselle and Madame Jourdain up yet?" Royal asked as casually as possible.

"Dey been up fo' hours."

"Are they in the house, or have they gone out?"

"Last time I saw dem dey was both in de conservatory." Indicating the bottle, Zenobia asked, "Yo' want me to take dis empty away with me?"

"Yes, dammit!" Royal snapped.

Anxious to encounter the two women, Royal hurried through his breakfast and bath. He was beginning to feel like a detective on the pursuit of an elusive criminal. He dressed quickly and was surprised to find that his hands were trembling. Nerves or alcohol? He made his way down the narrow hall and reached the conservatory. Swallowing hard, he rapped on the partly opened door and stepped inside.

The women, who were kneeling before a row of chairs, turned to look at him. "I'm sorry," Royal stammered. "I forgot it was Sunday. I've interrupted your prayers."

Royal's eye quickly took in the rearranged room. Flowering plants had been banked in tiers on both sides of an altar draped in blue satin. Atop the altar was a gold crucifix surrounded by flickering votive candles. The room was very humid, and evidently the plants had been recently watered, for the air held an earthy, loamy scent.

Suzanne and Angélique glanced at each other and then back at Royal. Suzanne stood up. "That's perfectly all right, M'sieur Brannigan. As you can see, we've taken the liberty of turning the conservatory into an impromptu chapel." She was flustered in both her voice and manner. "Since my husband's . . . death, it seemed appropriate, and it allows us the comfort of praying together."

Royal noticed Angélique glance quickly at her sister-in-law with embarrassment or irritation. Perhaps both. Suzanne continued rambling on, her eyes fixed on the marble floor. "Oddly enough, there is no chapel at Magnolia Landing. The plantation owners have discussed the possibility of building one for some time, but they cannot agree as to the site. I suppose we should have asked your permission, but it seemed—"

Angélique got to her feet and interrupted Suzanne's odd little speech. "What was it you wanted, m'sieur?"

Royal was perplexed; he didn't know what to answer. He could hardly state his true reason for being there—that he wanted to find out which of them he had slept with last night. He stared hard at the two women. They were very nearly the same height, approximately the same weight, and even their builds were similar. Their hair, now worn simply, in contrast to the elaborate coiffures of the previous night, was parted in the center and fell around their shoulders. It was exactly the same length, differing only in color.

Which one?

Royal said, "I just wanted to make sure you got home safely from the ball." The women did not respond. "I see that you did." They still did not reply. "I thought it was a very nice affair."

"Very nice," agreed Suzanne.

Royal's eyes traveled over her smooth, perfect skin. Was this the flesh he had kissed?

"Nice," echoed Angélique.

Royal looked closely at her full, sensuous lips, as pink as petals of cyclamen. Were these the lips that had so stimulated him?

"The food was excellent," he went on inanely.

"Yes," Suzanne agreed. "The Duc sets an excellent table."

Royal looked down at her fingers. They were long and slender. Had they explored his most secret places?

Angélique said, "I particularly enjoyed the gumbo." She smiled slightly, so that her even, white teeth glistened behind her lips. Did those teeth bite his flesh?

Royal took a step backward. "Well, I should leave you now."

He started to turn when Suzanne said, "Won't you join us, M'sieur Brannigan?" She gestured toward one of the empty chairs. Was she sincere? Did she really want him there? Did either of them?

"You do pray?" inquired Angélique.

"Often," Royal responded.

He wondered if they were ridiculing him. Had they planned the seduction together? And if they had, which one had come to his room?

"I'd be honored to join you."

The women stepped apart, making a place for him between them. As Royal walked toward his assigned position, he saw Zenobia standing in the doorway, her usually inexpressive face transformed into a mask of astonishment. He knelt, his shoulders touching the women's. Royal felt the heat of their bodies against his own.

Angélique said, "Shall we pray?" and they bowed their heads.

PART FOUR

Chapter Eighteen

Royal and Seth were seated beside each other in the driver's seat of the carriage. As the vehicle turned onto the Promenade, Royal adjusted his white planter's hat against the rays of the morning sun that managed to penetrate the thick foliage of the magnolia trees. Seth, in turn, adjusted his miniature version of the hat and continued his nonstop chatter as he drove Royal to the dock. Although his tone was chipper, his old man's face was pinched by anxiety.

"How long yo' gonna stay in New Orleans, Mr. Royal?"

"I don't know, Seth," Royal replied. "I guess as long as it takes me."

The little boy finally asked the question that had been on his mind all morning. "Yo' sho' yo' coming back?"

Royal patted him on the shoulder. "Of course I'm coming back, Seth. Heritage is my home now. I have no other."

"I sure wish yo' was taking me with yo'. I got dressed up jes' in case yo' changed yo' mind."

Royal was wearing the white suit he had worn to the midsummer ball, and Seth was dressed in the smaller version that Royal had had made for him.

Seth went on, "I reckon we look so much alike dat everyone probably thinks I'm yo' son."

"I'll bet they do." Royal smiled. "I'm sorry I can't take you this time, Seth, but I promise I will in the very near future. I have a lot of things on my mind that I have to sort out, and besides, it's not purely a good-time trip. I have to meet with the factor of Heritage. I want to get to know the other plantation owners—at least the ones who will accept me. I plan to visit the Sugar Exchange and learn everything I can about the industry. I want to be able to get the highest possible price for our product. Our future—yours and mine, as well as everybody else's on Heritage—depends upon it. So you keep that suit ready to go, and one of these days we'll go downriver together. Just me and you—I promise."

"Oh, I's real careful of my suit, Mr. Royal. I only puts it on every once in a while, when I needs to. Yo' know, at dem times when things don't go yo' way, and yo' starts feeling sorry fo' yo'self. Well, I just puts on dis suit and struts myself in front of de mirror, and befo' I knows it, I's thinking in yesses again."

"Thinking in yesses?" queried Royal.

"Yo' know, con-fee-dent and optim . . . optim . . ."

"You mean optimistic."

"Yes, sir, dat's what I mean—optimistic."

They reached the Magnolia Landing dock with time to spare. It was shortly after eleven-thirty, and the *Belle Créole* was not scheduled to leave until noon. Seth insisted on helping Royal with his luggage, and although Royal gave him the lightest of the two bags, the boy struggled under the weight of it. Royal caught up with him, slipped a hand through the handle, and sustained most of the weight.

Captain Calabozo was waiting by the gangplank, greeting his passengers as they boarded. Royal had not seen him since the night of the ball and thought that he looked ill. A little of the starch had been washed out of his personality, and he seemed to have lost weight. The material of his suit was limp with perspiration and could not stand up under the weight of the metal buttons, buckles, and studs. The captain seemed surprised and a little embarrassed to see Royal.

"Going to New Orleans, eh, M'sieur Brannigan? Business or pleasure?"

Royal thought he detected alcohol on the man's breath. "A little of each, Captain." He glanced at Seth. "You don't mind if my man helps me on with my luggage, do you?"

"Not at all," Calabozo replied. "You're in cabin twenty-seven."

Seth accompanied Royal to his assigned cabin off the promenade deck. The little boy looked as though he were about to cry. Royal knelt down. "Now, Seth, you're not to worry. I'll be back in a week, maybe a little longer, but I promise you I will be coming back."

"Well, if yo' promises, Mr. Royal," the little boy sniffed.

Royal slipped a silver coin into his hand. "Here—put that in your pocket. Anyone as dressed up as you ought to have some money on him. Now, you better get back to the plantation. I'm depending upon you to keep an eye on things while I'm gone, and if you try not to miss me, I'll bring you back a present. Would you like that, Seth?"

"I likes what yo' likes, Mr. Royal."

Royal watched until Seth was back on the wharf. He was about to go into his cabin to escape the noise and heat when he spotted several more arrivals hurrying toward the gangplank. He recognized Michelle and Léon Martineau from the Duc's ball. They were dressed far more conservatively than they had been then. He wondered why Marguerite Martineau wasn't accompanying them. Perhaps she hadn't yet recovered from her night of being lost and seeing ghosts.

Michelle tilted back her parasol, spotted Royal, and dazzled him with a smile of recognition. Léon, obviously not pleased, scowled at his wife and muttered something in her ear.

Following the couple aboard were a number of people Royal recognized as party guests who evidently had stayed on at Salle d'Or. He was thankful that Verbena Chevereaux was not among them. There was also a well-dressed slave woman, waiting on the wharf for the others to board first. When she looked up, Royal recognized her as the mulatto who was the mother of one of the Negrilions at the ball. Royal had seen her slip out of the kitchen to check on her son, and at the time he had been struck by her beauty. Now he noticed that her face was bruised; but even so, her statuesque form and exotic beauty remained startling. Just before she stepped onto the gangplank, she looked up again and caught him staring at her. Royal almost waved at her, but he restrained himself, knowing that the gesture could be misconstrued.

The pilot blasted the steam whistle, and a flock of birds that had been roosting on the wheelhouse scattered like spray from a shotgun. The *Belle Créole* moved slowly away from the wharf.

Royal went into his cabin, took off his boots, and stretched out on the narrow berth. He was happy to be leaving Magnolia Landing and hoped that the time away from Heritage would give him the chance he needed to think things through and to sort out his feelings concerning the events following the ball.

He still didn't know which woman had been his bed companion. On the Monday following the ball, Royal had resumed the learning pattern of his life at Heritage—mornings with Suzanne, afternoons with Angélique. He had begun the day in a positive frame of mind, certain that he would be able to ascertain which woman had visited his room. Part of his plan had been to be friendlier to both women, in order to compare their reactions. Suzanne had responded favorably. She had let down her guard, and if she had not been completely friendly, she had at least been civil. Angélique, on the other hand, had become suspicious, wary, and seemed more distrustful of him than ever. By the end of the day he was more confused than ever.

Had he been able, he would have touched their flesh or run his fingers through their hair. Perhaps the physicality of the act would have given him a clue—but of course he could not do that.

Royal's pride was somewhat bruised. Whomever he had been with, was one night of passion going to be the sum of their experience? Had he been used merely to satisfy a woman's lust? Or would she return and reveal herself to him? He had spent much of Monday and Tuesday nights awake and waiting, but no one had entered his bedroom. On Wednesday morning he had reluctantly come to the decision that now would be as good a time as any to make a trip to New Orleans. He did have business to take care of and wanted to order new clothing, but more to the point, his nerves simply demanded that he put some distance between himself and his bedroom. In any case, now that the sugar crop had been laid by and the slaves had been put to work gathering driftwood and cutting timber from the forests and swamps, there was little for him to do.

Royal's lack of rest caught up with him, and he drifted into a deep sleep, until he was awakened several hours later by the sound of a steam whistle. He put his boots back on and decided to take a turn around the deck, to wake himself up before the ship came into New Orleans.

On the shady side of the promenade, he saw the Martineaus once again. They were seated at a small, round table, sipping glasses of what appeared to be champagne. They noticed him, exchanged quick glances, and Léon got up and approached.

"M'sieur Brannigan, I am Léon Martineau. I know you only by reputation, and of course I saw you the other night at the Duc's midsummer ball. Won't you join my wife and me for a glass of champagne?"

"Thank you, M'sieur Martineau, I would enjoy that very much."

Léon introduced Michelle to Royal, and another glass of champagne was brought by a Negro attendant.

"What shall we drink to?" asked Léon. "Perhaps to M'sieur Brannigan's enjoying the favor of all the ladies in New Orleans?"

Royal knew that Léon had intended the remark mainly—though not entirely—as a joke. The three of them touched glasses, and Royal wondered why Léon had asked him over. He sensed that Michelle was attracted to him, as one good-looking person acknowledges another—almost as if to say, *aren't we the lucky ones?* He wondered if Léon realized that it was no more than that.

The champagne, however, seemed to relax everyone's inhibitions, and before long they were all calling one another by their Christian names. The Martineaus informed Royal that they would be staying at the Regent Hotel, and he in turn told them that he would be staying at the Plantation.

Léon asked, "Doesn't a man of your tastes find plantation life dull, Royal? I know we do."

"Not so far. Of course it's completely different from anything I've experienced before, and I quite like certain aspects of it." The corners of his mouth curled slightly in amusement, as he recalled the heated embrace of his mysterious visitor. "No—I'm anything but bored."

By the time the *Belle Créole* reached New Orleans, the three of them had become friends. Royal suspected that the couple's interest in him was partly due to his notoriety and their habit of thumbing their noses at convention; yet they so obviously enjoyed their youth and were so much in love with each other that he could not help but like them, even envy them a little.

As the ship slid over the sluggish brown current toward the waterfront, Royal and the Martineaus went to stand at the railing. Before them spread a wilderness of masts and iron chimneys, so many that the levee and the city itself were barely visible. Square-rigged ships, brigs, barks, schooners, and brigantines from distant ports were everywhere in sight, yet they were outnumbered by the steamboats, river galleys, and rafts of every description that had brought their cargoes downriver to the warehouses and markets of New Orleans.

The *Belle Créole* moved slowly through the flotilla of shipping, in search of a berth. Royal was reminded of a runt puppy trying to push its way through larger brothers and sisters to reach its mother's nursing teat.

They passed a stern-wheeler that some time ago had slammed into the pier. Her chimneys askew, her back broken, she listed at a sharp angle. Yet even this derelict had been put to use by some enterprising soul, who had converted it into a sleazy waterfront hotel to take advantage of the needs of the rapidly expanding population.

After a near-collision with a large naval frigate, the *Belle Créole* was able to edge into a narrow berth that was being used by a group of boys as a swimming hole. The naked urchins climbed back onto the wharf and jeered at the pilot, who blasted his whistle in reply.

Léon, his voice pounding with excitement, said, "I've never seen so many ships! There seem to be more of them each time we come here. Do you know that New Orleans now rivals New York City for the distinction of being America's biggest port?"

"The gateway to the West," said Royal.

"And to think," said Michelle, "that all this has been brought about by the invention of the steamboat."

Royal was surprised by the remark; he had not thought her interested in anything other than her own pleasure. He said, "I suppose you could say, Michelle, that the steamboat has done for New Orleans what the cotton gin has done for the rest of the South."

Michelle turned to her husband. "Léon, perhaps we should put our money into steamboats?"

Léon frowned. "We won't be here, remember?"

Royal thought she looked disappointed. Léon said to Royal, "This autumn I will come into my inheritance, and when I do, Michelle and I are planning to go live in Europe. So much more cosmopolitan, you understand."

"I've never been there," Royal replied. "But I can't imagine wanting to be far from New Orleans. This city's become like a drug to me, and I don't suppose I'll ever be free of it."

The other passengers were already headed for the gangplank, and after promising to get together when they returned to Magnolia Landing, Royal and the Martineaus parted company.

On the wharf, scores of newly disembarked passengers from several ships milled around, looking for relatives and collecting baggage. Others, stunned by the sights and sounds of the teeming waterfront, stood in wary groups, fanning themselves incessantly. The beggars, the unofficial greeters of New Orleans, filtered through the crowds, badgering new arrivals with plaintive pleas for money. Men from every walk of life and of every race, color, and nationality jammed the levees, and everywhere vendors were hawking their wares in loud, vigorous voices.

An infernal heat rose from the wooden planking underfoot in rippling vertical waves, provoking headaches and shortening tempers. People gasped for breath and moved about sluggishly. The humid atmosphere smelled of the sea, perspiration, and spoiled fish. Beyond the levee, the sound of twanging guitars and gruff shouts issued from the riverfront cabarets, a collection of rough-and-tumble buildings that appeared to lean one against the other for support. Here uniformed city guards patrolled the walkways, checking Negroes' passes, watching for pickpockets, and attempting to keep the provocative waterfront prostitutes in line.

Moving back and forth among all this, an army of sweating black men sang as they toiled beneath the merciless sun, trucking bales of cotton, hemp, and furs into dingy brick warehouses. Not too many years ago, the goods that passed across this same levee had gone to enrich French and Spanish pocketbooks. Now, above the doors of the warehouses, and on the signs of shipping offices, rooming houses, taverns, and less legitimate establishments, American names were appearing with more and more frequency. A new breed had flocked to the seductive land of gullibility and fast money, intent on making their fortunes in the great Creole city.

Royal walked through the teeming crowd in search of a carriage to take him to his hotel. A porter, a sloe-eyed young Negro, quoted him a good price and took his bags. Royal was about to climb into the vehicle when he saw the mulatto woman from the *Belle Créole*. She looked lost and distressed.

"Wait here," Royal told the driver. He walked over to the young woman, tipped his hat, and asked, "May I help you, mademoiselle?" She hesitated, and Royal realized that although he had seen her before, she did not know him. "My name is Royal Brannigan. I'm your neighbor at Magnolia Landing."

"You are M'sieur Brannigan?" the woman responded in English.

"At your service."

"My name is Lilliane. I'm from Villeneuve."

"I've met your son, mademoiselle. He's a friend of my Seth."

Lilliane noticeably relaxed at the mention of her son. "I'm afraid I've not been to New Orleans before, m'sieur. I'm trying to find my way to Bayou Road."

Royal suspected that she was going to visit Dr. Jacques, the king of New Orleans voodoo. Perhaps her nasty bruise had something to do with it. "It's not far from here," he said. "Why don't you allow me to drop you there on my way to the hotel?"

"It's on your way, m'sieur?"

"Of course," Royal replied. It was a white lie, but she would not know that.

"That is very kind of you, m'sieur."

Royal led Lilliane to his carriage and opened the door for her. "Oh, no, m'sieur—I must ride next to the driver."

Royal gave her his hand and helped her to the driver's perch. Then he gave the driver instructions to go first to Bayou Road and later to the Plantation Hotel. The driver nodded, waited for Royal to climb in, then snapped his whip over the heads of the spritely team.

When they had left the busy waterfront behind and reached the turnoff to Bayou Road, Royal heard the driver ask, "Where would you like to go, mademoiselle?"

"I'll get off here," Lilliane replied.

Royal got out of the cab and helped Lilliane to the ground. "Are you sure you don't want me to accompany you, mademoiselle? This area does not seem to be heavily populated."

"I'll be fine, m'sieur. And thank you for your kindness."

"I shall leave you, then. I hope you enjoy your trip to New Orleans."

"Thank you again, m'sieur."

Royal got back into the carriage and told the driver, "You can take me to the hotel now."

"Yo' sure came de long way around, m'sieur."

He called out the window, "Be careful, Lilliane."

She looked at him with her enormous gray eyes. They were bright and generous, and seemed capable of seeing the miraculous in the commonplace. Royal hoped that she wasn't going to be disappointed.

Lilliane approached the house on Bayou Road with a mixture of hope and trepidation. The building was a ramshackle affair, constructed of a variety of materials, including brick, cypress planking, and plaster. Apparently the original house had been a plain one-room cabin of cypress, to which several rooms had been added at random by someone who had little skill in either carpentry or masonry. The various additions jutted out at odd angles, and the whole mass squatted on brick pilings that rose several feet off the ground, protecting the house from flooding and night-crawling things.

The shutters did not fit the windows on which they were haphazardly hung. Old signs from warehouses and taverns had been hung at varying angles over the windows, to serve as makeshift awnings. The doors either overlapped the doorways or fell several inches short of their mark. Still, the house was not unattractive, Lilliane thought. Indeed, there was something charming about it. Colorful flowering vines had laced themselves around the building and were almost successful in covering the more glaring architectural defects. The surrounding land was unusually lush with grass, trees, and shrubs. The vegetation shadowed the house from the piercing sun, and when Lilliane stepped through a gate into the garden, she could actually feel the temperature drop by several degrees.

Aunt Lolly had described the house to her. "It like an oasis in the desert. Yo' can feel it welcoming yo'." The rotund slave had also told Lilliane something of the man who lived there. "He de only voodoo doctor yo' can trust. His gris-gris is de most powerful in New Orleans. He a free man of color, and dey say he a African prince, but he still care about his own people. He got de gift. He can solve dis problem fo yo', sister. He knows what yo' wants, and he can help yo' if yo' believes he can." She had also warned her, "Take some money. Dr. Jacques don't do no favors fo' nothing."

As Lilliane walked down the path, lizards scurried out of her way. She noticed that the witch doctor's garden was brimming with life. Birds frolicked in the trees, while snakes slid through the tall grass. Rabbits chased one another back and forth, and turtles lazed in the few patches of sunlight that managed to penetrate the miniature jungle. Lilliane stood there on the narrow porch, her hand raised, her skin tinted green by the shadows. Before she could knock, however, the door swung open with a loud creak that was inviting rather than frightening.

"Hello?" Lilliane said, but there was no response.

She stepped into a narrow hallway that had been formed by a long partition. The walls were pasted over with French newspapers and decorated with clumps of feathers, bones, dried flowers, snakeskins, and shells strung together on knotted ropes. The passage was dimly lit by a row of flickering candles placed in conch shells fastened to the wall. At the end of the hall was a very tall closed door.

Lilliane made her way down the corridor and rapped lightly on the door.

"Come inside, sister," a deep voice ordered.

Lilliane turned the knob and entered.

The dark room was steaming with incense, and the fumes made her eyes water. She blinked away the tears, and the first thing she made out were floor-to-ceiling shelves stacked with glass jars containing embalmed snakes, lizards, and scorpions. As her eyes adjusted, she could see rows of human and animal skulls, dried roots, herbs, and flowers. The overpowering smell was repulsive and erotic at the same time.

"I've been expecting you, sister."

Lilliane spun around as a man emerged from the shadows. His appearance so startled her that she almost retreated through the door. He was extraordinarily tall—nearly seven feet—and his height was emphasized by the black beaver top hat he wore. His shirt was heavily ruffled and dazzlingly white, his trousers were wine colored, and his vest was covered with eyes of overlapping peacock feathers. He wore heavy gold jewelry—earrings, bracelets, and necklaces. His skin was very dark, almost blue-black, and his features were stark, chiseled, and slightly menacing. He had three parallel scars on each cheek, curving from the temples to the corners of his lips. His dark, golden-flecked eyes were fixed upon her.

He reached out his hand and took hers. "Don't be afraid, sister. I'm Dr. Jacques. I know why you've come, and *I can* answer your prayers." He smiled at her, revealing teeth that were large, white, and even.

Lilliane allowed him to lead her back into the room. He guided her to a chair next to a small table, then sat down opposite her. "I know you, sister," he said. "I just don't know your name."

Lilliane explained who she was and started to tell him of her problems. He held up a hand.

"I *know* why you came. I want to help you, Lilliane, but you must trust in me. The loas give me the *power*. I can use that power to help others, but it will not happen without *faith*." His voice had a calming, almost hypnotic effect.

"I believe you, Dr. Jacques," Lilliane replied.

He closed his eyes and dipped his hand into a bowl filled with sand. His arm seemed to move automatically, and as it did, a thin trail of sand dribbled from his fist onto the dark tabletop, creating a pattern.

"Hear me, Freda Erzili, John the Baptist, Saint Rita, Dr. Moses, Damballah, Papa Legba, Saint Peter, Baron Cemetery . . . *guide my hand!*" He lapsed into Cajun, and Lilliane could make out only a few words. "*Mo gagnain soutchien la Louisiane, mallé oir ca ya di moin!*" It meant something about having the support of Louisiana, and that no one could resist him.

The chant ended, and Dr. Jacques looked down at the patterns he had made with the sand. He traced his fingers over the design and said, "You have had problems with your eyes." Lilliane's mouth dropped open. "I can help you." He traced another pattern. "You'll never be able to save enough money to buy your son's freedom." The young woman gasped and started to ask a question. He held up his hand for quiet. "The man who owns you is here in New Orleans. You must go back tonight, back to your plantation."

"There's a steamboat leaving at six o'clock. I was planning to take it."

"Yes," he replied softly. "I will drive you there. Now, come closer, sister, and I will tell you what you must do." In low, whispered tones, the voodoo doctor instructed Lilliane how to make the gris-gris work. From time to time he would pass the palm of his hand over her forehead.

"Do you understand, sister?"

"Yes, but what if I can't find—"

"What is needed will be there." He stood up and walked around the table until he was behind her. Pressing her eyes shut with his fingers, he said, "Keep your eyes closed, sister, and be still." She felt something wet and stinging penetrate her closed lids, but she did not cry out or move. Then, in a gesture that seemed more tender than mysterious, he turned her around and kissed each of her eyelids, saying, "There's nothing wrong with your eyes any longer, Lilliane."

Lilliane opened her eyes and was shocked to find that she

could see every minute detail of Dr. Jacques's face. There were no blurred edges, no faded patches. Everything was as distinct as if it had been drawn with sharp outlines.

"Walk about the room, sister."

Lilliane did as he said and was amazed that she could clearly see each letter on the bottle labels, distinguish one feather from another, count the rings on a slice of a tree trunk. Tears welled up in her eyes, and she rushed to Dr. Jacques. "This is wonderful," she cried.

He placed his hands on her shoulders. "Like me, you were born under the sign of Gemini. That means we have two lives. Your new life is about to begin."

"My new life?" she repeated. "What do you mean?"

"You have power. I sensed it the moment you stepped into my home."

"Power to do what?" she asked.

"Power to see things, do things, change things. But you need me to teach you how to use it."

"I still don't understand."

"You will." He slid his hands behind her head and in one quick motion removed her tignon. Lilliane's bright auburn hair came undone and fell over her shoulders, reaching nearly to her waist. The doctor ran his fingers through her tresses and murmured, "There's magic in your hair, sister. When you come to me again, come without your tignon."

Lilliane reached into her bodice and pulled out the knotted handkerchief that contained a portion of her secret savings. She started to untie it, but the witch doctor placed his hand over hers, saying, "I will not accept money from you, sister."

His meaning was obvious. She gazed into his eyes and saw reflected herself and the witch doctor. They were lying naked in a room filled with flickering candles. She nodded in silent agreement. Even though she had known no other man but Philippe, she was not afraid.

"Of course I would not expect payment until the gris-gris is successful," he said, replacing the knotted handkerchief. "You've never been in love, Lilliane?" She shook her head. "Then I will teach you what it is like." For a moment he looked as though he was about to embrace her, but then he stepped back and his manner became formal. "Come—I will drive you to the waterfront and see that you get on the steamboat safely."

"When should I return here?" Lilliane asked.

"You'll know," he replied enigmatically.

Dr. Jacques opened the front door for Lilliane. She abruptly turned around and asked him, "But what about Azby's freedom? You haven't told me if—"

He shook his head and replied softly, "One thing at a time, sister. One thing at a time."

Chapter Nineteen

Royal had checked into the Plantation Hotel and spent the remainder of the afternoon at his tailor's, ordering clothing more suitable for his life at Heritage. He had returned to the hotel without encountering anyone he could consider a friend, and after a bath he had reluctantly decided to join the New Orleans night life.

As he walked through the hotel lobby, he looked about for the little flower vendor. He recalled that the last time he had made a purchase from her, she had suggested a magnolia. Then he had gone to Odalisque and met Jean-Louis Jourdain.

Royal was disappointed that there was no sign of her. At first he was surprised that her absence should affect him so. She was such a familiar fixture that he had come to look forward to seeing her. Her cheerful greeting had always given him a feeling of stability in a city full of strangers and fleeting acquaintances.

Minette. He was surprised that the name came so easily to mind. He decided to inquire at the desk about her.

The desk clerk was a slender and nervous newcomer with an officious manner. "The flower girl?" he said. "We had to ask her to sell her goods elsewhere." He leaned forward and lowered his voice. "There were too many complaints about her."

"Complaints?" asked Royal. "What kind?"

"The Negro slaves were frightened of her. They claimed she had the evil eye."

"That's nonsense," declared Royal. "She's the soul of gentleness."

"Oh, I agree, certainly. But you have to admit, sir, that her eyes are—well, somewhat strange. In any case, many of our clientele experienced some resistance from their slaves because of her presence." He shrugged his shoulders. "Too bad—she was a colorful little creature."

Royal walked away from the desk clerk, bristling at the injustice of the act. Where would she go, a small child like that? At least here, in the lobby of the hotel, she had been protected from the elements. He tried to put the business out of his mind. After all, she was nothing to him, he told himself. She was just one of the countless street children who roamed the cities everywhere along the great rivers—one of the many who would grow up before they should, and grow old and die before their time.

The front veranda of the Plantation was a favorite gathering spot for the hotel's guests. Seated in a perfectly straight line of rocking chairs and attended by their slaves, the visitors indulged themselves in their favorite pastime—gossip. Royal noted that, as usual, the rocking chairs moved at exactly the same leisurely pace. The sight put him in a better humor, and stifling a grin, he proceeded down the stairs to the *banquette*, fully aware that all eyes were upon him.

As Royal walked through the narrow streets toward the Place d'Armes, he realized that he was also the object of attention and speculation on the part of the passersby. Those who had previously snubbed him for being a gambler and an American acknowledged him now that he was a plantation owner. Creole gentlemen who had formerly turned their heads tipped their hats to him. Creole matrons who had once crossed the street rather than pass nearby offered him their smiles. Royal figured that, despite his origins, he now was a potential catch for their unwed daughters.

At a corner he encountered a group of people who were watching the manipulations of a three-card monte dealer. The oily-looking entrepreneur was enticing the onlookers with a first-rate spiel, which appealed to both their skepticism and greed. "Step right up, gentlemen," he invited. "The winning card is the ace of hearts." He held it up for all to see before slapping it facedown on top of the barrel. "Now watch closely while I shuffle the cards."

Royal kept walking. Halfway down the block, a pair of Ursuline nuns in starched white wimples and gray habits glided solemnly toward him. Between them, swathed in gauze, walked a female figure. She looked like an Arabian bride. Royal stared at the strange apparition. As the trio neared, his gaze met that of the woman in gauze. Only her dark, almond-shaped eyes and a patch of fair forehead were visible. Royal could see that she was a young Creole, no more than twenty. There was a terrible anguish in her eyes, and with a pang Royal suddenly realized the truth—she had contracted leprosy. In accordance with New Orleans law, the nuns were escorting her to Lepers' Row, a place of banishment for those with the dreaded disease.

Each of the nuns was carrying a large basket, one apparently containing the woman's clothing, the other foodstuffs. People on the street quickly hurried to the other side as the trio approached, some crossing themselves, others spitting. Royal did not move. When they were next to him, he quietly asked the nearest nun if she would accept a contribution for the welfare of her charge. The nun smiled and nodded in response. He pressed a packet of money into her hand. The young woman in gauze thanked him with her terrible, sad eyes, and they passed on.

Royal stopped for a moment outside the Théâre d'Orléans, where a perspiring crowd had gathered to attend that evening's ball. A line of carriages stretched down the street, and several young Creole maidens on their way into the theater, their eyes gleaming like polished jet, offered Royal furtive glances from behind fans. Each girl was kept in tow by a matronly chaperone who carried her charge's dancing shoes so that they wouldn't get dirty. The girls primped and preened like exotic birds on display.

As Royal reached the Place d'Armes, the bells of Saint Louis Cathedral began to toll. Pigeons routed by the din forsook their nests in the triple towers of the cathedral and started circling overhead, finally coming to roost on the three wooden gallows that stood near the center of the square, like one-armed crucifixes.

Royal watched as groups of people streamed to the cathedral for evening mass. The main doors opened with a whoosh, and the congregation was sucked into the dark mouth of the church.

In front of the city hall next door, an aged Negress was selling calas, which were cooking in a pan over a small furnace. She sang her advertisement:

> "*Calas, tout chaudes, madame, tout chaudes!*
> Get 'em while they're hot! Hot calas!"

Next to her, a young mulattress, plump as a pullet, dispensed cups of freshly made coffee from her little stand and chanted:

"Coffee black! Coffee light!
Coffee fo' de black and white.
Some like it black,
Some like it white.
Some jes' like it all de night!"

Royal bought a cala and a cup of coffee. The vendors served him without breaking their songs. The silvery rattle of tambourines caught his attention, and Royal looked to his right. A procession of voodooists was dancing across the dusty square. The leader was a man Royal had seen many times before. Dr. Jacques, the self-ordained voodoo priest of New Orleans, was impossible to mistake.

This evening he was wearing a top hat, a ruffled shirt, and black evening clothes. As he moved to the rattle of the tambourines, his tails flapped in the wind, giving him the appearance of a huge prehistoric bird. Wrapped around his broad shoulders like an extravagant fur piece was a small, white goat. It was bawling and seemed to know what its fate would be. Royal guessed it would be sacrificed on the shores of Lake Pontchartrain during the height of a voodoo ceremony. The line of dancers moved and chanted as if hypnotized. Royal had the feeling that if the witch doctor chose to march straight into the river, all of them would happily follow.

As the impromptu parade passed the church, the voodooists, including Dr. Jacques, crossed themselves. Royal smiled at the sight, then watched as Dr. Jacques flipped each of the vendors a coin and sampled their wares. He ate the calas whole, washing them down with the scalding coffee. He kissed both women on the forehead and dipped his hat to Royal, then he and his flock moved quickly on.

A cannon was fired. It was nine o'clock—the time for all sailors, soldiers, and Negroes to get off the streets. Any of them found out after the cannon fire, unless bearing a pass from his employer or master, was taken to the prison. A watchman began crying out the hour, adding in a bored voice, "All is well."

Royal felt abandoned. The religious were in church, the

voodooists had gone to attend their ceremonies, and the remaining people wandering through the Place d'Armes were all in pairs. Husbands and wives, courting sweethearts, and lovers looking for a cool place to make love. Everybody was going somewhere. Royal had no appointments. Suddenly he wanted to see familiar faces and be in a familiar place. He wished he were back at Heritage, sitting on the veranda with Seth.

Royal turned around and began walking. He pretended that he was just strolling, with no direction in mind, but in his heart he knew where he was headed—to Odalisque. It was the very place he never thought he would return to, but tonight he was lonely.

He walked down Chartres Street until he reached Canal. He ignored the lower-class gambling establishments and headed directly for Odalisque, the garish pink building on the corner of Canal and Bourbon. Ahead, a large oil lamp held by a heavy iron hook projecting from a wall told Royal he had reached his destination. And standing beneath the hook and lamp, to his delight, was Minette.

A sign of good luck, Royal thought—then remembered that he didn't gamble anymore. He stopped and watched the freckled girl for a moment as she stood quietly next to the toy ship on wheels that housed not only her wares but her pet. The calico cat was staring over the ship's prow, observing the passersby with benign indifference.

"*Bonsoir, M'sieur Brannigan,*" said the patchwork girl. Even the cat turned its head and feigned interest.

"I'd wondered where you'd got to, Minette. Bad business, not letting you stay at the hotel."

She shrugged. "They did what they had to do."

"So now you're here?"

She nodded vigorously. "Yes, Madame Odalisque gave me permission. She told me I could make this my permanent spot."

"I must compliment her on her good judgment."

"Would you like a flower, m'sieur?"

"Yes, I would." He moved his hand over her selection and picked a half-opened red rose. He bent down so that she could pin it on his lapel. "And what is the message of this particular selection, Minette?"

"It asks a question: 'Won't you tell me your name?' "

Royal laughed. It was a harsh and bitter sound.

Minette frowned and said, "Would you prefer another flower, m'sieur?"

"No, Minette, I believe I've made the right choice."

"I think the red rose will go well with the colors of Odalisque."

"How do you know what the inside of Odalisque looks like?"

She blushed and replied shyly, "Is it not true?"

"It's true all right. Well, good night, Minette. I'm glad you've found a place to sell your flowers."

"Thank you, m'sieur, and *bonne chance*."

The Negro doorman opened the etched glass door, and as Royal passed into the hallway, Minette's disconcerting words echoed in his ears.

Won't you tell me your name?

His thoughts flashed back to that night. If only he knew which woman had come to his room! Royal forced the troubling question aside; he was determined to enjoy the glittering world of Odalisque.

The air was cooler inside because of the high ceilings and thick walls and the recently installed steam-driven ventilating fans. Royal went directly to the elaborate front bar. The bartender was new and didn't recognize him. Royal watched as the young man deftly mixed a series of intricate drinks favored by habitués of Odalisque—brandy smashes, rum punches, and mint juleps. He caught the bartender's attention and ordered an Irish whiskey. The bartender appeared disappointed that he hadn't requested anything fancier.

The whiskey didn't taste right to Royal, and he wondered if Odalisque had taken to serving a poor quality of liquor. Perhaps it was just his mood. He was feeling lonelier than ever. At that moment, Odalisque's raucous voice cut through the ongoing conversations like a scythe.

"Haugh!" she roared. "I'll be damned if it isn't the American!"

Royal turned and took in the spectacle that was Odalisque. The obese proprietress, seated on her huge rolling platform, was being wheeled toward him by Mataché. As usual, Boudin proceeded her, bearing a tray of candy.

Royal was so pleased to see a familiar face that he kissed Odalisque full on her puffy mouth. "It's good to see you, Odalisque."

The huge woman gurgled with delight. "Are you downriver for good, Royal, or just taking a break from the cane fields?"

"Just a short trip, Odalisque."

She looked at him appraisingly. "I hear you're doing just fine up at Magnolia Landing, considering you're an American."

"Considering everything, I think I am."

"Look at you, you Irish stud—you're handsomer than ever! The outdoor life must agree with you, haugh?" She leaned forward. The platform creaked menacingly, but Mataché steadied it with his strong hands. "I'm pleased that you're doing well, Royal." She added in a lowered voice, "It strikes a blow for our side."

"Our side?" Royal repeated.

Odalisque dropped her voice to a whisper. "Royal, I'm just plain old Maggie O'Leary from the Lower East Side of New York City."

"But . . . but . . ." Royal stuttered.

"Odalisque? She's my own creation. How else could I make a go of it in New Orleans? Thank God my first pimp was a Frenchie!"

Royal threw back his head and howled until tears came into his eyes. "You don't mean it!"

"I wouldn't tell anybody else but you, Royal, but it's just a great big, fat façade." She speared a soft candy from Boudin's tray and popped it into her mouth. "By the way, Royal, somebody's been coming around and asking about you."

"Gambler?"

She nodded. "I don't remember his name, but I sure know his game—a high roller with hair redder than mine, and *his* is natural. As a matter of fact, I think he's somewhere hereabouts tonight."

"St. Louis Sam!" exclaimed Royal.

"That's his moniker. Take a stroll around the place and see if you can find him."

"If you'll excuse me, Odalisque, I'll do just that."

"Now, don't go gambling away your plantation."

"I don't gamble anymore."

"Good for you, Royal. You have sense enough to know when to fold. After harvest, I expect you to bring me my very own barrel of molasses!"

Royal called over his shoulder, "They're not barrels, Odalisque, they're hogsheads!"

"Now, that's sure as hell appropriate," she chortled.

Royal made his way through the rooms of the establishment, searching for the man who had helped him bury his dearest friend, Charlie Hazard. The customers were immersed in their games and paid little attention to Royal. Only Odalisque's whores raised their eyes as he passed through the various gaming rooms. Royal guessed that St. Louis Sam preferred twenty-one or poker, or possibly roulette, though the odds weren't as good.

He entered the roulette parlor, which was, like all the other rooms at Odalisque, decorated in a shade of red. The walls and ceiling were hung with plum-colored satin and made Royal feel that he was inside a candy box. The croupier urged the patrons to place their bets. There were a murmur of voices and a shuffle of chips, then the wheel was spun. Royal heard the first faint click of the roulette ball, followed by eager words of encouragement from the gamblers, then a final dull rattle as the ball found its mark.

"And the winner is number eighteen, red!"

"Son of a bitch!" cried a gruff voice that sounded as if it had been put through a coarse strainer. Royal pushed his way past onlookers to where St. Louis Sam was bent over the table, raking in his chips. Royal touched him on the shoulder.

"Sam—St. Louis Sam?"

The old man turned, and Royal couldn't believe the change in his appearance. Gone were the threadbare clothes, the gaunt cheeks, and the downtrodden expression. This Sam was back in the chips, and evidently had been for some time. He had gained weight, and his face was flushed with high color. His unruly red hair was now held in place by a sweet-smelling pomade. He was dressed in an outfit of unspeakable gaudiness—a dark green coat and trousers shot through with metallic gold threads, a frilled shirt fastened with gold buttons, and a golden silk vest embroidered to depict stags in a forest.

The old man burst into a loud whoop and threw his arms around Royal. "Royal Brannigan! You're a sight to please the blessed saints! Come help me cash in these chips, and let's have a drink."

They went to the main salon. Sam ordered double Irish whiskies for both of them and offered an Irish toast. "*Slainte.*" Then he told Royal what had happened to him.

After burying Charlie Hazard, Sam had taken the grubstake Royal had given him and set himself up with a three-card monte game on the streets of Pittsburgh. He had earned enough money to return to the rivers, and had gone on from there. Lady Luck, he said, was sitting in his back pocket, and now he was riding the crest.

Sam finished his drink. "Money bought me a little bit of dazzle, Royal, but I figure it's sort of like gilding a wart."

Sam called for another round, and Royal, in turn, recounted the highlights of what had happened to him and explained his reasons for no longer gambling.

Sam said, "I can understand that, son. Hell, it makes no difference to me—I've won enough for tonight. There are other diversions here. You haven't given women up, have you?" Royal assured him that he hadn't.

They were about to leave the salon when Boudin, banging a gong, crisscrossed the room, shouting, "Auction! Auction!"

"What's this?" asked Sam.

"A rather sad spectacle, I'm afraid," Royal replied. "Every time Odalisque acquires a new whore—invariably young, fresh, and supposedly a virgin—her first evening is auctioned off to the highest bidder."

A light glimmered in Sam's pale blue eyes. "I'd like to see that, Royal. Do you mind if we stay?"

"No," Royal replied. He didn't want to stay, but he didn't want to disappoint Sam.

A professional auctioneer entered. He was young, but with crude features and a hard glint in his dark eyes and a cruel set to his jaw. An impromptu auction block was set up by clearing one of the heavy round tables and pushing it to the center of the room. A miniature set of stairs was placed next to it. The table was covered with a red velvet cloth, and a dozen or so small oil lamps were set around its edge, making it resemble a miniature stage.

The auctioneer swilled down almost an entire bottle of what appeared to be brandy, then, forcing his face into a semblance of congeniality, he held up a hand until everyone in the room was silent. The orchestra offered a drum roll, and, in a clumsy attempt at theatrics, the auctioneer bowed. When he straightened up, he threw out an arm toward the door that led to the kitchen. The door swung open, and a young girl entered. She was slender and not yet fully developed, and Royal guessed she could not have been more than thirteen. Her eyes were bright blue and doelike, and her skin was as creamy and unblemished as a new petal of a gardenia. Her waist-length hair was a soft shade of red, and she was dressed demurely in a white gown of eyelet lace.

Royal heard Sam suck in his breath and exclaim, "That's the prettiest little girl I ever did see—but she's only a child."

The girl, who was the very picture of naïveté, ascended the stairs and positioned herself in the center of the table. She kept her eyes downcast, and a faint smile puckered her mouth.

Word of the auction was circulated throughout Odalisque, and dozens of men, the majority of them overweight and older, were drawn to the main salon like a colony of ants to molasses. They gathered in sweaty groups to drink, ogle, and laugh. The auctioneer managed to quiet them, and then announced in a clear, ringing voice, "Gentlemen, I present for your pleasure . . . Nicole!" The girl executed a precise curtsy and favored her would-be clients with a generous smile, revealing two neat rows of tiny white teeth. "We'll start the bidding at fifty dollars."

There was a barrage of fifty-dollar bids, interspersed with guffaws and a few vulgar remarks impugning the girl's supposed virginity. As the auctioneer was trying to ascertain which bid to honor, someone shouted over the hubbub, "I'll bid one hundred dollars!"

Royal turned in the direction of the familiar voice. Philippe Duvallon, leaning against a table, and looking somewhat disheveled and a little bit more than drunk, was staring directly at him.

"A friend of yours?" asked St. Louis Sam.

"I hope not," Royal replied.

A grossly overweight man, his ruddy face shadowed by a gigantic planter's hat, belligerently offered, "One hundred and twenty dollars!"

A short man with a knobby forehead and a lascivious grin stepped out of his group. His reedy voice pierced the proceedings. "One hundred and thirty!"

Philippe calmly said, "Make that one hundred and fifty dollars!"

Sam turned to Royal. "I wonder how high he's willing to go?"

"I don't know, but let's find out, shall we?" Royal called out, "I bid one hundred and seventy-five!"

Sam was aghast. "But Royal, surely you don't want her?"

"No," Royal replied with a flicker of a smile. "But I want to see just how badly he does."

"One hundred and ninety!" cried planter's hat.

"Two hundred even!" gasped an elderly Creole gentleman who looked to be in his eighties.

Knobby forehead's voice rang out, "Make that two hundred and twenty-five!"

Philippe topped that with two hundred and fifty dollars. There were two more bids, of two hundred and sixty and two hundred and seventy-five. Royal casually added, "Three hundred dollars." He did not look in Philippe's direction but could feel his anger clear across the room.

Philippe's voice boomed out, "Three hundred and fifty dollars!"

There was an audible gasp from the onlookers, followed by a collective groan from the bidders.

The eighty-year-old tentatively offered three hundred and sixty dollars, but the fight was gone from his voice, as though he knew he was going to be outbid.

Philippe immediately upped the girl's price to four hundred. Royal made it four hundred and fifty dollars. Sam warned, "I believe everybody else has dropped out. You'd better drop out too."

"Not yet. He's not ready. Let's make him really pay for what he wants." Royal glanced at Nicole. She seemed to be getting a childish pleasure out of her popularity; she was smiling like a birthday girl.

"Five! I say five hundred dollars for the virgin!" Philippe roared, and slammed his fist on the table.

The other bidders grumbled their disappointment. Sam glanced nervously about. "They're out for sure. Damn, that young fellow's mad at you." He cackled and, caught up in the spirit of Royal's game, called out, "Five hundred and twenty-five dollars." There was a long pause, and Sam anxiously whispered, "God, I hope he's going to top me."

"He's good for another fifty or so," said Royal.

Philippe shouted, "Five hundred and fifty dollars!"

Royal pushed the bidding up to five hundred and seventy-five.

The auctioneer was perspiring with excitement. "I hear five seventy-five, I hear five seventy-five, going . . . going . . ."

"Six hundred," cried Philippe, in a wavering voice. Out of the corner of one eye Royal noted that his face was as pale as lard. He whispered to Sam, "Well, Sam, I think it's time to fold."

"I have six hundred dollars, six hundred, do I hear more?

Going . . . going . . . *gone!* Sold for six hundred dollars to M'sieur Duvallon!"

"Royal," Sam whispered, "he's coming over here."

Royal stood up and faced the angry Creole. "Congratulations, m'sieur," he said before Philippe could speak. "You've got not only the youngest whore in New Orleans, but also the most expensive."

"You'll pay a lot more for this, Brannigan," Philippe growled.

Royal calmly took out his pocket watch and checked the time. "It's almost twelve o'clock, m'sieur." He glanced over Philippe's shoulder toward the girl, who was still standing in the center of the table. "It's time for you to gather up your toys and go to bed."

Lilliane watched the kitchen clock with avid eyes and counted the strokes in a voice hoarse with anticipation. "Nine . . . ten . . . eleven . . . twelve!"

Quickly she pulled her shift over her head and hung it on the back of a chair. Following Dr. Jacques's instructions, she moved quietly about the room, turning out the lamps and lighting each of the twenty-two yellow candles—one for every year of her life. From time to time she would glance down the hall toward the closed bedroom door. Lilliane had the distinct impression that she was being watched, but then she remembered the witch doctor's words.

"The loas and the saints will be watching you. Don't be afraid—they are on your side."

Lilliane copied Philippe's full name on a small scrap of paper. Since she had never learned to write very well, she painstakingly copied each letter from an envelope she knew to be addressed to him. It was a time-consuming task, but Dr. Jacques had told her it was essential that the name be in her handwriting.

Setting the paper aside, she melted a small white candle in a saucepan. Beads of her sweat dropped into the pan. She plucked out the wick with a fork, then added a small scrap of material she had cut from a bed sheet stained with Philippe's semen. The fabric wilted in the hot wax. When the wax had cooled, Lilliane scraped it out of the pan and began molding it around the scrap of paper. She was good at working with her hands, and the wax soon took on a recognizable human form.

Using her sewing needles, Lilliane carefully carved the

facial features. She had been working on the project for over an hour when she realized that her eyes had not been bothering her in the least. She got up from the table and laid the finely wrought image of Philippe Duvallon on a small square of bright red material. In a hushed voice, she called on the voodoo gods and Catholic saints to answer her prayers. Then, in the same low, measured tones, she began chanting the words taught to her by Dr. Jacques:

"Jé innocent, jé innocent, bon a ye,
Jé innocent, jé innocent, bon a ye.
Nan point rien pleu fort passe Bon Dié.
Jé innocent, jé innocent, bon a ye."

A stiff breeze suddenly blew through the kitchen, moving the hanging pots, causing the candles to flicker and sputter, and drying the perspiration that coated Lilliane's body. Startled, she looked about the room. Although she couldn't see *them*, she knew *they* were there.

Reassured, Lilliane started the chant again. She knew only that it meant something about "innocent eyes" and "nothing stronger than God." As the strange words rolled off her tongue, she took a poker and began stoking the banked kitchen fire. The flames jumped high and burned with an eerie glow, filling the room with a yellow light. Lilliane cocked her head to one side and could hear Dr. Jacques's voice above the chant. The words were so clear that he might have been in the room: "Fear nothing, sister. You will not be hurt." She reached into the fire and, with her bare fingers, extracted a small, red-hot ember. Still chanting, she let it drop onto the crotch of the doll, and as the ember blackened and sizzled, the doll's appearance was altered. Its limbs were no longer straight, its face no longer handsome.

Lilliane wrapped the now-grotesque doll in the red fabric and secured it with seven sewing pins, all facing the same direction. She put on her dress, blew out the candles, and carried the doll into the bedroom, where she laid it to rest beneath her bed. She kissed Azby on the forehead. He had slept through everything. When she climbed between the sheets, Lilliane felt more relaxed than she could ever remember feeling.

* * *

Michelle Martineau was standing just outside the main salon at Odalisque. She had watched the auction with fascinated horror. But Michelle did not feel particularly sorry for the young girl who was the object of the heated bidding; rather she had conjured up a fantasy wherein she herself was in Nicole's place, and the men were bidding for her favors. The reverie hadn't really been satisfactory. For one thing, Léon wasn't one of the bidders, and in Michelle's fantasy no one except her husband could have been the winner of her favors.

She shuddered as Philippe passed, but he was so intent on the girl he was leading away that he didn't notice her. He fairly pulled his prize up the ornate staircase to the second floor. A giggle erupted from Michelle's lips. She looked around for some sign of Léon, and in so doing, took in the outlandish decor. If anything, Odalisque was in even worse taste than Salle d'Or. Yet in its own bizarre way it had a peculiar charm.

Léon had brought her here on a whim. For a fee, Madame Odalisque had lent her one of her own wigs, as well as one of her whore's gowns, allowing Michelle to move about the establishment disguised as one of the tarts.

Michelle examined her makeup in a nearby gilt mirror. The liberally employed cosmetics had convincingly transformed her. Her lips and cheeks were scarlet, her skin powdered to an almost tubercular whiteness, her eyes so outlined and shadowed that they resembled wilted sunflowers. The wig, however, was insufferably hot, and perspiration had caused the beauty patch to slide from her cheekbone nearly to her jaw. Michelle pushed it back into position, resumed her pose, and waited.

A huge fat man wearing a planter's hat stepped in front of her, blocking her view. He reeked of sweat and expensive cologne.

"What are you doing all alone, honey?" he whispered into her ear.

Michelle came up with a somewhat younger version of Odalisque. "Haugh!" she snorted. "Anyone can see that I'm waiting for someone."

"Not me?" The man looked disappointed.

"Not you. I'm terribly sorry, but perhaps one of the other ladies would benefit from your charming company."

The man lumbered off in search of another whore.

"Dammit," Michelle muttered, "where's Léon? I wish he could have seen that performance."

Michelle gasped. Royal Brannigan and another man were coming in her direction, and it was too late for her to turn away. They had their arms around each other's shoulders and looked as if they had been drinking quite a bit. Michelle had been amused at how Royal had driven up Philippe's bid, and although she wanted to tell him so, her presence here would not be easy to explain. As Royal drew near, however, he simply smiled at her, and the older man winked; then they continued weaving their way through the crowd.

Michelle let out a sigh of relief. Royal had not recognized her beneath the curly red wig and painted face. With a handkerchief redolent of perfume, she dabbed at the perspiration running from her temples.

Where *was* Léon!

Just then she felt a man slide his arms about her waist. She spun around. Léon was ludicrously dressed. Complete with false mustache, frilly shirt, fake diamond headlight, and spats, he was transformed into a typical riverboat gambler.

"What are you doing all alone?" he asked.

"Oh, Léon," she wailed in disappointment, "that's what the other man said." Léon looked hurt. She traced a fingertip over the fake mustache and said, "Well, come on—we might as well go upstairs. We've only got the room for two hours."

Chapter Twenty

Royal's week in New Orleans passed without any further encounters with Philippe. He had a wonderful time with Sam, drinking and swapping Charlie stories. He did not allow himself to gamble, and he did not desire the companionship of the city's women. He wanted only to be with the two women who intrigued him—Suzanne and Angélique. But which one did he want the most? His business finished, his wardrobe completed, Royal decided it was time to return to Heritage.

He sent notice upriver of his impending arrival, and the next morning, as the steamship pulled into sight of Magnolia

Landing, the first thing Royal saw was Seth sitting on the wharf, playing his banjo. When the boy saw that his new master was aboard, he strummed the strings to a fever pitch and began jumping up and down. Royal laughed and waved both arms, then clutched the railing and breathed in the fresh country air made fragrant by the heady scent of magnolias. He wondered if the Landing would always make him feel so welcome.

Royal rushed up the gangplank, picked up Seth, and swung him around. "It's great to see you, son!"

"I was afraid dat yo' weren't coming back, Mr. Royal."

"I had to come back. I had to bring your present to you, didn't I?" Royal stuck his hand into his pocket and drew out a gold chain. Dangling from the end of it was a gold pocket watch, which shone like a miniature sun.

Seth's eyes grew wide. "Is dat really fo' me, Mr. Royal?"

"Nobody else. Of course, this means you'll never have an excuse again for being late."

The boy grinned. "I 'spects I won't mind looking at de time now and den."

The suitcases and packages containing Royal's new clothes were loaded aboard the carriage, and he and Seth climbed into the driver's seat.

The sun was a patch of orange stitched onto a quilt of bright blue. The heat made the air wave and shimmer above the entrance to the Promenade. Royal had the impression that the carriage was entering a landscape of dreams. He hoped that they would be good ones.

"Tell me, Seth, what's been happening at Heritage?"

As Seth launched into a nonstop monologue, Royal leaned back in his seat and smiled to himself, thinking that nothing could be as pleasing to his ears as the little boy's stream of chatter.

The Duc Duvallon circled his latest acquisition, examining it from all angles. The enormous Chinese urn had arrived the previous evening by steamboat and had been taken to the ballroom, where it had been unpacked by slaves. It was nearly the same height as the Duc himself and was painted in oxide red and powder blue. Swimming around its side was a carp, the Chinese symbol for long life.

The Duc had made the purchase in response to the recent rage among plantation owners for anything old and Chinese.

Normally he viewed such objects with boredom and even distaste. He didn't care all that much for Chinese art and privately thought that a fish painted on a pot was not all that attractive. He vaguely wondered where he was going to put the damned thing. Not in the gardens. It was too valuable to be exposed to the elements. It would have to be someplace in the house where he didn't often visit. Perhaps the library. He hadn't been there since the night of the ball. A flicker of a smile skipped across his lips, then ran away.

He sat down on one of the ballroom chairs, crossed his legs, and scratched his neatly cropped mustache with a gloved hand. The urn somehow intimidated him, and he didn't know why.

The Duc sensed, rather than realized, that the structure of his ordered life was falling apart. Nothing had been the same since the night of the midsummer ball. He irrationally blamed his problems on Royal Brannigan. Everything had taken a turn for the worse when the American had arrived at Magnolia Landing. The Duc's only compensation was that he firmly believed Royal Brannigan would fail as a planter—and that when that happened, he would be there with ready cash to take Heritage off his hands.

Yet the Duc's heart was not in his projected schemes. There were too many problems at Salle d'Or that demanded his attention. Some slaves had contracted malaria while gathering wood in the swamps. Dr. Pradel was working night and day to avert an epidemic, but if any more became sick, the Duc would have to face the prospect of buying additional slaves, or even hiring Irish immigrants to do the work—and each of *them* could cost as much as a dollar a day. He had another worry. Apparently Philippe had picked up a touch of the fever. After his return from New Orleans, he had complained of not feeling well. Dammit, the Duc thought, he had told the boy again and again to stay away from the slaves. Philippe, however, claimed he hadn't been to the slave quarters since the night of the ball.

And Henriette continued her rebellious behavior. She seemed to take no interest in her son's health. Instead, she was always whispering and conspiring with Alcée. Supporting, he had no doubt, his daughter's rejection of Gilbert Gadobert. And the scenes! Alcée's outbursts were tantamount to tantrums. Not that the Duc was one to mind an occasional squabble, but no one had ever fought back before! He found his daughter's behavior quite unexplainable. Any other Creole girl would jump at the chance of marrying such a personable and wealthy young man as Gilbert Gadobert. Yet not only did she refuse to consider herself engaged, but she had become morose over his decision to transfer the griffe, Blaise, from the house to the fields. Philippe had told him of catching Blaise sneaking around the veranda the morning after the ball. The nigger was probably doing a bit of spying on the white women. Slaves were not to be trusted. Not where white women were concerned. Particularly slaves that were light-skinned and handsome.

The Duc glared at the urn. It gave him no pleasure, except the pleasure of having something that others wanted. Perhaps the heat was getting him down. The morning air pressed around him like a physical weight, and no matter how many times a day he changed clothes, he continually dripped with perspiration, which caused a rash to erupt in a most uncomfortable place.

As the Duc was shifting his weight in the chair, he saw Alcée walking along the veranda. He called to her, but she did not respond. He got up and ran to the open French doors.

"Alcée," he said sternly, "I am calling you." He noticed that she was wearing an old rag of a dress, no doubt to irritate him further. "Now, stop moping around. I'm your father, and I know what's best."

She halted and leaned forward, a swatch of chestnut hair swinging down to curtain her face—but she did not answer.

"You will not defy my wishes. Blaise will remain in the fields. I'll not have any high yellow sneaking around, watching white women undress."

She turned on him, her eyes blazing with outrage. "What white women, Papa? Do you mean Verbena Chevereaux, the white whore?"

Not believing what he heard, the Duc looked into his daughter's face and felt the strength of her personality. "How dare you!"

"Oh, she tried to get Blaise in bed. One dinner party last year when she got drunk. Naturally he refused."

"Did he tell you this? I'll have him punished for spreading such filth!"

"Filth? Verbena's the filth. You can't stop her, unless you strap her legs together when you ask her to the next party."

The Duc was shocked. "Where did you pick up such talk?"

"Why, at your social functions," she replied blithely.

A new and horrible thought entered the Duc's mind. "Alcée, Blaise wasn't spying on *you*, was he?"

She looked at him coldly. "What a ridiculous idea. Blaise already told you what happened. He wasn't spying on anyone. While he was helping clean up the yard, he noticed some glasses on the veranda and came up to collect them."

"Philippe didn't see any glasses."

"Philippe wasn't in a condition to see much of anything, Papa." She started to walk away. He grabbed her arm and pulled her hard.

"I'm speaking to you!"

"I'll listen when you have something to say!"

The Duc slapped Alcée across the mouth. She broke away from him, and he was immediately repentant. "Oh, Alcée, I'm sorry, I . . ."

"That's your way, isn't it, Papa? If you can't coerce somebody into doing something, then you use physical force. Well, don't think it will work with me just because you've browbeaten Mother for years. She's practically afraid to breathe. And you've turned your own son into an obnoxious duplicate of yourself. He's arrogant, thoughtless, and cruel, just like you."

"You'll marry Gilbert," the Duc threatened, but his words sounded weak even to himself.

"And what will you do if I don't? Tie me to the whipping post and give me fifty lashes? Or a hundred? Or a thousand? You can make me do nothing, Papa, except dislike you more each passing minute."

"Who," the Duc sputtered, "taught you to speak this way?"

Her voice was as soft as a whisper, but clear. "Why, you did, Papa," she answered sweetly, then continued on her way.

The Duc staggered into the ballroom as if he were suffering from an apoplexy. Anger and frustration exploded within him. "I should never have let that American into my home!" he cried out.

The words reverberated around the cavernous room and echoed in his ears. His eyes fell upon the Chinese urn. The carp stared at him unblinkingly. The Duc screamed once, then drew back his leg and kicked. The urn shattered, and the pieces went flying across the marble floor. But he didn't feel any better.

Alcée held back her tears until she was out of her father's sight. She ran up the stairs to the gallery and burst into her mother's room without knocking. Henriette was kneeling in front of her altar. She looked up and cried, "Alcée, what's the matter?"

Alcée stared at her mother in exasperation. Henriette's face resembled that of a tortured martyr in a medieval painting. "Mama," Alcée cried, "all the saints in heaven aren't going to solve our problems. We've got to solve them ourselves." She went to her mother and grabbed her under her arms. "Get up—get up off your knees, for God's sake! Yes, for God's sake and mine! Help *me!*"

"Why, Alcée, what can I do?"

"You can come away from your plaster statues and face reality. Stop pretending this life doesn't exist. You know that Papa married you for your money, and that was the only reason. And he's made you pay for it ever since."

Henriette lowered her head in shame.

"No, Mama, lift your head. It's not your fault—it's Papa's. He's the one who betrayed you. Mama, how many years have you hoped for some scrap of affection or reassurance from Papa?"

"I don't expect anything anymore."

"He's not a man—he's a tyrant. Look what he's made of Philippe—a drunken brute who beats the slaves for his pleasure."

"No," Henriette cried.

"Yes, it's true. He does, and you know he does. He's even killed several of them. I'm afraid that one day he's going to kill Lilliane."

"What do you mean?" Henriette replied, her face closing up.

"Mama, you know as well as I do that Philippe's been using that poor woman for years. Why, Papa bought her as a *present* for him on his sixteenth birthday! They have a son, Azby."

"No, no," Henriette repeated and brandished her arms in front of her face as if warding off evil spirits. Alcée grabbed her hands and pulled them down.

"You deny the child? You've seen him. He's Philippe's son.

Mama, you've got to accept that, if you're going to accept what I have to tell you!"

"What does that woman and *her* son have to do with this?"

"That woman's name is Lilliane. She's your son's mistress, and Azby is your grandson. Oh, Mama, don't react with your mind. Use your heart instead. You're not like the others. I know you're not."

Henriette drew back. "He—is—not—my—grandson!"

"He is. He is!" Alcée screamed. "And you'd better get used to having grandchildren of mixed blood, because there are going to be more."

Henriette pressed her hands over her ears. "Stop! I won't listen to any more!"

Alcée said quietly, "You already know. You just won't admit it."

"I know nothing."

"Mama, you can't remain detached from life, moving half-consciously in the physical world while your mind is with your saints in heaven."

Henriette picked up a fan and began working it around her face as if it were a delirious moth. "I hate this heat," she said, walking around the room. "It makes everything blurry. It's like looking through a dirty pane of glass."

Alcée took her mother's hand. "Come—come with me. I want to get away from the smell of all this incense." Alcée guided her into the dressing room and sat her down on a carved bench, then knelt in front of her. "Mama, I've something to tell you. I *must* tell you. Please let me not be wrong in trusting you."

"Why, Alcée, of course you can trust me."

"I hope so, Mama. You've changed, or at least I think you have." She kissed her mother's hand. "You've seen us together. Anyone with eyes could see, but then prejudice blinds people to the truth."

"I don't know what you're talking about," Henriette insisted.

"But you do, Mother, *you do*. I'm in love with Blaise, and he's in love with me."

Henriette fell to her knees and broke into a weeping fit so pitiful that Alcée started to cry too.

"Oh, God," Henriette said when she found her voice, "I knew. Yes, I knew, but I prayed that it wasn't so." She reached out to touch her daughter. "Oh, Alcée, don't take my meaning wrong. It's just that I don't want you to be hurt."

"But you wouldn't hurt me, Mother, and you're the only one who counts."

"You love him, then?"

"Oh, yes," Alcée cried rapturously. "I never thought I could love anyone so much in my life. He's a fine man, Mama, you know he is."

Henriette nodded. "Yes, I know he is."

"Love is so wonderful, Mama. It makes you feel so strange. It's as if the world had suddenly begun to spin faster and faster."

"I remember," said Henriette.

"Mama, you've got to help us."

"What do I have to do?"

"You do understand that we have to leave here—we have to go someplace so that Papa can't find us and bring us back. Someplace far away, like Canada."

"Some secret place," murmured Henriette, and realized that her own dreams of escape with Alcée were not to be. "Yes," she said suddenly. "And the solution to the problem is so simple."

Alcée threw her arms around her mother's shoulders. "Oh, Mama, I knew you'd help us."

"Yes," Henriette went on. "All we need is money."

Alcée almost fainted with relief. "Of course, that's the answer, Mama. Then you'll give us some? Just enough for passage to Canada. Why, Mama, what's wrong?"

"Alcée, my dear, I don't have any money. At least not at the moment." She stroked her daughter's cheek. "But I will get some, I promise you. I don't know how, but I will."

"I know you will, Mama. Oh, Mama, how can I bear to leave you!"

"But you must, Alcée. If you're in love with Blaise, then you must be with him. You can't stay," she said bitterly. "Oh, God, I wish you could. I always hoped that someday you and the man you loved would live at Villeneuve. I was so happy there."

Julia was sitting in a high-backed chair, staring at the pieces of paper that littered her desk. She dabbed at her face with a damp handkerchief and pushed the papers away from her. They were all bills from her creditors. Some polite, some demanding, some blatantly discourteous. Three were more recent than the others. One was for farm equipment—

axes, saws, shovels, and hoes needed for the Negroes' work of chopping wood and keeping the irrigation ditches in good repair. The second bill was for an extra supply of quinine, which Julia had sent for as a precaution after the outbreak of malaria at Salle d'Or. The third bill was for something more personal. In response to Theo's dinner invitation, she had ordered a length of inexpensive lavender muslin for a suitable dress. She planned to engage Lilliane to make it, because of her proximity and reasonable price.

The heat, combined with the mounting bills, caused Julia to be uncharacteristically irritable. With one swift motion, she swept the sheets of paper into a small tin box ominously labeled BILLS DUE, and exclaimed, "God in heaven, who could pay all these?"

Ottile knocked on the door and stepped inside. "Lilliane's here, Miz Julia. Shall I bring her in?"

"Goodness, no, Ottile—it's stifling in here. I'll meet with her on the back veranda. It's shady this time of day, and there might be a stray breeze lurking about. Offer her something cool to drink."

"What's wrong, Miz Julia? Yo' seem out of sorts."

"It's just this heat, Ottile. If only it would rain. The crops need it. I need it. We all need it." She looked at the tin box. "And all these bills. We've got to have a good crop this year. We've just got to."

"We going to, Miz Julia. Dose cane stalks are gettin' so fat and juicy dat dey jes' liable to burst open all by demselves."

Julia laughed. "Well, that would save us all a lot of work, wouldn't it?" She got up from the desk and ran her fingers through her hair, which the humidity had made curly. "You go on, Ottile. I'll be there momentarily."

When she emerged onto the veranda, the first thing Julia noticed about Lilliane was her hair. The sheer abundance of it startled her, especially since she was unused to seeing women of color without their tignons. It was the richest shade of auburn, glinting as though it had been sprinkled with gold dust, and like some exotic cape it further enhanced the beauty of Lilliane's tawny skin and luminous gray eyes.

Despite her mood, Julia was determined to be gracious. She swept forward and offered her hand to Lilliane. The quadroon took it cautiously.

"I'm Julia Taffarel. We've never met formally before, but of course we've seen each other from a distance. Thank you for coming. It's not the most pleasant weather for traveling."

"I didn't mind it, Miss Julia. It's not far."

"Goodness, did you walk over?"

Lilliane nodded.

"If only this heat would break. I've prayed for rain, but I fear it's not likely."

"Prayers can be answered, Miss Julia," Lilliane replied enigmatically.

Julia observed that the young woman did not seem affected by the heat. On the contrary, she looked cool and serene. The old woman wondered how she managed it.

"You have quite a gift, Lilliane. I admired the costumes you made for the Negrilions."

"Thank you, Miss Julia."

"I need a simple dress made." Ottile produced the fabric. "I ordered this from the New Orleans, sight unseen. I hope it will do."

"This will make a lovely dress, Miss Julia."

"I don't have any patterns, but I thought you might be able to work from a gown that I wore to the Duc's ball."

"I can do that."

"The problem is that I need it next week. Is that too soon?"

"Not at all. I have plenty of time. When I get it cut out and stitched together, I'll bring it back for the first fitting. You should have it in two days."

"That would be wonderful. Now, about the payment," Julia began. "I'm not a rich woman."

"I know that, Miss Julia. Whatever you want to give me will be fine."

"You do get to keep the money, don't you, Lilliane?"

"Oh, yes, ma'am."

Julia turned to Ottile. "Ottile, have Cato get a carriage ready to take Lilliane back to Villeneuve."

"That isn't necessary, Miss Julia."

"My dear, it's too hot to walk with these heavy packages. It's the least we can do."

"No, thank you, Miss Julia. I really prefer to walk." Lilliane gathered up the canvas bag that contained the fabric and the ball gown, and after exchanging goodbyes, she strode away across the lawn like a goddess.

"What a striking young woman," Julia remarked. "There's

something almost frightening about her. An inner strength. Ottile, didn't you feel it?"

"I felt something, Miz Julia, but I'm not sure dat I want to say what it is." Julia noticed that her old friend seemed upset.

"Ottile, what's the matter?"

"I never saw her hair befo'."

"It's beautiful, isn't it? She should never wear a tignon. It's too beautiful to keep covered up."

"A redheaded nigger is a witch. She got de power, Miz Julia. I seen it befo'. I recognize it."

"The power? What do you mean?"

"De loas and de saints walk with her, Miz Julia."

Julia was about to reprove Ottile for her superstitions when she saw the genuine fear on her servant's face.

There was a low rumbling of thunder, and both women looked to the sky in amazement. Just minutes earlier it had been a blinding blue, and now it was an opaque silver-gray.

"De same color of her eyes," Ottile pronounced.

The heavens opened, and the sibilant hiss of raindrops filled the air. The two women looked across the garden as Lilliane's image faded behind the misty veil of rain.

The children were gathered in the *cercle*, waiting none too patiently for Theo's unveiling of his latest puppet. Suddenly he stepped onto the platform that supported the puppet theater. Holding one hand behind his back, he asked, "Are you ready?"

"Oh, Grandpapa, *please!*" pleaded Fleur. "It's not nice to keep a person in suspense."

"Please, please, please," Blanche begged, running her words together like drips of paint.

Denis said nothing, but chewed nervously on a ragged cuticle.

The children's excitement at seeing the ghost had evaporated with the heat. They had spent too many hours playing games that no longer held any interest for them. They had explored and reexplored the grounds within the boundaries that Theo had assigned them, and they had performed their theatricals over and over until the lines had become automatic and tedious. They needed to put together a new production with different characters and fresh lines in order to chase the doldrums from their lives.

With a flourish, Theo produced the puppet that had consumed most of his spare time for the last week. "I give you . . . the ghost of Magnolia Landing!"

He controlled the body of the puppet with his left hand, using his other hand to manipulate the long, narrow black sticks attached to the puppet's wrists. From head to toe, his creation was about a foot and a half tall, and it had been designed from the description the children had given him. The flowing white hair was made of finely spun wool, the emaciated wooden face was painted a mottled gray, and the hollow, glowing eyes were fashioned of bits of mother-of-pearl. The tattered gray garments resembled loosely woven Spanish moss.

The children reacted in different ways. Blanche shrieked and turned her head away. Fleur stiffened in her seat. Denis stood up and said, "Grandpapa, that's exactly what he looks like!" An involuntary shudder ran through his broomstick-thin body.

"It's really quite excellent, Grandpapa," conceded Fleur. "You've captured the very essence of his horror."

"I can't look," cried Blanche.

"Nonsense," said Fleur. "It's just a puppet. Now, turn around and sit up."

Blanche reluctantly did so and gazed at the puppet through her sticky fingers. She gulped audibly and said, "He'll come for his baby, I know he will."

"Oh, Blanche, don't be a child. Ghosts can't have babies."

"So how do you know?" Blanche said. "You don't know everything, Fleur."

"In any case," said Theo, "it's not the ghost's baby. It's our newest puppet. Well, what are you waiting for? I'm expecting to see a brand-new production built around this ghastly creation."

"Oh, I've already started on a script, Grandpapa," said Denis. "I'm calling my new play *Journey into Midnight*."

"I still think that sounds silly," sniffed Fleur.

"I don't care what you think," replied Denis. "*I'm* writing the play."

"Perhaps you'll have it done by the time Miss Taffarel comes to dinner next week," said Theo.

"Is she going to be our new grandmama?" asked Blanche.

"It's too soon to tell." Theo grinned. "You'll have to meet her first and tell me what you think of her."

"We'll have to hurry," said Denis. "But I'm sure we can make it. Blanche? Fleur?"

The girls nodded their heads in agreement and began consulting each other.

"It's really true to life, Grandpapa," said Denis.

Fleur overheard her brother's remark and quipped, "You mean true to death!"

Everyone laughed at Fleur's comment except Blanche. She didn't understand the humor, and was otherwise engaged in trying to extract some hard candy that had become fused together in a tin container.

Marguerite pressed her cheek against a pane of her bedroom window and watched the gray rain falling from the sky. She did not enjoy the cooler air, nor did she consider the benefits that the sudden cloudburst would bring to the crops and gardens of Magnolia Landing. Rather, the gloomy weather served to reinforce her already somber mood.

There was a knock at the door, and Marguerite moved slowly across the carpet, as if each step were painful. "Who is it?" she whispered through the thick slab of wood.

"It Jake, Miz Marguerite. I brung more of dem boxes yo' was askin' fo'."

Marguerite unlocked the door, and a hulking slave carried a collection of empty wooden boxes inside. "Where yo' want dem, Miz Marguerite?"

"Just put them anywhere," she said vaguely. The slave set the boxes in the center of the room and left. Marguerite called out a belated thank you and locked her door once again.

Léon and Michelle had returned from New Orleans, and they had not even brought her a present. She gazed over the boxes she had already packed and those that she would be filling, and said caustically, "*I* won't be so thoughtless. I shall leave them a profusion of presents."

She went to the empty boxes, knelt down on the floor, and sorted through them, selecting those she thought were the proper size. After she had made up her mind what she wanted to put in each container, she went to her closet, took out one of her dresses, and began tearing it in strips. By the time she had finished, she was perspiring and gasping for breath. Not pausing to rest, she selected pieces of her personal bric-a-brac and carried them back to the bed and began wrapping them in the material. Once the items were neatly cocooned in the fabric, she packed them in the boxes.

While she worked, Marguerite kept up a fitful monologue. "This will make it easy for them," she said resolutely. "They won't have any trouble disposing of the leftovers of my life."

As Marguerite continued packing, she recalled the afternoon she had gone to Léon and Michelle's bedroom. She had planned to ask them for a driver to take her to Dr. Pradel at Salle d'Or—she needed the laudanum so desperately. Instead, she had overheard their conversation regarding their future plans. Of course they didn't want her with them in Europe, and she could not blame them. She was not loving, nor was she loved. She offered no sympathy and accepted none. She was just a boring old woman with outdated principles—somebody who always got dressed for company, even though company never came.

Marguerite had fled to her room in tears. She had never realized just how much Léon hated her until then. She had also realized something else—that she was too brittle, too unbending, to start anew. Her life had been shattered, and she could not put it back together.

"I wasn't always like this," she said bitterly.

Marguerite picked up from her dressing table a small oval frame that she kept tucked among her vast collection of cosmetics. She cradled the frame in the palm of her hand as she carried it to the window and held it up to the pearly light. The frame contained a miniature in oils of a young man, fair and heartbreakingly handsome. She touched her fingertips to her lips and carried that dry kiss to the lips of her only lover.

Charles Fortier had been a young captain in the military during the last war. He and Marguerite had been engaged to be married, but their youthful desire had been so strong that they had met secretly and given themselves to each other. Their marriage, however, was never to take place. Young Charles had been mortally wounded by a British rifle bullet that had pierced his throat. Marguerite had received other proposals, but she had never married, and never had she regretted her brief affair with her beloved Charles. Over the years her family had forgotten her tragedy, and Marguerite had become the standard fixture of many a Creole household—the unmarried *tante*.

"Charles, you always remain the same. You never get a day

older. If you had lived, I might have sustained the courage of my youth. But living from day to day requires more strength than I have left."

A sigh of anguish escaped her throat as she pressed the portrait to her breasts. Then, tenderly, she wrapped the miniature in a strip of cloth and tucked it into a small, extra-sturdy box.

Marguerite had decided what she must do. She had decided that suicide was the only solution to her life. By the very act of dying, she would put herself beyond the reach of disregard and disdain. She would avoid those terrible indignities of old age—the loss of independence, the end of privacy, and the abominable, inescapable pain.

While Michelle and Léon had been away, one of the drivers had taken her to Salle d'Or, and with a good deal of playacting, she had been able to cajole two bottles of laudanum from Dr. Pradel—and, when his back was turned, had managed to slip another out of his cabinet and conceal it in the folds of her dress. Back in her room, she had secreted two of the bottles for her suicide. The remaining bottle she had been using regularly to induce sleep. She had used half of the opiate. When the bottle was empty, she planned to employ the other two bottles the following night and, should God will it, sleep peacefully forever.

Marguerite had begun to view her bed as a funeral bier. As she continued packing, she glanced at it from time to time, to try to imagine herself as a corpse. She prayed that, when the time came, somebody would notice her absence and discover her body before it began to decay.

Exhausted from the heat and her labors, Marguerite sank into a chair, stared at the four-poster, and began softly crying. "Death will love me," she assured herself.

The thundershower ended as the carriage turned onto the driveway leading to Heritage. A distant rainbow framed the big house and seemed to reinforce the happiness Royal felt at returning to the plantation. Its prismatic beauty was duly noted by Seth, who exclaimed, "Yo' see, Mr. Royal, de Lawd God hisself is glad to have yo' back."

Royal was surprised to find Suzanne waiting on the veranda. He noticed that she had forsaken her drab mourning clothes and was wearing a colorful dress that matched the bright blue of the rainbow. Her usually cold eyes were suffused with warmth, and her firm mouth had softened. She was even smiling in his direction. As he climbed the steps to the veranda, she said, "Welcome back, m'sieur. I trust your visit to New Orleans was successful?"

"It was, Madame Jourdain. I met with M'sieur Lajeunesse, who agreed to continue acting as factor for Heritage. I also visited the Sugar Exchange and met some of my fellow planters—although they probably would not like to hear me refer to them as such. I also had some more suitable clothes made. I notice you're no longer wearing your mourning clothes."

Suzanne bit down on her lower lip. "I keep my mourning in my heart, m'sieur." She pushed up her sleeve to reveal a black armband beneath the bright blue material.

Royal realized that he had made a *faux pàs* and quickly apologized. "I'm sorry, madame, I didn't mean to imply . . ."

Seth came to his rescue. "Look at de present Mr. Royal brung me from New Orleans." He proudly held up the watch.

"A very lovely gift," commented Suzanne. She glanced at Royal. "I hope it was well earned. Seth, why don't you take the carriage around back and have M'sieur Brannigan's luggage and packages unloaded and put in his room. Then you can take the carriage to the stables. The horses look like they could use some water." Seth screwed up his face in disappointment at being dismissed.

"Yes, Miz Suzanne." To Royal he said, "I sees yo' later, Mr. Royal."

When Seth was gone, Suzanne remarked, "It seems that Seth has appointed himself your personal servant."

"That would seem so," replied Royal. "I like him immensely." He added with meaning, "It's nice to have a friend on the plantation."

"That's all very well, m'sieur, but Seth has not been trained as a house servant, and it is unseemly to have him running in and out of the house at all times."

Royal bristled and was about to remind Suzanne that he was now the owner of Heritage, and as such would make the rules. Instead, he asked her, "Would you do me a favor, madame? Would you take Seth in hand and train him to become my—what do you call it? Hand servant?"

"I'd be happy to, m'sieur. It will greatly benefit both of

you. Now, I was about to take coffee. Would you care for some?"

Royal readily agreed. "Will Mademoiselle Jourdain be joining us?"

"Angélique has gone for a visit to one of the neighbors," Suzanne replied with a flicker of a smile. "There will just be the two of us."

At Suzanne's suggestion they adjourned to the front parlor. There Zenobia served them coffee and lace cakes. She let her disapproval be known by walking heavily on her large feet, rattling the cups, and slamming down the tray. Suzanne pretended not to notice her surly manner, calmly chatting with Royal about New Orleans and their shared affection for their adopted city.

Although their conversation was somewhat strained—Royal felt like an actor in an improvised playlet—he was comfortable with Suzanne, and she seemed to be more at ease with him. He suspected that she was even enjoying his company. When coffee was finished, Royal thanked Suzanne and gallantly kissed her hand. The smoothness of her skin startled him. It was not the first time he had touched her flesh. There was no mistaking that velvety texture. It had to have been Suzanne!

Royal went to his room. His clothing and his new purchases had been unpacked and put away. He noticed that bowls of fresh flowers had been placed in the room. He knew that Suzanne daily selected, cut, and arranged the flowers for the big house, but never before had so much as a single bloom found its way into his room. "It's Suzanne," he said with finality.

Stung by the realization, Royal sat down on the edge of his bed. He wondered what could have caused Suzanne to act so outrageously. The aftershock of her husband's death? Her need for physical release? Odd, Royal thought, but he had almost hoped that she wasn't the one. It was true that he had enjoyed the sexual union, but it seemed so incongruous with Suzanne's character, or at least what he knew of her.

Royal had begun to discover that what he had originally perceived to be a cool and calculating manner had actually been a show of strength in the face of terrible tragedy, and he begrudgingly admired Suzanne for that. And the calm efficiency with which she continued to run the plantation had impressed him from the first.

Of course her treatment of him had not been particularly

pleasant, nor should it have been. But he had to admire the way she had handled herself and dealt with others. She was a strong-willed woman, but nonetheless kind and considerate of those she loved.

Whistling a spritely tune, Royal got up from the bed, selected a daisy from one of the bowls of flowers, and stuck it in his lapel. Daisies had been his mother's favorite flower. Royal smiled at the sudden realization. In many ways, Suzanne was very much like Finola Brannigan.

That afternoon a body was found floating along the banks of the Mississippi. The group of boys who regularly swam in the river had been forced from the docks because of the crush of arriving ships. They had moved down the levee to a point just beyond the French Market. The water was muddy here and clogged with rotten fruit and vegetables thrown away by the merchants, but on a sticky afternoon it was better than nothing.

The boys stripped out of their breeches and decided to make a game of diving for the discarded items, hoping to find something that was still edible. One of the lads, a tough little orphan named Sean, discovered the body. Its long red hair floated upon the water's surface like a blotch of crimson oil. She was naked, her body scarred and bruised like the rotting produce that bobbed around her.

The city watch was called to the scene. They wrapped the corpse in a dirty canvas blanket and carried it away. The coroner, a middle-aged man with a knobby forehead named Hippolyte Santerre, was shocked by the new arrival. He had been at Odalisque on the night of the girl's auction. In fact, he had been one of the bidders. He managed to conceal his consternation and informed his colleagues that the girl had been killed before being thrown in the river, most likely by a series of blows from a hammer. He did not mention that she had syphilis. The girl known briefly as Nicole was unceremoniously buried in a pauper's grave. To all intents and purposes she had never existed—except to the seventeen men who had slept with her.

Chapter Twenty-one

The kitchen slaves at Salle d'Or were staging a minor revolt. Every one of them steadfastly refused to take Philippe's breakfast tray to him. Ambrose, the chef, couldn't blame them. They had always viewed their young master as something less than human; now that he was ill, and malaria had broken out in the slave quarters, they had come to the conclusion that he was, as usual, the source of their misery.

Ambrose held up his hands to still the insurrection.

"Hush up, all of yo'," he said, attempting to infuse his weary voice with authority. The squawking of the five women subsided into a kind of whining choke, which reminded Ambrose of the noise a chicken made when its neck was being wrung.

A middle-aged slave name Poppy, the leader of the rebellion, folded her arms over her heavy bosom and said, "Dere ain't no use cajolin', Ambrose. Ain't none of us goin' near dat devil." The others murmured agreement. "Mayhaps he don't even have dis 'laria," Poppy went on ominously. "Mayhaps he got de Bronze John."

The other slaves gasped with fright.

"Now, jes' settle yo'self down, Poppy," said Ambrose. "M'sieur Philippe don't have de yellow fever. I seen enough of dat so I knows de signs."

"Den what could it be?" demanded Poppy.

Ambrose shrugged. "I's too much of de gentlemen to say. *I* takes his breakfast in myself."

He checked the tray. Because of the heat, the single red rose plucked from the garden earlier that morning was already beginning to wilt, and the cream had started to congeal. But the coffee remained hot. The other items on the tray were bread, a soft-boiled egg, and a crystal cordial glass that held a measure of quinine. The bitter brown liquid had been prescribed by Dr. Pradel for the treatment of malaria.

Ambrose carried the tray to the big house. He knocked on Philippe's door three successive times, and when he received no answer, he decided to take it inside.

The room smelled of sour perspiration and sickness. According to Creole custom, the French doors were tightly closed. Specks of dust floated lazily in the sunbeams. Ambrose placed the tray beside Philippe, but even the aromatic scent of the freshly brewed coffee did not stir him. Ambrose glanced impersonally at the young man's pale, drawn face. His hair and skin were wet with perspiration. He was not sleeping, but appeared to be in a feverish stupor.

"Dat ain't dis 'laria," Ambrose told himself with some alarm. "I's better tell de Duc."

The Duc was in his library doing the accounts when he received Ambrose's worried message. He immediately sent the old chef in search of Dr. Pradel, then, greatly concerned, rushed to his son's room, not even thinking to lock the library door behind him, as he customarily did.

The Duc's fears for his son were not groundless. Philippe's condition had worsened considerably the past two days, and his raging fever had not abated. He picked at his food, was losing weight, and complained of terrible pains in his muscles and joints. Pradel had originally diagnosed the ailment in general terms, as a *malaise*, a touch of swamp fever, nothing more, and had prescribed the imbibing of quinine three times a day. Philippe had faithfully taken the foul-tasting medicine, always washing it down with a generous quantity of brandy, but his condition had not improved. The Duc cursed himself for not sending for a doctor from New Orleans. Pradel was, after all, a slave doctor, not much better than a veterinarian.

Upon entering his son's room, the Duc was appalled by the fetid odor. He pulled back the sheet and saw that Philippe had dirtied himself sometime during the night. He called for two house slaves and ordered that they clean Philippe and change the sheets before the doctor came.

Ten minutes later, Dr. Louis Pradel arrived, carrying a small, stained canvas bag. He was an energetic little man of middle years who wore thick eyeglasses and had a shock of hair the color of dingy linen. The Duc had always been annoyed by the fact that Dr. Pradel enjoyed his work immensely. Exotic diseases seemed to delight him, and of late he had been positively ecstatic at the prospect of an epidemic. Grinning, the doctor now said, "I was just in the slave quarters. We lost three more—"

"Concentrate on my son," the Duc snapped. "I can buy new slaves."

Pradel ordered that the windows be opened to clear the foul air. He felt Philippe's forehead and judged his temperature to be well over one hundred. Then, starting with the young man's throat and neck, he began a thorough examination, poking and prodding and occasionally grunting, as doctors did. When he reached Philippe's crotch, he exclaimed, "Eureka!"

He motioned for the Duc to come nearer and proudly pointed out a pustular red ulcer on the foreskin of Philippe's penis.

The Duc wrinkled his nose in distaste. "He's got the pox!"

"That he does, M'sieur Duvallon," the doctor gleefully confirmed. "And now that it's shown itself, we shall commence treatment."

"But you said it was malaria!"

The doctor shrugged his shoulders. "The initial symptoms are similar. Besides, a little quinine never hurt anybody. It's not such a problem, m'sieur. As I recall, you've had it two or three times yourself."

The Duc frowned at the remark.

Dr. Pradel gently shook Philippe from his feverish sleep. "Good—you're awake. My boy, you don't have malaria after all. You have the pox. But don't worry—I have just the thing for it. You'll be up and about in no time."

The Duc was angry at Philippe. "Where in the hell did you pick that up?"

"I—I don't know, Papa," moaned Philippe, but his expression told otherwise.

The doctor flipped open his bag and removed a bottle of mercury compound. He poured out a spoonful of the heavy silvery liquid and said, "This stuff is voided unchanged in the feces, my boy. So don't think you're passing pearls."

As Philippe gulped down the medicine, the Duc growled, "And while you're being treated, I won't have you messing around with any of the slaves, do you hear? That includes Lilliane. It reduces their resale value by as much as three-quarters!"

Philippe groaned and turned his head away.

The Duc said, "I realize I'm taking away your favorite pleasure, but you'll just have to do without women for a while, and that's my final word on the subject."

"Damn that American," Philippe mumbled into his pillow.

The Duc was just about to ask him what he meant when the young man began gagging. He gave a heave, and the contents of his stomach came spewing forth all over the clean sheets. The mercury neatly separated from the rest of the mess and slid to the floor.

"Some find the compound hard to hold down," Dr. Pradel said cheerfully. "I guess we'll have to give him another dose."

Henriette was on her way to the kitchen to discuss the weekly menu with Ambrose when she noticed the library door ajar. Puzzled, she stuck her head inside and called out her husband's name. He didn't answer. She glanced down at the keyhole; the key was still in the lock. Henriette could scarcely believe her good luck. She knew that her husband kept his strongbox somewhere in the library, but she didn't know where. Now, at least, she might be able to discover its whereabouts.

Her mind raced. Should she take the key and lock the door? When her husband returned, he might believe he had locked it behind him and taken the key with him. Quickly deciding that desperate measures were called for, she slipped the key out of the keyhole and quietly closed the door, locking it from within.

Her body was shaking with her heartbeats. The library was the Duc's private sanctuary. He kept it locked at all times and rarely invited anyone there. Although she had not been expressly forbidden to enter, Henriette had never had any desire to intrude upon her husband's privacy. Besides, she had no use for any books other than her Bible, catechism, and missal.

She glanced nervously around the room. The drapes were drawn, and the only light was from a lamp on the Duc's desk. Her heavy breathing and the ticking of a clock were the only sounds.

Henriette tiptoed to the desk. She gingerly sat down on the edge of the Duc's chair and began going through the drawers. Each contained neatly labeled folders concerning various business transactions. Henriette noticed a file on the sale of slaves. She started to look inside, curious as to what the going rate was for a human being, but stopped short. She promised herself to come back and look through the files when she knew she had more time. She got up and moved swiftly past the freestanding bookshelves, deciding that the strongbox would not be located there, but rather somewhere behind the hundreds upon hundreds of books that lined the walls. Henriette felt faint with nervousness. She didn't know where to look first. Clasping her crucifix in her right hand as if it were a divining rod, she selected a place on the lowest shelf. She sat down on the floor and began removing books, taking out four or five at a time, then bending and looking into the empty space before replacing the books.

She couldn't see her husband's clock, but its ticking was unnaturally loud, as loud as the thumping of her heart. Tears of fright blurred her vision. She blinked them away and willed her mind and body to function.

She methodically moved down the row of books, not really knowing why she was taking such a chance. What if she did find the strongbox? What then? She didn't know the padlock's combination. Only the Duc did, and with his penchant for exactness, he had probably memorized it and not written it down anywhere.

Henriette had examined about half of the lowest shelf when she heard voices. She froze, staring across the room in horror. The doorknob turned, and her heart stopped. She heard the Duc curse.

"Well, I must have locked it—it's a habit. But where's the key?"

Pradel suggested, "Perhaps you dropped it on your way to Philippe's bedroom."

"I don't lose things," the Duc replied sharply. "Excuse me while I go up to my room and get the spare key."

Henriette scrambled to her feet, and as she did, the key fell out of her pocket and onto the Oriental carpet. She strained her eyes, but in the dim lamplight was unable to see where it had landed on the intricate design. Panic-stricken, she tried to estimate how long it would take the Duc to climb the staircase to his bedroom, find the spare key, and return. But he might use the back staircase, which was closer to his bedroom. Yet maybe he had the key secreted someplace where it would take him time to retrieve it. Maybe not. Her mind was a jumble of contradictions. All the while she moved about on her knees, running her hands over the thick nap of the carpet, searching frantically for the key.

He's climbing the staircase to the second floor.

Henriette gave a little cry and, dazed with fear, clutched at her chest. Her heart sank at the hopelessness of finding the key before the Duc returned. She crawled forward, sweeping both hands in front of her in an arclike motion. .Nothing! She swung around and began searching in the opposite direction, and as she did, her foot hit a narrow wooden pedestal supporting the marble bust of a Roman soldier, the one the Duc had bought because he fancied it looked like him. The pedestal tilted, and the bust began to shift. Henriette clamped both her hands around the column and steadied it, and the bust settled back into place.

He's in his bedroom.

She caught sight of something metallic glinting to one side. She sucked in her breath and reached for it. It was a woman's gold hairpin—Verbena Chevereaux's, no doubt.

He's got the key in his hand, and he's starting back down.

Henriette was just about to give up in despair when her knee pressed into something hard—the key!

He's reached the bottom of the stairs.

She got up and ran across the carpet to the French doors leading to the veranda, praying that the same key would fit the lock.

He's almost to the door.

She yanked back the drapes and worked the key into the lock, just as another key was being fitted into the main door of the library. Both keys turned at the same time. One door opened as the other closed. The Duc and Dr. Pradel entered the library, and Henriette, gasping for breath, heard her husband say, "And just what is this new treatment for impotence?"

Clutching the key in her hand, Henriette hurried down the veranda, not daring to stop or look back. When she turned the corner, she collapsed against the side of the house, gulping in mouthfuls of air until she was breathing normally once again. She opened her hand to make sure the key was still there. She had clenched it so tightly that she had cut herself and drawn blood.

One of the house slaves approached from behind, and Henriette jumped.

"My goodness, Miz Henriette. I didn't mean to frighten yo' none."

"That's all right, Saisie. What is it?"

"It dat Lilliane from over at Villeneuve. She askin' to see

de Duc, but he in de library with de doctor, and I don't dare to disturb him."

Henriette was about to tell the girl to send Lilliane away when Alcée's remembered words stopped her.

"Mama, you can't remain detached from life. . . ."

"Take her up to my room, Saisie."

"Yo' room, Miz Henriette?" The slave was surprised.

"Yes, I'll meet with her there."

Henriette hurriedly climbed the stairs that led from the veranda to the gallery. She entered her room through the French doors and went directly to her altar. She slipped the library key under the statue of the Virgin Mary, then went to her bath and wrapped a cloth around her injured hand.

There was a knock at the door, and she opened it to admit Lilliane. "Come in, please."

After a long silence, Henriette realized that she was staring rudely at the young woman. "Forgive me—I've never seen you without your tignon."

"It's too hot to wear a tignon, Madame Duvallon."

Rippling waves of amber tresses framed Lilliane's face and the upper part of her body. Henriette had never seen such abundant hair, not even on a white woman. Suddenly she realized that Lilliane *was* beautiful. It was odd, she thought, but she had never before noticed the beauty in Negroes.

"My husband is busy. Can I be of some help to you?"

"I came to ask for a pass so that I could go to New Orleans."

Henriette noticed that Lilliane did not state her reasons for going, but she did not ask. "I can do that for you," she said, not quite knowing why she felt so pleased to be of assistance to the young woman. "When do you want to go, Lilliane?"

"This coming Saturday. And I would like to stay over, if possible. It's difficult getting a steamship back the same day."

"Of course. But do you have a place to stay?"

"Yes, I have a friend."

Henriette sat down at her writing desk, took out a small sheet of heavy paper, and wrote the official sounding words. She signed her name with an unexpected flourish. Then she lit a small candle, melted a bit of sealing wax onto the corner of the paper, and imprinted it with the Salle d'Or seal. She handed the paper to Lilliane. The woman's eyes were filled with gratitude, and something else that Henriette could not define.

"Thank you, Madame Duvallon."

"Lilliane, if there's ever anything I can do for you, I want you to come to me, do you understand?"

Lilliane nodded. "Yes, ma'am. There . . . there is one thing." She swallowed hard. "If ever I'm sold, could you try to see that my son and I are sold together?"

The unexpected words made Henriette feel both heartsick and embarrassed. "Of course," she replied. "I promise that if you're sold, you will be sold together." She glanced at her altar and her placid saints and hoped that if the time came, she would be able to keep her promise.

"Thank you, Madame Duvallon."

"You love your son very much."

Lilliane nodded in response; she seemed so over taken by emotion that she couldn't trust herself to speak.

"I love my daughter too," Henriette stated simply. "Very much."

Lilliane started out the door, then turned back and said in a surprisingly firm voice, "Thank you for the pass, Madame Duvallon. You won't regret it." Then she closed the door behind her.

Still sitting at her writing table, Henriette put her head in her hands. She couldn't begin to imagine the slave woman's terrible fear of someday being parted forever from her child—yet she herself was going to have to part with Alcée, although she hoped desperately that it wouldn't be forever.

For once, Henriette did not turn to her saints for comfort. Instead, she sat there weeping, for Lilliane and Azby, for Alcée and Blaise, and for herself—for all those whose lives were controlled by others.

The bell towers of Saint Louis Cathedral were sharply defined against the hazy afternoon sky. Those New Orleanians out for a stroll in the Place d'Armes moved slowly beneath the shade of the sycamore trees and avoided the expanse of parched grass open to the sun. Talk was at a minimum. Most of the men wore broad straw hats, and the women carried parasols to ward off the heat and glare of the day. Even so, their clothing was stained with perspiration.

Lilliane walked directly across the square. The languid strollers stopped to stare at her, their tongues prompted into action. She had washed her hair before leaving Magnolia Landing, rinsed it in lemon juice to make it shine, and scented it with crushed magnolia petals. She had parted it in the center and back-combed it so that it stood out from her head like a corrugated pyramid. The rays of the sun got caught in its tresses, making them glow as if on fire. She had fashioned herself a new outfit for her second trip to the Crescent City, a daring dress for a woman of color to wear. It was made of cotton and was the orange of a summer sunset. The sleeveless bodice had a scooped neckline that revealed the swell of her breasts. A wide belt in matching fabric cinched her narrow waist, and the full skirt was made fuller by a pink, ruffled petticoat. She wore no jewelry because she owned none.

Lilliane stopped near the entrance to the cathedral and listened to the sound of a chanting priest, his voice rising and falling in rhythm to the heat waves that shimmered above the square. The odor of incense was heavy in the air and stung her nostrils.

The men standing nearby were intrigued by Lilliane's exotic beauty, the women offended. One outraged matron coerced a city guard into asking the mulatto for her pass. Smiling benignly, Lilliane produced the folded paper from the bodice of her dress and handed it to him. The guard made a show of scrupulously examining it, and when he handed it back, he whispered an apology.

She left the Place d'Armes and headed away from the river, until the crowded buildings gave way to the beginnings of a swamp and Bayou Road. Here the atmosphere changed. The air became so heavy with moisture that Lilliane looked to the sky to see if it had started raining. She squared her shoulders and walked toward the strange house of the witch doctor. Today she was to present him with her payment. Lilliane had expected to be nervous, but she wasn't. She trusted Dr. Jacques. Her eyes had not bothered her since the first visit, and the fix on Philippe had worked. She hoped that Dr. Jacques would also be able to do something for Azby, so that her son would not have to spend the rest of his life a slave.

As Lilliane neared her destination, she noticed for the first time that the lushness of the witch doctor's garden was in marked contrast to the rest of the area. The ramshackle houses farther down the road were surrounded by yellow-tinged shrubs, and the few trees were blighted and bereft of leaves.

Lilliane was also puzzled that there was no one in sight. Aunt Lolly had warned her of the lines of people, black and white, who were always waiting to see Dr. Jacques. But there had been no one about the last time, either, and once again the yard was empty except for the creatures that inhabited it. As she walked up the path, birds sang their welcome, and frogs croaked like little old men.

As before, the door opened to admit her. Lilliane moved swiftly down the narrow hall, as if drawn magnetically to what waited beyond the tall door. Once again a deep voice commanded her to enter. As she opened the door, Lilliane gasped with surprise. Every surface—the tables, the shelves, the windowsills—was covered with blazing white candles. It was exactly the image she had seen in Dr. Jacques's eyes during her last visit. Yet despite all the candles, the room was as cool as a cave behind a waterfall. The voodoo man stood in the center of the floor, smiling at her. "I've been expecting you," he said, repeating his first greeting, but in an altogether different tone.

"What if it wasn't me, Dr. Jacques?" she asked.

"Just Jacques. I know you, Lilliane. I think I've known you all my life, but I just didn't meet you until a few weeks ago."

"But I don't know *you*—not yet. They say you're a Senegalese prince."

He laughed. "Well, at least they got that right! Yes, my father was a king of the Bambaras, the finest Negro race in Senegal." He moved around the room, employing his hands to illustrate his story. They became, in turn, iron leg clamps, the rippling waves of the sea, a storm-tossed ship, an effeminate man, a pair of pistols, and a bird in flight. "I was eight years old when I was kidnapped by Spanish slavers. I was sold at some Spanish port—I never knew its name. Then I was shipped to Santo Domingo. My master there was *sweet* on me. He taught me how to read and write Spanish, English, and French. When I was eighteen and he was dying, he made me a present of my freedom. I became a pirate and roamed the seas of both hemispheres, finally ending up here in New Orleans."

"But how did you become a witch doctor?"

"You don't *become* it. You're born it. My father taught me to recognize the magic in plants and animals—how to read the back of a leaf, to tell the weather by the depth of a gazelle's hoofprint. In the West Indies I was taken under the wing of the *houngan*—the voodoo man. He taught me about herbs and potions, spells and fixes. An old woman in the Orient whose fingernails reached to the floor taught me to tell fortunes and predict the future. Once I realized I had the power to answer people's prayers, I let it happen, and I became Dr. Jacques, the *voodoo king!*"

"They say," Lilliane whispered, "that you're the most powerful man in New Orleans."

"Well, now, *being* powerful and *having* power are two different things—but I'll go into that another time."

"People are willing to pay for your services, and I hear they pay a lot."

"I charge what they can afford, be it a jar of swamp honey or a chain of beaten gold. Hell, religion's the biggest *show* in the world! Voodoo, Catholic, Hindu, Islam—it's all the same. The people want to see something for their money, so a little mumbo jumbo is necessary. They don't want just a cure for what ails 'em—that's too easy. You got to give 'em a little entertainment." He became an old woman: "Oh, please, Dr. Jacques, yo' got to cure dis rheumatiz fo' me." A high-born Creole lady: "M'sieur, I have reason to believe my husband is having an affair." An American businessman: "Dammit, I can't keep it hard. All I can think of while I'm doing it is my multiplication table." A waterfront whore: "Please, don't let me be pregnant." A little white girl: "Make the nuns stop picking on me." A Portuguese sailor: "Make me stop screaming every time I take a piss." He became her: "Dr. Jacques, help me gain my son's freedom." He became the voodoo man again: "I got 'em coming, and I keep 'em coming. They all want something, and I have it!"

Dr. Jacques took off his top hat. His kinky hair shone with oils. He walked toward her, cupped her face in his huge hands, and kissed her forehead. As he did, his fingertips worked their way into the depths of her hair. "You fixed your hair for me, didn't you, Lilliane?"

"Yes," she breathed.

"Can you feel the magic in your hair?" She nodded as he worked his fingers deeper into her tresses. "Did you know that your hair keeps growing long after you're dead and buried? The hair is the threads of the soul. And it has power. Can you feel it growing?"

"Yes, I feel it."

"Think of it, Lilliane—the strength of Sampson. The salvation of Mary Magdalene. It was in their hair! Don't let anyone cut your hair except yourself, and then burn the trimmings. Someone could use them against you."

"Why would anyone want to do that?"

"Because you have the *power*, Lilliane, and you're going to be much envied. And when people envy, they want to take things away. Do you understand me?"

"I'm not sure."

"But you do understand that I'm not going to take anything from you this afternoon? I'm going to *give* you something. I'm going to make you feel better than you've ever felt in your life."

He lifted her hair so that it fanned out around her shoulders, and murmured prayers to Freda Erzili, the voodoo goddess of love and passion. He thanked Freda Erzili for delivering Lilliane to him and promised that, in appreciation, he would make Lilliane cry with pleasure.

"Can you let yourself be loved, Lilliane?"

"I know only one kind of love, and that's what I feel for my son, for Azby."

"There are so many kinds, Lilliane. The most joyous is the love between man and woman. You're going to need that if you're going to hold on to the power. Look into my eyes and tell me what you see." She did. His pupils seemed as small as pinpoints. The irises were large and yellow, like pieces of amber.

"I see . . ."

"Yes, tell me what you see."

"I see . . . people dancing." The picture was accompanied by the sound of a steady drumbeat, the stamping of feet, cries and shouts, and the slap of tambourines.

"What else do you see?"

"I see myself," she gasped, "leading the dance."

Dr. Jacques blinked his eyes, and the image disappeared. "Do you want to lead the dance, Lilliane?"

"What dance?"

He smiled. "Why, the dance of life." His fingers toyed with the neckline of her bodice. "You made this dress for me," he told her.

"Yes. Do you like it?"

"It needs some decoration, but we'll take care of that later. Take off your dress, Lilliane, the dress that you made for me."

He leaned against the table and watched her as she removed her clothing. She wasn't ashamed, as she always was with Philippe.

His eyes were glowing like a cat's. Lilliane undid the hooks down the back of the bodice and slipped her arms free. The material slid across her nipples, making them tingle. She stepped out of the dress, then removed the petticoat and her smallclothes. She stood before him nude, her discarded garments piled around her ankles like a florid wave.

Dr. Jacques lowered his gaze to the center of her femininity. "You're very beautiful, Lilliane. Such beauty should be rewarded." He produced a bottle of rum from behind him, uncorked it with his teeth, and spat the cork on the floor. He took a long swig and handed the bottle to her.

Lilliane took it and lifted it high. The liquid burned her throat, but it was a pleasing sensation. As she drank, she watched the voodoo man undress, and he watched her watching him. He undid the buttons of his frilly shirt, took it off, and dropped it to the floor. Then he began unbuttoning his tight black trousers, peeling them downward as if he were shedding a second skin.

Lilliane felt the rum ignite in her stomach, sending waves of warmth throughout her body. She could feel it in her breasts, in her thighs, in her buttocks, and in each strand of hair.

Lilliane's eyes traveled down his body. His skin was as black as coal. His shoulders were broad, his muscles sharply defined. He had a trim, narrow waist, slender hips, and legs so long that they seemed to account for more than half of his height. He was completely hairless, except for the woolly patch between his legs. He was nothing like Philippe, who was pale, puny, and soft, with skin the color and texture of unrisen dough.

She set the bottle on a table, in the middle of a dozen burning candles.

Dr. Jacques took several steps toward her, took her face in his hands, and began kissing her. Between tender bites he said, "Trust me, Lilliane. I won't hurt you. I'll never hurt you."

He slid a hand down between their bodies and pressed his palm over her femininity, then slowly began using his fingers to stimulate her.

Within moments Lilliane began moaning and pushing against

him. Slowly he pulled her to the floor, which was covered with a thick red rug. The room was suddenly filled with the echo of a laugh.

Dr. Jacques said, "That's just ol' Freda Erzili wishin' us luck!"

He lay on top of her and gently opened her thighs. He pressed his lips against hers and asked, "Now what do you see?"

"I see only you."

He spread her thighs farther apart, and when he entered her, she was ready. Lilliane groaned with pleasure, and Dr. Jacques said, "I've been traveling all my life, and now I'm finally home!"

Chapter Twenty-two

The candles had burned halfway down, and supper was nearly over. All day Aunt Lolly had been in a state of anxiety over having Julia Taffarel as a guest at Victoire, and she was taking her responsibilities even more seriously than usual. Julia, seated directly across from Theo, could overhear the rotund mammy in the next room, fussing at the serving girls as they shuttled back and forth to the table:

"Harmonie! Don't stack dose dishes so high. Yo' gets dem all broke. . . .

"Vermillion! Pour Miz Julia some more coffee. Can't yo' see her cup is almost empty?

"Libertine! Take de wine bucket and fill it up with ice. Dat one is all melted down. And it look like we need some more dessert."

"Aunt Lolly is very dedicated," Theo remarked after all the servants had left the room. "You're our first real guest at Victoire in . . . well, I'm embarrassed to think how long."

"We had the farm equipment representative to dinner last October, Grandpapa," Fleur reminded him. She turned to Julia. "He had dreadful manners, Miss Julia. He chewed with his mouth open and made a terrible noise."

Theo said, "Fleur places great store in good manners."

"Well, so do I, Fleur," said Julia. "And I certainly appreciate someone of the younger generation who does too." Fleur looked very pleased with herself.

Julia continued, "Aren't they wonderful? Mammies, I mean. Their influence on our Creole family life cannot be overestimated. I know that my own dear Ottile has been everything to me—mother, sister, friend."

"Aren't you awfully old to have a mammy, Miss Julia?" asked Blanche.

Julia laughed. "Yes, I am. But she's not really my mammy anymore. She and her husband are now my family. I gave them their freedom years ago, but they've chosen to stay on with me, I'm thankful to say."

"I would unhesitatingly give Aunt Lolly her freedom," Theo said. "Lord knows she's earned it."

A minute later Aunt Lolly appeared, carrying a second trayful of her special dessert—vanilla custard covered with a puree of red raspberries. She placed a dish in front of Blanche, who had made short work of her first portion.

Unexpectedly, Theo asked, "Aunt Lolly, how would you like your freedom?"

The old mammy looked stricken. "Didn't yo' like de supper, M'sieur Theo?"

"Why, of course. We all did. I just thought—"

"Don't give me a blood rush! What would I do with freedom? Is yo' fixin' to get rid of ol' Aunt Lolly, M'sieur Theo?"

"Never! This is your home, and it will always be. Nobody's going to give you your freedom if you don't want it."

"Den I can stay here?"

"Forever and ever."

"Dat's good." Aunt Lolly smiled. "Now, who wants more dessert?" She moved around the table and served all the others a second portion, whether they wanted it or not. She placed her hands on her broad hips and said, "If yo' all wants anything else, yo' just ring de bell, and Aunt Lolly will be right here. And I don't want to hear no more talk about freedom." Then she sashayed out of the room.

Julia turned to Theo. "I didn't mean to start something."

"Aunt Lolly's like a lot of slaves, Julia. They're afraid of freedom, because like everyone else they fear change." He asked his grandson, "Denis, are you children all set up in the theater?"

"Yes, Grandpapa," Denis replied. "We rehearsed again this afternoon. Even Blanche knows her lines."

"Wait until you see my costumes, Miss Julia," said Fleur. "I made them all myself."

"I'm looking forward to the production," Julia replied. She glanced from face to face, seeing a bit of Theo reflected in each of the children: Denis, with his curiosity about the world around him; Fleur, with her sense of propriety; and Blanche, unabashedly fond of the good things in life—particularly food. This is how it should have been, Julia found herself thinking. A family gathering, a fine meal, loving grandchildren. She looked across the table at Theo. He was regarding her over the rim of his coffee cup. She wondered if he was thinking the same thing—that he could have been her husband, that this could have been their dining room, and these three charming youngsters could have been their grandchildren.

Denis got up, his arms swinging loosely at his sides, and announced, "Excuse us, Grandpapa, Miss Julia, but we're going to get ready now. Give us about five minutes."

When they had left, Theo poured himself and Julia snifters of brandy. "What do you think of my grandchildren, Julia?"

"In a word, delightful. You've done quite well by them, Theo."

"I had a lot of help from Aunt Lolly. She loves the children as if they were her own. You know, I think I *am* going to see my lawyer and have papers drawn up granting Aunt Lolly her freedom. Just in case anything should happen to me. Of course I'll make comfortable provision for her. I would hate to think of Aunt Lolly ever wanting for anything."

"I think that's a wise idea, Theo."

"Perhaps we'd better leave for the premiere. The children will be getting impatient to show off their talents." He helped Julia out of her chair, and together they left the dining room.

"I'm pleased that you kept up your wood carving, Theo," said Julia. "I still have that little wooden box you made for me."

"I still enjoy it, and I'm teaching Denis. He'll be handy at it, once he learns patience. All three children seem to be good with their hands. Fleur's costumes are excellent, as she'll be the first to tell you. Blanche's props are perhaps a little bit lumpy, but they show a definite flair and imagination."

"Tell me about the play Denis has written."

"It's supposed to be a surprise, so I can't really talk about it. But he calls it *Journey into Midnight*."

"A very adult title."

"Well, I don't think it's exactly a children's play. But I haven't attended any rehearsals, nor have I read the script."

As Julia stepped across the threshold of the clubhouse, she experienced a feeling of apprehension, but she brushed it aside. Blanche, her mouth still smeared with vanilla custard, ushered the arrivals to their seats directly in front of the raised stage.

"Hope you enjoy the show," Blanche said, and skipped away toward backstage.

Julia was impressed. "They're very professional."

There came the ominous sound of a ringing bell, and Denis announced from behind the stage in a solemn voice, "*Journey . . . into . . . Midnight.*" As the curtains slowly opened, Fleur and Blanche provided the sound effects of a wailing wind.

The oil lamps revealed a scene familiar to Julia. A painted backdrop depicted the Promenade in almost perfect perspective. Julia stirred in her chair and glanced uneasily at Theo. He smiled and whispered, "Excellent set. That's Denis's work."

Something inside Julia told her to leave, that she should not watch the play any further.

Two puppets appeared from the wings—a man and a woman in formal dress. They were discussing the Duc's midsummer ball.

Woman: I'm really looking forward to the Duc's ball.

Man: Yes, I hear he's outdone himself this year.

Woman: Such a generous man, the Duc.

Man: A paragon of taste.

Theo whispered to Julia, "As you can hear, my grandson is a satirist."

A gibbous moon was dropped into place.

Woman: It's a pity the wheel came off our carriage.

Man: But it's a pleasant night for a stroll.

Woman: Aren't you afraid of the ghost?

Man: Nonsense. There are no such things as ghosts.

Julia was having difficulty breathing. She dropped her head and began massaging her temples. Theo noticed her actions.

"Aren't you feeling well?"

"Just a headache."

At that moment the ghost puppet appeared, wailing like a banshee. Its hair was wild and streaming, its arms outstretched, menacing. The two other puppets screamed, and Julia heard herself cry out.

"Julia, what's the matter?" Theo asked.

Unable to take her eyes from the hideous puppet, Julia reached out for Theo's support. She half rose from the chair, then her knees crumpled and she fell against him.

"I'm sorry," she gasped. "I feel ill. Could you take me out?"

Theo picked her up in his arms and carried her toward the door.

When they were outside in the evening air, Julia asked to be put down. She leaned against Theo's shoulder, and he felt her forehead. "Why, you're as cold as ice."

"I'm probably coming down with something," she murmured. "There's so much malaria about."

"Let me take you into the house, and you can lie down."

"No, thank you, Theo, but I think I'd like to go home. Apologize to the children for me, won't you?"

"I'll drive you."

"No, please. Cato's waiting with my carriage. If you'll just call him for me. He's probably in the kitchen, gossiping with your servants."

"Are you sure you're all right?"

"Yes, really, I am." She managed a half smile. "I'll feel much better when I'm home and can take off these corsets. If you'll just help me to my carriage and fetch Cato."

"Very well—I'll do as you say."

After Julia was seated in the back of her carriage, Theo went in search of Cato. The elderly slave came rushing to his mistress's side. Julia assured him that she was all right, that she just had a touch of something and would be better once she got home. She apologized to Theo once again and asked him to explain her poor manners to the children, but she could not meet his gaze. Theo kissed her hand, then closed the door, and the carriage moved off.

Julia slumped against the seat, her hand pressed over her forehead. It was no use, she told herself. Her dream of a new life with Theo was dead. She couldn't pretend any longer that things could be different. She now knew with heart-wrenching certainty that the decision she had made over four decades ago had sealed her fate. She was mad Julia Taffarel, the eccentric recluse of Magnolia Landing, and would remain so until she died.

* * *

Lilliane watched the lizard as it left its hiding place among the morning-glory vines and crept into the open window. It scurried across the rough plaster wall, changing colors as it passed over water stains, holy pictures, and bits of hanging voodoo paraphernalia—a pair of hollow gourds, a necklace made from cats' teeth, a patch of alligator skin.

She could not help but liken the lizard to Dr. Jacques, who had crossed many seas on his way to New Orleans and borrowed from the lore of many lands to create his own character, his own religion.

Lilliane stretched her legs and yawned, breaking into a smile. She had never experienced such loving before. It had released something deep within her, some spirit that had been waiting like a caged bird to be freed. They had made love in every room of the house, in every position imaginable. The pungent aroma of their sexual adventures was everywhere, overpowering even the incense burning at the altars Dr. Jacques had provided for his favorite saints and loas.

Toward dawn they had stopped to eat a bowl of gumbo that the voodoo man had prepared himself. Then they had gone to his bed—a huge, billowing mattress stuffed with cornshucks and owl feathers—and there they had made love one final time before the cock's crow.

Lilliane's hair had grown during the night. She could tell the difference in the length—at least an inch, surely—and the texture was thicker and more lustrous than the day before. It was curled around their still-interlocked bodies like a large red cocoon. Lilliane turned to look at her lover. Dr. Jacques slept with his mouth open, peacefully sucking in great quantities of the cool morning air. Lilliane unwound her hair from his body and slipped out of bed, hoping she could remember the location of the kitchen. Since most of the rooms had two or even three entrances, it was easy to get confused. After wandering through the maze of doorways and corridors, she finally found it. She stoked the fire in the iron stove and added wood, then opened an outside door to let in the cool, fresh air from the garden. She put on a pot of coffee to boil and, after assembling the necessary ingredients, whipped up a batch of drop biscuits, which she put into the oven. While the biscuits were baking, she peeled several oranges, filled two bowls with the sections, then shaved a mound of coconut and sprinkled it on top of each.

As she worked, she reflected that she had never been so free of anxiety in her life. She thought that perhaps she was in love with Dr. Jacques. She smiled as she recalled his words. "I know why you've come." For the first time in her life, Lilliane felt that her prayers were going to be answered.

The coffee was brewed and the biscuits were browned. Lilliane sat down at the table and began to eat. She was famished. She found a tub of butter, which was nearly liquid but not rancid, and dipped the pieces of hot biscuit into it. A toad, most likely one of Dr. Jacques' tenants, hopped onto the sill of the garden door and eyed her. Lilliane broke off a small piece of biscuit and tossed it in front of the toad. Its long tongue flashed out, and the treat disappeared in a blink.

"I see you've met Papa Joe."

Lilliane turned around. Dr. Jacques was standing in the other doorway, wearing nothing but a huge grin. "I smelled the coffee and the biscuits. That'll get me out of bed every time."

Lilliane rose from the table and went to him. He placed his hands on her waist and swung her around. They both laughed for the pure joy of being in each other's company. The witch doctor sat down at the table, and Lilliane served him.

"I had a little difficulty in finding the kitchen," she said. "Who added all the rooms?"

"Me, mostly."

"I like your house, Jacques, but I wonder why a man like you doesn't live in the grandest house in New Orleans."

"Always live in a simple house, Lilliane. You can have chairs of gold if you like, and chandeliers hanging everywhere—" He glanced up. "Even in the kitchen, if that's what you want. But keep your front porch humble. Otherwise you'll put off your customers. The simple folks won't come to no mansion for a cure, and the rich folks would be offended if I lived in such a place."

Lilliane was startled as a parrot flapped through the garden doorway and alighted on Dr. Jacques's shoulder. It cocked its head to one side and trained a beady eye on her.

"This is Red Eye. He's come to have a look at you."

"And do I pass muster?"

"He knows you make me happy."

"Do I?"

"Oh, yes, sister. I knew you would. The loas told me. But telling and doing are two different things. Nobody could have told me it was going to be this good." He bit into a biscuit, washed it down with black coffee, and pronounced, "Hey, Miss Lilliane, you make a strong cup of coffee and a mighty light biscuit. Why don't you marry me?"

Lilliane was stunned. He had spoken the words that she wanted to hear, and yet there were so many complications. "Jacques, are you serious?"

"I'm plenty serious."

For a moment, Lilliane did not know what to say. "Well, there are problems. I'm a slave. And there's Azby."

"Azby's going to love me. All children do. And as for the other, why don't you believe me, Lilliane, when I tell you that everything is going to be all right? You know a hard-headed bird don't make good soup. Now, don't cause me to take back my proposal."

"How can you be so sure?" she asked, her voice shaking with her heartbeats.

"I told you I've been waiting all my life for you. This is a golden chance, Lilliane. Take it. Most people just live, suffer, endure, and die; but sometimes along the way you find someone special, and that makes it all worthwhile. We belong together. Come bring your son and live with me. I want to make you my queen. You have the gift, Lilliane. I knew it the minute I saw you. We'll set New Orleans spinning on its tail. We'll make a barrel of money. Voodoo is a very profitable business."

"I thought it was a religion."

"It is. And religion is a business—don't you ever forget it."

"But I don't know anything about spells and fixes."

"Yes, you do. It's all inside, just waiting to come out. I'll make it happen. Say yes, Lilliane. I've been waiting for you for a long time."

"Yes is a word I like saying to you, Jacques," she replied carefully.

Dr. Jacques jumped up from the table. "Come on, Lilliane. It's a brand-new day that's never been touched. Let's take a bath together, and then I'm going to take you to Congo Square!"

He took her hand and led her through the kitchen door to the back garden. Under a huge oak tree, and enclosed by a series of discarded doors that had been nailed together, sat a large stone tub.

"That's your bathtub?" Lilliane laughed. "It looks more like a trough."

"It was," Dr. Jacques replied. "Get in—I'll show you how it works."

Lilliane climbed inside and sat down at one end of the tub. Dr. Jacques joined her, then pointed upward. Wedged between a forked limb of the live oak was a barrel with a series of holes drilled in the bottom. The witch doctor pulled a cord, a flat piece of tin shifted on the inside, and all of a sudden tiny streams of water came pouring out.

"It's delightful," squealed Lilliane. "What is it?"

"My master in Santo Domingo called it a shower." He handed Lilliane a cake of scented soap. "Me first," he said. "After all, I am providing the soap and the water."

After each had soaped the other's body, Dr. Jacques pulled the cord once again, and the warm rainwater rinsed them. They dried each other, then went inside and got dressed. Lilliane put on her bright orange dress, and Dr. Jacques selected a pair of tight black pants, a ruffled fuchsia shirt, and a frock coat.

The witch doctor took Lilliane into another room and opened a wooden chest. Lilliane gasped with astonishment. The chest was filled to the top with jewelry—dozens of ropes of pearls, mixed together with necklaces, bracelets, and rings of gold, silver, and every imaginable variety of precious and semiprecious gem, including coral, amethyst, topaz, carnelian, onyx, and lapis lazuli.

"Are they real?" she asked.

"Some's real and some's paste. But what difference does it make, as long as it shines? Pick out what you like. It's all part of the show."

Lilliane selected a huge pair of gold hoop earrings and put them on. Dr. Jacques urged her, "Don't be shy. Here, let me help you." He draped a handful of necklaces around her long neck, slid a half-dozen bracelets onto each of her bare arms, selected a jeweled barrette for either side of her head, wound chains of gold and silver around her waist, and studded her fingers with rings. Finally he secured a band of tiny golden bells around each of her ankles and wrists. "Now they can hear you coming."

"I feel like a gypsy," she laughed.

The voodoo man stepped back. "You still need something. I know! Some sparkle in your hair." He undid the lid of a jar and sprinkled specks of a silvery substance through her tresses. "Diamond dust," he explained.

"It looks like mica to me."

"Lilliane, if you believe it's diamond dust, then it is. Now, what is it?"

"Diamond dust," she replied.

Satisfied with his protégée's appearance, Dr. Jacques dug into his treasure trove and began choosing pieces of jewelry to wear himself. Finally he produced a top hat banded with peacock feathers, adjusted it to a jaunty angle, and pronounced, "Now we're ready for Congo Square."

Just before leaving the room, Dr. Jacques pulled from a tabletop a large Chinese scarf embroidered with dragons and folded it into a triangle. He handed it to Lilliane and said, "Cover your hair."

"But . . . I don't understand."

"Never reveal everything all at once. You'll know when to remove it."

As they left the house, Dr. Jacques said, "Today we'll walk. No carriages. I want my public to see us."

"Where are all your clients, Jacques?"

"They know that Sundays I'm at Congo Square."

"But there weren't any people here yesterday afternoon or the time before."

He grinned. "Word got around that I was expecting somebody special."

As they walked down Bayou Road toward the Place d'Armes, it seemed to Lilliane that everyone, black and white, free and slave, acknowledged Dr. Jacques. Children of all hues rushed up to him. The shy ones touched his coattails and ran off giggling. Others who were more forward asked him direct questions, mostly pertaining to growing pains and school problems.

Lilliane observed with relief how good the doctor was with children. He was patient, loving, and always gave them a positive answer, sending them away smiling.

On Condé Street, a group of prisoners from the jail, mostly runaway Negro slaves, were cleaning up the sewage that was dumped into the open gutters in front of the houses every day. Dr. Jacques stopped to speak with them. The mean-looking guard adopted a civil smile and stepped aside. Dr.

Jacques offered the prisoners words of encouragement and told them that when they were released they should come see him, and he would help them find jobs.

They turned right at the Place d'Armes, heading up Saint Peter Street, away from the river. Although their destination was still six blocks away, they could already hear the roll of the bamboulas and the rumble of the drums, seducing them, along with hundreds of others, to Congo Square.

Everything in this part of the city was new and strange to Lilliane. Her bewilderment must have showed, for as they walked, Dr. Jacques took her arm and reassured her, describing the layout of the city and telling her that the newer, American, section was several blocks to their left. A generation ago, under the French and Spanish, he explained, slaves had been allowed no freedom of movement or assembly in the city. After the Louisiana Purchase, however, the Americans had taken over and brought a new viewpoint to the laws and customs regulating the life of the black man. For their own entertainment, Negroes were allowed to gather on Sundays at various places, the most celebrated being a large open field in the very heart of the city, at Rampart and Orleans streets. The area became popularly known as Congo Square, and the weekly dancing there soon was as much an entertainment for the whites as it was for the blacks.

As Lilliane and Dr. Jacques came in sight of the crowded square, they could hear the cries and shouts of the dancers.

"*Dansez Bamboula! Badoum! Badoum!*"

The voodoo king said to Lilliane, "They're sounding extra good today. They can sense that something special is going to happen."

The square itself, Lilliane could now see, was bordered by sycamore trees and surrounded by a picket fence that held four gates. What grass there was had long since been worn away by hundreds of stamping feet. Rows of white people were gaping over the fence at the acrobatic male dancers, who were wearing the cast-off finery of their masters, together with anklets of dangling bits of tin or other metal, which jingled as they jumped. Most of the Negro women were dressed in madras tignons and calico shifts, to which they had added feathers or gaily colored strips of ribbons.

The cries of the food vendors intermingled with the voodoo songs. Carrying great trays around their necks, they moved on the periphery of the crowd, selling pineapple beer and lemonade, little ginger cakes called mulattoes' bellies, sweetmeats, rice cakes, and pralines. Gris-gris hawkers offered their good-luck and bad-luck charms to eager buyers, many of whom had come to the square for just such a purchase.

Squealing black children ran through the legs of the white onlookers. Creole and American gentlemen were perspiring freely through their pastel suits. Ladies wore gauzy veils to ward off the dust and body odor, to protect their pale skin from the sun, or, in some cases, just to remain anonymous.

Dr. Jacques and Lilliane were admitted through a gate by a police official who tipped his hat respectfully. As the witch doctor entered the square, slaves rushed to his side, asking him for favors. He treated them kindly but with a certain distance, dispensing advice but more often telling them to come and see him at his home.

A cheer went up from the dancers when they saw their voodoo king, and as they stopped dancing, the musicians stopped playing. Clasping Lilliane's hand in his, Dr. Jacques walked her around the center of the plain, tipping his hat and making pleasant comments to those who had gathered there. Soon everyone had grown quiet, even the children, the vendors, and the white audience. They sensed that something unusual was about to happen.

Dr. Jacques removed his frock coat, then his shirt, and tossed them behind the musicians. The male dancers, taking a cue from him, removed their shirts and tied them around their waists. Bottles of rum were passed from dancer to dancer. Lilliane suspected they had been supplied by Dr. Jacques.

Leaving her standing near one of the drummers, with instructions to join in when she felt like it, Dr. Jacques signaled the musicians. A prolonged rumbling commenced as one of the drummers applied two huge beef bones to the head of a cask covered with goatskin. This was soon joined by tom-toms and Congo drums, tambourines, bamboo flutes, bells, banjos fashioned from cigar boxes, and rattles made from gourds and the jawbones of asses, the loosened teeth of which clattered when struck.

The dancers took their places once again, and Dr. Jacques joined the males, who began moving back and forth, stamping the bare ground in unison and emitting shouts of "*Dansez Bamboula! Badoum! Badoum!*"

The intensity of the music steadily built, and the men

began leaping in the air and performing gymnastic feats. The witch doctor lept higher and shouted louder than any of the others. When he landed, the earth seemed to shake beneath him, and Lilliane could imagine the tops of the sycamores trembling as he cried, *"Badoum! Badoum!"*

The women lined up facing the men. Swaying their bodies from side to side, they chanted the words to a primitive song that had its beginnings in Africa. Punctuated by moans and cries of exaltation, the song worked slowly toward a climax. The whole square became a swirling mass of undulating brown, yellow, and black bodies. The pulse of the rhythm was infectious, and even the white people who had come merely to observe were tapping their feet and swaying their bodies, although in most cases with conscious restraint.

Lilliane had remained one of the observers. But as the dance progressed and became more frenzied in its intensity, she was infused not only with the incessant beat, but also with a sense of what Dr. Jacques expected of her. She shook her thighs and rolled her hips, threw back her head, and allowed the spell of the music to stimulate her senses to an almost sexual arousal. She stared unblinkingly into the blinding eye of the sun, lifted her arms toward the hard blue sky, and let the scarf slide from her head. She caught it, quickly tied it around her waist, and shook her hair loose.

The spectators gasped when they saw Lilliane's hair, and those dancing nearby made space for her to join them. Over the top of the crowd, Lilliane could see Dr. Jacques. He was smiling at her and beckoning. It was her time. Tossing her head from side to side so that her hair floated about her like a sparkling cape, she moved among the dancers, improvising her own steps and body movements. She raised her arms. The tinkling of the wrist bells instilled a touch of femininity to the driving music and drew even more attention to her.

The musicians focused their attention on Lilliane and began altering their rhythms to suit those dictated by her body. They kept their eyes riveted to the newcomer, nodding with her every movement. They were playing for her and for her only.

Lilliane circled the square, fixing the audience in the steady gaze of her luminous gray eyes. The women dancers retreated to the sidelines, still clapping their hands in time to the music. Out of the corner of her eye, Lilliane saw Dr. Jacques standing beside the musicians. It was her show now, and he was giving it over to her. He tipped his hat. His face was beaming with pleasure, but not surprise.

Lilliane started weaving in and out of the line of male dancers. They, in turn, began stomping harder and jumping higher than they had before. She seemed to charge them with an almost visible electric energy as her hair stroked their bare shoulders.

Sometimes she touched them, sometimes she whispered encouragement. She conquered each one as she passed, caressing subtly with words and gestures, subduing one after the other with her commands.

Shouts of excitement rippled through the white crowd, as the onlookers congratulated themselves for picking that particular day to attend the spectacle. Even the food, drink, and gris-gris vendors stopped counting their money to view the phenomenon.

As she danced, Lilliane felt as if a veil had been lifted from her eyes, a weight from her shoulders. For the first time in her life, she was experiencing the joyous feeling of freedom. She now knew that meeting Dr. Jacques, coming to Congo Square, the dance—everything in the last two days—was but a preamble to the start of her second life. Now she understood. She knew that somehow the witch doctor would liberate both her and Azby from their bonds. To be able to trust someone was a new adventure for her, and she was filled with unlimited optimism. It was a joy beyond description to know that her prayers *were* going to be answered.

Smiling at her audience for the first time, Lilliane began rolling her hips from side to side, reaching out her arms to those who danced, drawing them closer. Through her movements, she began telling the story of her life—all their lives—illustrating their bondage, the brutality of enslavement, and the rapture of freedom.

The male dancers broke their line, somersaulted toward Lilliane, and formed a circle around her. The women rushed forward, placing their arms around each other's waists and forming an outer circle. Shouts rose from all directions, and the dance grew wilder and wilder. It was as if the celebrants seemed intent upon shaking off the shackles of their slavery right then and there. All Congo Square was dancing to Lilliane's tune.

Lilliane raised her arms and slapped her hands together, and suddenly everything stopped. The dancers fell to the ground around her. The entire plain was littered with panting bodies, all paying homage to the young woman. The musicians forgot their instruments and turned toward Lilliane. The onlookers were completely still. Lilliane pivoted on her heels, her hair and skirts swirling slowly around her as she turned in a full circle, acknowledging their adoration.

New Orleans had a new voodoo queen.

The female figure moved silently through Heritage. The flawless white face, unmarked by time, looked at each room in turn. The unblinking eyes searched the big house, searched for someone who was no longer there.

With a cry of exasperation Angélique let the doll slip through her grasp. The delicate porcelain face struck the floor of the miniature music room, and a thin, almost imperceptible crack appeared, running from the hairline to the jaw. Angélique stared in horror at the injured doll, which represented herself as a child. She turned away from the dollhouse and began crying unassuageable tears. They streamed down her perfect face and seeped into her gasping mouth.

"Jean-Louis is dead and buried," she told herself, but it was a reality that she had difficulty accepting. She had seen his body, his shattered face; she had inhaled his decay and attended his funeral. And several days later, in a secret ceremony of her own, she had buried Jean-Louis's porcelain image in the freshly turned ground above his real body.

Rest in peace, my beloved Jean-Louis. You were the only person I ever loved.

For one terrible moment, Angélique thought she had spoken aloud. It wouldn't do for anyone to hear her. She wiped her wet cheeks with a sleeve of her dress, reminding herself that there were strangers who walked free in the very house of Jean-Louis's birth.

Memories of her brother had been corrupted by hate, but now that hate calmed her. The tears were still flowing, but in a gentle, unbroken stream.

Heat lightning bounded across the horizon, and the room was suddenly illuminated. Angélique looked toward the open window. The air was filled with a metallic scent, and the sky was a dark greenish tint. Everything seemed bigger, clearer, yet somehow less substantial.

Jean-Louis's suicide had come as an inconceivable shock to her, especially since she had known that his marriage to

Suzanne was nearing its end. A few months longer and Suzanne would have gone home to her parents in Georgia, and then Heritage would have been theirs once again, forever and ever.

"Why didn't you hold on, Jean-Louis?" she said bitterly.

But he was gone, and now she was a guest in her own home.

Angélique reached out to the dollhouse. It was the one solid reality in her shifting world. A wave of nausea passed through her. She shut her eyes and took deep gulps of night air. When she opened her eyes, she made herself concentrate on those things she could touch and feel—the columns, the walls, the rooms of Heritage.

Time was running out. It would soon be harvest, and her dream of regaining Heritage would be over.

There was only one way that she could become mistress of the big house again, and that was through Royal Brannigan. She would have to make him fall in love with her. How easily men were controlled by their passions, she thought as she recalled all those she had known intimately. Corso Lajeunesse had been the first of many houseguests who had enjoyed her favors. And when the guests were old or ugly or unappealing, she had turned to the overseer, Rafe Bastile, who had surprised her with the ferocity of his lovemaking.

Yes, her marriage to Royal Brannigan would be the next-to-last act—then she would once again be the mistress of Heritage.

Smiling to herself, Angélique righted the fallen doll. She traced her finger over the thin crack in its head and pushed its hair—her own hair—forward so that the defect was concealed. She placed the doll at the front entrance to Heritage.

Angélique got to her feet and caught sight of herself in the mirror. She had forgotten it was there. For a brief moment she saw not a person of flesh and blood, bone and sinew, but the reflection of the doll—with her dead blond hair pushed forward to cover the crack in her skull.

She caught her breath and, with a hand to one cold cheek, moved toward the mirror. The doll's face faded, and she became herself.

Angélique pushed back her hair and examined her face, but there were no marks, no imperfections.

"That's better," she said. "This is how I really look. This is Angélique Jourdain, mistress of Heritage."

The moment of confusion had passed, and Angélique was

left with a strong sense of self-possession. She blew out the oil lamp, and shadows skittered about the room like dark and elusive imps. As she walked down the hallway, the sound of her taffeta robe trailing over the parquet floors followed her like a malicious whisper.

Royal started to close the drapes against the coming storm when he abruptly changed his mind. He got undressed and slipped into bed, knowing instinctively that he would not remain alone for long.

A short time later he heard the sound of the doorknob being turned with a very soft creak, and then the sudden change of air as the door was opened. Someone had come into the room. There was a rustle of material as an article of clothing was discarded and dropped to the floor. He could see her shape as a denser blackness in the dark. The shape grew fluid and glided toward him.

Just as the visitor reached the side of the bed, the lightning flashed and a band of yellow-white light fell across Angélique.

Royal was both shocked and disappointed. He had expected Suzanne—but then Angélique smiled at him. Her hair was flowing loose, a swinging curtain of gold. Her exquisite body was bathed in the heat lightning's glow, and every curve and indentation stood out in sharp relief. His eyes narrowed in desire, and he reached out for her.

Chapter Twenty-three

The heaviness of high summer descended upon Magnolia Landing. The late August sun was a hot, crimson orb that sucked every drop of moisture from the atmosphere, leaving it unfresh and tainted. The recent outbreak of malaria among the slaves at Salle d'Or had been successfully contained, yet a feeling of vague discontent sat over the land, as if feeding off the anger, frustration, and madness brought on by the heat.

Although it was only nine o'clock in the morning, Denis, Fleur, and Blanche were already drenched with perspiration.

Laden with the paraphernalia of their day's outing, they trudged toward the Promenade. Denis, wearing nothing but a loose pair of cotton pants, poked at the scorched lawn with an old bamboo cane of his grandfather's that he had appropriated. The cane concealed a long, narrow sword and had been used as a protective device by Theo in his younger days on the lawless streets of New Orleans. Ever since the encounter with the ghost, Denis would not consider taking his sisters anywhere unless he carried a weapon.

Fleur wore a wide-brimmed straw hat that had belonged to her mother. She had stuffed strips of newspaper into the crown so that it would fit. Although the straw was limp and the decorative silken flowers had wilted with the passage of time, the hat kept her well shaded from the sun. She carried a picnic basket full of food that Aunt Lolly had prepared for them.

Blanche trailed behind carrying another, smaller, basket that held an assortment of desserts. She was in a cranky mood and whined constantly, hoping to provoke Denis into giving her a piggyback ride. Because of her fair skin, she had been made to wear a long-sleeved blouse and a pair of pants that Denis had outgrown. She had been further humiliated by the compulsory addition of a floppy hat woven out of palmetto, which offered her face shade but caused her head to itch.

The children were on their way to a small pond hidden in a wooded area between Villeneuve and Salle d'Or. The pond was fed by an underground spring, and even in the dog days of summer the water there remained crystal clear and perfect for swimming. Aunt Lolly had put up a fuss about it, claiming that it was too far for them to walk and that they would surely come down with sun pain. The children had had sun pain before—it was an affliction peculiar to that part of the country, consisting of a throbbing pain at the back of the head brought on by overexposure to the sun—but that certainly would not deter them.

In any case, Aunt Lolly's protestations had gone for naught, for Theo, who had been distracted and withdrawn since the night of Julia's abrupt departure, had unexpectedly given them his permission to go. The mammy, overruled, had retreated to the kitchen to make their lunches and pout.

The pond had been discovered by Denis and Coffey the previous August on one of their explorations around Magnolia Landing. Azby, from Villeneuve, had tagged along, and it was he, Denis recalled, who had come upon the clearing nearby littered with the remains of bonfires and burned-out candles. Coffey had identified it as a gathering spot for slaves who slipped out on certain nights to worship their voodoo gods in secret. Denis would not admit he was frightened by the nocturnal use of the site, and Coffey, who knew something of voodoo, had named the place Damballah Pond, after the snake god. Naturally these details had been kept from Theo and Aunt Lolly.

The children waited at the edge of the Promenade for a dusty line of wagons to pass, bringing water up from the river. Their plan was to stop by Villeneuve and see if Azby could accompany them. It was past ten when they approached the brick kitchen building. Denis began strutting with the cane, showing off for Azby, but he drew to a halt when he saw that the kitchen door and all the shutters were closed, which was surprising for such a hot day. Fleur rapped on the heavy wood, and all three of them called Azby's name. When the door finally opened, however, it was not Azby who answered, but Lilliane. She had on an apron and looked busy cleaning or moving things around. Her expression was guarded and her manner unfriendly.

Denis explained the reason for their visit.

"He can't come out today," said Lilliane brusquely. "He's busy. I've got chores for him to do."

"It's too hot for chores, Miss Lilliane," said Fleur. "Besides, Aunt Lolly's packed an absolutely scrumptious lunch, and she made enough for Azby too."

Lilliane softened. "Well, I'm sorry, children, but Azby really is busy. He'll be pleased to know you were thinking of him." Then, without another word, she shut the door.

The girls looked to Denis. He shrugged his shoulders, turned on his heels, and pointed the cane in the direction of the pond.

Fifteen minutes later, after crossing the deserted gardens of Villeneuve and cutting through a cane field, the children reached a stand of live oaks bordering a swampy area. The trees were draped with streamers of gray moss, and their widespread limbs offered a welcome measure of shade. The usually lush vegetation, however, showed the effects of the recent drought. The leaves on the trees were edged with yellow and drooped listlessly. By now the children were desperate for a swim in the cool pond, and with each step their excitement increased.

"Keep a watch out for snakes," warned Denis.

"It's too hot for snakes," said Fleur from beneath the giant pancake of a hat.

"It's too hot for me," wailed Blanche. "When do we get there? I want the pool!"

"We're almost there," said Denis.

As they drew closer to the swamp, the dense vegetation became so thick that it blotted out the sky. A narrow path unwound before them, and with Denis in the lead pushing branches aside, the children hurried forward until they found themselves under a dome of willows. There, just ahead, in a shady glen curtained on all sides by the cascading green branches, a spring trickled out from between gnarled old roots and spilled down like a miniature waterfall into a pond encircled by lush ferns and clumps of wildflowers.

The children broke into a run. When they reached the edge of the pond, they hurriedly stripped off their clothes and, laughing and shouting, jumped into the refreshingly cool water.

They splashed about and dived under the surface, and then Fleur challenged the others to a race across the pond. All three were good swimmers, but Denis held back and allowed his sisters to reach the other side first. They came out of the water sputtering and squealing with delight, then climbed up on the grassy bank and allowed the warm air to dry their bodies.

"What do you suppose happened to the ghost?" pondered Denis. "No one's reported seeing him since the Duc's ball."

"Where *do* ghosts go when they're not scaring people?" wondered Fleur.

"Maybe he got tired of being a ghost and died," Blanche offered philosophically.

Denis and Fleur laughed so heartily that Blanche, thoroughly offended, jumped back into the water and began swimming toward where they had left the picnic baskets.

Fleur said to her brother, "We'd better start swimming, too, or there won't be anything left to eat."

They dived into the water and beat Blanche to the opposite side. Denis, eyeing the position of the sun, said, "It must be getting near noon. We might as well eat."

"But first we must dress," said Fleur. "Well-brought-up persons do not lunch naked."

"Naked! Naked! Naked!" chanted Blanche as she pirouetted around the dessert basket.

Henriette cried out when the clock in the foyer began striking noon. Her heart seemed to stop, and her extremities stiffened as if they had suddenly turned to stone. She willed herself into movement and rushed out onto the veranda. Directly above her, on the second-floor gallery, Saisie, Alcée's personal maid, was watching for the *Belle Créole*.

"Any sign yet?" Henriette called up, her voice trembling.

"Not yet, Miz Henriette," Saisie replied. "It probably late, with de water so low and all. Don't yo' worry—I got my eyes stuck on de river, and I lets yo' know as soon as I sees a boat."

"Thank you, Saisie."

Another house slave came up behind Henriette, and again she almost jumped out of her skin.

"I's sorry, Miz Henriette," the girl said, "but dat Lilliane and her son done arrived at de back door, and dey asking fo' yo'."

"Take them into the front parlor."

If the slave was surprised by the request, she did not show it. Instead, she merely shook her head to herself, as if resigned to Henriette's peculiarities.

Henriette remained on the veranda a few moments longer. She closed her eyes and silently prayed that the *Belle Créole* would suddenly appear on the muddy Mississippi. But when she opened them, it still wasn't in sight. She was about to go inside when she spotted a small cloud of dust turning into the driveway toward the big house. She ran back to the edge of the veranda and shaded her eyes against the sun.

"Yo' see dat?" Saisie yelled down, and Henriette nodded. The cloud of dust got bigger and bigger as it neared. For one agonizing moment she thought it might be her husband and Philippe returning from downriver, where they had gone to attend a slave auction.

But by the time the cloud was halfway down the driveway, certain details emerged. It was a carriage, covered with the dust of a long journey, and it was very oddly built indeed. The cab was large and ungainly, like a miniature house perched precariously on a chassis not designed to support it. The back wheels were much larger than the front ones, and the fenders were . . . well, Henriette could hardly believe her eyes. The fenders were actually decorated with feathers, flags, and bouquets of flowers! The bizarre vehicle pulled to a stop, and Henriette saw that the driver was totally concealed by a coat with the collar turned up, a smashed-flat hat, a pair of tinted spectacles, and a scarf that was wound around his face to his nose. All of which was covered with a film of road dust. She thought wildly of a drawing she had once seen of an Egyptain mummy.

With surprising agility the driver leaped down from the box and began divesting himself of his dusty apparel. Henriette gasped at his height—he must have been seven feet! She watched as he took off the squat hat and his hair sprang up from his head in glistening black curls. He unwound the scarf from over a broad, grinning mouth. Next he shed the dusty traveling coat, revealing tight gray pants and a frilly magenta shirt. He removed the tinted glasses, and his eyes fixed their gaze upon Henriette. The grinning mouth spoke to her.

"It is twelve noon. I am Dr. Jacques, and you are Madame Henriette Duvallon." He bowed deeply, then bounded up the steps in one stretch of his long legs. He offered his hand, and Henriette didn't know what else to do but take it.

He grinned crookedly. "Don't worry, Miss Henriette, I've brought cash. Have Lilliane and Azby arrived yet?"

"Y-yes," stammered Henriette. "I've had them shown into the parlor. Won't you follow me, ah—ah, Doctor."

He smiled at her so warmly that, even though she was intimidated by his presence, she began to feel more confident that her plan was going to work. She led him to the parlor and waited at the door so that Lilliane would have a few moments to introduce him to Azby.

The witch doctor approached Lilliane and Azby. There was no mistaking the light in Lilliane's eyes; she was clearly in love with this extraordinary man. But Azby looked frightened and unhappy. Henriette watched as Dr. Jacques politely took Lilliane's hand and kissed it, then turned his attention to the little boy. The voodoo man reached behind Azby's ear and—presto!—produced a little yellow bird. The bird flew in circles above the boy's head. Azby looked entranced.

"A present for you, my boy." Dr. Jacques extended his finger, and the bird came to rest on it. "This is Bonaparte. He's your new pet. Go on, take him."

Azby put out his finger. The bird hopped onto it, walked up his arm, and perched calmly on his shoulder.

Henriette could see that Lilliane was delighted with the first meeting of the two men in her life. Yet despite the apparent happiness in the room, Henriette was struck by a sorrow that brought tears to her eyes. This beautiful little boy was her grandson. She had never acknowledged him in any way, and now he would be leaving Magnolia Landing forever. It was quite possible that she would never see him again.

Henriette stepped out of sight so that she could compose herself. Yet her tears made her all the more determined that nothing should go wrong with her plan for saving Alcée and Blaise from her husband's machinations.

Out of deference to Lilliane and Azby, Dr. Jacques and Henriette went to the Duc's library to conduct their business. The voodoo man examined the deeds of sale she had drawn up—modeled word for word after those she had found in the Duc's desk—and was satisfied that everything was duly signed, sealed, and in order. He then handed Henriette a packet containing the money they had agreed upon.

"You're a good woman, Miss Henriette. And believe me, the saints, the gods, and the loas are going to reward you for your kindness." He covered her hand with his and looked directly into her eyes. "You've had much unhappiness in your life, but all that will change. Your daughter and her man will be safe. And you'll find what you are searching for."

"W-what do you mean?"

"You'll know when you find it," he replied cryptically. "I suppose we'd better be going. I know you have much to do. And, Miss Henriette, I want you to know that you are welcome to visit our house in New Orleans at any time."

Henriette swallowed hard. "Thank you," she replied. "I don't know what my future plans are as yet."

"Well, now, Miss Henriette, the good Lord helps those who help themselves. And if you just keep on doing that, you have nothing to worry about."

While Lilliane and Azby's meager belongings were being loaded into the carriage and Dr. Jacques redonned his dusty driving attire, Henriette went to Lilliane. The two women looked at each other for a moment, neither knowing what to say. Then Henriette embraced Lilliane. "I hope, my dear, that you're going to be far happier than you ever were at Villeneuve."

"Thank you, Madame Duvallon. If it wasn't for you, none of this could have ever happened."

Henriette didn't trust herself to answer. She knelt down in front of Azby, who was so diverted by the yellow bird that his fear of leaving had completely disappeared.

"You're a fine boy, Azby," she said, directly meeting his gaze for the first time. She saw traces of herself in his young countenance and had to bite her lip to keep from crying. "Your mama's very proud of you, and I'm very proud of you too."

"I didn't know you knew my name," said the little boy.

"Why, of course I did. I've always known it," replied Henriette. "And now I'll keep it in my heart for always."

Denis, Fleur, and Blanche had finished the picnic lunch. They had eaten too much and were feeling sluggish. Each of them was waiting for another to make a suggestion as to what they should do next. They couldn't swim. Theo's rules were strict about swimming on full stomachs, and theirs were certainly full.

Fleur was the first to speak. "Come on, Blanche, let's gather up the dishes."

Blanche, grumbling, struggled to her feet, and the two girls began packing away the remnants of the picnic.

Denis got up and stretched to his full height. He was not one to give in to lethargy, and he looked around for something that might stimulate his interest. He began walking toward the nearby clearing where the voodooists met. Perhaps he could find some artifact he could take back and show to Coffey.

As soon as he pushed past the willow branches into the clearing, his eyes fell upon a series of small, rust-colored discs scattered around the remains of a fire. He bent down and touched one. It crumbled into dust. He sniffed his fingers. They smelled like copper. He recognized the scent of dried blood.

Denis continued across the clearing until he reached the ashes of another fire, next to which was a crude arrangement of flat rocks that he guessed was an altar. But all he found there was a fat white candle burned to the end of its wick, a scrap of paper on which a symbol had been drawn in charcoal, and some small bones he took to be those of a chicken. Nothing to elicit Coffey's envy.

Denis got down on his hands and knees and began searching around and under the pile of rocks. He was ready to give the search up when he spotted something hard and metallic half buried in the earth. He began digging and withdrew an amulet about two inches in diameter, attached to a crude chain. He brushed off the dirt, and a design was revealed—a wiggling line, which he knew from Coffey's information was the symbol for the snake god Damballah.

Denis was staring hard at the amulet, hoping it would impart some voodoo secret to him, when he was startled by the sound of a black cloud of crows taking to the skies, cawing and fluttering their wings. He looked up. They resembled inkblots against a sheet of perfectly blue paper. Something in the swamp beyond had frightened them. Denis hung the amulet around his neck and hurried back out of the clearing. Stationing himself behind a tree, he waited until he could make out three men in the distance, wading quickly through the shallow waters of the swamp. Denis didn't like the looks of them. Instinct told him not to let himself or his sisters be seen.

He ran back to the pond. "Quickly," he said. "There are some men approaching."

"Voodooists?" asked Fleur, the excitement rising in her voice.

"No, white men. They don't look right. I think we ought to hide somewhere. Gather up the stuff." Denis picked up Blanche and the cane. "Fleur, dammit, get the basket!" He looked wildly about for someplace for them to hide. "Over there, in the saw grass!"

Blanche began moaning with fright. "Shhh," Denis warned as they waded into the tall grass and sat down facing the pond and willows. Denis unsheathed his sword, then rearranged the saw grass as best he could over them. Just as he sat down they heard gruff voices.

"Nobody breathe or make a sound," Denis whispered.

The three of them watched wide-eyed as the ragged men burst through the willow branches and stopped at the edge of the pond. The strangers looked around warily, then at one another. They were all dressed alike, in dirty, sweat-stained shirts and equally soiled pants, similar to the kind that slaves wore in the fields. The tallest of the three appeared to be the leader. He was large and muscular, with a crudely handsome face. He had dark, wavy hair, a fleshy, broad nose, and thick, unnaturally red lips. His piercing eyes were those of a mesmerist.

The second man was thin and scraggly, with overworked muscles that stood out like giant blisters on his unfleshed frame. His hair was shoulder length and so greasy that its color was impossible to determine. His skin was mottled with what appeared to be heat rash, or possibly poison ivy.

The third man was small and chunky, with short, tightly curled hair that was a raw shade of red, and yellowish skin.

The good-looking one was the first to speak. His voice was deep and commanding, with the trace of an Irish accent. "That looks like fresh water. Who wants to test it? Spoke?"

The thin man shook his head.

"Finn?"

Finn, the red-haired man, replied, "What the hell, I'm so thirsty I could drink just about anything." He ran to the edge of the pond, submerged his face, and came up coughing. "It tastes fine to me. If we only had a little whiskey to go with it, eh, Darcy?"

The handsome man grunted, "All you ever think of is liquor."

Darcy and Spoke joined Finn at the edge of the pond. The men drank for what seemed to the children an impossible amount of time. Then they lay back against the bank, breathing hard and stretching out their legs. It was then that the children noticed the leg-irons. The chains attached to them had been sawed away.

"Convicts," Denis gasped. The word was out of his mouth before he could stop it. The three men lifted their heads and looked about.

Darcy narrowed his eyes. "Did you hear something?"

"Just an animal," said Finn.

"Or a bird," added Spoke.

Darcy got to his feet. "You two and your birds and animals. If I hadn't listened to you, we never would have gotten caught. Since when does a guard look like an owl?"

Darcy circled the pond with long but quiet steps, as graceful as an Indian. He reached the edge of the willows and peered into the saw grass.

Denis tightened his grip around the handle of the sword and glanced at Blanche with an expression that warned her to stay quiet. Tears of fright were oozing from the corners of her eyes. Fleur had bitten down on her lower lip and shut her eyes as if praying. Denis could hear his own heart thumping as the convict took a step into the grass.

Just then a lizard scurried over Denis's bare foot, nearly causing him to cry out. The lizard zigzagged out of the grass, and the convict snorted and brought his great booted foot down on the creature, smashing it flat. "I hate reptiles," he muttered as he walked back to the group. The children were too frightened even to exhale.

"Come on, you bastards! On your feet. We've got to find a hiding place before dark."

Finn and Spoke reluctantly got up. They stumbled away from the pond, following Darcy, and the three of them disappeared into the willows.

The girls waited for Denis's signal before moving, but he sat quietly a full ten minutes before giving it.

"Everybody breathe easy." He stood up.

"We've got to get home and tell Grandpapa," said Fleur, who also stood.

They both turned to Blanche, but she didn't move. Her body was rigid, and her eyes were glazed. Not a yard away from her was a coiled cottonmouth. It was as thick as a man's arm and held the little girl in the gaze of its seedlike eyes. It raised its arrow-shaped head and opened its jaws, revealing the soft, white interior of its mouth and sharp, deadly fangs.

Henriette hurried down the hall to her daughter's room. Alcée was packing clothes in a trunk. She looked up and asked anxiously, "Has the ship been sighted?"

"Not yet." Henriette leaned against the door, her hand over her chest. "I don't know if I'm going to survive this day."

Alcée went to her mother. "You'll survive it, Mama. You're strong. I don't know what I would have done without your support."

"I know I'll survive, dear. It's just a little hard on one's nerves."

Alcée embraced her mother. "It looks like our prayers were answered. The money Dr. Jacques paid you is more than enough to get Blaise and me to Canada."

"And all this time I've been asking the saints to help me. All I really had to do was help myself."

Alcée laughed. "You certainly did help yourself, Mama. When I think of all those things you appropriated from the house and gave to Captain Calabozo to sell in New Orleans! That will keep us going until we find work."

In spite of her anxiety, Henriette laughed too. "I keep thinking that someday Alexandre will purchase something that was already his. But it was the best I could do, Alcée. I *did* find his strongbox, you know, but I couldn't get it open." Her expression suddenly changed. "Oh, God, what if he and Philippe should come home early?"

"Mama, that's not going to happen. It's a long way to the Mirabeau Plantation. The auction will go on for hours. And you know how Papa is. He'll want to stay and socialize."

"But Philippe might come home early. He's not fully recovered yet."

"He seems to be. He's just as mean as ever. Mama, stop worrying. The ship will be here soon. And we'll be on our way before they've even started back."

Henriette glanced into the trunk. "Why, Alcée, you haven't packed any of your pretty ball gowns."

"Mama, where we're going we won't be attending fancy dress balls. We'll be working hard just to keep body and soul together. Besides, I don't really want them. Give them to the maids. Let them have something nice to wear when they go to Congo Square. Oh, that reminds me." She went to her closet and withdrew a large hatbox. "This is my Christmas present to you, Mama."

Henriette took the box and laid it on Alcée's bed. She untied the lid and opened it, to discover the macramé portière that Alcée had made.

"I had to work extra hard on it, Mama, to get it done before we left."

Henriette lifted it out of the box and burst into tears. "Oh, Alcée," she murmured. "Oh, Alcée."

Alcée went to her mother and put an arm around her shoulders. "It's all right, Mama. Someday we'll be together again. I know we will."

"I guess," Henriette sniffed, "it just didn't hit me until this moment that you actually won't be here."

"Mama, don't. You'll make my leaving so much harder."

Henriette straightened up. "I'm sorry. It's beautiful, Alcée. You always were so talented with your hands. And you're not to worry about me. I can handle your papa."

"You know, I believe you can."

Henriette went to the door and glanced anxiously toward

the stairway. "I hope Saisie's keeping her eyes opened. Where *is* that steamboat?" She paced to the French doors, wiping her tears away with the backs of her hands. "I think it's wonderful that Captain Calabozo is going to stand up for you."

"Yes, he's a wonderful man."

"And he'll make sure that you get the best accommodations on a northbound ship—" Henriette's voice broke, and she had to turn away from Alcée.

Freedom, the spider monkey, scampered through the open French doors and jumped on Alcée's bed. After chittering a greeting, he began looking around for something to eat. Alcée kept a bowl of fruit atop her dresser for his unannounced visits, and Henriette, who had grown fond of the animal, picked up a bunch of grapes and handed them to him.

"You're sure you don't mind looking after Freedom, Mama?"

"Not at all. I've become quite used to the little beast." She scratched the monkey on the head.

"It would be much too cold for him in Canada."

"I don't know what you or Blaise are going to wear up there. We didn't think ahead. We should have had some clothes made."

"Mama, don't worry. There'll be enough money to buy a few basic garments. Blaise and I don't need much. We won't be trying to impress anybody. You see, Mama, in Canada we can be honest. We don't have to lie about Blaise's bloodline."

"You're going to tell people?"

She nodded. "Yes. They'll either accept us or they won't. At least it's not against the law up there."

Henriette took her daughter's hands and said, "I know you're doing what's right, Alcée. You're going away with someone you love who loves you back. It's not pleasant to love somebody when they don't love you in return. I know. I've lived with that all these years."

"Mama, you can't still love him."

"I don't hate him, Alcée. Sometimes I wish I could. He's only done to me what I allowed him to do. Well, I won't allow him to do anything to me again. I intend to live the rest of my life according to my standards, not his."

"Good for you, Mama."

"Steamboat a-comin'!" Saisie's voice echoed from upstairs.

Henriette ran into the hallway. "Is it the *Belle Créole*?" she called back, although she had hardly enough strength to make her words heard.

"Yes, ma'am, it sho' is," the slave answered. "I know dat boat anywhere."

"Good. Stay there, Saisie. Keep an eye out for you-know-who."

"Yes, ma'am," the slave replied resolutely.

Henriette went back inside Alcée's room, stopped suddenly, and looked at her daughter. "The steamboat's here."

"Yes, Mama, I heard," Alcée replied quietly. "I'll go get Blaise."

When Alcée had gone, Henriette knelt beside the closed trunk. She stretched out her arms as if embracing it and held on tightly. "Dear God, please give me the strength to see this through."

Chapter Twenty-four

The river road bordered the east bank of the winding Mississippi, connecting fifty miles or so of plantation land to New Orleans. It was kept in sporadic repair by the owners of adjacent plantations, but in the hot months of summer, when there was little entertaining and few deliveries, most Southern gentlemen concerned themselves mainly with a shady place and a cool drink. The road was ignored, and it became a continuous trough filled with ocher dust.

By the time Dr. Jacques's carriage was halfway to New Orleans, it resembled a freshly baked brick on wheels. Every few miles he stopped to wipe his glasses and clear his head of the choking dust. Lilliane and Azby were sequestered in the cab. Although the curtains were tightly drawn over the window openings, the reddish-yellow dust had filtered inside and lay in small drifts about their feet.

The carriage reached a bend where the road narrowed and veered abruptly to the left. Dr. Jacques slowed the horses and was about to take the turn when a coach-and-four came bounding around the corner at a ferocious speed. He reined the horses and gave the oncoming carriage as much space as possible, but the back wheels of the two carriages scraped, sending off a shower of sparks and jolting Dr. Jacques's lighter vehicle to the side, dangerously close to the riverbank. His right back wheel dug into the dry shoulder, and the soil began to crumble. As clods of earth slid down the bank, Dr. Jacques cracked his whip, and the carriage jerked forward. A section of the bank gave way and tumbled into the muddy water of the Mississippi.

The larger carriage continued on at its breakneck speed until it was out of sight. Once Dr. Jacques ascertained that his own carriage was on solid ground, he pulled the horses to a stop and jumped down. He yanked open the door. Lilliane and Azby were sprawled on the floor. Bonaparte was flying above their heads, loudly protesting.

"Lilliane, Azby—are you all right?"

"Yes, yes, we're both fine, Jacques."

"The bastard almost ran us off the road."

"I saw him coming," Lilliane said. "Do you know who that was? That was the Duc Duvallon. My God, Jacques, he's returning early! We've got to warn Miss Henriette."

The witch doctor shook his head. "There's no way we could overtake a coach-and-four, Lilliane. But don't you worry—Miss Henriette only looks fragile. She's got a spine of steel."

He helped Lilliane and Azby back into their seats and tried to brush the dust from their clothes. It was a futile exercise. He ran his fingers through the little boy's now-yellow curls. "Have you ever had a shower, Azby?"

The boy shook his head. "What's that, Dr. Jacques?"

"It's like having your own personal rain cloud on a hot, hot day."

The little boy's face brightened with expectancy, and the incident with the Duc's carriage was quickly forgotten.

"How do you get the sky to do that?"

"It's simple. I'll teach you when we get home." The voodoo man shut the door, climbed back on the driver's box, and the carriage was off once again toward New Orleans.

The cottonmouth unwound itself with intricate grace and slithered closer to Blanche.

"Denis, the sword!" Fleur said without moving her lips. "The sword!"

Denis whispered hoarsely, "Don't move, Blanche," but he needn't have, for his little sister was petrified. Slowly he raised the narrow blade, clenching the handle tight in his right hand. His brain screamed: *I'm going to miss!*

The snake reared back, then thrust forward. Denis swung at the same time. He watched the action as if it were in slow motion. The cottonmouth tensed, seemed frozen in space, and then the head flew off to the left as the body, still writhing as if alive, collapsed onto the grass. Denis dropped the sword and cried out with relief and joy. He grabbed Blanche's arms, yanked her to her feet, and dragged her from the saw grass. Fleur picked up the sword, distastefully wiped the blade against the grass, and replaced it in its bamboo sheath. She gathered up the baskets and followed Denis.

He was shaking Blanche, who seemed to be in a trance. All of a sudden the little girl's face became animated, and she began bawling. Denis gathered her up in his arms and held her tight. "It's all right, Blanche. It's all right."

Her crying ceased as quickly as it had started, and she spluttered, "That was the biggest damn cottonmouth I ever saw." Both Denis and Fleur could not help but laugh.

"We shouldn't encourage her profanity," said Fleur between giggles. Then she dropped everything she was holding, threw her arms around her brother's neck, and kissed him hard on the cheek. "Denis, you were wonderful. I doubt that Grandpapa could have done better."

Denis flushed, embarrassed by Fleur's praise and her rare display of physical affection. "Come on," he said, "let's get out of here. We have to warn everybody about the convicts."

Henriette let herself back into the Duc's library. The room, being at the rear of the house and always curtained and closed, was surprisingly cool. She stopped for a moment and allowed the sudden change of temperature to wash over her. Then she sat down at her husband's desk, leaned over, and opened the bottom right-hand drawer so that she could replace the bills of sale she had used as a guide in making up Lilliane's and Azby's papers.

She lifted out the heavy pasteboard file, set it on the desk, and put the forms she had borrowed back into their appropriate places. She started to return the file when she noticed something she hadn't seen before. It was a small metal ring set into the bottom of the drawer. She realized that the drawer had a false bottom. She pulled on the ring, and a hinged panel of wood lifted up. Lying beneath it was yet another folder.

She glanced over her shoulder, through the narrow opening between the draperies, and saw Alcée directing the loading of her luggage into the open carriage Lilliane had driven from Villeneuve. It would serve to transport her and Blaise to the Landing.

"There's no time," Henriette told herself and started to replace the top files, when a nagging feeling caused her abruptly to set the files aside and remove the contents of the secret drawer.

Her fingers were trembling so badly that she could barely untie the ribbon that secured the file. Finally, in exasperation, she used her teeth to undo the neat bow, knowing that she would never be able to retie it. Inside were the deeds to the various properties the Duc owned—including Salle d'Or, four city blocks in New Orleans, a tract of land near Lake Pontchartrain, and—Henriette gulped—Villeneuve. She opened this last paper. It was the same deed she had brought with her to her marriage. It had not been changed into her husband's name, and she wondered if it had to be, under Louisiana law. Henriette did not know whether, once in her possession, it would stand up in court. But she removed it nonetheless and tucked it into the bodice of her dress. She actually managed to get the bow retied, and replaced all the papers. Just as she shut the drawer, Saisie came running into the library. Her brown face was bleached several shades lighter.

"Oh, Miz Henriette," she screamed, "it's de Duc! He's coming up de driveway!"

Henriette's heart stopped. "Are you sure?"

"Oh, yes, ma'am."

"Saisie, do something to stop him—anything!" She tore open the drapes. Blaise had joined Alcée. They were dressed for their voyage upriver, she in a pink traveling suit, Blaise in an old suit of Philippe's that had been altered to fit him. He could easily pass for white. Henriette unlocked the French doors and rushed out onto the back veranda. "Quickly! Quickly!" she cried. "The Duc's returning! Are you ready to leave?"

"Yes, Mama, but . . ."

"I'm not coming to the dock, Alcée. I'll stay here and somehow delay your papa. Wait here in the carriage until

Saisie comes to tell you that it's all right. Then you drive like the wind." She embraced Blaise. "Goodbye, my son. Take care of my little girl. She's the most precious thing in the world to me."

"I will, Miss Henriette. I love your daughter with every fiber of my being."

Henriette nodded and touched his cheek. "Yes, I know you do."

She went to Alcée and smiled bravely. "I've never liked prolonged farewells anyhow, dear. I'll just say goodbye until we meet again."

"Until we meet again, Mama."

The two women hugged tightly, each unwilling to let the other go. Finally Henriette broke away. "Now hurry, my dears. Get in the carriage and wait for Saisie's signal."

Henriette rushed back to the library. Before stepping inside, she turned to look for one last time at her daughter and the man she loved. Clamping her hand over her mouth to keep from crying out in pain, she went in and relocked the French doors, then hurried across the room and through the other door, which she also locked behind her. As she ran through the house toward the foyer, her heart was in her throat. What could she do to keep her husband and Philippe occupied so that Alcée and Blaise could make their escape?

She reached the foyer and saw the Duc's carriage through the side window. He had arrived. She looked around as if expecting him to materialize suddenly, like an evil spirit. She rushed to the door and threw it wide. The Duc was standing on the front steps, staring in consternation at Saisie. Henriette didn't know whether to laugh or cry. The loyal slave was writhing on the veranda, in the throes of a make-believe fit. The Duc, furious, looked at his wife.

"Henriette, get out here! Do something with this creature! She's blocking my way. Where's Alcée? She's supposed to see to this girl when she's having these seizures."

Despite her heartache, Henriette could barely suppress a smile. "Alcée's visiting her friends upriver at the Vedette Plantation."

"She picked a fine time for visiting," snapped the Duc. "Why didn't she take this thing with her?"

"You'll have to help me hold her, Alexandre."

"Me? I've just gotten home."

"Please. She's liable to swallow her tongue."

"Very well," he grumbled. "What do you want me to do?"

"Just grab her ankles and hold fast."

Henriette picked up a wooden doorstop and knelt beside the girl. She put the piece of wood in Saisie's mouth, and as she did, the two women smiled conspiratorially.

"Where's Philippe?" she asked her husband as casually as possible.

"Philippe? He stayed on at Mirabeau Plantation. There is a dance tonight."

"Feeling better, is he?"

"Much. Tomorrow he'll be bringing back the slaves we purchased."

"Then the trip was successful?"

"Yes, dammit! When does this thing stop kicking?"

"Just hold on, Alexandre. She's calming down."

Henriette signaled to Saisie that her theatrics could come to an end. The girl's twitchings and moanings subsided, and the Duc straightened up and stomped into the big house.

"Good performance, Saisie," Henriette whispered. "Now I'll go into the house, and as soon as I've engaged the Duc in conversation, you run around the veranda and tell Blaise and Alcée to get going."

Henriette hurried inside and called after her husband, "Alexandre, give me a minute of your time. I need to speak to you about something."

The Duc was halfway up the staircase. "What is it now, Henriette? I'm hot and dusty. I want to take a bath." He glared at his wife.

For a moment Henriette's old fears came back, and she was struck dumb.

"What is it? Don't just stand there like a tree. Speak up, you dumb bitch."

Henriette's anger flared, and she found her voice. "I was thinking of having the front parlor repainted, Alexandre," she shouted. "And I was wondering what color—"

"What in the hell are you talking about painting for now? I told you I want a bath. Are you losing your mind, Henriette?"

He started back up the steps, but the sound of the carriage made him turn around once again. Henriette gasped. She realized that from his vantage point he had an unobstructed view through the fanlight over the door. She heard the carriage roll by.

"What's that?" the Duc asked sharply. "That was Alcée and Blaise!" He started back down the steps. "What's going on, Henriette? You just told me she was visiting Vedette. Where's that yellow bastard taking her?"

Henriette backed away, her courage evaporating. "Why, she must have been delayed," she stammered. "I thought she had gone earlier. She must . . . she must . . ."

The Duc reached the bottom of the stairs. He grabbed his wife's wrist and twisted her arm so that she was forced into a kneeling position.

A sudden realization spread over the Duc's face like a fever. "They're going off together, aren't they? Of course! I was a fool not to realize it before! The way she always stood up for him. The morning after the ball. He was coming from Alcée's room!" He looked down at Henriette in disgust. "And you were in on the whole thing." He slapped her across the face with the back of his hand. She struggled but could not break away from his grasp. He threw her aside and started for the front door.

"*Noooo!*" Henriette screamed. She got to her feet and ran to the hall closet where the Duc kept a loaded shotgun in case of prowlers. She flung open the door, grabbed the heavy gun, and rushed out onto the veranda. The Duc was climbing into his carriage. Henriette leveled the rifle at her husband. "Alexandre!" she cried. "Get down from that carriage or I will kill you!"

The Duc turned around. When he saw the rifle in her hands he was incredulous. "Henriette, you're mad! Put that thing down. It's loaded."

"Yes, I know."

"You really are insane! Letting your own daughter go off with that nigger."

"They love each other. They're going to be married."

"Over my dead body!"

"If it so pleases you, Alexandre."

"You wouldn't dare."

Henriette squeezed the trigger. A blast of lead shattered the passenger step on which the Duc was standing, and he nearly fell to the ground. He looked at her again, his expression changed. He no longer looked superior.

"The next time I fire, Alexandre, I swear I'll kill you. You'll not ruin my daughter's chances for happiness as you've ruined everything else in your life."

"He's just using her. All niggers want white women."

"Yes, you would think that. Now come back up on the veranda."

The Duc did as Henriette directed. She moved to a position behind him and said, "Now walk around the veranda to the back of the house. And walk slowly. My nerves are very high-strung today. I wouldn't want my finger to slip on the trigger."

"I'll go after them," he said. "I'll find them, and when I do, I'll kill that nigger and bring Alcée back here. And she'll marry Gilbert Gadobert."

"Just keep walking, Alexandre."

"And where do you want me to go, Henriette?" There was almost a note of amusement in his voice.

"Go toward the kitchen."

They rounded the veranda to find Saisie standing on the back steps. The slave backed away as the Duc approached, and he growled, "Are you in this too, you freak? I'll sell you to the worst—"

"You're selling no one, Alexandre." Henriette jabbed him in the back with the barrel of the rifle. "How does it feel to be hurt?" She jammed it hard, twice more. "Now walk down the stairs toward the back of the kitchen."

As they passed the kitchen door, the slaves came out. Ambrose and the others were stunned and frightened by the scene they saw taking place. "Go on about your work," Henriette ordered in a voice they had never heard her use before. To her husband she said, "Stop there."

He was standing next to a shed where extra chamber pots were stored for guests. "Open the door and get yourself a pot, Alexandre."

He turned his head toward her. "Get my own chamber pot?" he sputtered.

"Yes, you're going to need it. Go on, pick one up."He reluctantly did so. "Now continue through the vegetable gardens. No, don't step on the cucumbers!"

Farther on was a large mound of earth that had a door built into its side and four wooden stairs leading downward. The Duc stopped in front of the door and waited for Henriette's further orders.

"The root cellar will be nice and cool, Alexandre. You'll be very comfortable. Now open the door and go inside." He did as she ordered. Henriette stood in the doorway and watched her husband as he looked around the small, damp room. "Light a candle, unless you want to sit in the dark." He did so. There were shelves of preserved foods, barrels of potatoes and apples, and strings of onions. "There's plenty to eat if you get hungry."

She slammed the door and bolted it.

"How long do you intend to keep me in this place?" the Duc asked from the other side.

"For twelve hours, Alexandre. That way you can't follow Alcée and Blaise. They'll be married by the time you get out. Remember marriage, Alexandre? Love, honor, obey? They're going to Canada, where they can live free from prejudice and hate. They're free, Alexandre. And now I'm free!" Henriette picked up an empty crate and placed it in front of the stairwell. She sat down facing the door, with the gun across her lap.

She glanced toward the kitchen and saw Ambrose peeking around the corner, his face blank with astonishment. "Ambrose," she called gaily, "bring me a drink. Bring me a nice tall drink!"

Blanche tripped and went sprawling, skinning her knees and scraping her palms on the seashells that covered the Promenade. She began to cry. Fleur and Denis picked her up and, half walking, half carrying her, stumbled up the driveway until they reached Victoire. Woozy from running in the heat, they fell upon the steps, gagging for breath and calling their grandfather and Aunt Lolly. Alerted by a house slave, Aunt Lolly rushed outside. "What de matter?"

They all began talking at once. A disjointed nightmare came spilling out of their mouths, a tale filled with voodoo, amulets, convicts, cottonmouths. Aunt Lolly looked hard at the children. "I won't have yo' bothering yo' grandpapa with such nonsense," she said. "First all dat business about de ghost, and now dis. I swear I don't know what we going to do with de three of yo'!"

Denis said, "But, Aunt Lolly, I have the amulet." He reached for it, but it was no longer hanging around his neck. He must have lost it in the saw grass. Aunt Lolly shook her head.

Theo, who had been in his study, heard the commotion

and came out onto the veranda. "What's all this, Aunt Lolly? What's wrong with the children?"

The mammy put her hands on her hips and rolled her eyes heavenward. "I told yo' dat yo' shouldn't let them go, M'sieur Theo. Now dey all feverish and sunstroked and telling wild tales."

Blanche, crying with renewed vigor, ran up the steps and wrapped her arms around Theo's legs. He picked her up and held her, then said to Aunt Lolly, "You're right—they're all red. They probably have a touch of sunstroke. You'd better bring them something cold to drink." He stared at Denis sternly. "Denis, you're the oldest. What's all this about? What are you children doing running around in the heat?"

"Grandpapa, we saw three escaped convicts at the pond!"

"Did you, now? And how did you know they were convicts?"

"They were wearing leg-irons."

"And then," Fleur interrupted, "Denis killed a cotton-mouth that was about to attack Blanche, and we ran all the way back here to tell you."

He looked at them through narrowed eyes. "Couldn't you make up your mind as to which story to tell me?"

Denis was hurt. "Grandpapa, don't you believe us?"

Aunt Lolly tsk-tsked and shook her head. "Like I said, first de ghost, and now dis. Yo' chillen ought to be ashamed of yo'selves."

Theo said, "Denis, Fleur, Blanche—I will no longer tolerate your lying."

Denis cried, "Grandpapa, Aunt Lolly, don't either of you believe us?"

The two adults looked at each other in exasperation. Theo said, "I want you children to go up, get undressed, and get into bed now. You're overtired, and possibly you are suffering from sunstroke. Aunt Lolly will remedy what ails you." He put Blanche down.

"But, Grandpapa—" Fleur protested.

"Fleur, be quiet. I won't have you children running wild all over the countryside, getting into trouble, making up stories, and upsetting the household. Now, I don't want to see you at supper. Aunt Lolly will bring you something on a tray. In fact, I don't want to see you again until you're ready to apologize to both of us for upsetting us like this. Now get on with you."

The children obediently filed into the house. Denis was the last. He heard his grandfather say to Aunt Lolly, "I don't know what I've done wrong, Aunt Lolly. Perhaps if their parents had lived."

"Don't blame yo'self, M'sieur Theo. Yo' did de best yo' know how."

The *Belle Créole* had made good time. As soon as Alcée and Blaisc had arrived at the Landing, Captain Calabozo had ordered his men to cast off, and the steamship had reached Baton Rouge in the late afternoon. Alcée and Blaise, accompanied by the captain himself, had gone directly to the church and the waiting priest, who now intoned the words: "I call upon all of you here present to be witnesses at this holy union, which I have now blessed. 'Man must not separate what God has joined together.' "

Captain Calabozo nervously glanced around the small chapel, half expecting to see the Duc and his son come bursting through the oak doors, brandishing pistols and shouting foul words. But no one arrived, and the ceremony went on uninterrupted. There were only Alcée and Blaise, the captain himself, and the priest—who happened to be a close friend of Henriette's—plus a scattering of devout souls who had come to pray and, curious, had stayed on to watch the ceremony.

Captain Calabozo turned his attention back to the service. The chapel of Saint Anthony was nowhere near as large or as grand as New Orleans's Saint Louis Cathedral, but north of here the country was sparsely populated, mostly by Protestants and poor hill farmers. The priest was a slim, exceedingly handsome young man with pale blond hair and pure, evenly cut features. He looked as a priest should look, the captain found himself thinking—as an innocent grown up. He spoke the words in a clear voice and with youthful enthusiasm.

"May you be blessed in your children, and may the love that you lavish on them be returned a hundredfold."

The captain looked at Blaise and Alcée, who were standing in profile, facing each other. The candles on the altar cast a glow about their faces, almost like halos. The captain thought that the love the couple held for each other gleamed in their eyes so strongly that it outshone all the candles in all the churches of the world.

"May the peace of Christ dwell always in your hearts and

in your home; may you have true friends to stay by you, both in joy and in sorrow. May you be ready with help and consolation for all those who come to your need; and may the blessings promised to the compassionate descend in abundance on your house."

The captain felt proud but sad. He was proud that he had been able to help Henriette and the young couple, but he regretted deeply that he had no one with whom he could share his own life. The ceremony was almost over. He planned to accompany Alcée and Blaise back to the *Belle Créole* and invite them to his cabin, where he had a bottle of chilled champagne and a small cake that he had brought upriver from New Orleans.

Then he would see that they were safely aboard another steamship that would take them as far north as Cairo. After that, they would be on their own. He closed his eyes and silently offered a small prayer that their journey would be safe and that they would find peace, happiness, and fulfillment in Canada. He only wished that Henriette could have been here with him to witness the ceremony and see them off.

The service ended, and the captain was suddenly ridiculously happy, as if he were young again and had just been married to a young woman as lovely and kind as Alcée Duvallon Christophe. At the signal from the handsome priest, the church bells began to peal. It was a joyous, spontaneous sound, and it reinforced Captain Calabozo's belief in happy endings.

Although it was early evening, the sun continued to burn in the brazen sky. The penetrating light and the stifling heat made Angélique feel dizzy as she rode Arab through the cane fields. She dug her heels into the ribs of the horse, prodding him to move faster through the tall green rows.

The events of the past several weeks had wrought a noticeable change in Angélique Jourdain. There was a brighter gleam in her eyes and a harder note to her voice. Nothing was working out as she had planned. The facts affecting her existence at Heritage, as she perceived them, were all jumbled together in one part of her consciousness, battling each other like desperate enemies, and her grasp on reality was becoming increasingly tenuous.

She realized now that she would never make Royal Brannigan love her, let alone marry her. They were bound together by lust, but that was all. He was hers only in the dark hours after midnight, when the baser instincts took precedence over the reasoning light of day. She knew that he did not like her any more than she liked him.

He liked Suzanne.

And she liked him in return. It was evident in their every word and gesture, the way they looked at each other, the tone of their conversation, the hesitant, almost embarrassed, way that each spoke of the other when the other wasn't present.

Suzanne's feelings were especially obvious, Angélique thought bitterly. She was falling in love with a man she should have hated, and with Jean-Louis barely cold in his grave. It was clear Suzanne had never really loved Jean-Louis—not as *she* had loved him.

No, Suzanne loved Royal.

She'd even taken the *immortelle* from the front door and had ceased wearing mourning. Oh, yes, pastels were so much more flattering. All the better to capture the American's attention. Angélique twisted her mouth in the parody of a smile and mimicked Royal's lilting speech. "That's a mighty pretty dress, Madame Jourdain."

Madame Jourdain!

The smile turned to an ugly sneer as Angélique was suddenly struck by the realization that Royal never called her anything when they were in bed together. Never once had he used her proper name. It was as if, in saying it, he would somehow dispel his desire for her.

Angélique wondered whether Suzanne suspected. If so, she gave no indication of it. And if she did find out? Angélique had no doubt how her sister-in-law would react. She would be oh-so-forgiving. It was her nature. She had forgiven Jean-Louis time after time when he had returned from New Orleans or from one of the other flesh pots along the Mississippi. He was always ready to atone for his sins, and she was always ready to forgive. Who, she wondered, had been the weaker of the two? The one who sinned, or the one who was sinned against? It hardly mattered now. Only one thing was certain: If it hadn't been for Suzanne—Suzanne *and* Royal—Jean-Louis would still be alive.

"Suzanne and Royal," she chanted over and over as she whipped her horse onward.

And where was this newly blossomed friendship leading? Angélique knew, even if Royal and Suzanne had not admitted it to themselves. He would ask her to marry him, and she would accept. It was the natural course of events for two such *decent* people. And just where, she asked herself bitterly, would that leave her? She would still be a guest at Heritage, at her own home. She had failed to make the American love her, and there was only one alternative left.

She reined in at the front of the small brick house where Rafe Bastile lived. Quickly hitching the horse to a post, she climbed the narrow flight of steps to the porch. The door was partly open. Angélique did not knock but walked right in. Rafe had just finished his workday. He had stripped out of his clothes and was sitting naked at the kitchen table, drinking whiskey. Rivulets of sweat poured down his body, leaving lighter trails in the dusty grime that covered his flesh.

He stood up as Angélique entered. She walked directly to him and placed her arms around his waist, oblivious of the perspiration and dust that stained her dress. In a moment she, too, was naked. They fell to the floor, gasping and panting, like two animals caught in a death grip.

The setting sun was covered by a thin mist, turning everything a dull yellow. Not even an errant breeze stirred the leaden air. Despite the heat, Suzanne chose to walk up the hillock to the Jourdain cemetery. She carried a large basket of flowers from the Heritage garden to put on her husband's grave. When Suzanne reached the top of the hill, she paused to catch her breath, then continued on toward the grove of dogwood trees and the cemetery. The statue of the kneeling angel shimmered in the haze of the heat and appeared to be floating above the ground.

She reached the grave site, put down her basket, and sat on the parched grass. The ivy she had planted on the grave on a previous visit had not taken root. The plants had been baked by the hot sun. To Suzanne, the brittle brown leaves seemed to represent her life with Jean-Louis. She was surprised she could finally admit her relief at no longer being married to him. Their life together had been a year-long nightmare. Suzanne wondered how much more she would have been able to endure, had Jean-Louis not committed suicide. Her life was better now—yet what would happen to her come harvest? She knew that she was in love with Royal Brannigan, and that fact both shocked and pleased her.

If he asked her, could she marry him? Suzanne smiled at the irony of it. She honestly couldn't answer. After Jean-Louis, did she even know what marriage really was? Disturbed with herself that she felt so little for her dead husband, Suzanne got up and began pulling away the dead ivy. She attacked the lifeless plants with a fury, yanking them out by their roots and tossing them helter-skelter.

Suzanne noticed something revealed by the broken soil—a flash of pink in the dull brown earth. She brushed aside the earth, and the doll was uncovered. She immediately recognized it as the image that had represented her husband as a child. Before the wedding, Jean-Louis had taken her on a tour of Heritage and, in the children's room, had pointed out the dollhouse and the lifelike dolls of himself and Angélique. At the time, she had thought them charming, but now, staring at the doll, Suzanne felt sick with revulsion. Its porcelain flesh was covered with a network of cracks. The mechanism that had supported the eyes had given way, and the sockets were hollow, empty. The hair—Jean-Louis's own—was matted and discolored by the soil. And there were no clothes.

Had they rotted, or had they been removed?

She wondered who could have buried the doll here, and for what dark purpose? One of the slaves? Did it have something to do with voodoo?

She felt as if Jean-Louis's grave had been desecrated, but was loath to touch the inanimate object. Quickly she covered it up once again and scattered the flowers she had brought with her, now already wilting in the basket. She hoped that the purity of the blooms might somehow sanctify her husband's grave. When she was finished, Suzanne looked into the face of the stone angel as if expecting answers, but that serene countenance imparted nothing.

Royal had finished supper and was smoking his cigar while Nicey cleared the table. From time to time he would glance at her and try to analyze her inscrutable expression. He wondered if she knew about his affair with Angélique. Did the other house servants? He was almost sure that Zenobia knew. Something in her manner toward him had changed. She was still brusque, but he could detect a certain anxiety in the way she looked at him that indicated . . . what? Pity? Fear? The only two people at Heritage who he was sure didn't know of the midnight visits were Seth and Suzanne. He wondered what would happen when they found out, as they surely must. Would the little boy lose faith in him? Would Suzanne reject their new friendship and retreat from him, cutting off the possibility of there ever being anything more?

Nicey asked, "Will dere be anything else, M'sieur Royal?"

"No, thank you, Nicey. You may go."

Royal poured himself another cup of coffee and relit his cigar, which had gone out. He stifled a yawn. The workday had been exhausting, but a new irrigation ditch had been completed and more fuel wood laid by for the sugar making. And so far none of the slaves had come down with the malaria that had struck Salle d'Or.

Royal went to the veranda, hoping for a fresh breeze, but everything was unnaturally still. The newly risen moon had bleached the gardens to a luminous pallor, and it seemed to Royal that the entire world was holding its breath, waiting for something to happen.

Royal suddenly realized that he was dreading the oncoming night. He hoped that Angélique would not come to his room. Though his desire for her had not diminished, he felt a growing uneasiness in her company that he couldn't put a name to. He felt that somehow she had acquired more knowledge of him than he cared to give, and he didn't know to whom he'd given it. He didn't know Angélique. They were bound precariously together by lust, nothing more.

They rarely spoke in bed, but when they did, Angélique always tried to turn him against Suzanne, by either insinuation or mockery. Her apparent affection for her sister-in-law was a sham. Yet he knew it would be useless to tell this to Suzanne; she simply would not believe him—perhaps she would even hate him for telling her such things. As he had gotten to know Suzanne better, Royal had realized that one of her most ingratiating qualities was to attribute to others the virtues that she herself possessed.

Angélique was the complete opposite. Royal believed that she was unbalanced, if not mad, and wicked, if not evil. How, he wondered, could this impossible triangle end but in tragedy?

Chapter Twenty-five

Sitting on the center of the dressing table, the twin bottles of laudanum stared at Marguerite like two elongated brown eyes. Separating them was a narrow crystal goblet that took on the semblance of a nose. Across the room, Marguerite lay in her bed, returning the gaze of the imaginary face. It vaguely reminded her of someone from the past. Possibly someone who had once meant something to her.

Marguerite had dined alone in her room, as usual. She had been avoiding taking her meals with Léon and Michelle for weeks. They hadn't been curious enough about her self-imposed isolation to take notice, even to inquire about her health.

"They're like children," Marguerite said aloud. "Arrogant, selfish. They have no compassion for anyone except themselves, and just like rebellious children they break all the rules and cry only when they're caught and punished."

When would their punishment come? she wondered. Certainly they would not view her own death as any kind of penalty for their thoughtless behavior. No, it would be merely a temporary inconvenience for them.

Marguerite got up from her bed, straightened the covers, and looked about the room at the boxes she had so meticulously packed. She wondered what Léon and Michelle would do with them. Certainly they wouldn't take the trouble of unpacking them and looking through her pathetic belongings. Perhaps they would just have them carried up to the attic and put in storage until they sold Bellechasse and prepared to leave for Europe. Then her things would probably be either thrown away or left unopened for the new owners to peruse at leisure and wonder why someone had taken so much trouble to protect such worthless bric-a-brac. Marguerite almost smiled as she imagined their amazement and consternation.

Her eyes came back to the imaginary face sitting on her dressing table. Marguerite was not a person to put things off. Not even her own suicide. She went to her closet and withdrew the dress she had chosen to wear. It was a garnet silk ball gown, hopelessly out of fashion and much too young for her. But of all her gowns it had always been her favorite.

Marguerite dressed carefully, selecting her best undergarments, her fullest petticoats, and a pair of shoes that very nearly matched her gown. Then she went to the dressing table and sat down. She pushed the bottles and the glass to one side and slowly lifted her face to the mirror. It seemed she had suddenly grown five years older. Her wrinkles reminded her of a map representing some pale, obscure country. Gravity and discontent had caused her chin to sag, and it pulled her mouth down at its corners.

Marguerite was prompted into action. "I'm not going to glory looking like this," she announced. She picked up a hairbrush and began vigorously brushing her hair, arranging the sides in an upsweep and letting the back fall about her shoulders in a decidedly youthful style. Then she opened the drawer and began taking out all the jars, bottles, and containers of cosmetics that she hadn't used since the afternoon she had decided to end her life. She arranged everything in correct order, and then, with a fierce determination, she went to work on her face.

Léon and Michelle lay naked on opposite sides of the bed, sullenly staring at the *ciel de lit* hanging above them. A band of cupids frolicked among painted clouds. The night was so hot and uncomfortable that they had been able to sleep only fitfully; worse still, the couple couldn't even bear to touch each other's flesh.

"I envy those cupids, Léon," Michelle said. "They look so cool."

"Don't they? Would you like some more champagne?"

"It's not helping, is it?"

He shook his head. "No, nothing's helping. If we were living in Europe, we could escape the heat by taking a trip to the Alps."

"All that snow," murmured Michelle. "I'd love to roll naked in it."

"I have an idea—let's go down to the rose maze. The water in the fountain should be cool. We'll bathe each other, and we'll—"

"But, Léon, we've done that."

"Not at night, not in the dark."

"It might be fun," she conceded, "and certainly refreshing."

They climbed out of bed with an urgency that they hadn't felt all day. Michelle hurriedly put on a filmy dressing gown and slippers as Léon struggled into trousers, shirt, and boots.

"I don't know why we're bothering to get dressed," he said. "Everyone's asleep."

"You never know when Aunt Marguerite might be lurking about."

"You're right," Léon said. "She's been in the strangest mood recently."

"So you've taken the time to notice. She's mad at us for some reason or other."

"It's probably me she's mad at. The old maid."

"Make it up to her tomorrow, Léon. I don't like it when she's unhappy. We'll invite her on a picnic or something."

"A picnic! Can you imagine my aunt on a picnic?"

"Yes, I can. You know, Léon, sometimes I don't think she's quite as staid as she seems. You never give her a chance."

Léon, tired of discussing Aunt Marguerite, said, "Let's misbehave, Michelle." He tweaked one of her nipples with his thumb and forefinger.

Michelle squealed. "Léon Martineau, I'm going to get you for that!"

They ran out of the room and down the back stairs, racing each other toward the rose maze. Léon got there first and, panting and laughing, waited for Michelle to catch up. When she did, he pinched her again. Laughing even harder, he ducked into the entrance to the maze.

"Léon," she wailed, "just wait until I get my hands on you!"

"I'll beat you to the center!" he called over his shoulder.

Michelle stood with her hands on her knees to catch her breath. "Lord, it's too hot to run!"

After a minute or so, she followed her husband into the passageway. The hedges loomed high on either side, blotting out all light except that provided by the moon. With her head throbbing from the champagne and the heat, she took a wrong turn and found herself facing a wall of yellowed leaves. Frustrated, she called out for Léon, but he didn't answer. She could imagine him laughing to himself. She backed up, her footsteps crunching on the gravel, and tried to figure out where she had gone wrong.

Pausing to listen for her husband, Michelle heard something brush against the other side of the hedge. "Léon," she scolded, "stop playing games with me." Irritated, she stamped her foot and began walking once again. Immediately she heard other footsteps join her own. They sounded too heavy to be Léon's, and the realization raised the small, fine hairs on her forearms. Michelle shuddered and rubbed her flesh. There was no reason for her to be afraid. Léon was just playing games. Wasn't he?

She'd show him. She decided to retrace her footsteps and start all over again, but she made another wrong turn, and instead of finding her way back to where she had started, she was in yet another cul-de-sac.

Michelle was exasperated and frightened. "Damn! Now, let's see, if I ever find my way back to the beginning, it's right, left, right, left, two rights, two lefts, and then repeat."

She turned around and took a firm step, and heard a clink of metal. Puzzled, she knelt down and felt the gravel, wondering if her foot had struck something. But even as she searched, she knew full well that the sound had come from the other side of the hedge. Michelle quickly stood up and began walking fast, then trotting. There were other running footsteps, echoing her own.

She stumbled and fell against the hedge, scratching her shoulder. Petals showered like summer snow from the full-blown roses. She got up and broke into a run down the leafy corridor, and once again other footsteps accompanied hers. It was as if her shadow had pulled away and was running beside her on the other side of the hedge. "Léon," she called out in a choked voice. "Léon!" Suddenly someone began to whistle a sprightly melody. Michelle panicked. Léon never whistled. Ahead the corridor split apart, and Michelle paused, not knowing which way to turn. Tears of frustration blurred her vision. She picked one path and dashed straight into it. She stopped abruptly when she found it was yet another blind alley. She thrust her hands into the hedge, but the branches were too thick, too well trained, and she was a captive.

When she turned to retrace her steps, somebody stepped onto the path, blocking her way. He was whistling. Michelle screamed and clutched at the hedge, cutting herself on the thorns. He was tall, handsome, and brutal looking. He tipped an imaginary hat.

"At your service, miss," he said with an Irish lilt, his thick lips curving into a smile.

"Who are you?" she demanded.

His eyes scanned her body appreciatively. "There's no need for first names, miss."

"How did you get in here?"

"Well, now, I always did like puzzles, miss." He took a step toward her, and she heard the metal clink. She looked down and saw the leg-irons and a few links of chain attached to one of the shackles.

"Stand aside and let me by," Michelle said in a weak voice. To her surprise and relief, he stepped aside. She started to pass him when he caught her arm, swung her around, and pressed his body against hers.

"And where would you be going, miss? Maybe you've gotten yourself lost." He put his face close to hers.

She could feel the stubble of his beard and smell his sickening, sweet breath, which reeked of alcohol. She tried to draw her head back, but he clamped his hand around her neck and held her fast. Michelle brought her knee up with the intent of hitting him in the testicles, but he was so tall that she merely grazed them. He grunted with pain and momentarily loosened his grip. Michelle broke away and began running.

"Léon," she cried over and over as she ran toward what she hoped was the center of the maze. She glanced fearfully over her shoulder and didn't see the man following her. Perhaps if she could find Léon, they could somehow alert the plantation to the presence of the convict.

"Right turn, left turn, right turn, left turn, two rights, two lefts." Breathless, she made it to the center of the maze, and the first thing she noticed was Léon lying next to the marble fountain. Michelle thought that he was still playing games and wasn't aware of her danger. "Léon, get up!" She knelt down and began to shake him. It was then that she felt the blood trickling from the back of his head. "Léon!"

"He's out for a while, lady."

"Just a little tap on the head."

Michelle looked up. Two men had appeared from the shadows. They also wore leg-irons. One was thin and ugly, the other was small and had bright red hair. He held a hoe in his hand. The blade end was stained with blood.

"What have you done to him?" Michelle screamed.

"Take it easy, lady," said Spoke.

"It was just a tap," Finn reiterated.

Michelle, outraged, advanced on the men with her hands clenched. Finn and Spoke retreated a step.

"Giving my men a bit of a battle, miss?" came a mocking voice behind her. Michelle swung around to face the tall, handsome convict.

"She's a spunky lady, Darcy," giggled Spoke.

"Yep," agreed Finn, "right spunky."

Darcy came up behind Michelle, slid his broad, callused hands around her, and covered her breasts. He squeezed them hard, and Michelle let out a gasp of pain.

"Don't do that," she groaned.

"Spunky," agreed Finn and Spoke in unison.

Michelle whirled around and pushed Darcy away from her. "How dare you! How dare any of you! Now, get off Bellechasse and leave us alone before I start screaming and the entire household comes running."

"Oh, I don't think that's going to happen, miss," said Darcy. He gestured toward a white cloth spread open on the grass. A lantern highlighted the silver candelabras, gold-rimmed plates, heavy silver cutlery, and other valuables piled upon it. It all belonged to Bellechasse.

Spoke giggled. "We watched you havin' your dinner, lady. You and . . . and . . ." He indicated Léon with a twist of his narrow head. "Him. It looked real good. Better than prison food, I'd wager."

Finn said, "And good liquor too. We know. We finished it for you."

For some reason the words didn't register. "There are the house slaves," Michelle said. "They'll come to our aid."

"They're not goin' to come to anybody's aid," said Darcy.

"What do you mean?" cried Michelle.

"I mean nobody's goin' to come to your aid, miss. We took care of them, nice and quiet-like. The only niggers left are the ones down by the cane fields, and they ain't likely to hear you scream."

"Oh, no," groaned Michelle. "Ginny, Marie, Jolie, Uncle Prosper . . ." Her voice trailed off as she staggered forward and fell upon her knees. She noticed the bloodstains on Finn's trousers.

"Niggers are like snakes," said Finn. "You can't kill 'em 'cept with a knife or a hoe." To punctuate his remark he swung the hoe through the air and brought its blade down with a whoosh, pinning the hem of Michelle's dressing gown to the earth.

Darcy bent down and ripped the thin material free. "Nice goods, eh, lads?"

"Nice," said Spoke. His breath reeked of alcohol and was coming in ragged gasps.

"Very nice," added Finn.

"Let me see to my husband," pleaded Michelle.

"Go ahead," said Darcy.

Michelle crawled over to Léon and examined the back of his head. There was a nasty bump, and the skin was broken, but the cut was not deep. She tore off a piece of her nightgown, dipped it in the fountain, and started to wash the blood away when Darcy grabbed her arm and pulled her to her feet.

"That's enough nursin', miss."

"What are you going to do with me?" asked Michelle.

"What do you think?" Darcy replied with an ugly smile. "A pretty little miss like you, cavortin' in her nightgown. What did you expect to happen?"

"I was with my husband," said Michelle.

"And now you're with us," Darcy replied evenly.

Michelle's black eyes blurred with tears as she watched Finn and Spoke undo the buttons of their pants. She looked from face to face in horror as the men converged upon her. They pulled her to the ground and began tearing at her dressing gown. Once the fabric was ripped away, their dirty hands and fingers probed her body, their rancid mouths licked and bit her flesh.

Michelle gave up without further struggle, and there was even a kind of peace in her resignation. She wouldn't humiliate herself by begging for mercy. She knew that there would be no mercy.

Someone's hands were clamped around her throat. Michelle thought, almost with relief, that they were going to strangle her first.

But they didn't. Darcy moved behind her head and pinned his heavy knees on her shoulders to keep her from moving while he tortured her breasts. Spoke jumped on top of her, his bony hips cutting into her flesh. His thrusts were accompanied by his shrill giggle. Darcy lowered his head and clamped his mouth over Michelle's as Spoke quickly worked himself to orgasm.

Spoke pulled away with a satisfied groan, and it was Finn's turn. Instead of immediately entering Michelle, he pressed his face against her stomach and began biting it so hard that some of the teeth marks exuded blood. Michelle screamed in pain, but her screams were muffled by Darcy's ravenous mouth. Michelle tried to will her mind on her past life—gay parties and pretty dresses and kind friends—but it was no use. Her degradation was brought back again and again with each brutal lunge.

Finn rolled away. He and Spoke retreated to the pile of goods and began arguing over the spoils in a high staccato jabber. Michelle felt Darcy's body shift. He released her temporarily, swinging himself around so that he was lying directly on top of her. She looked at him with loathing and spat in his face. His smile didn't alter as he wiped away the spittle. "Don't just lie there," he said pleasantly. "Fight me. Scream all you want. There's no one to hear you but me." Michelle flailed her arms against his back. She squirmed and twisted, trying to get out from under him, but he was too heavy. The gravel cut into her back and buttocks as he pushed all of his weight against her. "Léon," she called out weakly. She managed to turn her head so that she could see him. His prostrate form stirred, and her hopes soared. "Léon!" she screamed.

This time her cry awakened Léon, who turned in time to see Darcy take his wife. Léon forced himself to his knees, clenched the side of the pool, and pulled himself to his feet. Then he staggered toward them.

Darcy saw him coming. "Spoke! Finn!"

Léon heard the footfalls and whirled around, but not in time. Finn's blow with the hoe handle glanced off his left temple, and he crumpled forward. Blinded by blood in his eyes, Léon grappled at the air and tried to rise again. Finn hit him once more, this time with the shank of the hoe.

Michelle cried her husband's name.

"That's better," Darcy murmured as he reared back and rammed himself into her.

Michelle screamed again—a high shriek that pierced the night. She continued screaming, only half conscious that her cries had prompted Darcy's orgasm.

Marguerite had just finished outlining her eyelids with kohl when she heard Michelle call Léon's name. She dismissed it as a cry of passion, nothing more. Besides, there had been strange noises from downstairs all night. She had grown used to Léon and Michelle's sometimes noisy antics and wouldn't have been surprised if they were making love on the stairs. She pushed herself away from the dressing table and inspected her work. The cosmetics had been employed liberally. The result, although garish, was not unattractive. Her face resembled not so much a living face as a skillful painting. Marguerite was pleased with the result. She moved the glass goblet to the center of her dressing table and started to reach for one of the bottles of laudanum when she heard a piercing scream. At first she thought it was the cry of an animal, but the anguished howl persisted, becoming terrifyingly human.

Marguerite ran out onto the veranda and rushed to Léon and Michelle's room. The French doors were open, the lamp was still burning, but the bed was empty. The cries *had* to be coming from Michelle. Her hair flying loose, Marguerite ran wildly through their room and down the stairs, calling to the house slaves.

She hurried down the dark hall toward the slaves' bedrooms. Her foot caught against something, and she sprawled flat on the floor. The fall knocked the breath out of her. She shook her head and reached back to see what she had tripped over. There was no mistaking the rotund form of Uncle Prosper's wife, Jolie. Marguerite's hand came back moist and sticky. Her eyes, now adjusted to the dim light, registered the carving knife embedded in the woman's chest. "Jolie! Oh, my God!" She scrambled to her feet and gaped at the body in horror. "Jolie . . . Jolie . . ." Marguerite urged, as if speaking the slave's name would somehow bring her back to life.

Marguerite staggered backward and pushed open the first door, barely daring to breath. Ginny, a young house slave, was sprawled in the center of the floor. There was red all over her—on her face, her chest, and all down the front of her dress. Marguerite's eyes registered what her mind was bent on not comprehending.

Reeling with horror, she went from room to room. Each of the servants had been slaughtered like cattle. The final door she opened was to the largest room, the one shared by Jolie and Uncle Prosper.

The stench of blood was overpowering, and she had to fight against the urge to be sick. In the feeble moonlight she saw Uncle Prosper's body. Like a sick dog, the little man had crawled into a corner to die.

Marguerite pushed her hands over her cheeks and up to her temples. "Oh, my God!"

Uncle Prosper had been stabbed repeatedly, and ribbons of blood still issued from the multiple wounds. His head was turned toward the window, and his eyes were still open.

Marguerite clutched her own throat and fell to her knees. "Oh, Uncle Prosper!" Tears welled in her eyes and dropped on the little man's cold flesh as she reached across him to close his eyes. Despite her fear, Marguerite was filled with outrage that her beloved slaves had been so senselessly slaughtered.

"Oh, God, please!"

Marguerite detected a note of hysteria creeping into her voice. "No!" she cried. "I will not fall apart. I must not."

The wheels of her mind, which had been spinning wildly, took hold again, and she began to think. Michelle and Léon were out there somewhere, and they were in danger. She hurried from Uncle Prosper's room out onto the veranda, and breathless with anxiety, she ran for the rope hanging from the great brass plantation bell suspended between two of the columns.

Marguerite grabbed hold of the rope and began pulling. The bell tolled, and the sound reverberated through her body. She yanked the rope again and again until she felt the hempen fibers burning her palms, but she didn't stop. She continued yanking the rope even when blood began trickling from her hands.

"What's happened, Miz Marguerite?"

Marguerite screamed and swung around. It was Jake, a large, burly Negro who did heavy work around the house and slept in a room in the stable. He had an old musket in his hands. Marguerite backed away from him, thinking that there had been a slave uprising.

"Easy now, Miz Marguerite. I was out possum hunting, dat's all."

Marguerite cried with relief. "Oh, Jake. Jake, something terrible—" She panted for breath, and he looked toward the house. "No, no, don't go in," she said. "They're dead, all dead. Murdered."

The hulking Negro began to cry. He had a special affection for Ginny. They were to have been married at Christmastime.

"There's nothing you can do. They're all dead. But Léon and Michelle might still be alive."

"M'sieur Léon, Miz Michelle . . ."

"I heard Michelle screaming. She's somewhere in the garden. And Léon must be with her."

"Where, Miz Marguerite? What direction?"

Marguerite tried to focus her mind. "I think it was coming from the rose maze."

"Yo' stay here, Miz Marguerite."

"No, I've got to come!"

Marguerite and Jake hurried across the garden toward the maze. They were about halfway there when they saw three men emerge from the entrance, apparently alarmed by the ringing of the plantation bell.

One of them, shorter than the others, was carrying a lantern, and each had a tablecloth stuffed with goods swung over his shoulder. Marguerite recognized the tablecloths and guessed what they held. She also saw the leg-irons. "Jake," she cried, "shoot them!"

The men spotted the hulking Negro and the middle-aged woman. They also saw Jake raise the musket to his shoulder. The short one dropped the lantern in fright. The tall one shouted, "Let's get out of here," and the three of them took off running.

"Shoot them! Shoot them!" urged Marguerite.

Jake lowered the rifle, turned to Marguerite, and said, "I can't, Miz Marguerite. It only got one shot, and I missed de possum."

"Well, at least you scared them off," snorted Marguerite. "Hurry, into the maze. Léon and Michelle must be there."

"Does yo' remember de way, Miz Marguerite?"

"I'm not senile yet," she snapped, and picked up the lantern.

They stopped at each junction in the path before proceeding, examining the cul-de-sacs to make sure the young people weren't there. Marguerite called their names, and as she and Jake neared the center, they heard a thin moan.

"Hurry, Jake," she prodded. "Hurry!"

As she ran, Marguerite made all sorts of promises to God if He would only let them be alive. In the face of disaster, her own problems had become pathetically insignificant.

Despite Jake's size and giant stride, Marguerite reached the center before him. A final prayer fell from her lips as she held up the lantern.

Michelle was lying naked on the ground, staring unblinkingly at the sky. Blood stained her stomach and thighs, and Marguerite realized that she'd been raped. But her chest was rising and falling. She was alive. Léon, his face crusted with blood, was crawling toward her, his hand outstretched.

"Aunt Marguerite," Léon cried with relief. Marguerite ran to her nephew, knelt down, and touched his head. The cuts seemed superficial. She moved to Michelle. The girl's face became animated, and she burst into tears.

"There, there, child. It's all right. Aunt Marguerite's here."

Léon reached his wife, and they embraced. Tears poured down their cheeks.

Marguerite got to her feet. "Léon, can you walk if I help you?"

"I'll walk, Aunt Marguerite."

Marguerite pulled the remains of Michelle's dressing gown around her and instructed Jake to pick her up. The slave swept her into his arms as if she were a sack of flour. Marguerite, supporting her nephew, helped him to his feet.

"Did you see the men?" he asked her.

"Yes. They took off running."

"The rest of the household . . ." he began fearfully.

Marguerite shook her head.

"Not everyone!" cried Michelle.

"I'm afraid so. They killed them all."

Michelle sobbed against Jake's broad chest.

"Who rang the plantation bell?" Léon asked sadly.

"I did. Jake had been out hunting. The sight of him and his rifle chased them off."

Léon seemed to gain strength with each step, his anger infusing him with energy. "I'm going to get them," he said quietly.

The four of them reached the maze entrance, and as they moved across the lawn toward the rear of the house, two men on horseback galloped into sight. Marguerite was relieved to see Theo and Royal. They were both armed and looked as if they had dressed in a hurry.

"We heard the bell," cried Theo. "What's wrong? What's happened here?"

"Convicts—escaped," gasped Marguerite. "They killed our house slaves, stole some goods, and attacked Léon and Michelle."

The two men dismounted and rushed across the lawn. "Léon, Michelle, are you all right?" asked Royal.

"We're alive," Léon replied grimly.

Theo's face was ashen. "My God," he said. "My grandchildren told me that they saw escaped convicts, but I didn't believe them. I thought it was another story, like the ghost."

Marguerite said, "Don't blame yourself for not listening to the children, Theo. I was there, I saw the ghost, but I denied it."

"You saw it?"

She nodded. "And if I had only admitted it, the children's word would never have come into question."

"How many men were there?" asked Royal.

"Three—and they don't have guns," said Léon. "Will you help me go after them?"

"Of course," Theo replied. "But you're injured, Léon. You're in no condition to—"

"My wife has been raped! My slaves murdered. I must avenge myself!"

"Yes," urged Michelle. "Go, Léon. Catch them and kill them. I want you to promise me—" She broke into sobs.

Léon took his wife from Jake and whispered to her, "I'll catch them. I swear it to you, Michelle." He turned to Jake. "Get me a horse and some firearms—and rope, plenty of rope."

"And hurry, for God's sake," added Theo.

Léon, his voice breaking with emotion, appealed to Marguerite. "Aunt Marguerite, you'll stay with her?"

"Of course, Léon," she said. "You know I will. I always will."

It would be difficult to pick up the trail of the convicts before daylight, but Theo's military experience stood him in good stead. He led Léon and Royal across the gardens of Bellechasse, heading diagonally to the south. Theo believed that the criminals would make for the river road and New Orleans, where they could sell their stolen goods. To the east and north were forbidding swamps, and to the west was the river.

The three men rode to the edge of a cane field that bordered the gardens. The field covered a wide expanse up to a thicket that edged the river road. Theo reined in his horse and said, "I think we should split up here. We'll spread out and cover as much of the field as possible. Whoever discovers the convicts should fire a shot."

"I hope they're not waiting for us in there," said Royal. "They have the cover and we don't." He turned to Léon. "I wonder why they didn't steal guns when they had a chance?"

"I keep the firearms hidden behind a secret panel. Only the house slaves and I know where they are."

"Well, we can count ourselves lucky on your foresight," said Royal.

"It wasn't my idea," admitted Léon. "My father did it to protect me as a child."

"Your father was a smart man, Léon," said Theo. "Now let's get going."

The men split up and drove their horses into the cane. Each taking a section of the field, they zigzagged through the rows, finally coming together once again on the opposite side, where the thicket began. Theo pointed to a clump of broken ferns. His eyes scanned the dark, junglelike mass of vegetation. In low, measured tones, he said, "I suggest that instead of dismounting and fighting our way through the undergrowth, we circumvent the thicket completely. We can head directly south, keeping in the cane fields along the river road until we reach a point where there is no cover and they have to show themselves."

"That makes sense to me," said Royal. They looked toward Léon.

Léon, his jaw firmly set, his boyish face still encrusted with blood, merely nodded in response.

The men reentered the field, and led by Theo, they rode at a steady canter down a long alley of cane, then detoured around a swampy area bordering the river road. After twenty minutes Theo signaled that they should veer right. The cane field ended in a patch of woods, and the three of them found themselves facing an open stretch in the dusty river road.

"Let's wait here," said Theo. "The woods will offer us cover, and unless my guess is wrong, by now our boys will be tired of slogging through sugar cane and forest and will chance a shortcut on the road."

Theo, Royal, and Léon withdrew their pistols from their waistbands and waited.

It didn't take long. Not more than ten minutes later, the stillness of the night was broken by the sound of somebody whistling a jaunty Irish ballad. Theo motioned to his companions to be still and await his signal.

A moment later three ragged figures with sacks slung over their shoulders ambled into sight. They were walking abreast of each other, obviously secure that no one was following them. When they were fewer than ten yards away, Theo, Royal, and Léon emerged from the woods, their pistols leveled at point-blank range. With an audible gulp the whistle died, lodged in its owner's throat.

Chapter Twenty-six

Henriette glanced anxiously at the sky and said to Saisie, "Not a cloud, unless one counts that little wisp over there to the south, and it's no bigger than a mare's tail."

"Don't underestimate de littlest ones, Miz Henriette. Dey always de ones dat surprises yo'."

The two women picked up a large bucket of river water and lugged it to another flower bed. Using metal dippers, they began watering the plants by hand. They were trailed by the monkey Freedom, who mimicked their actions with a palm leaf, dipping it into the water and shaking the gathered drops on the plants. Henriette straightened up and said, "It's a shame we can't do something about the grass. It looks like an old brown blanket. I thought that September would bring rain, but none seems to be forthcoming. I don't know how the garden will survive without it."

"Oh, it'll survive, Miz Henriette. One good rain will bring it back to life."

"Anyway, it's good to be working in the garden again, Saisie. Alexandre always said it was unseemly for the wife of a duc. Everything that gave me pleasure seemed to be unseemly."

Henriette could not help but smile as she recalled her last days at Salle d'Or Plantation. Exactly twelve hours after Alcée and Blaise's abrupt departure, she had released her husband from the root cellar. Then, after demanding and getting Saisie's bill of sale, she had informed the Duc that she was leaving him, that she was returning to Villeneuve and taking Saisie with her. She planned to resume active management of her family plantation and did not expect any interference from him. Furthermore, she had said, if he attempted to visit her home, she would "shoot the legs right out from under him," and if he tried to make trouble for her, she would create a *scandale* the likes of which New Orleans had never known. She had told him that she knew of virtually all his infidelities, including the latest one with Verbena Chevereaux. She didn't tell him about taking the property deed from his desk or selling Lilliane and Azby. She figured he would find out for himself soon enough.

Just then the two women heard a carriage approaching, and Henriette, her smile vanishing, said, "Saisie, perhaps you'd better fetch my rifle."

"Dat's not de Duc, Miz Henriette." Saisie's eyesight was sharper than that of her mistress. "Dat's Captain Calabozo."

Henriette ran her fingers through her hair and quickly removed her apron. Beneath it she was wearing a plain cotton dress. "Goodness, I must look a mess."

"No, yo' don't, Miz Henriette," Saisie replied. "In fact, if yo' ask me, yo' never looked better."

The captain jumped from the carriage before it had come fully to a stop. He was waving an envelope as he ran across the lawn toward Henriette. "A letter from Alcée," he cried. "From Canada!"

After complimenting Henriette on her appearance, he handed the letter to her. "She sent it in care of me, to make sure you got it."

"Come, let's go up on the veranda, and I'll read it aloud," said Henriette. "Would you like a drink, Captain?"

"Just some water, please."

"Nothing stronger?" asked Henriette.

"No, I'm not drinking anymore."

Henriette said, "Saisie, if you would be so kind as to bring the captain a glass of water, I'll wait until you return to read the letter."

Saisie hurried off. The captain and Henriette walked toward the veranda arm in arm.

"How are you getting along, Henriette?" the captain asked.

"Very well, Bartolomé. I believe I like living alone. I have my meals when I wish, eat what I like, dress as I please, and I don't have to play hostess to a lot of people who mean nothing at all to me."

"I hope that doesn't include me, Henriette."

"Of course not, Bartolomé. You are my good, dear friend and will always be welcome at my home."

"Thank you. I don't mean to pry, Henriette, but . . . are you getting along financially?"

"If I have a problem, I have a houseful of things to sell," she replied gaily.

Saisie arrived with a tall glass of water. Henriette sat down on the top step, and the captain and Saisie sat on either side of her. Henriette examined the envelope and whispered in amazement, "From Canada." She removed the sheet of paper and read aloud:

"Dearest Mama,

Please forgive my short missive. I've so many things to do, I don't know where to begin. I'll write a long letter next week, filling you in on all the details of our new lives. For now I just wanted to let you know that we arrived safely and are settling in.

The steamship took us up the Mississippi to Cairo, and from there we took a smaller boat up the Ohio, to Madison, Indiana. The rest of the way we traveled overland by wagon, finally ending up across the border just north of Detroit, in a little settlement called the Rapids.

We were able to buy a small tract of land at a very good price from an old fur trapper who wanted to return to France. The property is in sight of Lake Huron and has a small but perfectly livable house that we both adore. Blaise is so thrilled at actually owning something. The people here speak French and are friendly and accepting. Many of them have Indian blood, and perhaps that is why they're more understanding than some others we've met. We're working hard, getting ready for the winter, which I understand can be quite fierce. We're fishing and trapping and chopping more wood than the slaves used to cut for the sugar making back home.

Blaise has found work at a fur warehouse near to here. That will enable us to earn enough to buy those things we need that we cannot catch or grow.

The country is beautiful and so vast. It's nothing at all like Louisiana. We miss you terribly and pray nightly for you. You've given us so much happiness, and I know we'll never be able to repay you, but I believe that God will reward you in His own way. Please send our love and best wishes to Captain Calabozo and Saisie, and give Freedom a hug from us. In the spring Blaise plans to start building an additional room onto the house. If the signs are right, we're going to need it by the beginning of summer, for your grandchild.

With all our love,
Alcée and Blaise."

Henriette put down the letter. "A grandchild!" she exclaimed, tears glistening in her eyes. "And I'll probably never get to hold it and love it."

Captain Calabozo stood up. "Yes, you will, Henriette. I promise that you will, if I have to fire up *La Belle Créole* and take you up to Canada myself!"

A shipment of one hundred empty hogsheads ordered by Royal had arrived on the *Belle Créole*. Come harvest time, the large oak casks would by used for storing and shipping the processed cane. Each was over five feet tall and would hold approximately one hundred and twenty-five gallons of crystallized sugar, or an equivalent amount of molasses.

Royal and Seth waited in the first of several wagons while a dozen sweating slaves finished loading the hogsheads. The dockworkers as well as the slaves wore lengths of muslin tied over the lower halves of their faces to keep out the choking dust that covered everything in sight.

As Royal took out a handkerchief and mopped his brow, Seth glanced at the two dust-covered magnolia trees that marked the entrance to the Promenade. "I's sure glad dey took down dem convicts, Mr. Royal. Upon my word, dey was overpowering de magnolias."

"Their presence served a purpose, Seth. Criminals will think twice before coming up here again—particularly now that we've instituted a guard patrol."

"I wish I was big enough to be a guard."

"You will be, someday."

Seth asked, "I was jes' wondering, Mr. Royal. What happened to dem convicts' bodies?"

"They were buried together in an unmarked grave."

Seth shuddered. Royal, anxious to change the subject, asked him the time, knowing full well the little boy delighted in telling him.

"Let's see, now," Seth said. He held his watch high and pretended to have trouble reading it, thus allowing the other slaves a good view of his gift. "I'd say it just about three o'clock."

"Then we ought to be able to get these hogsheads back and unloaded and still have plenty of time to bathe before dinner. Do you want to have dinner with me tonight, Seth?"

"Yo' mean it, Mr. Royal?" The little boy's ancient face looked almost young.

"Of course I do. We'll eat on the veranda."

"And we has ourselves a few drinks."

Royal laughed. "Well, whiskey for me and lemonade for you." As Seth put his watch away and carefully arranged the fob chain, Royal thought that he would indeed be grateful for Seth's undemanding company that evening—and just as grateful that nobody else would be visiting his room. By unspoken agreement, the affair between him and Angélique had ended. She had stopped coming, and he had stopped expecting her. Their passion had burned itself out, leaving nothing behind.

Royal was glad, for her visits had come to seem like a bad habit. To his relief, when he and Angélique now encountered each other, she was polite, almost friendly, but nothing more. It was as if their heated affair had never happened, as if it had been no more than a fantasy. Sometimes Royal actually found himself believing as much.

Yet one problem remained. Royal knew that somehow the truth of the affair would come out, and when it did, it would destroy his friendship with Suzanne. And the way Suzanne continued to occupy his thoughts only made matters worse.

The last hogshead was loaded, and Royal led the wagon train down the Promenade. After a short but dusty ride, they reached the Heritage turnoff, then veered left onto the narrow, rutted road across the cane fields to the plantation's refinery and storage buildings.

Royal halted the wagons at the crest of a slope behind a cavernous brick warehouse. Rather than continue down the road to the front of the refinery buildings, he would have the hogsheads unloaded here, where they could be slid end-first down a makeshift wooden ramp leading straight to the open rear of the warehouse. Rafe Bastile, stripped to the waist, was waiting at the top of the ramp. He was so suntanned that, except for the distinctive knee-high boots and planter's hat, he almost looked like one of the slaves. He would supervise the unloading of the wagons, while Royal, in the cooler warehouse below, would direct the stacking operation.

Even with the ramp, however, it turned out to be slow, hot work, for the heavy hogsheads had to be slid, not rolled, down the incline one at a time, so that they could be safely stopped at the bottom. Then they had to be rolled into place and stacked one atop the other, four high, with the help of a hand-powered crane. As the afternoon wore on, Royal, impatient to be finished, took off his shirt, tied it around his waist, and joined the slaves in carrying the hogsheads from the base of the ramp into the warehouse. He noted Bastile's annoyance at his performing what the overseer considered "nigger work," but ignored it. Royal did not like Bastile—in fact, the two of them still addressed each other in coldly formal terms—but he had to admit that the man was good at his job.

"Mr. Bastile," Royal called out, "do you think we'll be finished by six o'clock?"

"Six, six-thirty, M'sieur Brannigan," Bastile replied.

Royal walked across the loading platform at the bottom of the ramp to the water barrel. Seth was making himself useful by dispensing drinks to the slaves. "I'll have a dipperful, Seth."

"Yes, sir, Mr. Royal."

As Royal drank he glanced toward the top of the ramp. For an instant he thought he saw Angélique standing next to Bastile, both of them looking down at him.

He blinked and she was gone. Royal quickly dismissed the vision, not particularly caring if he had indeed seen her. He handed the dipper back to Seth and started walking back across the platform when there was a sound like thunder and he heard Seth scream, "Mr. Royal! Watch out!"

Royal looked up in time to see a pair of hogsheads rolling out of control down the chute, heading straight for him. He was shoved hard from behind and went sprawling, the breath knocked out of him. He felt the vibrations of the heavy casks as they landed a few yards away.

When he was certain that no more hogsheads were forthcoming, Royal got to his feet and turned around. There was a man lying facedown at the bottom of the ramp. With a shock, Royal realized it was the person who had pushed him out of harm's way. He knelt and turned the motionless figure over. It was Josh, one of the slaves he had befriended. The entire left side of his head had been crushed by one of the hogsheads. Royal untied his shirt and covered the broken face. Blood seeped through the material of the shirt, like a scarlet flower opening.

Royal looked up the hillside to Bastile, who was staring back down, as if defying Royal to accuse him.

"I'm coming for you, Bastile!" Royal screamed.

Fueled by his anger, Royal raced up the slope. Bastile, he was sure, had released the casks on purpose, but had succeeded in killing the wrong man. The vision of Angélique flashed through Royal's mind. As soon as he reached the top, he roared, "Why did you try to kill me?"

Bastile started to turn away, then, unexpectedly, drew back his fist and punched Royal squarely on the chin, knocking him backward into the side of the ramp. Breathless and shaken, Royal expelled a mouthful of blood and saliva and lunged at Bastile. The hefty overseer absorbed the charge and broke free, then held his ground. The two men crouched and began circling each other like animals, their eyes blazing with hatred. Bastile made a dive, but this time Royal was ready, bringing his knee up and catching his opponent beneath the chin. Bastile stumbled to the ground near the top of the ramp. Spitting out dust, he quickly hauled himself to his feet, but instead of going for Royal, he lunged to one side, coming up with a machete that had been lying under the ramp.

Bastile grinned as he clasped the machete in his huge fist. With a grunt, he lunged forward, swinging the weapon.

Royal jumped aside just as the deadly hooked blade hissed past. He scrambled back toward the ramp, his eyes searching wildly for a weapon.

The slaves had gathered in groups to watch the white men fight. Although they hated Bastile, they were not about to come to Royal's aid. If the American lost the fight, they would have to deal with the angry overseer.

Bastile advanced steadily, slicing the machete as if he were cutting cane, backing Royal down the slope alongside the ramp. Royal tried to leap over the ramp, to put it between himself and Bastile, but he lost his footing and found himself sliding backward down the wooden chute. He grappled in vain for a handhold as he slid to the bottom, where he landed with a painful thud on his backside. In a daze, Royal turned over and tried to focus his eyes. Suddenly a splash of water shocked him back to his senses. He saw that Seth had thrown the water, but before he could get to his feet, Bastile came plummeting down the slide feet-first. Heavy boots struck Royal in the side of the chest, knocking him flat. Out of the corner of his eye, Royal saw the glint of a blade and rolled away as the machete struck the wooden platform just inches from his face.

Bastile had been so sure of his blow that he had put all his force behind it. As the burly man regained his balance and worked the blade free, Royal jumped to his feet. He heard Seth call his name and glanced to his left. "Mr. Royal, catch!" Seth tossed a machete, and Royal caught it by the handle just as Bastile's blade came free.

Bastile growled a curse at the boy, and again the two men circled warily. They were about ten paces apart. At exactly the same moment, they rushed each other, their machetes clanging together. They grappled for an instant and separated, both unharmed, and Bastile hissed through clenched teeth, "You should be dead, American. You and your nigger boy."

Royal reacted immediately, attacking with a speed and ferocity that startled the overseer. Bastile backed and dodged, glancing behind him to avoid the stacked hogsheads.

Bastile blocked one of Royal's slashes and eased himself to the left. Royal was off-guard for an instant, and Bastile struck lightning-fast, the hooked point of his weapon catching Royal across the right shoulder, ripping into the flesh. Royal stepped back and glanced at the widening red line.

Confident now, Bastile began showing off, darting and feinting left and right. Speed was his tactic, and despite his bulky physique, it was also his strong point. The hate in his eyes left no doubt that he intended to kill Royal.

Once again the machetes clashed, Royal blocking Bastile's powerful lunges the best he could while backing away. By now his entire right side was streaked with blood.

Bastile forced Royal toward the stacked hogsheads. Sensing that the kill was near, he began swinging savagely. Royal had no choice but to press back between two of the huge casks. They were stacked directly against a wall, however, and he could retreat no farther. With a wicked grin, Bastile sliced and jabbed again and again, and it was all Royal could do to deflect or block the blows with his own blade. Realizing he had but one hope left, Royal shoved his body backward like a wedge, separating the stacks of hogsheads on either side of him. The casks shifted apart and began to teeter, and Royal felt his back against the brick wall. As someone shouted "Dey goin' to go!" Royal forced himself sideways against the wall and pushed the bottom hogshead outward with his shoulder. Bastile screamed, but his cry was cut off by the tumbling crash. Royal crossed his arms over his head and stayed pressed against the wall.

When the dust cleared, Bastile was lying in a crumpled heap under two of the fallen casks. Royal rushed to his opponent and knelt beside him. Bastile's chest had been crushed, and he could barely breathe. Blood was flowing freely from his mouth and nose.

"Why?" Royal demanded.

Bastile regarded him through eyes that were rapidly growing opaque. He spoke in a gurgling voice. "Angélique—she promised me . . . master . . . of Heritage." Then his eyes slid shut, and he was dead.

The veranda was deserted and dark, save for a patch of lamplight issuing from the dining room. Royal pushed open the French doors and entered, accompanied by a hot gust of wind.

Zenobia was standing next to the sideboard. Suzanne was seated at the table, having her supper. Angélique's chair was empty. Both women looked at him, their faces registering shock.

Royal had come directly from his fight with Bastile. His bare chest was covered with dirt and streaked with dried blood from his shoulder wound, and he was seething with fury.

Suzanne shot out of her chair. "Royal, what's happened?"

He regarded her for a moment before replying. She was wearing the same blue gown she had been wearing the night he had first come to Heritage, bearing the body of her husband.

"That's the first time you've used my Christian name," he said. "It's a pity it's not a more pleasant occasion."

Suzanne rushed to him and touched his shoulder. "You're hurt! Zenobia, bring some water and bandages."

"Don't bother, Zenobia," said Royal. He glanced at the empty place setting and asked sharply, "Where is she?"

"Angélique? She isn't feeling well. She's not coming down to supper."

"She was feeling well enough earlier when she tried to have me killed."

"What do you mean?"

"She talked Bastile into attempting to murder me by promising to make him master of Heritage. I'm afraid he got killed in the process."

Zenobia dropped a plate. It struck the floor without breaking and rolled under the table.

Royal snapped his head toward the slave. "What do you know about all this?"

Zenobia lowered her hooded eyes and looked away.

Royal turned back to Suzanne. "Were you in on this too?" He grabbed her by the shoulder. She smelled of flowers and sunshine. "Were you?" he shouted. "Did you want Heritage back so badly that you would have me murdered?"

Suzanne pushed him away. "You must be mad to make such accusations."

In a gentler tone he said, "It's Angélique who's mad. She wants Heritage for her own. And she will stop at nothing to get it, including your destruction and mine. She hates you, Suzanne. She always has. She's just been wearing a mask."

Suzanne glared at him, her lower lip trembling. "And just where did you acquire this knowledge?" she demanded.

"In bed."

Suzanne staggered backward as if she had been struck. "Zenobia, leave the room—"

"No, stay here," Royal ordered. "I have a feeling that she knows more than both of us."

Suzanne stared at him, horrified. "You—you seduced Angélique?" She shook her head vigorously, her dark hair lashing her face. "What kind of man are you? She's ruined, spoiled forever—"

"Spoiled, yes. She's that, all right. I wasn't the first."

"What do you mean?"

"What do you think I mean? She wasn't a virgin."

"You're lying." Suzanne protested, but her tone was weak. "You've got to be lying."

Royal went on as if he hadn't heard her. "The first time it happened was the night of the ball. I was drunk. The room was dark. She came to my bed. I was lonely, worried about succeeding, and uncomfortable in this hostile place. But most of all I was lonely." He paused a moment to consider his words. "It was too dark to see. I thought it was you."

Anger inflamed Suzanne's cheeks, and tears burst from her eyes. "Me?" she cried. "You thought it was me? That I would behave like a slut!" She collapsed in Angélique's chair.

Royal reached out to touch her.

"No, don't!" She wiped her eyes with her balled fists. "It could not have been me. Not me. And do you want to know why?"

Zenobia protested, "Don't, Miz Suzanne. There's no need—"

"Yes, yes, there is a desperate need—for honesty—in this house. So, M'sieur Brannigan, would you like to hear some truth-telling?" She picked up Angélique's wineglass, seemed surprised to find it empty, and put it back down. "You see, my marriage was never consummated."

"Never consummated!"

"I am still a virgin." She threw back her head and uttered a bitter laugh. "So you see, it couldn't have been me." She gestured helplessly and accidentally knocked over the wineglass. "Not me!"

Royal glanced at Zenobia. The slave woman was stone-faced.

"I spent my wedding night alone," Suzanne went on. "Jean-Louis got so drunk at the reception that he passed out. I attributed his behavior to nerves, high spirits. I'm always good at making excuses for other people. That night we slept in separate rooms. The next morning his attitude toward me was changed. He was cold, distant. Night after night I waited for him to come to my room. But he didn't, and I thought the fault must be mine. What had I done to make him turn from me? I suffered the most common of personal tragedies, m'sieur. I loved somebody who didn't love me in return."

"He did love you, Miz Suzanne. I knows he did," said Zenobia.

"He had a peculiar way of showing it. I kept waiting and hoping that he would come to me, but he never did. Finally my love began to turn into something else. It was a new emotion for me, m'sieur, one I'd never felt before. My love began to turn to hate. Yes, I hated him." Suzanne pressed her head against the back of her chair. "And I hated myself, too, because I didn't know how to help him. Do you know what I felt when you brought him home in that casket? I'm ashamed even to say it now. I felt relief. Relief! Our suffering was over."

She turned on Royal. "And you come to me with these lies about Angélique. Had it not been for her, I would not have survived that terrible year. And you try to make her out to be some kind of monster. I won't—I *can't*—believe it."

Royal said to Zenobia, "You know the truth. Tell her. *Tell her!*"

Zenobia replied solemnly. "It true, Miz Suzanne. I knows. Dat night I saw her standing in front of his door—naked."

"And you know other things too," Royal said. The Negress looked away. "You hoard secrets, don't you, Zenobia?"

"I was trying to protect Miz Suzanne."

"Protect? She doesn't need protection. She's strong. Stronger than both of us."

Suzanne stood up. "It—it can't be. We'll go upstairs and confront Angélique. She'll deny everything."

"I have no doubt she will," said Royal. "But I want to see her alone." He put his hands on Suzanne's shoulders and gently pushed her down in the chair. "You stay here, Suzanne," he said. "You, too, Zenobia."

"You won't hurt her?" Suzanne asked fearfully.

"That's for her to decide," Royal replied, and walked out of the room.

Royal had been upstairs only once and did not remember one room from another. All the doors were partly open, save for one. He walked quickly around the curved gallery overlooking the foyer, glancing into each room in turn. Only one remained—the closed door at the end of the gallery. He tried the handle. It was locked. He stepped back and rammed his booted foot against it. The wood splintered, and the door flew open.

Angélique was sitting in the center of the parquet floor, her back toward him. Royal's eyes quickly scanned the large room. He took in the shelves of toys and stuffed animals, the carved rocking horse, the child's daybed, the tiny rosewood table set for tea. He looked back to Angélique. She hadn't acknowledged his presence. He stepped inside the room to get a better view of her. She was sitting next to a large dollhouse, an exact replica of Heritage. Nearby an oil lamp sat on the floor. The dim yellow light cast eerie shadows over Angélique and the object of her attention.

She held a doll in her hand, and as Royal neared, he realized that it was a representation of Angélique herself as a child. Like the doll, Angélique was wearing a white dress trimmed in lace. Her expression, he could now see, was startled, as if she had been frightened by a loud noise. Her eyes, more protuberant than ever, resembled pieces of green glass. Royal wondered if she had dressed herself to look like the doll, or dressed the doll to look like her.

Without looking up, Angélique said in a light, purring voice, "She has very pretty hair." She turned and looked up at him. From her expression, he could have been a stranger. "Doesn't she?" she demanded.

"Get up, Angélique."

She obeyed, keeping her eyes downcast in a demure manner. She held the doll in front of her as if it were a talisman and had the power to ward off evil. Two bright splotches of color inflamed her cheeks, and her voice began to tremble in excitement.

"I wore this dress to the wedding," she said, turning in a full circle to show it off. "Everyone was shocked. Only the bride wears white." She repeated the words in a child's singsong voice: "Only the bride wears white."

She stopped abruptly and smoothed the folds of her dress with one hand. "She should *still* wear white." She threw back her head, and the room was filled with her shrill laughter. "Still—wear—white!"

The laughter stopped as suddenly as it had begun. She knelt by the dollhouse and carefully placed the image of herself on the veranda, spreading its arms so that it looked like a welcoming hostess. Her eyes unfocused, Angélique tilted her head to one side, as if listening to someone whispering in her ear. "Yes, I should have been the bride," she agreed. "I should have been . . ." Her voice grew suddenly harsh, as if the words burned in her throat. ". . . mistress of Heritage!"

Royal noticed out of the corner of his eye that Suzanne and Zenobia had stepped into the room. They were in shadow, and Angélique did not see them. With a gesture of his hand he cautioned the two women to remain quiet and stay where they were.

For a long time Angélique didn't say anything. Royal, hoping that he was exercising good judgment, prompted her with a question. "Is that why you wore a white dress, Angélique? Because you should have been the bride?"

She turned her bright green eyes upon him and smiled coquettishly, as a little girl smiles when complimented by an adult. A giggle spilled from her pursed lips. "Of course *she* thought it was a charming idea."

"Do you mean Suzanne?" he asked quickly.

She nodded. "She said that it was as if we were true sisters already." She frowned. "I didn't want a sister. I didn't want anybody but Jean-Louis." Angélique suddenly threw back her head and howled his name. "Jean-Louis!" The sound reverberated around the room. Then she began to sob, but tears did not come to bring her relief.

Royal glanced at the two women behind him. Zenobia's head was lowered, her arms crossed. Suzanne, her face deathly white, was staring at her sister-in-law.

Despite everything Angélique had done, Royal was moved to pity. He reached out his hand to her, but she quickly drew away, a hiss of breath escaping her lips. She stood up and regarded him with disdain, and then the poison began to spew forth.

"Well, *I* was the bride after all, wasn't I? Theirs wasn't a marriage, it was only a wedding. Have another glass of champagne, Jean-Louis. We must drink a toast to your new bride." Her voice grew more bitter with each word. "And another to her beauty. And another to her good health. And another to her—" She smiled triumphantly. "Jean-Louis never could hold his champagne." She knelt down again and, with both hands, pantomimed his prone form. "No, no, you mustn't take him to the master bedroom. How unfair to his bride. Take him to his own room. Let him sleep it off. He'll feel better in the morning, I'm sure." She shook her head slowly. "It's a shame, and on his wedding night too."

Angélique turned again to the dollhouse and fixed her gaze on an upstairs bedroom, which, by its color scheme and miniature furnishings, Royal surmised had been Jean-Louis's.

"It was dark and he was drunk," she whispered. "He thought that I was she." And then she began pantomiming taking off her clothes.

Suzanne cried out. It was a sound full of shock and pain. Royal walked quickly to her side, took her in his arms, and held her tight. The three of them watched in horrified fascination as Angélique, now "undressed," backed away from the dollhouse and sat down on the child's daybed. She had begun to tremble with physical excitement. She lowered her eyelids and parted her wet lips, and her face became contorted with desire.

When she lay back on the bed, Suzanne, unable to bear any more, cried, "My God, Angélique, stop it. *Stop it!*"

Angélique looked up, surprised and hurt. With a sulking expression, she rose from the bed and began walking about the room. She trailed a hand over the shelves of outgrown toys and games, paused to straighten a place setting at the tea table, then moved on to the carved rocking horse. She stroked its wooden mane and gave it a gentle push so that it began moving back and forth.

From the shelf she picked up a music box and pressed it to her heart as she wound it. She set it back down, opened the lid, and a tinkling waltz began to play.

Angélique curtsied to an imaginary partner and, lifting the hem of her gown, began to dance around the room. As she circled the dollhouse, the mechanism in the music box, old and rusted, skipped notes and quickly wound down, becoming a plodding parody of a waltz. Angélique, oblivious of the dying tempo, waltzed wildly around the floor. Her swirling skirts brushed against the oil lamp, causing it to topple.

Suzanne cried out, "The lamp, Angélique, the lamp!"

The oil poured out and was ignited by the flame. The puddle of fire lapped against the veranda of the dollhouse, quickly igniting the doll's dress, then its hair. Angélique ran to the dollhouse and shrieked in agony, as if she herself were burning.

Royal shouted to the women, "Get some water!"

Zenobia and Suzanne rushed from the room. Royal ran to the windows, yanked down the brocade drapes, and began smothering the flames.

Suzanne and Zenobia both returned bearing pitchers of water, which they dumped on the dollhouse. They stood watching as the doused embers sputtered and finally went out. The room was left in almost total darkness. Zenobia lit another lamp. It was only then that they realized that Angélique was no longer in the room.

"She's gone," Suzanne said. "Angélique's gone."

"I gets her," said Zenobia. "De Lawd have mercy on dat woman," she mumbled as she strode from the room.

Royal turned to Suzanne. Her face was ashen, her eyes wet and unblinking.

He reached out for her, thought better of it, and withdrew his arm.

"I'm not fragile, Royal. I won't break."

"What are you feeling?" he asked gently.

She pressed her hand to her forehead. "Shock, mostly. Revulsion. Pity. But also relief. All this time I felt that I had done something wrong. Something I couldn't see or understand." She shuddered. "I can't stop shaking."

Royal put his arms around her and held her.

"I can't—understand," she said, "can't forgive what Angélique did. She not only destroyed my marriage, she destroyed Jean-Louis."

"She must have always harbored those feelings for her brother," Royal said. "And she used other men as a substitute for him. Including me and Bastile. Suzanne, can you ever forgive me for what I've done? I promise you, it's been over for a long time."

"There's nothing to forgive, Royal. As you said, you were lonely, and she came to you. God, what can I do? I don't know how I can go on living with Angélique, knowing what I now do."

"She needs care," Royal began. "There are places—"

"No! No matter what she's done, I will not let her be put in a madhouse. Heritage is still her home. We're the trespassers. Oh, I can't think now. I simply cannot plan ahead."

"We'll do what's best for her, Suzanne. But we have responsibilities to the plantation and to ourselves."

He took her hand and held it tight. She absently looked down at their intertwined fingers and asked, "How could she hate me so much? I don't deserve that, Royal."

"It's not you, Suzanne. She would have hated anyone who came between her and her brother."

"It's a strange feeling to know that someone hates you."

"And to know that someone loves you?"

She looked at him sadly, but the light had been taken from her eyes. "How can we even hope for a future with things as they are?"

"Dammit, *I do* hope for a future. No, I *demand* it. Listen to me, Suzanne. *Listen!* You have a right to happiness. She's robbed you of one husband. Are you going to let her rob you of another?"

Suzanne parted her lips to reply, but she never got the chance. Zenobia rushed into the room, out of breath.

"I can't find her anywhere," she panted.

Suzanne looked at Royal, her eyes filled with dread.

It was a warm, dry night, but a steady wind from the Gulf brought with it the smell of the sea. An orange crescent moon hung low over the horizon, occasionally obscured by clouds that were otherwise invisible against the night sky.

Angélique walked quickly across the parched grass. Her surroundings appeared foreign to her, as if she were seeing them for the first time. Her feet knew where they were going, even if her mind did not, and she was content to let them decide her destination.

She reached the greenhouse. Two male slaves, both gardeners, were closing up the building, their day's work done. They tipped their straw hats and offered her a good evening. She knew better than to answer them, however. She mustn't respond or even acknowledge them. That would be admitting that she was there. They gave her uneasy glances as she passed.

Angélique raced on, gasping for breath. She paused, looking behind her to see that the men had not followed her, then hurried on down the crescent brick staircase. She passed the sunken sugar cane kettles. Usually filled with rainwater, they were empty except for puddles of green slime, and the surrounding vines had been shriveled by the heat. No birds sang there now.

Angélique reached the glen of bamboo and fern. Her footsteps raised dust from the dry earth; brittle leaves brushed her face. The ladder of waterfalls was silent, the bottom of each pool barren and dry.

It was growing dark, but it didn't matter. Her destination was now as clear to her as her purpose.

She wanted to hurry, but that would never do. Someone might see her, and it was important that she remain unnoticed. The blood pounded in her temples as she saw the stables looming ahead. Despite her resolution not to draw attention to herself, Angélique broke into a run toward her strange and terrifying destination.

She shoved open the door with both hands and stumbled inside. The aroma of the stables embraced her like an old friend. The scent of the hay and the horses always pleased her, but now it gave her confidence and resolve as well.

"Miz Angélique."

She whirled around. Seth was standing there, looking frightened. "Go away," she said. She knew how to deal with slaves. One gave orders.

"But, Miz Angélique . . ."

She snatched the lantern from him. "I said go away. *Now!*" The little boy backed off and was swallowed by the darkness of the stables.

Angélique searched in the tack room and found what she was looking for—an ax handle, some rags, and a container of lamp oil. She wrapped the rags tightly around the length of wood, humming a snatch of the music-box waltz as she worked. When the lump of rags was the size of a child's head, she tied it off, laid her handiwork on the floor, and poured out the lamp oil, soaking the rags through and through. Then, using the lighted lantern, she ignited the rags and went to get the horse Arab. The stallion shied as she neared him with the flaming torch, but she soothed him with words and strokes of her hand, and was able to lead him outside and mount him bareback. She held on to his mane as she directed him toward the cane fields. As she rode, she let the torch lick at the passing tree branches, savoring the crackling sound they made as they burst into flame.

She reached the edge of the main cane field and stopped,

just within reach of the dry stalks. She stretched out her arm and ignited the tasseled tops of the cane. The dry fibers burst into flame, like miniature fireworks. She threw back her head and laughed out loud. It was not ordinary laughter, and its sound caused the horse to back and rear. Angélique calmed him once again by rubbing her cheek against his neck and offering soothing words.

She rode down an alley of cane, igniting the tassels as she went. She turned and looked behind her. The entire row was blazing. She reached one of the irrigation windmills. Propelled by the brisk wind, the blades were turning at a good pace. She brushed the torch against the dry wood and canvas of one of the vanes, and it immediately burst into flame, igniting the others in turn. The windmill creaked to a halt, blazing against the night sky.

Soot from the burning canvas began swirling through the air, alighting on Angélique's hair, skin, and dress. She wiped her cheeks with the back of a hand, leaving streaks of grime, turning her face into a primitive mask.

Angélique surveyed her work. Fanned by the strong wind, flames swept across the cane fields faster than a man could run. Patches of brilliant orange jumped from row to row, like waves of breaking surf.

She turned Arab around and rode down another cane row, spreading the fire. When she reached the area where she had entered the field, she reined the horse to a stop. Seth was standing between her and the stables, wide-eyed with horror. He ran toward her, waving his hands and screaming.

"Miz Angélique!" he cried. "What is yo' doing? Yo' gots to stop!"

Angélique galloped at him and hit him on the side of the head with the flaming cudgel. The little boy crumpled to the ground.

Angélique rode along the periphery of the field until she reached a store of stacked wood. The dry timber ignited immediately. As she watched it burn, the wind veered to the east and changed the direction of the flames. Angélique turned around and found herself facing a crackling wall of fire. Arab bolted, and she was thrown.

Jagged scythes of flame cut across the fields, burning everything in their path. Creating its own wind now, the fire raced down row after row of cane, even leaping the irrigation ditches. Great billows of smoke rose and merged with the clouds, covering the sky as burning clots of ash fell upon the fields like a hellish rain.

Chapter Twenty-seven

The plantation bell tolled just once and then was silent. Royal, Suzanne, and Zenobia came rushing out of the big house. As far as their eyes could see, the cane fields were in flames.

"My God," cried Suzanne. "What's happening?"

"Quickly, Zenobia, alert the house slaves," said Royal. He started across the lawn.

"Where are you going?" shouted Suzanne.

"To the stables. I must get the field hands."

"I'm coming with you."

They raced across the lawn, and as they neared the plantation bell, they saw a slave boy lying on the ground, propped against the foot of the stone structure.

"Seth!" Royal knelt by his little friend. "He must have rung the bell."

Seth's honey-colored skin was blackened by the smoke, his clothing dotted with holes burned by flying sparks. His head was singed and bleeding. Royal took him in his arms and gently lifted him up. The boy's eyes opened, and he began struggling.

"Take it easy, son," said Royal.

"Mr. Royal, I thought yo' was de ghost!"

"The ghost, Seth?"

"De ghost he come along, pick me up, and I guess he carry me here. Why would a ghost do dat, Mr. Royal?"

"I don't know, Seth."

"And watch out fo' Miz Angélique. She gone crazy."

"You saw her?"

"She was riding Arab in de cane fields. She set de fire, and when I tries to stop her, she hits me in de head."

Royal and Suzanne exchanged glances; it appeared that the

boy was delirious. Royal said, "Zenobia, take Seth inside and see to him. Quickly!"

The Negress took the little boy from Royal and rushed toward the house.

Suzanne asked, "What can I do?"

"Keep ringing the bell to warn the other plantations. I'll bring back the field hands and have them dig a firebreak at the far edge of the garden. We're in real trouble if the wind shifts. Right now it's blowing northeast, toward the swamp."

"And Taffarel."

"The swamp should extinguish the flames."

They heard hoofbeats and looked in the direction of the sound. Arab, riderless, was galloping toward them, his eyes wild and his coat singed. Royal pulled Suzanne behind the stone arch, out of the frightened animal's way. Her expression told him that she was thinking the same thing: that the appearance of the horse confirmed Seth's story—at least the part about Angélique.

Suzanne twisted her head toward the fire. "Oh, God, Royal, she's in there. Please bring her back, no matter what she's done. Bring her back."

He kissed her quickly on the cheek. "I'll try—but first I've got to go to the slaves. They'll be frightened and confused, and with Bastile dead, there's no one to tell them what to do."

Royal raced through the gardens, taking a shortcut to the stables instead of following the formal path. Thorns and branches tore at his flesh and trousers. The leaves around him were trembling, as if they were afraid, and with a sinking heart Royal realized that the wind had shifted toward the south. If it continued, then surely Heritage, too, would be destroyed.

Suddenly he became afraid. Perhaps it was sheer exhaustion, combined with the threat of losing everything he owned and loved, but all at once Royal felt as if he had been struck a physical blow, and he stumbled and fell to the ground. Numbed by fear, he lay still, his face pressed against the earth. In the distance he could hear the fire rage. . . .

It would be so easy to stay here, he thought, *so easy to give up, to cast aside hope*. From out of the recesses of his mind, his father's parting words came to him: "*You've never failed to disappoint me*."

Royal grabbed a low branch and yanked himself to his feet. He emerged from the undergrowth next to the stables, and only then did he dare look at the fields. They had become a turbulent sea of red and orange. The skeletal blades of the windmills, silhouetted black and motionless against the fire, stood out like broken crosses in hell. Even if the big house itself survived the conflagration, there would be nothing to harvest come October.

When Royal entered the stables, one of the attendants, a middle-aged slave named Eben, was waiting for him. "I saddled Alezan fo' yo', M'sieur Royal. I figure yo' be needing to ride him."

"Thanks, Eben. Have you seen Angélique anywhere?"

"No, M'sieur Royal."

"If you do, bring her back to the house, even if you have to carry her against her will. Do you understand?"

"Yes, M'sieur Royal, but—"

"No buts—just do it. Now listen carefully. You and the other stable hands lash the horses together in one long line and take them to the Promenade. Is there a rifle in here?"

"Yes, sir."

"Please get it for me, and make sure it's loaded."

Royal doused Alezan with water and mounted him. He took the rifle from Eben and rode from the stables, heading toward the slave quarters, which were just to the south of the cane fields.

As he rode past the blaze, Royal searched in vain for Angélique. Through the thickening smoke he could barely make out the form of Rafe Bastile's house, which had already been engulfed by the flames. He wondered whether the slaves had taken the overseer's body there.

The slave quarters themselves had been spared so far, but only because there was a wide expanse of open ground between them and the cane fields. The cabins' inhabitants were milling about outside, and as Royal approached, he scanned the dark faces. Some of the men were fighting among themselves, trying to assert their positions. Many of the women were crying or hysterical. Some had gathered their children together along with household goods, pets, and domestic animals, and were standing in frightened groups, awaiting instructions.

Suddenly a hideous scream rent the air. An old woman

apparently had strayed too close to the flames and been hit by a falling ember, for her clothing was smoldering, her hair aflame. Royal jumped from his horse and rushed to her aid. The poor woman collapsed a few feet in front of him, and although Royal and a few slaves rolled her in the dusty earth, they knew that they were too late to save her life.

The other slaves were on the verge of panic, and Royal saw that it was important for him to take charge immediately. He grabbed the rifle from his saddle and fired it into the air. The Negroes quickly grew still.

"I want all the drivers to line up in front of me. Now!"

The drivers—those men who oversaw groups of other slaves—rushed to the forefront.

"I'm counting on you men!" Royal shouted over the roaring blaze. "Take charge of your regular work groups. I want you to hurry them to the big house and clear a wide area all along the edge of the gardens. Cut down any trees or bushes you have to. If anyone falters in his work, I will shoot him on the spot. Now get your tools and go!"

While the drivers were organizing the men, Royal sought out Aunt Carrie, a large, rawboned woman in her late fifties who was the acknowledged matriarch of the slave community. He found her trying to calm a group of children. "Aunt Carrie," he shouted.

She turned to him. "Yes, M'sieur Royal? What does yo' want Aunt Carrie to do?"

"Have the women take the children and animals and go to the front of the big house. Have the younger women pump water from the wells. Fill every container you can find. Is that understood?"

"Yes, m'sieur."

Royal remounted and made one last check of the slave quarters. He urged Alezan along the rows of cabins, making sure that no one had been left behind. A young girl, no more than twelve, had returned for her pet kitten. She clutched it to her breast as she staggered out of one of the buildings. Royal helped her onto Alezan, then rode past the rows of slaves marching toward Heritage. Their heads were bowed, their faces shocked. Royal wondered what would become of them now that he had lost the crop. How would he feed them? Clothe them? He reached the big house, gave over the girl to one of the house servants, and found Suzanne.

"Any sign of Angélique?" she asked.

He shook his head. "In the morning I'll organize a search party, and we'll know for certain."

A sob escaped her lips. "I can't bear to think of her trapped in the fire."

Royal said, "I need your help, Suzanne. The wind's shifted and the fire's coming this way. Have ladders placed against the house, and round up all the young boys who like to climb trees. We're going to have to keep the roof wet if the sparks start flying. Have Zenobia set up an area on the front veranda for anyone who might get injured. Have beds, bandages, and ointments ready."

Royal rode back and forth among the men digging the firebreak. Under the supervision of the drivers, they were working quickly and hard, but Royal feared it would be too late. Everywhere he looked the sky was a swirling mass of red and black. Ashes filled the air like swarms of huge insects, and the smoke was growing thicker. Large plumes of it began billowing toward the slaves, stinging their eyes and searing their nostrils and throats. Royal shouted at them to keep their faces covered and urged them to keep working.

After a few minutes, the acrid smoke became too thick for the work to continue. Royal called for the slaves to retreat toward the big house. He rode behind them, and when they reached the back lawn, he dismounted and tied Alezan to a tree. He walked quickly to the veranda and climbed one of the ladders, to get a better view of what they were facing. In the distance, the blaze had swept all the way to the swamp and was burning the cane fields of Taffarel to the north. So far, Victoire, to the south, had been spared. Royal had to wait for a gust of wind to sweep away the smoke before he could see what he feared: that the flames were almost to the gardens and outbuildings of Heritage. Soon they would reach the stables, and then it would be only a matter of minutes before they engulfed the orchards, the gardens, and the big house itself. It looked as though all was lost.

Royal descended the ladder and went to Suzanne's side. The slaves, prompted by their childlike piety, had gathered together in groups and were kneeling down to pray. Their tearful words, spoken in a hundred different voices, mingled with the ominous sound of the fire.

Royal and Suzanne, humbled by this simple act of faith, knelt with them, bowing their heads in prayer.

Somewhere a young man began to sing in a crystal clear tenor:

"Jesus is my captain,
I shall not be moved."

The other slaves, swaying from side to side, joined him, and the song rose over the roar of the flames.

"Jesus is my captain,
I shall not be moved.
Just like a tree
Planted by the wayside,
I shall not be moved."

A vivid flash caused Royal to jerk his head up. He scanned the skies, but saw nothing. Just the billowing smoke. He lowered his head once again when the unmistakable rumble of thunder overrode the slaves' singing. A tiny drop of water glanced off Royal's shoulder, and then another, and another. He stood up and looked at Suzanne, hardly daring to hope. Both their faces were sprinkled by a succession of raindrops. Suddenly the sky split apart, and the rain poured down upon the awed congregation.

The slaves began cheering. Some of them wept. The rain increased to a deluge, but no one moved for cover. Instead, they gathered around Royal and Suzanne.

Royal just stood there, watching as the fire was quenched. He put his arm around Suzanne.

"Go back to your homes," he said to the slaves. "Go home, be with your loved ones, and give thanks."

Suzanne was rain-soaked and streaked with soot, but Royal thought that nobody in the world could look so beautiful. He embraced her, and their tears mixed with the rain. He said, "I've got to ride over to Taffarel and see if Miss Julia is all right."

"Yes, yes. Of course you must go."

They stared at each other for a moment, not daring to put into words what was on their minds. What were they going to do now that the crop was destroyed? How were they going to continue to hold on to Heritage? Suddenly, Royal took Suzanne in his arms and kissed her hard and long. "I'll be back as soon as I can." He took Alezan's rein and mounted, nudged the horse in the sides, and raced off in the direction of Taffarel.

As Royal rode through the rain, past the still-smoldering cane fields, he surveyed the damage. He estimated that all of his cane crop, and three quarters of Julia's, had been destroyed.

He reached the big house and knocked on the door. Ottile answered almost immediately. Without speaking, she led him into the foyer. Cato was standing sentinel by the open parlor door. He nodded sadly as Royal passed.

Halfway into the room, Royal stopped in his tracks. Julia was kneeling next to a body that had been laid out on a blanket beneath the portrait of Claude Taffarel. At first the possibility that it was Angélique flashed through Royal's mind, but as he took another step forward, he could see that it was a man, about Julia's age. His hair was long, white, and had been singed by the fire. His chalk-white flesh and pale clothes were streaked with soot and burned by cinders.

Julia looked up and said, "The ghost of Magnolia Landing is finally at rest."

Royal helped her to her feet.

"Ghost? I'm afraid I don't understand."

"He's my brother, Royal. Claude was stricken with leprosy just before I was to be married to Theo. Forty-one years ago."

Suddenly it all started to become clear to Royal.

"I panicked, you see," Julia said. "Royal, I couldn't let him be sent to Lepers' Row, and that's what the law dictated. I had to care for him. I just couldn't marry Theo and take the risk of spreading the disease. I feared it was hereditary."

"They don't believe that anymore, Julia."

"They did then. I had no choice but to break off my engagement. I told everybody that Claude had died—everybody except Ottile and Cato, who knew the truth."

"But all these years. How did you—?"

"How did I keep it a secret?" Julia looked toward Cato and Ottile, who were standing just beyond the doorway. "We couldn't have, if it hadn't been for Claude. The disease changed my brother, Royal. It not only destroyed his looks, but it turned him inward. He became an entirely different person. He couldn't stand to have anyone see him. He began sleeping through the day and getting up only at night. Naturally, we couldn't keep him cooped up inside all the time. On occasion he would venture out, and over the years he was seen by a number of people. And that, my dear Royal, is how the legend of the ghost of Magnolia Landing was perpetuated."

Royal helped Julia into a chair and sat opposite her. "I suppose I loved Claude too much," she went on. "I should have loved Theo more. It wasn't fair to either of us to do what I did, but—" She gazed at her brother's corpse. "All that is past redemption."

After a while she looked up. "That portrait is all I had left of him—a beautiful memory. These past few years, Claude had become more difficult to handle, and I was only waiting for him to pass on. I would have been happy to join him . . . until you came to the Landing." She drew herself up in the chair, and her voice became steadier. "Recent events have brought about a change of heart, Royal. I now want to remain with the living. But that's not so easy, is it?"

Royal shook his head.

"Claude saved your Seth."

"Yes, I know," Royal said. "He told me. You see, Seth saw Angélique—saw her set the fire. He tried to stop her. She knocked him out and left him to be burned alive."

Julia raised an eyebrow. "Angélique? But why?"

Royal wondered how he could answer that question. "I guess she couldn't bear the thought of my owning Heritage," he said at last. It was close to the truth.

"I never did like that girl. What happened to her?"

Royal shook his head. "I don't know. She might have been killed in the blaze."

Julia frowned. "That would be divine retribution, after what she did to Seth. It was lucky Claude was nearby. He carried the boy back to Heritage and rang the plantation bell. When he saw you and Suzanne, he became frightened and ran back to Taffarel, but he must have inhaled too much smoke, because by the time he reached home . . ." Julia's voice broke, and her eyes filled with tears. "There was nothing I could do for him. There's nothing I can do for him ever again."

Royal reached out and took her hand.

Julia rubbed the tears from her eyes. "Well, Royal Brannigan, what are we going to do now? It's a hard fact we have to face, but there's going to be no harvest for either of us."

"I know, Miss Julia."

She sighed and shook her head. "How are we going to run our plantations for yet another year? Keep our workers fed and clothed? Where are we going to get the money to replant, rebuild our refineries, replace our windmills? Even if we irrigate by hand, we'll have to buy seed cane, hogsheads, tools. My toolshed was burned down. Do you have any idea how much a hoe costs these days? One dollar and twenty-seven cents!"

Royal lowered his head and was silent.

"Royal Brannigan!" she admonished. "You're not giving up!" She stood and pulled him to his feet. "We've got resources, you and I, and if we combine them, we just might get through this."

"I don't know what you mean, Miss Julia."

"Then I guess you've lost your imagination, along with your crop. Come with me."

Puzzled, Royal followed her down a darkened hall and into the dining room. She lit a lamp and pointed triumphantly to a cracked vase sitting on the sideboard. It contained an arrangement of artificial flowers fashioned from beads and wire. "I don't believe in safes," she said. "That's the first place thieves look." She yanked the wire stems out of the vase and laid them on the sideboard, then carried the vase to the dining table and upturned it. A long rope of pearls slid out. "Now, tell me, Royal. What do you see?"

"It's your strand of pearls."

Julia shook her head. "No. It's food, farm equipment, living expenses, and even new hoes!"

"But, Julia, I couldn't . . ."

"That's not my proposition," she interrupted. "I said this was to be a *combination* of resources. Selling that necklace wouldn't fetch enough money to keep both our plantations going even two months."

Royal looked at her, still completely befuddled.

There was a twinkle in Julia's eye, and a sly grin played on her mouth. "But it would fetch enough money for what your friend Charlie Hazard would call a grubstake."

Royal, astounded, backed away from her. He started to laugh, but cut it short when he saw that she was serious. "Miss Julia, I told you I've given up gambling for good."

"Nonsense. Once a man gets the gambling fever, it stays with him."

"But I can't. M'sieur Jourdain's suicide—"

"Oh, don't play that tune for me, Royal. You didn't have a thing to do with that young man's death."

Royal thought of Angélique's confession and knew that he no longer had to carry even a portion of guilt in his heart.

"I may have lost the touch, Miss Julia," he offered lamely.

"That's nonsense, Royal—you know it, and I know it." She picked up the pearls and held them to the light. "Beautiful, aren't they? Claude gave these to me in honor of my impending marriage to Theo. Despite all the hardship, all the poverty I've been through, I vowed that I would never part with them. But now it seems to be the only sensible thing to do . . . for both our sakes." She let the pearls fall to the table and laid her hand on Royal's shoulder. "Don't sacrifice your happiness as I did, for a false notion of duty. I had a duty to Claude, yes, but I also had a duty to myself and to Theo. And you also have a duty to yourself and—" She smiled knowingly. "Unless I'm wrong, to someone else as well. To all the people who call Heritage their home. Now, I've provided you with a grubstake, and it's up to you to save all our hides."

Royal raised his head and looked directly into Julia's bright blue eyes. "I'll do it," he said tentatively. And then with more force, "I'll do it. Dammit, I'll do it!"

Julia picked up the necklace, dangled it from her index finger, and then began spinning it in a circle. "Round and round it goes, and where it stops—" She winked at Royal. "Nobody knows!"

Royal stood without making a sound, looking into the mirror. He was fascinated by himself, by the return of his old image. It was strange, but not altogether unpleasant, to see himself once again attired in his gambling clothes—a black suit, a frilly shirt, an elaborate vest. But the impression that he was looking at somebody else stayed with him. Did any of that former man remain? Could he be ruthless? Could he win? Julia Taffarel had entrusted him with her future and given him an opportunity to have one of his own. Would Lady Luck walk again at his side? He could only pray that she still enjoyed his company.

"You look very handsome."

Royal turned. Suzanne had come into the room. She offered him a brave smile and said, "Seth has brought around the carriage."

"I'm almost ready."

Suzanne folded her arms across her chest and bowed her head. "Royal, I know you're doing the right thing for all of us, but I can't help wishing you'd stay."

Royal went to her and wrapped his arms around her. "Suzanne, I don't want to go, but I must."

She looked up at him with tearful eyes. "Everything's happening so quickly. I don't know if I can adjust to all the changes."

"You will, Suzanne. You have to. It's up to you to keep Heritage running until I return."

"It's just that . . . well, I know this sounds strange, but I don't know how I'll manage without Angélique."

"I understand," Royal said gently.

"I'm just finding it so hard to accept her death." She brushed her hand across her eyes, as if to wipe away the recurrent image of the hideously charred body. "Horrible . . . horrible to die like that." She shuddered, adding, "And I don't suppose I'll ever accept Angélique's duplicity in my heart."

"Then don't, Suzanne. Try to remember her as you thought she was."

Zenobia knocked on the door and stepped into the room. "Yo' goin' to miss de steamboat, M'sieur Royal."

"Thank you, Zenobia. I'm coming."

The slave shifted her feet uneasily and started her sentence several times before getting the words out. "I—I—I jes' wanted to wish yo' good luck, M'sieur Royal." She picked up his suitcases and hurried out the door.

Suzanne smiled. "I think Zenobia's finally taken a liking to you."

"I hope so. As Seth says, she's a tough old bird. Well, I'd better get going. I don't want to miss the departure of *La Belle Créole.*" He smiled halfheartedly. "Captain Calabozo has been keeping on schedule recently."

Suzanne turned away with an anguished sob.

"Don't, Suzanne. You're making it harder for me to leave."

"I'm sorry, Royal. It's funny, but a long time ago I devised a plan to make you like me. I thought if I were pleasant and compliant, you might consider leasing Heritage to me and leave Magnolia Landing. But now that you're really going, I can't keep from crying."

Royal kissed the tears from her eyes. "Those are for me?"

She nodded.

"Then I'm deeply honored. We won't be parted for long, Suzanne. If Lady Luck is still on my side, I hope to be back by Christmas."

"Oh, no longer, Royal. I couldn't bear Christmas without you."

"Then I make a promise to you. Somehow, someway, I'll be back in time to help you celebrate."

Suzanne's face brightened. "I'll have a party. I'll invite all of our friends from the Landing."

"Let's hope we have something to celebrate."

"Oh, Royal, just come back to me. That will be reason enough for me to celebrate."

Royal clenched his jaw tight, afraid of what words might spill out. He offered Suzanne his arm and led her to the front veranda.

Seth was sitting in the driver's seat of the waiting carriage, dressed in his white suit. When he saw his master come through the door, he pulled out his pocket watch, dangled it in the air, and said with a forced smile, "Mr. Royal, it time we was leaving."

"I'm coming, Seth." Royal took Suzanne in his arms and held her so close that the beating of their hearts became as one.

"I can't say goodbye," she said.

"There are no goodbyes for us . . . ever," Royal replied. He kissed her just once, softly, and full on the lips. Then he broke away from her, bounded down the stairs, and climbed onto the seat next to Seth. "Get going, Seth," he said in a choked voice, "before I change my mind."

The carriage began rolling away from Heritage. Royal looked over his shoulder and saw Suzanne running after them. "Seth, stop the carriage!" she called.

The little boy reined in the horses. Royal jumped out of the carriage and hurried toward Suzanne. She fell into his arms.

"I had to tell you something," she gasped. "I'm glad my plan didn't work. I love you, Royal Brannigan."

Royal's face broke into a broad smile. "I think Lady Luck just smiled on me."

Epilogue

December 24, 1830

A mist of snowflakes swirled about the open deck of the steamship. Royal shivered and turned up the collar of his greatcoat against the chilling wind. He took out his pocket watch, flipped open the lid, and whispered, "Merry Christmas, Charlie, wherever you are." The twelve miniature cards, ace through queen, informed him that it was nearly eleven o'clock in the morning. Blinking away the snowflakes, Royal literally counted the minutes until his return to Magnolia Landing.

Royal had kept his pact with Julia Taffarel, but at what cost to himself! He no longer viewed gambling as the glamorous occupation he had once thought it, but rather as a dangerous obsession for the frivolous, the greedy, and the desperate. He had witnessed men destroyed, marriages shattered, lives lost. All this he had seen before, but he had not understood.

He looked older now, and was well aware of it. Etched into his memory and upon his face were the hard experiences of the past three months. Although the casinos, the cities, the steamships, the taverns had, in his mind, blended one into the other and lost their individual identities, the faces of the losers remained distinct. He would never forget them.

Royal had played the game with a vengeance, taking on all comers, pushing the stakes as high as he dared, and sometimes sitting at a table around the clock. But his dedication and perseverance—if indeed those words could be applied to the pursuit of gambling—had paid off handsomely. He had been able to send a stipend regularly to both Suzanne and Julia, and before leaving New Orleans, he had deposited substantial sums in both the Taffarel and Heritage accounts.

Royal had received an unwanted bonus in the bargain—he had become what the theater people referred to as a celebrity. Of course he had been known and recognized in gambling circles before, but now he found that his notoriety had become general, even outside of New Orleans. The inevitable result was that he could not go anywhere without being instantly recognized. Men, no matter what their prowess at poker, challenged him, if only to claim they had played a hand with the famous Royal Brannigan. Women of all ages propositioned him. Children tagged after him and could be dispersed only by a handful of tossed coins.

Royal ached for the anonymity of plantation life. He wanted to be back among people he knew and trusted, people who had come to accept him for what he was. People like Seth, Miss Julia, Theo and the children, Léon and Michelle, and even Zenobia. But most of all he was looking forward to spending the rest of his life with the woman he loved—Suzanne.

Royal looked up and saw Captain Calabozo making his way down the cabin-deck promenade toward him. The captain, Royal thought, looked happier, healthier than when he had last seen him. His uniform, navy blue with brass buttons, was less flamboyant and more flattering to his newly trim physique.

"Ah, M'sieur Brannigan, you seem to be the only one on deck. The weather has kept most of the passengers sequestered in their cabins, or gathered around the smokestacks, warming their backsides. You're impatient to get home, aren't you?"

"Yes, I certainly am," said Royal genially.

"Lots has happened since you left the Landing, in case you haven't heard."

Royal smiled to himself. Although the captain had changed in appearance, he was just as loquacious as ever—the self-appointed host of his ship.

"I'm sure you wouldn't mind catching me up," Royal said dryly.

The captain moved closer to Royal. He looked about, checking for listeners—a needless gesture—and began in a breathless voice, "They say it wasn't her body."

"Whose body?" asked Royal, knowing full well whom the captain meant.

"Why, Angélique Jourdain. Personally, I think it was a runaway slave—one of the Duc's. After all, she was burnt to a crisp. It could have been anyone."

"But it wasn't anyone," Royal said evenly. "Suzanne positively identified her sister-in-law by the bracelet she was wearing."

The captain mulled that over for a few seconds, obviously reluctant to give up his theory. Then he presented another tidbit of information. "Alcée and Blaise are doing fine up in Canada. Alcée's expecting in late June, and Henriette couldn't be happier."

"She's still at Villeneuve, then?"

"Yes." A touch of pride crept into the captain's voice. "Several afternoons a week, when I'm up here on my run, she has me over for coffee and cakes. The Duc doesn't bother her. He's very embarrassed about the whole situation. He's not even been entertaining lately, if you can believe that! I hear that he and Philippe just sit up in that big house and drink. However, the Duc has been to visit Madame Jourdain on several occasions."

Royal's eyebrows shot up. "Has he?"

"He's getting anxious about your return. I hear he's going to make an offer for Heritage." The captain stepped back and grinned. "But from the look of you, I don't think you'll be selling."

"Not now. Not ever. And how are the Martineaus?"

The captain frowned. "They're fine. The three of them are behaving like a true family. Léon has taken over the reins of the plantation and is running Bellechasse on a full head of steam, as we rivermen say."

"That's good to hear," said Royal.

"And, oh—did I tell you about Theo and Miss Julia?"

"Not yet." Royal smiled.

"They see each other constantly. If he's not at Taffarel, she's at Victoire. It's been a long time coming, but I wouldn't be surprised if there was a wedding at Magnolia Landing."

"I wouldn't be surprised if there were two."

The captain's face broke into a surprised grin. "You and Madame Jourdain?"

"If she'll have me."

The captain took Royal's hand and shook it vigorously. "Congratulations, m'sieur. You know, I never did thank you for taking care of me that night of the ball. Henriette told me everything. You're a gentleman, M'sieur Brannigan, even if you are an American."

Royal suppressed a smile. "Thank you, Captain, for the good wishes and . . . the compliment."

"Do they know you're arriving?"

"Yes, I sent word upriver."

"Then I better get below and see that the stokers keep the boiler fed. I wouldn't want you to be late. And I'll see that your cargo gets unloaded first. I've never seen so many Christmas presents! A very different cargo from the first time I transported you upriver."

"Yes," Royal replied to himself as Captain Calabozo hurried away. "A *very* different cargo."

Royal leaned over the railing and stared at the twisting eddies of the Mississippi. As the gray water rushed by, voices whispered in his mind's ear. He tilted his head to one side and eavesdropped to the pieces of dialogue that charted, as clearly as signposts, the tangled pathways of his memory:

"Then you are an American, M'sieur Bran-ee-gan? . . ."

"People from the Landing don't like Americans. . . ."

"We will be holding funeral services tomorrow afternoon. I hope you will have the good manners not to attend. . . ."

"You may own the plantation, M'sieur Brannigan, but you don't own me. . . ."

"I hope that you will be happy here at Magnolia Landing . . . so few of us are. . . ."

"You should be dead, American!"

"The ghost of Magnolia Landing is finally at rest. . . ."

"I love you, Royal Brannigan. . . ."

Royal looked up and was surprised to see that the ship was in sight of its destination. The buildings, the trees, even the wharf and the people waiting on it, were covered with a dusting of snow, making the Landing seem like a toy village, a setting for a fairy tale. And then, as the ship drew nearer, he made out a figure in bright blue, standing at the edge of the wharf. Suzanne!

Royal began waving and running along the promenade. He bounded down the staircase to the main deck. Back at the foot of the wharf, he could now see, Zenobia and Seth were waiting. The formidable mammy was restraining the little boy from rushing to dockside.

The ship's side scraped the pilings, and Royal, too impatient to wait for the gangplank, took off his bulky greatcoat, threw it to the deck, and leaped across the brief expanse of water, landing almost directly in front of Suzanne.

Suzanne was more beautiful than he remembered from his dreams. They stared at each other, transfixed, for a moment, before embracing.

Royal said, "How far I've traveled with only your name on my lips, and your love in my heart to sustain me." He smiled. "I told you I'd make it by Christmas. I brought presents—"

She touched her fingertips to his lips.

"Hush, you're all I wanted or will ever want for Christmas, my beautiful American."

Their lips parted and they kissed. Soon, other arms were hugging Royal, and he knew that he was home . . . finally home.

READ THIS THRILLING PREVIEW
OF A BOLD NEW SAGA
FROM THE CREATORS OF WAGONS WEST

AMERICA 2040

BY EVAN INNES

As the author of WAGONS WEST, I love to write about the conquering of the American West and the good folks who brought law, order, and civilization to the unknown wilds. In America 2040, I've found a mixture of all the qualities of WAGONS WEST, but set in the future—courageous men and women forced to flee to the far planets to settle and live, while the Earth teeters on the brink of nuclear war. AMERICA 2040 tells about men and women like you and me, who are determined to carry on American morality and love of freedom and family on uncharted lands light years away. AMERICA 2040 is a terrific exciting book!

Dana Fuller Ross
Author of WAGONS WEST

To American President Dexter Hamilton, entering Greater Moscow in the spring of 2033 was a fifty-year leap into the past, an enigmatic separation from his familiar, changing, bustling world. The impressive modernity of Gagarin Airport, the city's newest civilian and military aviation facility, had not prepared him for the real Moscow.

There was snow in the city, grayed, trodden, piled. Along the motorcade route he and his entourage caught glimpses of real antiques: diesel-powered trucks spouting the contaminants of burning fossil fuel to cloud the chill air. People swaddled in animal furs. Drab, stern, slab-sided apartment buildings that had been built shortly after World War II.

Under a lowering, slate sky, the Kremlin loomed redly beyond the frozen Moskva River. To Hamilton, and to millions, the triangularly shaped fortress housed most of what was evil in the world. The relationship between Russia and the United States remained tense, hostile, suspicious, and dangerous, but Dexter Hamilton wanted to be the American President who halted the eternal arms race and delivered the world, forever, from the threat of nuclear incineration. To that end, he was to meet with the Soviet leader, Premier Yuri Kolchak.

The President was young to be serving in that office, only forty-six, having been born in 1987. His silvering hair—a tight, curled mass that clung to his well-formed head—seemed to be a tacit signal that, although young, here was a wise, experienced man.

Behind the smile-crinkled blue eyes, the classic nose, the upturned mouth, there was the strength that had given him the governorship of North Carolina, then a seat in the Senate, and finally the Oval Office.

When the limousine hummed through guarded gates, past heavily armed and stalwart men handpicked for Kremlin duty from the huge Red Army, Dexter Hamilton was guided from the car by a woman general. He walked with long, quick strides, eager to begin the summit meeting with Premier Yuri Kolchak.

Premier Kolchak was waiting for him behind a wide, gleaming table in a conference room. The Premier was a darkly handsome man, but there was something in his eyes that bothered Hamilton, a quality he'd seen before. Then the memory came back to him: When he was quite young he'd owned a little dog that had wandered into a field and been swept up in a tomato picker. The dying, mutilated dog lay stunned and shocked. In Kolchak's eyes were those same qualities—a pain that seemed to approach madness. Was there truth to the rumor that the Premier was seriously ill?

Several minutes after the meeting has begun, Yuri Kolchak rises abruptly from his seat, obviously taken ill. He is led away hastily, without explanation or apology. Hamilton is escorted back to his suite, where, except for a serving girl bringing dinner, he is left alone for the night.

The next morning there was a knock on the door of his luxurious suite in the Kremlin, and a smiling, dark-haired serving girl in livery appeared. Pleasant aromas of coffee, real eggs, and ham came from the serving cart she was standing behind. A great number of covered serving bowls were on the cart, certainly enough for more than one man.

Just then he heard a deep, resonant voice coming from behind the girl.

"Good morning, Mr. President. You slept well?"

Premier Kolchak was dressed informally in tunic, trousers. At forty-seven his slightly Slavic face was smooth, and his dark and bristly hair showed no hint of gray. He extended a hand. Hamilton took it. Each grip was firm.

"Forgive me for surprising you," Kolchak said as the serving girl disappeared out the door. "But if I had taken time to warn you that I was coming, we'd have to invite our aides and observe protocol." There was no explanation of the previous meeting's cancellation.

"I understand," Hamilton said. Kolchak took a seat and Hamilton sat across the table, and they began to eat.

"My people don't understand your real purpose here," the Premier said.

"Well, Yuri," Hamilton began, "you like straight talk, so here it is: I'm here to talk peace. I want to talk about what we have in common. We're all passengers on a small, increasingly overcrowded planet. It is time we took down the bombs from the space stations and junked the missiles and the space weapons. The men who bring peace to the world will be sung in history down through the ages. Let's make those men you and me."

"I could learn to like you," Kolchak said. "I will give you anything you want from this conference."

The statement seemed simple enough, direct enough, but there was something wrong.

"Because you see," Kolchak said, his dark, hard

eyes boring into Hamilton's, "whatever you achieve in this present conference does not matter." The Premier had finished eating. He leaned back, wiped his lips on a linen napkin, let it fall to his knee. "What matters is what you and I say here in this room." He smiled. "I hope you will be receptive and reasonable."

"I'll do my best."

"For centuries," Kolchak said, "elitist and imperialist countries have delayed the destiny of the masses. We can no longer allow that. Soon, Mr. President, the downtrodden of the world will be free to share in the fruits of their own labors. Within my lifetime, the revolution will be total." He paused. "With one single exception. We will allow the continued existence of the United States as a governmental entity. In time, with the rest of the world's workers freed from their masters and living in equality with their fellows, you will see reason and work with the rest of the civilized world." Ever since the use of the first atomic bomb on Japan, men had dreaded that someday, in some country, a madman would be in a position to push the button. This, Hamilton felt with a despair that made him want to strike out, was the man.

"Mr. Premier, this must be the first time in the history of my country that a President has been so threatened."

Kolchak shrugged. "We can no longer allow you to prevent the legitimate aspirations of the peoples of this world. We have liberated many countries. We will liberate more."

"Are you speaking of South America?"

"That, first."

South America was dominated by the emerging

imperialistic giant Brazil, whose armed forces had overwhelmed Cuba, ending Communist rule there. However, Communist insurgents continued to rebel against Brazilian authorities in the Caribbean and South America. An American fleet was stationed in the Pacific, but as of yet there had been no direct confrontation with the Russians.

"Are you declaring war?" Hamilton asked. "For we will fight you over that continent."

"There will be a war only if you choose to interfere. If both our countries let loose all our military power there will be little, if any, life left on Earth. But that doesn't really matter."

"What, in God's name, does matter?"

Kolchak leaned forward, his face pale, his lips twitching in obvious pain. "The triumph of right."

"Your brand of right, of course?"

"Of course. There is no other. Now will you pull out of South America and let events take their course?"

"No."

Kolchak leaned back, sighed. "Then, Mr. President, prepare yourself for some very difficult decisions."

"We've faced tough decisions before," Hamilton said. "I'll admit that you're scaring the living daylights out of me, but we won't stand aside and let you gobble up what's left."

Kolchak smiled. "Understand this, Mr. President. Before I die, the world will be Red or dead, and quite frankly I don't give a"—he used a Russian obscenity unfamiliar to Hamilton—"which it is."

Hamilton heard himself saying words, inane words. "May you have a long life, Mr. Premier."

"No, my friend, you will not escape the responsibility in that way."

"You *are* ill," Hamilton said softly.

Kolchak, with a cold smile, nodded.

"Perhaps we could help in some way. Our medical research—"

"Is no better than ours."

"How long?" Hamilton asked.

"Fewer than nine years."

"I'm sorry," Hamilton said. "But we have time to think about it, to talk. Yuri, there's no winning a war. My God, man, we've both got enough warheads in space to do the job twice over. If you push the button I'm dead, but I'll have time to push my own button and you're dead."

"But I'm dead regardless of what happens," Kolchak said. With a wicked gleam in his black eyes, he added, "All I care about is that the world is ours . . . or else it does not exist at all."

President Hamilton returns to Washington, where he briefs the head of the CIA and orders him to make the assassination of Yuri Kolchak a top priority. Then Dexter Hamilton and his scientific advisor, Oscar Kost, explore other ways to avert annihilation of the American people and their way of life. Their search takes them to Vandenberg Air Force Base in California, to learn about Project Lightstep, a top-secret operation.

Dexter Hamilton and Oscar Kost were introduced by a two-star general to Harry Shaw, a small, dark man, with a wide forehead and thin mouth that was, nevertheless, capable of a wide smile.

"This is a genuine pleasure, Mr. President, Mr. Kost," Shaw said.

"The pleasure is mutual," Hamilton said. "I have

to confess that I know absolutely nothing about this project. Please start at the beginning."

"I'll try to make it brief," Shaw said. "When I was an undergraduate I worked with platinum metals and their ability to store heat and energy, but it wasn't until I got my hands on a supply of rhenium that I began to make any progress. I decided to hit a few molecules of rhenium with antimatter, and as a result we almost obliterated Los Angeles. The reaction was contained, but just barely," Shaw added.

Hamilton didn't see the significance. A bigger and better bomb would not make Yuri Kolchak take his finger off the button. Nuclear bombs could already destroy all life on Earth, so why bother with something else?

"Harry," Hamilton said, "just tell me rhenium's other applications."

"It's currently the energy source for an experimental space vehicle disguised as a simple planetary probe. It's out beyond Pluto right now. If we've succeeded, that vehicle, propelled by rhenium, has made a round trip to within a few million miles of the star closest to our system, Proxima Centauri. That's thirty trillion miles in a billionth of a second."

Hamilton felt a sudden surge of joy. He glanced at Kost. Oscar's hooded eyes were gleaming. For the first time since his meeting with Yuri Kolchak, Hamilton felt a swelling of hope in his breast. As the countdown clock jerked its second hand closer to the critical moment when the experimental space vehicle's computer-screen transmission would be received by Vandenberg, a fantastic and exciting dream grew inside Dexter Hamilton: If Yuri Kolchak sent the whole world up in smoke and dust and fire, there would be still one last hope for the human race.

"One minute and counting," an amplified voice said, breaking the tense silence.

Hamilton's eyes were on the clock.

"Thirty seconds . . . twenty—"

Screens came to life, flickered, were blank. There was an air of supreme tension in the room, a breathless hush except for the counting voice.

"—five, four, three, two, one—!"

A large screen flickered, static lines flowering, diminishing, and then the screen was filled with fire—harsh, golden, roiling, boiling fire.

"Oh, God, no," Hamilton said. Seen close up, a sun is an awesome furnace, the golden fires of thermonuclear reaction forming slowly roiling masses on its curved surface.

"Wait," Harry Shaw said, his voice cracking with excitement. "We're not on the scopes. We're on radio telemetry."

And slowly, slowly, the screen changed, the fire gradually becoming more distant.

"The camera is changing lenses!" Shaw yelled. "We were too close!"

A cheer went up.

"It worked! Thank God, it worked!" Harry Shaw yelled, doing a little dance. It worked! Man could travel faster than light. With some luck, and some tricky, very secret planning, there could be people, Americans, out there traveling through the far reaches of space.

Now there was hope. At least some would survive. Hamilton would see to that. He could not trust Yuri Kolchak to leave the United States alone. Kolchak would want total world domination, and Dexter would never bow down and live under Communism. There'd be a part of the United States of America alive, out there in space. And if the missiles began to lance down from the orbiting space stations, at least a seed stock of humankind, if the form of Americans, would be alive.

The colossal rhenium-powered spaceship, secretly constructed under the Utah desert over a period of six years, is ready for lift-off. In the interim, Yuri Kolchak's health and the international political situation deteriorate. President Hamilton addresses the nation and the world, on the brink of nuclear war, disclosing at last history's best kept secret, the Spirit of America.

From cameras outside, a view of the White House was flashed upward to satellites, and a band played the "Star Spangled Banner." The anthem was being fed to the sound monitors in the Oval Office. As the last notes of music died, the director stabbed a finger toward Hamilton, who sat immobile, his calm, kind, distinguished face in repose, his eyes looking directly into the cameras. At last his drawling voice broke the almost unbearable tension.

"My fellow Americans. Today, December 24, 2040, this great nation of ours is about to embark upon humankind's greatest adventure.

"Even as I speak, while hundreds of thousands of our servicemen and women are massed in South America because of that age-old curse of mankind—war—other brave men and women are preparing to leave behind family and loved ones, their homes, their native country, even the planet of their birth.

"Today, one thousand Americans will leave Earth to open a new frontier among the stars.

"We Americans have a history of facing and

overcoming the unknown. Our forefathers dared a great ocean and overcame great obstacles to establish this nation, under God, and in freedom. They came to face the fierceness of a raw, vast land, and they established a nation that is unique, a nation wherein each and every individual has equal rights.

"Today our freedom faces its gravest test. Even now, our avowed enemies in South America threaten to overwhelm us, and the largest battle fleet ever to be assembled is massing off the western coast of the South American continent.

"I cannot tell you, my fellow citizens, what tomorrow will bring. But I can tell you this: The spirit of America will not die. The force and the dream that made this country great will live on in those brave pioneers who today will leave Earth to venture into the unknown.

"America now offers hope to the billions of people, citizens of every country. For the great ship that will journey to the far stars can, with international cooperation, bring the blessing of plenty back to our wasted world. American science, American genius, and the American dream have opened up a vast new empire, which can provide us with badly needed living space, a safety valve for our overpopulation, a source of rich, new raw materials to quiet our hunger and restore to us, and to the world, the standard of living we once knew.

"As President of the United States and as your spokesman, I extend the hand of cooperation and friendship to our enemies. The destiny of humankind cannot continue in bitter warfare until there is nothing left but ashes and cinders. No, we have a higher destiny. Our destiny lies among the stars."

Hamilton's face was seemingly at peace, his eagle's eyes looking straight into the camera.

"And now, my fellow Americans, let us experience this great moment together."

The first view was from a distance. Desert. Low mounds in the background, and then, from a hovering helicopter, the first view of the ship. It looked like some fantastic toy buried in a round hole in the ground. Only when the airborne camera pulled back to a long shot and it was possible to see vehicles, antlike people, the temporary town, was it possible to gain an idea of the ship's vast size.

From the top it looked like a huge wheel and had been painted red, white, and blue. On a blank expanse of metal near the core were Old Glory and the words *UNITED STATES*. And on the outer wheel, proudly, in huge letters that gleamed in gold against white, *Spirit of America*.

It came to life slowly. First a billowing rush of smoke pouring up from the circular pit around its sides, obscuring it, and then tongues of flame.

Was it merely illusion or did that impossibly huge mass move?

Smoke. Flames. Rocketry had reached its zenith. Fuels of high mass-to-bulk ratio had been developed during the space-station-building epoch. Combustion times had been extended. But never before had such a mass been lifted from Earth's gravitational pull. Never before had so much fuel been expended in so short time.

The ship crawled upward, and the flames decreased, and *Spirit of America* emerged from them, huge, round, lifting slowly, slowly, and that sound familiar to all Americans was rumbling and roaring, the awesome power sound of bellowing rockets as it had never been heard in such intensity. And now it was accelerating slowly, slowly, too fantastic to be anything but trick photography, and yet it was real.

The ship bellowed straight up for long minutes, and then, as the cameramen began to switch to their long lenses, it tilted slowly and angled off toward the east. It was so big that the longest lenses could follow it into orbit. True, the ship was but a bright speck of reflected sunlight when, after the rockets had ceased firing, it swam through the darkness of near space, a bright star to be seen with the naked eye, but it was there, and after the long tension of watching the takeoff, a billion Americans cheered.